savage
blood

ALEX CHANCE

arrow books

Published by Arrow Books 2011

1 3 5 7 9 10 8 6 4 2

First published in Great Britain in 2010 by William Heinemann

Arrow Books
The Random House Group Limited
20 Vauxhall Bridge Road, London, SW1V 2SA

www.randomhouse.co.uk

Addresses for companies within The Random House Group Limited can be
found at: www.randomhouse.co.uk/offices.htm

The Random House Group Limited Reg. No. 954009

A CIP catalogue record for this book
is available from the British Library

ISBN 9780099532842

The Random House Group Limited supports the Forest Stewardship Council®
(FSC®), the leading international forest certification organisation. All our titles that
are printed on Greenpeace approved FSC® certified paper carry the FSC® logo. Our
paper procurement policy can be found at:
www.randomhouse.co.uk/environment

Typeset in Electra LH Regular by Palimpsest Book Production Limited,
Falkirk, Stirlingshire

Printed and bound in Great Britain by
CPI Cox & Wyman, Reading, RG1 8EX

For my parents, Patricia and Anthony.

Prologue

Everyone calls barbarity what he is not accustomed to.

Michel de Montaigne
Essay, 1, 31.
1580

'On Savage Island, the men have the heads of dogs,' said Thein.

The American calling himself Edward Quinn sat up a little straighter. *Professor* Edward Quinn of the University of Chicago, no less. 'You've been?' he said, injecting hope into his voice.

Thein shook his head. He didn't want to lay it on too strong. 'My brother sometimes fishes the far waters. He sees from a distance. He says the air is heavy, even on the nearby sea. Even the sea is cursed.'

'Cursed? In what way?'

'Shipwrecks? Sea monsters? My brother drinks. We will not bring him.' Thein drained his third Kingfisher without irony, condensation on the bottle becoming greasy in his fingers. In the corner of the bar, Hindi music videos flickered on a silent and badly tuned television.

'His boat is here? We can go tonight?'

Thein stared the American in the face. It was shiny with the heat and harsh lighting.

Eager, this one.

'Not in Port Barren.' Thein sat back in his chair. 'Small boat, up the coast. But we sail before dawn. Navy patrol are inept, but they stop us if they see you. No white-skinned fishermen.'

3

Quinn appeared to make up his mind, gestured across the empty room for more beer. The owner was ready; Thein and the strange American were his only customers.

'*American anthropological survey*,' said Thein. He spoke slowly, rolling the syllables of what was almost certainly a lie around his mouth like stale *pan*. 'You can do that on your own?'

'Excuse me?'

Thein resisted an urge to spit out the imagined bad taste. Of all the languages the Myanmar could have brought to the table, he had chosen to negotiate in his careful, excellent English, but had deliberately opted not to mimic the American's accent. Perhaps he should have played it more dumb.

Stay with him. You could eat and drink for a month. Eat and drink like a king.

'I mean,' said Thein, 'only you for the voyage?'

Professor Quinn snorted. 'My research team just got off the ground. Goddam weather in Europe held them two days.'

'Snow?'

'Volcanic Ash. You believe that? The monsoon I can prepare for, but you can't predict the airports.'

Thein didn't know what to believe. He marvelled as a vast *Anopheles* mosquito appeared on the plump vein dividing the professor's damp forehead and began her eager preliminaries.

How are you not noticing?

The beer arrived. Thein waited for the Bengali to retreat.

'*Cannibals*,' he said, in a low voice.

'I don't want to land on the island. I just want to look.'

'They say if you even get close enough to see, the next instant you are surely dead.'

'And how's that?' said the man. 'Arrows?'

Thein shrugged.

'How would you know this if no one ever returns?'

The Myanmar grinned, proud of his two gold caps, wondered

when to introduce the topic of money. He didn't anticipate too much haggling.

This man wants it bad. Bad enough to lie. Bad enough to forge permission beneath an important letterhead. Should I care who he really is?

Edward Quinn swigged his beer, the wet label already peeling.

The mosquito clung on. Thein sympathised.

He'd seen Western tourists in the islands before, but they were rare; most were still discouraged by the remoteness and expense. Thein had learned to seek out the adventurous few and give them what they wanted. Usually a driver, someone to get them to the isolated and beautiful beaches, of which there were many. But Thein Suu Ay was more than a guide, he was an opportunist. Once, some Dutch backpackers had joked that they wanted to fuck a genuine Okojuwoi girl; in half a day, Thein had tracked down a *Jaman* half-breed, lousy with cholera. He draped her in bark-fibre fringe and, for good measure, threaded some orchids through her pubic hair. The tourists had left satisfied. But those tribes that remained on the main island were becoming tame; gifts and communication from the outside world were making them stupid, if still somewhat unpredictable.

The natives on the Savage Island were different altogether. Untouched, unknowable, apparently lethal, and cut off by that God-forsaken reef. And protected in equal measure by Indian red tape and the most fearsome mythology in the Bay of Bengal.

Thein wasn't fazed by any of it. 'Twelve thousand rupees,' he said, opening his palm.

Professor Edward Quinn grinned.

The bar was only walled in on three sides. Behind the broad shoulders of the American, the haphazardly strewn lights of Port Barren, such as they were, tumbled down to a sea of black glass.

'The men on Savage Island have the heads of dogs,' said Thein, and this time, he did spit.

*

The following night, the jungle surrounding the tiny cove throbbed with unseen life.

A light flared on the belt of sand, fleeting as a stray firefly. Thein had taken the American's money and treated himself to a new lighter, good cigarettes.

As if signalled, a shadow emerged from the thick trees: a vast, five-legged beetle, freeing itself from a muddy animal track. Thein smoked while one of the legs detached itself from beneath what was an upturned boat, the eldest Pandit brother walking towards him.

'Return it here,' said the fisherman. 'Not to the dock. I'll be waiting.'

Thein watched the small vessel being lowered into the water with a critical eye. The other men seemed nervous, reluctant, sweat shining on bare chests – except for the American, of course.

'Did you hear what I said?'

Thein turned, irritated. Sanjay, the eldest of the four brothers, looked no older than a boy; shirtless, shoeless, his skin cobalt in the light of the moon. He spoke in broken English, presumably for the benefit of Quinn, who was already ankle deep in the shallows, checking the inboard motor.

Thein waved dismissively, a lofty gesture he had copied from the tourists. He wasn't about take a lecture from an Indian child with muddy feet.

'We're supposed to be repainting,' said Sanjay. 'Harbour master knows we don't sail at night.'

'No one will stop us. The professor will keep his head down, at least until we are across the channel.'

Since sealing the deal, Professor Quinn had acted more like an excited boy scout than any kind of scientist. To the confusion of the hired help, he'd insisted on helping to carry the boat, had packed and repacked his backpack, and had painstakingly laid out camera equipment on the solid earth floor of the hut where they had spent the first half of the night. On top of this, he had been irritating Thein all day: on the slow drive up from Port Barren; on the empty, bug-infested passenger ferry between Great and North Islands. Questions, always questions. Who else had been to Savage Island? Who had died there? When, why, how? Things a qualified researcher surely should have known already.

To make matters worse, Thein's own brother had ruled himself out of the trip with some pathetic excuse that only proved how terrified he was of sailing in that direction, and Thein had been forced to employ alternative help. The Pandit brothers were cheap, but they acted as though Quinn was in charge, which pissed Thein off mightily.

He sighed, tapped out another smoke.

Sanjay grimaced at the blaze of the Zippo.

'*Jaman* territory,' he whispered, gesturing towards the dark, breathing forest. 'We are not supposed to be here, government orders. I already risk my life to wait.'

'Do you not like money?'

'There are savages.'

'No trouble here, not for years. And anyway, all *Jaman* have been driven further north.'

'Some would still attack if they found us,' countered Sanjay. 'Yet these savages are not as bad as those on the island. Not as bad by half. At least we know something of the *Jaman*.'

'Bare natives, with asses painted yellow. And fast asleep now.'

Edward Quinn had stopped fussing with the boat, was looking across at them.

'If it comes to it, we will not be able to make rescue,' Sanjay said, daring to raise his voice a little. 'Neither the police nor even the army – they will not go near.'

'Yes, yes. Government orders.'

'The helicopter, maybe it will fly over your skeletons, dry on the beach.'

Thein laughed, a hollow bray that rattled scrubfowl in nearby palms. 'You should write a brochure,' he said quickly. 'For the tourists.' But despite the humidity, the hot dampness in his shirt, Thein shivered. The kid was making him nervous.

He glanced skyward to cover this momentary weakness.

'Ah,' he said, licking his lips. 'I am no fisherman, yet I believe I know a spell of decent weather when I see it.'

Sanjay ignored him. 'You are only going to look?' He spoke as loud as he dared, though the professor was no longer listening. 'You are not planning to make land?'

'How many times?' said Thein. 'We will *observe*.'

'Child-eaters.' Sanjay was showing the whites of his eyes, doubly reflected off the bone-pale sand. 'Men without gods. Child-eating killers, and seven feet tall.'

He put himself between Thein and the boat, wanting Thein to understand.

Forget everything you thought you knew, said Sanjay, in Bengali.

Thein shrugged. Later, he would have reason to remember the boy's face at that point – frozen in terror, with the ignorance and superstition that was the lifeblood of the islands.

No, wait, it was more than that. This was genuine, palpable, potentially contagious *horror*, and he wasn't even making the trip himself. But then, these fishermen lived amongst the native people, had shared that much more history.

Thein relented, allowed some sympathy to enter his voice. 'We will only observe. We are *not* going to make land.'

It seemed to take for ever.

They navigated by starlight across the impenetrable depths, powered by the put-puttering of an eight-horsepower engine, Professor Quinn snoring beneath a thin tarp. They had no radio, no life vests, and no back-up vessel.

The three boys who were sailing the boat did not speak English, but they hardly seemed interested in talking anyway, so Thein occupied himself trying to spot the first sign of dawn, while counting the ever present Morse blasts of sheet lightning in the distance.

Both first light and landfall arrived at the same time; a dull fire in the east revealing the irregular shadow of an island lurking to the west. Thein actually believed he could smell the land – nothing distinctive, just something different after hours and hours of warm, flat sea.

Perhaps Edward Quinn could smell it too. He sat up quickly, rocking the boat and startling one of the fishermen, the cloth at the rear of his headband whipping around as he turned. Thein felt the boy's hollow, accusing stare. He had been getting similar looks throughout the night.

Was it irritation or fear?

What is wrong with these people?

Now the American was looking at him too, expectant day-tripper to overpaid tour guide.

'They say we will sail once around,' Thein lied, making a circular motion with his finger.

'Only once? I need time to see the island, to photograph.'

Thein shrilled a lengthy order sternwards and received a desultory, one-syllable response.

'Yes, we will circle only once,' he said. 'Then, we will head back.'

Ominous dark clouds to the west seemed to lend authority to this idea, so Thein pointed them out, pleased at the convenience.

Edward Quinn, handsome and maddeningly neat in his recently purchased khaki, simply smiled his enigmatic smile, and they sailed on.

Nothing, no one.

There was more life in the surrounding sea. Small, sleek dolphins danced in front of the bow as they chased schools of nimble flying fish. Thein could see to the bottom now, and the turquoise water nearer the island was shallow enough to reach down and disturb an alternative universe. There were astonishing tracts of multi-coloured coral; mini-cities of clownfish, parrotfish and thorny seahorses, occasionally divided by a kick-line of plump, translucent squid.

The fishermen ran out nets as they sailed, on one occasion pulling in a huge pinky-orange snapper, which twisted and bucked, and, finally, held Thein's gaze as it expired. There was a hairy moment when another line snagged on thick underwater mangrove, and from then on the boat stayed further out from the reef, a good quarter of a mile from the shore, from the island of death.

Edward Quinn remained glued to his binoculars the whole time, scanning, making little excited sighs and whistles, urging on each new cove, each new bay. But with every reveal came fresh disappointment: beach after pristine beach with no sign of life.

After four hours, and a lunch of stale samosas and hot Frooti, Thein was beginning to wonder if they even had the right island. Natives on the main Okojuwois were rarely so shy.

The day dragged, the sun hot and bloated. Quinn slapped on sunscreen.

By the time the little boat had rounded three sides of the island, Thein believed he could sense something different about the professor. It wasn't that his energy was dissipating, or his enthusiasm, even though whatever mission he had planned was obviously failing. It was more that he appeared to be gearing up for something, perhaps to speak, maybe to admit defeat. He looked nervous, fidgety, and Thein, who had spent a lifetime honing his ability to decipher the wants and feelings of others in order to exploit them for financial gain, dedicated himself to figuring it out.

Guilt? Does he think he's wasted our time?

Better: does he want us to come back tomorrow?

Thein smiled, shading his face with his hand.

Another day's cruising would suit him fine; there had been no work for him besides contracting the Pandit family, and provided the brothers would capitulate, the mechanism would be in place for regular trips around the island. There had been no sight of any patrol boats or navy vessels, and if Edward Quinn was going to be in the Okojuwois for as long as he claimed, if he had a *team* of some kind coming out to join him, then Thein could be in business for months to come; perhaps until the monsoon, until his yearly return to Yangon.

Maybe he wouldn't even have to sail out himself each time: the fishermen could learn, could work out what was expected of them. They could all be in the money just because one rich American wanted to stare at some empty beaches.

Thein wiped a little sweat off his forehead and proposed an imaginary toast to the savages of their eponymous island, a near-legendary collective of jabbering murderers who had the good sense to stay in the jungle.

And long may they hide.

He was looking away from the island and licking his lips, preparing to make his pitch to Quinn, when one of the fishermen spoke.

A single word.

One urgent, panicked, warning.

Thein spun around, watched in slow-motion as the American's tan elbow rocketed towards his face, the thick bicep behind it knotted with muscle. Then he saw stars, more stars than had filled the night sky. Thein sagged like he'd been punctured, became aware of his cheek pressing into the dampness in the bottom of the boat. There was surprisingly cool water where the shadows had lain.

Quinn pulled a gun. There was hasty movement all around him, and cries, and shouts.

Then there was nothing.

*

The heat was profound.

Thein awoke in the bottom of the boat, stared into a cloudless blue sky.

He sat up, rocking slightly. Gazing out across the water, he could see distant waves breaking on the reef, the open sea beyond. But it was quiet here, the sea barely lapping.

The reef? We've landed.

We're ashore.

Fear fluttered down his spine, danced across his testicles.

Wait. Be smart now.

His mouth was full of fluid. Thein Suu Ay wiped his lips across his forearm, came back with a red smear, thick and viscous. Coughing hard, he lent over and slobbered gummy blood into gin-clear water, watched it go wispy amongst tiny, darting fish.

Spots were swimming in his vision. Concentrating made them go away.

Okay.

The boat had been pulled halfway up onto the beach, like someone had made an effort to get it onto dry land but had then given up. Thein stood, picked his way out of the vessel.

He faced a dense wall of jungle across a short stretch of sand. Trees and branches intertwined like a hateful orgy of snakes, and they appeared to absorb the light.

Thousands of imagined eyes stared out.

Savage Island.

And it *was* awful here, really awful, somehow as awful as the legends claimed. The air was heavy and narcotic, many sweet poisons.

Footprints on the beach, four sets, three going one way, one another. They all looked like they'd been running, hard. Thein recognised the American's Birkenstocks as the solitary tracks. They led down the shoreline and, presumably, around the headland.

That fucking American.
Why were they running?

The child appeared shortly before sunset.

Thein, dehydrated and woozy, had been unable to start the motor. There were oars in the boat, but he would never break the reef, and attempting to row thirty miles in changeable weather with no fresh water was tantamount to suicide. The best he could hope was that one of the much-touted patrol boats would pick him up before things got too bad.

But you'll never break the reef. Look at those waves.

The alternative was to follow the footprints; it was not an attractive option. If the fishermen wanted to sail off the island, they would have to come back. If the fishermen had been taken captive, Thein was in no condition to mount a rescue. If the fishermen were dead – well, that wasn't worth thinking about. His fellow travellers had obviously been running from something, but Thein, exposed and unconscious in the boat, had been left unharmed.

Why?

Perhaps he was safe in the boat. Perhaps he was safe on the water.

Perhaps the water had protected him.

The child was naked, dark-skinned, and a little over four feet tall. He was prepubescent, although Thein could make out traces of developing muscle in his chest and abdomen. More unexpected was a small white birthmark on his temple, reaching over his left eyebrow like a little brushstroke.

The boy had emerged in silence from a gap in the jungle, and in his hand was the disembodied head of one of the fishermen, carried upside down by a short, gristly cord of spine. It must have been quite heavy, yet was held easily, almost casually.

The fisherman was very freshly dead.

Thein blinked.

Both eyes had been gouged, and the mouth yawned like a carelessly stowed puppet. There was blood, more blood than made sense. It ran out of the nose and the mouth and the ears and the eye-sockets and pit-pattered onto the pale yellow beach as the child walked towards him.

The boy had no weapon, yet still Thein stumbled backwards in terror, practically fell into the boat as he pushed it out, made a hell of a lot of clatter.

He found he had lost an oar, watched it float away, uselessly.

It only took a few seconds for the child to reach the water's edge, and then he and the boy regarded one another.

He's NOT going to come into the sea.

They must be afraid of the sea. At least here, I'm safe.

Thein was just remembering to breathe, when the boy shouted, one quick, high-pitched noise, and to Thein it sounded horrible, like barking. It made him want to clamp his hands to his ears.

Dogs, they have the heads of dogs . . .

The boy dropped his grisly load onto the sand, and Thein watched the head roll, sand sticking to the wet bits, which was most of it. Given the sight, it was strange that the vomit, Thein's own, would take him so entirely by surprise.

The boy was shouting again, jumping up and down, his little penis bouncing against his tummy. Too late, Thein realised what had distracted the child, why he was shouting out to sea.

Dark lines on the water.

Canoes. Dozens of them.

They poured into the bay, backlit by a sunset of red fire.

Heat from one concentrated source, and pain in the sockets of his arms.

Then, panic.

I can't open my eyes they've glued my eyes they've taken my eyes

But, eventually, his left opened, the lid gummy with puke and congealed spit. Thein's pupil contracted as he stared into the heart of a large fire, a few feet away.

Far above the clearing, stars twinkled. He could see them because he was hanging upside down, suspended from a tree. His wrists were tied below, and his arms were slack and aching.

A noise, a voice nearby, though it sounded more like a wheeze, a release of breath.

Thein turned his head, saw another one of the Pandit brothers. He was strung up similarly, like meat.

Like meat.

But this fisherman looked physically unharmed, although his face was contorted into a mask of fear. The noise he was making was also very strange, having mostly worn out his vocal chords with screaming. He was staring, his eyes wide and wild.

Staring at Thein.

Thein embraced a strange wave of calmness, wishing the man wouldn't stare so hard, and tried to say so. But this effort to communicate seemed to make the fisherman expel his silent screams even more violently, and he bucked and jolted in a distressing way.

Thein was reminded of the snapper that they'd hauled aboard the boat only a few hours before, his casual disinterest in the way it had died at his feet.

He's screaming at me. Why is he screaming at me?

It was as if the fisherman couldn't believe Thein was alive, or perhaps that Thein being alive was somehow making it worse. But making *what* worse?

Thein turned his head in the other direction and saw the third fisherman similarly tied, but having been flayed of almost all his skin. He too was still alive, and dripping out into a green, shiny plastic bucket. He whipped on his rope like a pinned eel, and his eyes were lidless and dry.

Improbably long teeth snapped in a skull of red gore, the lips being God-knows-where.

On impulse, Thein craned his neck backwards to look towards the ground, discovered another naked island boy staring up at him with juvenile curiosity, the fire dancing in his eyes. Thein could recognise that this was a different child, because this one had no white birthmark, although the two young natives together would have looked very similar.

In that instant, something like understanding passed between them.

Thein tried to form a sentence – *What did you do with Edward Quinn?* – but could not manage to get past the first four words.

The boy said nothing.

'Where did you get the bucket?' said Thein.

This sentence came out far better, because he really wanted to know.

The child skipped away, and the fire crackled and blazed.

Thein screamed when the first incision was made around his ankle, and the skin of his left leg was drawn back slowly, like electrical tape.

He screamed again when the blood ran down his back, his neck, and into his eyes.

Thein still had plenty of energy for screaming.

Part One

Some years later

One

Atlanta, Georgia, USA.

It was difficult to pinpoint the precise moment when Dr Charlie Cortez decided to cheat on his wife. Certainly the desire had been accumulating in his loins as he walked into the strip joint beneath the crappy motel on Ponce De Leon, but it could have been days, weeks, even months before that. It wasn't exactly a mid-life crisis; at thirty-eight he imagined he was too young, and Charlie had kept in great shape, still had all his own hair – but he'd had a burgeoning feeling that something was missing, that his life so far was lacking, that he had a right to *more*.

As his therapist had told him when he confessed his guilt at desiring other women, marriage wasn't tantamount to lobotomy, or chemical castration. Hell, Vanessa was practically daring him to cheat by not putting out as much. She certainly shouldn't have been surprised to discover him here, not that she would ever know.

It was approaching midnight, and the music was pounding into his skull.

Dan Demus, a preppy colleague boozehound – whose friendship Charlie should have grown out of – hit him hard between the shoulder blades.

'Dude,' he said, 'you wanna tell me what I'm looking at?'

Charlie couldn't hear over the Kid Rock track and was a little spaced out from an interminable shift in the ER, so Dan gave his face a light swat with loose knuckles, and gestured towards the counter. Two Goth dykes were making out over a line of vodka shots, muscular buttocks pinning ruined barstools to the bare concrete floor.

'Shit,' said Charlie.

'Fuck,' said Dan, bad language serving to reassert their collective manliness on what was essentially alien terrain. For whatever reason, they'd set out to misbehave tonight, but already felt somewhat out of their depth.

'Someone should put this shit on YouTube,' said Charlie.

'I'm gonna go talk to them,' said Dan.

'Of course you are.'

'What? They know we're watching. They know full well.'

'Forget it, Demus. This isn't for our benefit,' Charlie said, but Dan wasn't kidding. Still lip-locked, the white-faced chick with her face in their direction rolled her dark eyes heavenward in mock ecstasy. Then, she set her gaze across the dance floor. Set her gaze on them.

A pale arm snaked out, crowded with art. A black fingernail beckoned.

Dan was striding over already, would surely screw it up with his dumb-ass grin and scholarship-winning confidence. When Dan was drunk he got overconfident, and then he'd been known to get grabby, though it would probably take quite a lot to get thrown out of a dive like this.

'In for a penny,' said Charlie, chugging his beer.

'This is Leo, this is Tiffany,' Dan said to Charlie, after Charlie had picked his way through the crowd. They were yelling, they all had to; Kid Rock had segued into Marilyn Manson.

Dan leaned in and screamed like a goosed demon. 'I think Leo has a COCK in her pants!'

The booming laugh that followed threw his head way back, and Charlie wanted to hit him; the girls were cuter close up.

'Wait three songs,' shouted the Goth called Tiffany, nodding towards the stage, where a middle-aged stripper had suspended herself upside down around the dancer's pole, breasts dropping into her armpits. 'Then you'll see what Leo has. Best mover we ever had.'

'You work here?'

The girls nodded, and Charlie found himself staring at Leo, her big dark eyes. She seemed to be the youngest woman in the joint by maybe ten years, and she was moving her labret piercing with her tongue in a way he found irresistible. She was skinny and beautiful with wine-red lips, her face framed by thick blond hair. Her skin was almost translucent, and a roadmap of delicate veins crisscrossed a bulging cleavage.

'I thought strippers were supposed to be *good-looking*,' Dan, yelled but they all ignored him.

Without warning, Tiffany pulled Charlie towards her, grabbed his balls through his pants with one hand, surprisingly strong.

'What's a nice black boy like you doing in a place like this?'

'Puerto Rican American.'

'Dark for a Hispanic.'

He gulped more beer. 'Spare me your ignorance.'

'A nice black boy, and in shirt and tie, no less. Don't imagine I'll find any biker tats on your shiny brown body. You after a taste of the exotic?'

'Exotic like a sewer,' Charlie said, flicking a cigarette butt from the peanut bowl.

'See Leo here?' Tiffany was hissing in his ear; her breath was hot, boozy, moist. 'You see this girl? She doesn't sleep. She can't. She hasn't slept in, like, a week.'

'She's sick?' said Charlie.

'No, she's *hardcore*.' The hand began to massage, found his prick, it was stiffening; he couldn't help himself. Charlie looked at pale little Leo again, she was watching them with acute concentration, dark circles beneath long, heavy lashes.

Leo knocked back a shot, shivered endearingly, then smiled like an ingénue.

'She gets especially hardcore for boys like you,' said Tiffany. 'You know, *bigger* boys. You let your white friend lead you astray.'

Despite the music, the strobe lights, the insistent hand on his dick, Charlie flashed on his wife at home in their apartment. Vanessa, kissing him on the cheek on his way out the door. Vanessa, chastising him for leaving his muddy golf shoes in the hallway while he washed up for dinner. Vanessa, sitting up in bed, thoughtfully investigating the inside of her ear with a Q-tip.

Then, with remarkable clarity and in surround sound: Vanessa, unveiling one of her mood-swings when she was hungry, thirsty, sleepy, horny. *I have a right to my feelings. My feelings are legitimate. Don't lecture me about being tired. I give the lectures around here, mister . . .*

'Upstairs,' said Tiffany, producing a key from somewhere. 'We have a room.'

'A room?'

'You know what to do.'

Charlie glanced at Dan. He was leaning across the counter, drunkenly extolling the virtues of Panama City Beach to the giant barman. It was spring break next week, Charlie heard him say; *pussy season in Florida*, as if Dan would do anything about it beyond Googling for reality porn. Red-faced and sweaty, clad from top to toe in J. Crew, he was looking more and more like potential carrion.

'We should never have come here,' Charlie whispered. 'Whose idea was this?'

'What's that, hon?' said Tiffany.

'Nothing.'

The music changed again – Ray Wylie Hubbard singing 'Snake Farm'.

'Go now, and don't worry about your friend.' Tiffany's smile was crooked. 'He'll have a real nice story to tell when you find yourselves back in your real lives.'

After kissing his closed eyelids, she slithered off him and strode on leather boots towards the bathroom. Charlie winced as he rolled the condom off his softening penis, marvelled at his productivity on what had already been a five-beer night. Too lazy to move, yet already attempting to stave off the guilt gathering around the corners of his consciousness, he dropped the oozing rubber onto the night table. There were bottles and bottles of pills there, and Charlie blinked at them.

'She wasn't kidding, your friend,' he said. 'When she said you never slept.'

He could hear the sound of running water. 'Huh?' came the voice.

'Active ingredients,' said Charlie, louder. 'Triazolam. Hypnotex. *Lunesta*. Jesus, you have to take all these sedatives?'

Leo appeared in the doorway. The neon outside flashed on-off across her naked body.

'It doesn't make any difference,' she said. 'I haven't slept in three weeks. I haven't slept properly in six months.'

'Everyone needs to sleep sometimes.'

'I don't expect you to believe me. I haven't slept a moment in three weeks.' She was slurring her words pretty badly. 'Not for a single moment.'

Damn, this chick is fucked up.

'How did you get this many pills?' he said.

She shrugged, smiled. 'What are you, a doctor?'

Charlie didn't answer immediately, examined the bedcover instead. It was marked with squashed bugs and other assorted stains, this despite the sympathetic lighting.

Charlie Cortez was so proud of being a doctor, had every right to be. He was pleased with how far he'd come, of how hard he'd worked; and yes, pleased with the glazed, ignorant admiration that flashed across the eyes of almost all he told, from the wealthy and influential to the sick and the desperate, and often both categories of patient at once. Charlie realised then that *I'm a doctor*, or *I'm Dr Cortez* were probably the things he said more than anything else. More than *please*, more than *thank you*, far more than *I love you*. He probably wouldn't have had it any other way. *I'm a doctor* was his immediate password to legitimacy, to respect, and sometimes, before he even knew it was happening, strangers would open their secrets to him and bare their souls.

He didn't much feel like saying it now, though.

'I have to get out of here,' Charlie whispered. 'None of this ever happened.'

Leo walked over, unsteady on her feet, but a strange little smile played across her lips. She was hiding something behind her back. Charlie hoped it wasn't some kind of sex toy, she seemed like she might be the type.

'You should relax a while,' she said. 'Stress can kill, y'know?'

'So what's it like,' he said, shifting position, 'to never sleep?'

'Interesting.'

'How so?'

'It means . . . I can see things.'

She was holding a scarf, spotless white silk. She took his dark wrist in her pale hand, threaded the material through the strong bars on the headboard.

Charlie, getting excited again despite himself, permitted her to tie him up. Above them, a dusty ceiling fan stirred the stale air.

'What do you see, Leo?' he said.

'Call me Leona.'

'Leona.'

'I see *lots* of things.' She traced the sweat beads on his skin, chasing them into tight abdominal grooves. God knows why he took so much care to stay in shape; him, a married man who had finally found the courage to pay for sex.

'What do you see right now?' he said.

'You really wanna know?'

Charlie nodded, tested his strength against the silk, watched his muscles jump. It was a little disquieting to realise just how good her knots were.

'Right now . . . I see *fire*.' Leona closed her eyes.

'You have another rubber?' He nodded southward. 'I only brought one out with me.'

She stood up, walked to the dresser.

The dagger that she drew from the drawer was decorative, antique, and the blade coiled, kind of. Jewels in the handle coruscated in the half-light.

'Damn,' said Charlie. 'You really *are* hardcore.'

'Please, scream as loud as you like,' she said. 'The management here is used to it.'

Far below them, Charlie could hear the bass thump of the night-club: distant, hypnotic, tribal.

Dr Charlie Cortez, teeth gritted, pushed the Lotus Evora far harder than he should onto the Downtown Connector, relishing the roar and response of the engine. It was still night, and the sleek blue bullet flashed through wide pools of streetlight and past the moon-blanked glass of slower traffic, a steel blur in the fine mist of pre-dawn. The seventy-five/eighty-five is a beast of a road, sixteen-lanes wide in some places, but Charlie had greater worries than the traffic.

The girl in the seat next to him was laughing at his earnestness, his concentration. She was naked but for their sex-stained bedcovers, and the whole car stank of fucking.

'Why are we driving so quickly, Charlie?'

'I always drive quickly,' said Charlie. 'I have to.'

'What are you running from? *Who* are you running from? I'm already here.'

'We have to get to the hospital.'

'There's no cure for what we have, Charlie Cortez. No cure but music, lights and laughter.'

'Shut up.'

'No cure but *death*, Charlie Cortez. And it'll take more than pills to get us there.'

'Everyone has to sleep sometime.'

'Even me?'

'Everyone.'

'Don't get confused, Charlie.'

Leona dropped the sheet, and Charlie found himself staring at the tattoo on her flat belly, a snake poised to strike. The lights outside wound images across her body, a sensuous, writhing nakedness upon which he projected his shame and lust.

She reached across to him, one hand immediately busy in his crotch, the other on the wheel.

Gentle but insistent, little Leo tugged at the steering, and they sheared across lanes, the Evora mowing the ridged paint that demarked the HOV lane, then vibrating on the rumble-strip that was the extreme edge of the road.

'*Now*, Dr Cortez.'

The car buzzed a violent, urgent warning up his spine.

'I never told you . . .' Charlie screamed. 'I never told you I was a doctor . . .'

She took control completely as he grabbed for her; he couldn't help himself. A peaky breast filled one hand, and his other skewered into hot, irresistible slickness. Charlie caught a glance in the rear-view mirror, the glimmering glow of Midtown rolling ever further away; the huge, futuristic, hard-won civilisation of his city.

The car smashed through the thick barriers dividing the north-south lanes as though they were cardboard, and there was the screech of tyres and a howl of horns.

When Charlie tried to reach for the wheel and save their lives, she was far too strong for him, and she *wouldn't let go.*

'We're going the *wrong way*,' Charlie yelled, and oncoming lights bore down.

Real or imagined, a scream is a disturbing thing to experience under normal circumstances, let alone in the mental twilight between waking and sleeping.

Charlie Cortez, wrestling with the choking luxury of sweat-heavy Egyptian cotton, was brought to the bright, freshly painted reality of his spare room with hideous immediacy.

Again, he heard screaming. Real screaming. He wasn't in a nightmare any more.

Get up.

Fighting to free his long limbs from the bed with all the sticky inelegance of a newly birthed giraffe, Charlie found himself brought up short by Milo, the eldest – by one minute – of his non-identical fourteen-year-old twin boys. Slim and confident in his semi-nakedness, Milo was standing in the doorway in a matching, albeit miniaturised, version of his father's black Armani underwear, regarding Charlie through thick-framed spectacles. To Charlie, who had just experienced intercourse in a crashing automobile, it was all a little much.

'How long have you been standing there?' he said, not knowing what to do with his arms, but resisting the urge to fold them across his bare chest.

The scream rang out again, tinged with what? Impatience? It was Vanessa, probably from the kitchen.

'Please,' said Milo. 'Must I live in a house of hysterics?'

He turned his gaze to the bed, upon which drooped Charlie's soggy meringue of night-terror sheets.

'What are you doing in here?'

Here being the guest room: and it was a reasonable question. While nobody was looking, the guest room of their apartment had taken on an impersonal hotel-like quality, and the staged, generic comfort added to the surreal nature of the exchange.

Charlie fought for clarity while a pneumatic hangover forced spots to swim across his vision.

What was her name?

She was called LEONA.

What did you do to her?

No, what did SHE do to YOU?

Charlie remembered a wet heat, a shared need, but when he licked his lips he found no taste of her. This was disappointing, for some reason.

But you DID have sex with someone last night. You crushed your marriage vows.

The spots before his eyes began to take the appearance of melting marshmallows.

And just how did you get yourself home, Dr Cortez?

'Ah, late night yesterday,' confessed Charlie to his son, tapping his chest as though that would dislodge the burgeoning nausea. 'Very late. I didn't want to wake your mom.'

Milo shrugged. 'You're entitled to a Friday every now and then.'

'Glad to have your consent.'

'Big night, then?'

'Big enough.'

Milo shot him a glance of fresh scrutiny, and Charlie realised he'd have to throw the boy a catch of acceptable size to curb much more questioning. 'Demus threw up in the parking lot behind Burger King.'

Dan Demus was always good for a tangy excuse. Hard to remember

exactly why he was banned from visiting the family in person –
burping the alphabet, teaching the boys Texas hold-em, bringing
over an old *Playboy* because he insisted he once went to high school
with the cover girl – there were tales aplenty to draw upon.

Milo grinned. 'Demus is such a jerk-off.'

Charlie allowed his mouth to twitch into a smile. Dan, of course,
was the innocent party in this instance, and the boys had not even
laid eyes on the flame-haired psych resident in six months. The
guilt was all Charlie's, but it was not the false accusation of his
friend that was chewing at his conscience.

Alliance with his son re-established, Charlie winced theatrically
as Vanessa shouted again, and Milo laughed. Her voice was
decreasing in hysteria, but it still sounded as though a tormented
lioness was trying to pronounce his name.

Charlie strode into the master bedroom and grabbed his towelling
robe.

The apartment, a modern condo in the heart of Midtown, was
an expensive compromise. Both Charlie and Vanessa had grown
up in Metro Atlanta, and both could recognise a good investment.
But where Charlie had visions of raising his kids in a house on a
tree-lined street in Buckhead, Vanessa had her heart set on a busy,
high-rise, central address. The place was nice, if sterile: lots of
chrome and granite. They were in a skyscraper above an international hotel, so the views were spectacular, but the arrangement,
while satisfying Vanessa's sense of social advancement, had imbued
in Charlie a feeling of impermanence, and the staff at the pool
used by residents alongside the hotel guests had never bothered to
learn his name.

Charlie found his wife in her robe also, palms down on the
polished unit in the middle of the kitchen. Vanessa looked weary
in the way she always seemed to out of make-up nowadays, and
was hanging her head as though she had been engaged in mental
battle for some time.

'In the sink,' she said to him.

The cockroach that resided there was a good inch-and-a-half long, and a hue of brown, sickeningly shiny. The beast was probably a king amongst its peers, not only having negotiated sixteen floors of vertical modern plumbing, but also possessing the mythical power to disjoint itself in such a way as to fit through a sinkhole small enough for the Jolly Green Giant to generate besetment.

Now it rested, motionless but very much alive, in a thimbleful of water.

Charlie managed to disguise his pleasure at this unexpected distraction.

'You gonna deal with it already?' said Vanessa.

With the morbid regard of the mortally hung-over, Charlie immediately ascribed the roach a personality, imagined he could see it, actually *witness* it, panting with the exertion of it all. Hard not to admire a creature that had experienced a more complicated night than he.

Not particularly keen on his task, Charlie's hand stalled, wadded kitchen paper in hand. The cockroach waggled two disconcertingly long antennae at him like an infant questing for the breast.

Vanessa moved over for a better view of the battlefield and searched her husband with eyes still heavy-lidded from sleep.

'Where were you last night?'

'Strip club,' he said without hesitation.

'You wouldn't dare.'

'No,' he said. Reverse psychology, always a winner.

'You stink of smoke. Card game?'

'We lost track of the time. I wasn't late, but I didn't want to wake you.'

She nodded. 'How'd you get home?'

Good question, Charlie.

After the motel, the reminder of the night was a blur, a mixture of dream and reality. It was of real concern to him, as he didn't feel he had drunk all that much.

Wet heat, shared need.

Her name was LEONA.

Did this particular hangover have a strangely narcotic quality? Had she put something in his drink? Maybe one of those horse-strength tranquillisers lined up on the bedside cabinet? Might also explain the Hollywood quality of his nightmare.

A nice black boy, in shirt and tie, no less. You after a taste of the exotic?

'Charlie?' Vanessa sounded concerned.

'Yeah,' he said. 'Spaced out for a moment there.'

He was pretty sure that Dan had driven him home, although Dan couldn't have been in a condition to drive either. But there were issues this morning that had an order of priority, and by confusing them in his compromised state he could run into trouble. Right now he seemed to be acing the interrogations of his family, so it was best to concentrate on this winning streak; he could unravel his own confusions later.

'Designated driver,' said Charlie, eventually. 'Ah, Davey Manuel.'

It was sufficient. To Vanessa, everything suddenly made sense.

'You drop a fortune on a British sports car and then let your idiot friends drive it? *Designated driver*? Did you think of your insurance? I was gonna meet Michelle for lunch.'

'You can still take the car.'

'Davey Manuel who smokes cigars? You get that vehicle to the valet, mister.'

'Take the Forester.'

'There's a dent in the side door.'

'Remind me who put that dent there?'

'For *chrissake*, Charlie, can we get to the roach now?'

'We?'

'Please, Charlie,' she said. 'I have to work this morning. I don't need this.'

'Rather you than me.'

Vanessa put her hands on her hips, and her robe fell open a little. A white negligee was revealed, one hard, dark nipple pushing through the silk. She caught his glance and covered herself up just as quickly, pulling the cord tightly around her middle.

'You're damn right, rather me than you,' she said. 'I don't know why I care so much. No one else seems to.'

Vanessa was a children's writer; her employment as such the result of a curious turn of events. Two bottles of Merlot one evening on her parents' postcard-pretty porch with a friend who worked on a minority press, and she'd wheeled out an impromptu story about a *talking worm* of all things; something she claimed to have made up for Milo and Jesse while they were still in the crib. This worm – who spoke with a stereotypical Southern *yes ma'am, no ma'am* accent – was the Good Samaritan in annelid form, capable of becoming a washing line (to help a little girl dry her clothes), a footbridge (to help a little boy escape a vicious swarm of bees) and, by hopping on a basketball, a half-assed exclamation mark (for no real reason at all).

Charlie had been present at this improvised pitch meeting, and his suggestion of a bootlace episode had been roundly laughed at, which bothered him more than it probably should have. He especially remembered the snub when, many years later, the short series of books became an unexpected success, finding a way into kindergarten libraries up and down the country. A second series was commissioned, and the upshot was that Wilkins the Worm, despite not being real – and a worm – was now a full-blown member of the Cortez family, and, through Vanessa, had become capable of making demands. These demands were tough on them all; Vanessa particularly, who had never previously voiced a desire to be anything other than a homemaker.

Suffer from stress, Wilkins seemed to say to her. *I need you to WORRY about me. I need you to spend more time with me, working on me, telling my tales.*

And, as time passed, it seemed that Wilkins had a few choice words for Charlie as well: *You'd better be quiet, sonny-Jim. Know why? I make more money than you.* It was true.

This after *years* of medical school.

I make more money than you.

Years of struggle, of test taking, of pulling all-nighters, of pleasing his teachers, his bosses, his patients. Vanessa's contribution to their bank balance, neither expected nor particularly required, now dwarfed Charlie's. And she'd fallen into it, by having the good fortune to be able to produce five-hundred-word books that, suddenly, everyone wanted to read.

But Charlie couldn't complain. Every time he wanted to ask the question, to express his dissatisfaction, Wilkins was ready with the only response that seemed to ring true: *If you can't be glad for your wife, that must mean that you don't love her.*

Dr Charlie Cortez, thrashed in the man-stakes by a cartoon worm.

Vanessa's love of the small and crawly didn't extend to cockroaches, however.

'What are you waiting for?' she was saying to him. 'He's getting his breath back.'

'He's half-dead already,' Charlie said, integrating into the present. 'I talked to the super, they pour gallons of poison down the drains. You think those paying guests downstairs are tolerating this?'

'They poison our *building*?' Vanessa liked to envisage herself in a happy, dancing skyscraper. She'd live on *Sesame Street* if she could.

'Building's fine,' said Charlie. 'Bugs get everywhere. Wet winter.'

He had never crushed a face-up cockroach before. His ball of kitchen paper descended once more. The cockroach righted itself and promptly trotted towards the wall of its stainless-steel oubliette like an ass-slapped mule.

'You *see?*' wailed Vanessa. 'He's getting away!'

Charlie felt an insistent tug on his bare arm. Jesse, his other son, was trying to pull him out of the way.

'He'll climb that smooth surface, easy,' Jesse said. 'He'll be up, then he'll fly.'

'He'll *fly?*'

'Don't frighten your mom.'

'Kill it!' wailed Vanessa.

Charlie brought down the wad, wincing at the myriad *cracking* noises.

'Dad, you only got the head.'

Charlie brought up the tissue. The body of the cockroach flailed.

'You know, cockroach don't need a head to live,' Jesse confided to Vanessa.

'*What?*'

'Oh yeah.' Jesse rattled a half-empty bag of potato chips that lay open beside the refrigerator. 'If he just ate a big meal, Mr Cockroach, he just goes about his business without a head.' He shrugged. 'Thought everyone knew that. He can't grow himself a new one, but not having a head don't bother him one bit.'

'*Doesn't* bother him,' corrected Charlie, bringing down the tissue again. The body of the cockroach gave an electric spasm.

'For God's sake,' said Jesse, and he brought down his bare fist on the body of the beast.

Crunch.

Delighted by the disgusted reaction of his parents, Jesse did it again and again, until bug debris littered the plughole and pieces of the wreckage were pressed into his skin.

'If you want something done . . .' He flashed his broad, winning smile.

'Go wash your hands,' said Vanessa quietly. 'I'll make breakfast.'

Still smiling, Jesse grabbed the bag of chips and loped towards the hallway. Milo already had the TV on: the boy could watch the blowhards on CNBC for hours. There'd be the usual argument in there soon enough, Jesse having already lined up the Saturday *NCIS* marathon on USA.

Alone together in the kitchen, Charlie fought for something else to say to his wife, but couldn't find any words, not one.

So it was that Dr Charlie Cortez brushed his teeth and thought about sex and death.

Perhaps it was typical of him. Charlie couldn't just cheat on his wife with a regular upmarket escort like a normal rogue on his salary, or screw a willing Candy Striper like so many of his middle-aged colleagues had. He had to pick himself a beautiful, doomed, suicide blonde, who fucked like a demon and clung on with tears in her eyes as though she really needed him.

It was all an act. That's what they do.

An act?

The good ones show you what you want.

Was that what he wanted, to be needed? By a pill-popping prostitute?

Yet despite Leona's collection of pills, she was like no drug addict that Charlie had ever encountered. She didn't even seem sick, more like she was going, what . . .

Mad?

The way she talked put Charlie in mind of those patients who had accepted terminal illness, had acknowledged that they didn't have long to live.

I haven't slept properly in six months.

This girl wasn't concerned: it was as though she had entered an exclusive club, had found an exalted plain, could access some hard-won knowledge or ancient wisdom.

I see things.

She didn't want his sympathy, she sneered at his pity, she mocked his awkwardness, and when he finally got her to untie him, when he got her to drop the knife, to lose the dominatrix act more for her safety than his, he tried to hold her and show her it was okay, despite his booze and her pills, the stains on the sheets, the ugly circumstances that had thrown them together.

Charlie *did* want to be needed, just for a moment, and it didn't matter where or why; she had the power to show him *who he was* for those torrid few minutes, and in return, Leona just wanted his . . .

Love?

Disgusted, Charlie banged the cabinet door hard enough to rattle the lifestyle potions within. The face, his face, that swung into the mirror, with bloodshot eyes and foaming mouth, looked ridiculous to him.

And who are you?

I'm a doctor.

The line was growing as stale as the life that existed to support it. That was Charlie's gift to his family: consistency, dependability, faultless performances, day after day. Charlie Cortez, the hard-working, thankless supporting actor to Vanessa, the troubled, grandstanding, star. Not to mention the twins, with their biological uniqueness. Always worthy of comment, they were a double act that never failed to impress.

It was time to branch out, to find fresh self-definition. Not in sordid liaisons like the previous night – for the sake of safety, and for the good things in the life he knew, it was important to seal off Leona as a desperate, if remarkable, excursion – but *something*.

The important thing was to talk to Vanessa. Repress thoughts of Leona and talk to Vanessa. That would be most appropriate. They might not have been expert communicators, but Charlie hoped that their marriage had retained sufficient honesty for them to depart from predictability for once and make it up as they went along, like he imagined other people always did.

Whoa, hold it right there. Honesty?

You were balls-deep in a WHORE last night, sonny-boy.

The voice had changed. Inner-Charlie was so easily beaten. Comment now flowed forth in Wilkins the Worm's southern-fried accent.

Charlie rinsed, spat, reached for the towel.

Two hands began to beat a light tattoo on the other side of the bathroom door.

'Charlie,' said Vanessa, 'I need to get in there. I need to *pee*.'

Unscrewing the safety cap on the mouthwash, Charlie Cortez delivered the lines on that morning's script as faultlessly as he always did.

'I'll be one second,' he said, then: 'Can't you use the other bathroom, baby?'

'I *can't*.' She was whispering, but the voice sounded so urgent as to be in the room with him. 'Please, I need a tampon.'

There was never a good time.

'Door's unlocked,' said Charlie.

Perhaps he would talk to Vanessa later.

Thursday.

Despite what had been a far more grizzly car accident on the I-20 than it had looked from the traffic-copter, the trauma bays had miraculously emptied by the end of the morning, so for once Charlie found himself eating in an hour appropriate for lunch. There was a line for hot food in the canteen, but Vanessa had packed him something healthy in Tupperware that would have to be augmented later by candy from the machine.

Dan Demus rarely missed a meal, and Charlie found him sitting alone, having laid out an expansive picnic on the largest table in the room.

'You know what the nurses call the computers on wheels?' he said, as Charlie took his place.

'COWS,' said Charlie, half-heartedly eyeing the limp lettuce in his own bowl.

'Not any more. Remember that pertussis kid whose mother had refused the vaccination?'

'The kid who died?'

'Yeah. Well, his mom thought they were talking about her. You know, "Go fetch the COW". She logged a complaint, made a fuss.'

Charlie sighed. 'I don't know what offends me more: the inane complaint or the fact that her kid died because she was too stupid to vaccinate.'

'She hates needles, didn't want to see a needle in her kid.'

'But she just *loves* whooping cough,' said Charlie.'

'Whoa there. What's biting you? You've not been the same since – now, when was it?'

'Last Friday.'

'Of course, last Friday.' Dan's blue eyes sparkled like the inscrutable, jovial bastard he was. 'Didn't I put your mind at ease there? Wasn't it your Uncle Dan who got you home, drove you in your car, tucked you in? Little boy grew up, allowed himself to have fun, it was about time.'

'I think that girl *drugged* me, Dan. I'm almost sure of it.' Charlie lowered his voice. 'Ground-up sleeping pill in my drink, she had hundreds of them there.'

'Right, because she wasn't attractive or anything. You talked about these pills before, and I said you seemed fine. Perhaps more spaced out than I've ever seen you, but fine.'

'You were drunk.'

'A very little bit,' said Dan, grinning. 'Look, you've suffered enough for your wrongdoing, paid sufficient penance. You've been dragging your sin through this hospital like Marley's chains for the better part of a week.'

'Right.'

'So lighten up some, you'll live longer.'

'I feel bad. And you know what? I can't stop thinking about her.'

'That's you there, buddy.'

Charlie fished around in his pocket, found his pager.

'Code Blue,' he said, moving.

'Tonight,' said Dan, conversational because it wasn't his emergency. 'Shellfish and beer. Let's start the weekend early.'

'Not on your life,' said Charlie.

'Half-price pitchers at the Big Fish until eight,' Dan called after him, and some diners turned to look. 'My treat . . . You should never refuse me, Cortez; I know what's bad for you . . .'

Charlie Cortez, private life forgotten for a moment, pushed through the double doors into Grundy's Level 1 Trauma Center, picking up a couple of colleagues along the way. Chris Light, white-coated and sporting the kind of hi-top fade rarely seen since the early 90s, was a third-year medical student from Morehouse on his emergency medicine rotation. He was good, and Charlie hoped he would stick around. Chris actively encouraged his nickname – 'Sparky' – because of his surname, his indefatigable energy or his eccentric haircut.

Nurse Francesca Lee, short, steel-jawed and matronly, had worked at Grundy Memorial since the beginning of time, and was famous for scolding the doctors. Charlie would never forget his first day as a resident, walking out of a patient's room and writing an order for a urinal at the nurses' station. Francesca had read it over his shoulder, then brought her hand down flat on the desk hard enough to make him jump.

'Patient needs a urinal, Doctor?'

'Right.'

'Can you tell me that writing this order took less time than it would've taken you to hand the patient a urinal yourself?'

'I . . . no.'

'Thought so,' Francesca had said, hands on her considerable hips. 'We're gonna get on just fine, you and I.'

Charlie had done business in different hospitals since then, in different departments, but he was always happy to come back to work with Francesca. She had the safest pair of nursing hands in emergency medicine that he'd ever seen, even if he'd never actually experienced her smile.

Now she whipped back the blue curtains of the bay like a barker with a well-hyped sideshow act, and Charlie was treated to the sight of an obese and pasty-white Asian-American man. He was stripped to the waist, unconscious in the recovery position, but was practically hanging off the gurney. A pretty young paramedic called Alice hovered around the body, intrigued by the rolls of fat bulging from the patient's back.

'Frank Tsang,' Nurse Francesca said to Charlie. 'Pulse one hundred and forty, but improving. Night and day of heavy drinking. I got details from his wallet, found no wife, no next of kin. He lives in New Jersey, here for some consumer electronics fair. Wanna see the pail?'

'The pail?'

'Alice?'

'When we found him,' said Alice, 'he had, like, a waste basket with him.' The paramedic picked up a light grey plastic bucket by the side of the gurney, gave it a shake. There was plenty of blood sloshing around. It appeared quite black, and a trio of different-sized bubbles clung together.

'What do you think, about two thousand ccs?' said Sparky, watching as Charlie noted the crimson tidemarks of various vintages.

'He vomited all this blood?'

'Pretty bad, huh?' Alice said. She was looking kind of peaky herself.

'Probably not as bad as it looks, but you were right to page.'

'Dr Carmine has a nursing-home patient,' said Francesca. 'Serum sodium up at one hundred and seventy-nine. I don't know where Dr Hubbard is.'

'Okay, I've seen a college student or two like this,' Charlie said, adjusting his stethoscope in the habit that was his way when diagnosing. 'Sparky, you know what a Mallory-Weiss tear is?'

'Torn mucous membrane. Ah, bleeding in the oesophagus caused by excessive, sustained coughing.'

'Or probably vomiting, from the look of him,' said Nurse Francesca. 'Who gets this drunk by the early afternoon?'

'Nurse?'

'Sorry Doctor, don't know what came over me. He quit puking, wanna do a EGD?'

'Sparky?'

'Ah, EGD and a CBC. We should check the count.'

'See if anything unusual turns up,' said Charlie. 'And we need to rule out intestinal bleeding, but I'd be surprised if I'm wrong. He must have ingested to expel this much. Probably scared himself half to death in the process. These damn expos, the way the delegates cut loose.'

'I'm on it,' said Sparky, but still he stared at Tsang, who was now gently snoring. He was growing distracted by something, moved towards the patient for a closer look.

'Sparky?'

'I don't think we're looking at a standard drunk.'

'What's a standard drunk?' said Charlie.

'Well,' said Sparky, pointing with his pen, 'did he puke blood on the trolley?'

'What?'

'Look there. You see a spread?'

'Alice?'

The paramedic snapped like she'd been scolded. 'There was no blood on the trolley,' she said. 'No blood in the wagon. He was conscious when he was puking.'

'I was told,' said Charlie.

'Frank here could always hit the bucket, even joked about how good his aim was.'

'He told you he'd been drinking?'

'Right. He was slurry, disoriented, but basically okay. This never happened to him before.'

'So he said.'

'Right.'

'You never saw this patient before?'

'First time,' said Alice. 'But you learn how to spot the truth.'

'Perhaps you'll explain it to me sometime.'

'Yes, Dr Cortez.'

'Alcohol, but nothing else?'

'So he said.' Alice glanced across at the nurse, no help there.

Charlie had put his gloves on, carefully moved the dark pants material. Sure enough – wetness, a seeping puddle of blood, fresh this time.

'Okay, he's bleeding down here, not much, maybe an abrasion if he fell on his ass. Where did you find him?'

'Motel parking lot. Manageress called it in. Cops didn't show. Would have just been drunk and disorderly, but for the blood thing.'

'We need to get his pants off.'

Alice was looking distinctly unsure, like she couldn't believe she'd missed something, but she went to get shears while Charlie double-checked the airway and repeated Chris's flashlight test.

'Damn,' said Nurse Francesca, after a couple of desultory tugs at the clothing. 'Someone should tell this man to go up a dress size.'

It took time, but eventually, a thick wad of hastily applied bandages was revealed beneath the tight slacks, wrapped hard and fast around a thigh the size of a Christmas ham. Blood was seeping through in a shape that resembled the state of Tennessee.

'Bandages explain why there isn't more red stuff,' said Chris Light, goggled up and with his stethoscope poised over the patient's heart. 'But this wound is fresh.'

'So what exactly *do* we have here?' Charlie said to himself, peeling back the gauze. He wasn't particularly worried, given the rising pulse, steady breathing and relative lack of flow. But he was curious; here was a second complaint scarcely older than the first, and a complaint that had been treated with reasonable competence before the paramedics arrived, if with rather excessive speed.

'It looks like someone tried to take a juicy slice out of him,' said Nurse Francesca, who had missed her lunch break. 'A nice thin cut from the rump.'

'Nurse, please.'

'He'll want stitches, you think?'

'Where *is* Dr Hubbard?'

'Patient's coming around,' said Chris, up at Tsang's head. 'One-thirty over eighty.'

Charlie handed bandages to Francesca to press into the incision. There was already a small flurry of other nurses, unwinding dressings, prepping an IV and spiking the bag, turning over a fresh trolley.

'Frank?' Charlie said. He was gentle, his hand pressing against Tsang's plump, sweating cheek. '*Frank?*'

He got the texture of stubble, noted the dried spittle in the corner of the patient's mouth; this was definitely an all-nighter. Charlie hoped the big man wouldn't try to buck himself onto the floor as he woke. 'Frank, do you know where you are?'

'Nuhh . . . you're all *black*,' said Tsang, his stare glazing under the bright lights.

'Atlanta welcomes you also,' said Nurse Francesca.

Charlie laughed a little, it was going to be okay. 'Frank Tsang, you're in Grundy Memorial Hospital.' Then came a variation on his famous line, the succinct delivery of which could charge any situation – no matter how desperate – with health-giving surety: 'Frank, my name is Dr Cortez.'

This time, it didn't get the expected reaction.

'*Please,*' said Frank Tsang, delirious, his voice barely a mumble.

'Please what, Frank?'

He was looking at Charlie, but his eyes now fizzed and his pupils were contracting and expanding.

'Scream as loud as you like,' said Frank. 'The management here is used to it.'

Even without the moonlit alcoholic filter and aggressive blaze of neon, the Clearmont Lounge and Motor Hotel possessed a timeless, otherworldly quality, the type of gathering place that has existed for the wantonly marginal in all great cities since civilisation agglomerated in an orgy of base desires.

Charlie Cortez nudged his Subaru Forester over the broad sidewalk and into the narrow, shadowy lot. The windows of cheaply rented rooms stared down at him from the imposing tall brick structure, blank and expressionless. Charlie was glad he had demurred to Vanessa and allowed her to take the sports car today; this was not the moment to be climbing out of an expensive status symbol, even if he had dared risk it a week ago.

Despite the warmth of the early spring afternoon, Charlie suppressed a shiver. Sin collected around these parts of town and in towns like it, was drawn to it, yet was whitewashed nightly, and now this particular motel and nightclub sat stony-faced before a multitude of accumulated secrets, at least one of them Charlie's own.

For shame, Charlie.

There were cops there; a weary duo of uniforms emerging from the concrete stairwell that led to the basement club.

'I'm Dr Charlie Cortez,' Charlie said, stepping forward.

The two cops were blinking after their time in the underground murk. They took in Charlie, his clean shave, his neatly brushed suit from Barney's. One was tall and thin, the other short and fat, but both were pale and moustachioed, with short-cropped blond hair. When they paused at the top of the vomit-hosed steps, they held their loaded belts in exactly the same way. It wouldn't have been more surreal to Charlie if they had spoken in rhyme.

'What seems to be the problem, Doctor?' said tall-and-thin.

'Frank Tsang,' said Charlie. 'A patient of mine. He was admitted to Grundy an hour ago.'

Tall-and-thin looked over at short-and-fat. Short-and-fat caught the glance and rotated his fleshy head towards the sky in a way that suggested he might be concerned about rainfall.

'Mr Tsang was vomiting blood,' said Charlie. 'A drunk, we think. But he had a deep laceration to his right thigh.' Charlie demonstrated on his own silk-suited leg. 'The paramedics found him in this parking lot. The wound would suggest assault.'

'He couldn't have done it to himself?'

This had occurred to Charlie. He couldn't say exactly why he didn't think this was the case, only that he had some deep-seated certainty about Leona. It was more than just Tsang's repetition of her words, words that had resounded in his consciousness like a whisper from across the void. Perhaps he had some strange understanding of her madness, something they had shared together, something—

Be quiet, whispered Wilkins the Worm, like a corrosive Jiminy Cricket.

'Sir?'

'Given the nature of the wound,' said Charlie, 'I would say that self-harm was unlikely. People normally target their arms, their wrists, their hands. I've never experienced someone who sliced into their upper thigh.'

'You say he was drunk?'

And the rest, thought Charlie. He didn't have Tsang's tox-screen yet, but if the man had been anywhere near Leona . . .

Pills on the nightstand, bottles and bottles of pills.

Charlie just nodded.

'So what exactly is your concern,' said tall-and-thin, 'Dr . . .'

'Cortez,' repeated Charlie.

Good question.

'Well, simply put,' said Charlie, 'we're concerned about infection.'

'Infection?' said short-and-fat. He spoke with solid, dull authority.

'Tetanus to be exact. We don't have a weapon. We don't know what cut him.'

'Tetanus?'

'Yes,' said Charlie. '*Costridium tetani.*'

Somewhere in the back of Charlie's mind, an off-Broadway theatre full of anthropomorphic cartoon worms received this gratuitous use of Latin with a sarcastic round of applause.

The cops exchanged another look, and short-and-fat expelled his breath in a long whistle.

'I'm Burke,' said tall-and-thin, thumbing the name pinned to his chest. 'This is McManus. Did your dispatcher call the cops?'

'Yes. No. I don't know. Doesn't the hospital always do that?'

'Was it assault?' said Burke. 'On Mr . . .'

'Tsang. No, wait . . .' said Charlie, remembering. 'Drunk and disorderly.'

'He was bleeding out of his ass, and no one called it assault?'

'He wasn't bleeding out of his *anus*. It was his thigh, already bandaged.'

'Someone assaulted him,' said McManus, '*then* applied bandages?'

The urgent crackle of a police radio suggested that more important things might be starting to happen elsewhere.

'But *recently*,' said Charlie. 'We didn't notice the bandage until later, and the weapon—'

He was interrupted by a noise at the base of the stairwell. The heavy metal doors to the bar surged open, slamming against brickwork with an industrial echo.

'You gonna harass my customers as well as my staff?' yelled the bosomy, middle-aged bleach-blonde who emerged. 'I can see it all right here on the security cameras. You want me to sue the city for harassment?'

'Ma'am . . .'

The woman squinted up into the light, tried to make out Charlie's face. 'Mister, you don't let these two morons put you off. We're open, we're always open. Half-price juleps until five.'

'Since when?' said McManus.

'I gotta push a vacuum around some, but the jukebox got free plays.'

'Deal of the century, so long as you like John Fogerty,' muttered McManus.

'You still here?' said the woman.

'This man's a doctor, don't be hustlin' now.'

It was her voice, rather than her appearance, that rang a bell in Charlie's mind. She looked different out of her Goth costume and dark wig. This was Tiffany, Leo's friend, the one who had set them up in the first place.

'Look, Doc,' said Burke, the look on his face suggesting they wouldn't be conversing for very much longer, 'we're not here for a drunk and disorderly, and we're not here for assault. I don't know your Frank Tsang.'

'Excuse me?'

'Your patient, I don't know him. We get info that some harsh weed got sold out of one of these rooms upstairs, and although we know that don't happen mostly, we have to check it out. Tiffany knows that, right, Tiff?'

Tiffany was picking her way up the wet concrete stairs. She seemed like a creature unused to the light.

'Can't run a decent dive bar any more,' she said to Charlie. 'The competition will do anything to fuck you up. No drugs here. Not now, not ever, the lies that get told—' She stopped herself, finally recognising him.

McManus grasped the opportunity to adjust his underwear, having enjoyed a better look at Tiffany's cleavage in the natural light. 'Well then,' he said, 'we'll be checking with our dispatcher.'

'Thanks,' said Charlie.

'Take care now,' said Burke.

A little time passed.

'Well, she ain't here,' Tiffany said to Charlie as the cop car departed, gumballs spinning in anticipation of some fresh crime fighting.

'Leona? How did you—'

'Because you have it bad, nice boy.' She lit a cigarette and expelled smoke, then picked at something on the end of her tongue, maybe a stray hair. 'You aren't the first, probably won't be the last.'

Charlie couldn't think of anything to say.

'You think I haven't seen it before?' said Tiffany.

'Seen what before?'

'The desire.'

'Desire for what?'

'She talked about you, you know. Afterwards.'

'She did?'

'What do you care? Did you get what you wanted? Did you get what you *paid* for?'

Charlie struggled to hold her gaze.

'But you're back, and not for the generous way my barman pours.'

'You own this place?'

'Me and my husband.'

'I think Leona attacked a man,' said Charlie Cortez. 'Fat Asian-American guy, name of Frank Tsang. Probably a client.'

'I called the paramedics.'

'You?'

'I call the ambulance all the time. This idiot you're talking about, I didn't know his name, but I found him out here, just assumed he was dead drunk.'

'Frank Tsang.'

'We don't do names. He was attacked?'

'Bleeding but bandaged,' Charlie said. 'He'd been cut.'

'I saw no cuts. I saw red puke. I saw a fat guy projectile vomiting.'

'Someone bandaged him up.'

'Not me.'

'My nurse got his employer on the phone,' said Charlie. 'Did a little background check. Why would an Asian-American man with no history of self-harm or knowledge of first aid, lacerate his own leg then dress it in a professional fashion?'

'You'd be surprised how much mystery blood gets spilled in this little parking lot. You think this is to do with Leona?'

'What do you think?'

'I don't talk to the cops.'

'I'm not the cops.'

'Right, you're a doctor. And you suddenly grew a conscience about a fat conference reject, worried that what got him laid landed him in a hospital bed.'

For the second time in the same conversation, Charlie was lost for words. It didn't seem to matter; Tiffany was busy thrashing another spark out of a phlegm-coloured lighter.

'Kindred fucking spirits, the two of you,' she mumbled.

'Can I speak with Leo? Leona?'

Tiffany shot a fresh cloud, and they watched it dissipate toward the heavens.

'Okay,' said Tiffany. 'But don't be causing her any more grief.'

'Grief? Why would I do that? What do you mean?'

'Nothing. Only that I know pain when I see it. And that girl has had enough for this lifetime.'

Charlie had no memory of the inside of the motel, an anonymous maze of faded wallpaper and ash-spoiled carpet. Leo's room was on the second level, no number on the door.

Three hard blows, and Tiffany's shrill, commanding voice: 'Leo, you in there?'

No answer.

'Leona?'

A few seconds later she was fumbling with a master key. Charlie surprised himself by reaching for her wrist, and she started at the unexpected touch, jangling her costume jewellery.

'What,' he said, 'you're just going to march in there?'

'You have a better idea?'

'She could be sleeping.'

'Leo never sleeps.'

'Right, she never sleeps.'

'And she never leaves, hardly. Not for weeks. We need to see if she's all right.'

'But still . . .'

'But still what? But still we got a goddam *doctor* here for a reason that's unknown right now, but is probably about to become very apparent. You a stupid man, sir?'

'No.'

'You see all the bottles of pills when you screwed this little girl?'

Charlie nodded.

'Door's open, Doctor.' She stepped back. 'You just make sure you're the best thing that happened to her in a while. If that girl ain't in trouble herself, she's surely capable of attracting it.'

Charlie took a deep breath and pushed his way into the room.

Disparaging as Vanessa frequently was of Charlie's preposterously expensive sports car, she did relish the occasional J-Lo type moment outside the Providence Christian Academy while waiting for her boys to come bounding out in their smart uniforms. She stood, resting a little on the sleek hood, hands on hips, shapely butt ensconced in tight white jeans. Her Vuitton sunglasses reflected what she imagined were the longing stares of other moms in their lesser Buicks, their Corvettes, their BMWs; these women were not capable of having careers of their own, not strong enough to survive without tolerating the whims of unreliable men or sticky-fingered nannies, not quite *goddess* enough to have birthed more than a single strong individual at one time.

Having been separated into different classes, the boys usually emerged separately, but today they appeared in the shadow of the neo-Gothic portico at once, and Vanessa felt her usual pang of pride and love. She waved, all smiles, bouncing a little on the balls of her feet, stilettos pinching.

'How was your day, babies?' she said, cupping a smooth face in each hand.

Milo shrugged, said nothing. He scrunched his nose up at this public display of affection, shifted his glasses to a more comfortable location on his face. He was going to be a politician, or a famous newsman, or—

'Well,' said Jesse, flashing his faultless teeth, 'I don't have head lice.' Jesse was the sportsman, or the action photographer, or the war hero.

'That's good, Jesse,' Vanessa whispered, wondering if anyone else had heard. Lice didn't feel like a suitable topic of conversation for the star trio.

'Rhonda Hedges has lice,' Jesse went on. '*Nits*. And she hardly even has, like, hair.'

'She has braids,' said Milo.

'Milo fancies her,' said Jesse.

'Do not.'

'Milo fancies Mrs Reynolds, the substitute teacher.'

'Do not.'

'What? Garth said you told her she looked *nice*.'

'Was I adopted, Mom?' Milo said in his mock whine. 'If not, you could lie once in a while.'

Milo came out with this strange line at least once a week. He was joking, but it still hurt. Vanessa glanced around at the other parents. They were bundling children into utility vehicles, juggling babies back into safety seats, fighting for the opportunity to pull out onto the street.

'Okay,' she said. '*Pastries A Go-Go?*'

'Yeah!' said Jesse.

'I might manage a latte,' said Milo.

There was never any question of who would squeeze into the small back seat. While Jesse perched in the front, eyes everywhere, eager as a Labrador on family vacation, Milo placed himself in the back as though chauffeured, never far from a comic book or his beloved *Time* magazine.

Vanessa signalled and drove into a space between other fast-moving cars. Pleased with the shape of the traffic on North Avenue, she risked an extra push on the accelerator, felt the big motor respond as she sped towards a light that had just turned green.

'You know,' she said to anyone who cared to listen, 'lice are nothing to be ashamed of. They only like clean hair.'

'*Mom!*'

Jesse's shriek froze her heart in her chest. Out of nowhere, there was mortal danger.

An Atlanta school bus, a solid yellow cheese-box, was making a cumbersome left, straight across their lane. The driver hadn't seen her.

Vanessa was already nailing the brakes with both feet and throwing a protective but useless arm across Jesse's chest.

O fuck fuck fuck no

Electronics fought to help her correct a skid that threw the sunglasses off her forehead and caught a scream of maternal agony in her lungs.

We're all going to die . . .

She closed her eyes and waited for the impact, for their little safe world to compress in a twisted mass of metal as milliseconds stretched into what felt like hours.

Please God my boys spare my boys

Vanessa was brought back to life by a cacophony of car horns.

They trilled out in a blast of discordant reality, and when she opened her eyes, she found herself unhurt, her boys untouched, and their car stretched diagonally across the intersection.

There had been no impact.

A glance to the right confirmed the presence of the bus, still lumbering through traffic. Tiny shocked faces were kneeling up on the back seat to watch the devastation they were leaving behind.

Vanessa looked across at Jesse, his chest expanding and contracting beneath the seatbelt that had surely saved him. His breath was ragged, heaving, and she could make out the strong bones of his ribcage as they rose and fell. He was staring straight ahead, but then he looked at her, eyes wide.

'Whoa,' he said.

'Milo?'

'I'm fine,' came the shocked voice from the back. Vanessa could see him in the mirror, at first glance he looked okay. He was staring intently into his lap, glasses askew on his face.

Strangers appeared at the windows of the car like ghosts from the mist, a concerned black man in dirty white tank top, an enraged-looking white woman by his side mouthing something about *what a lunatic, my husband is reporting him right now, do you want to open the door, can we help?*

'Mom?' said Milo.

'I'm here,' said Vanessa. 'I'm here.'

'No,' said Milo. '*Mom?*'

Vanessa remembered to breathe. Her chest was aching where the belt had dug in. She unbuckled, spun around to face Milo, sweat beading on her forehead.

For some reason, her son was holding a knife. It was beautiful, and encrusted with jewels. It looked like an artefact from an ancient world.

'Milo?'

Hands were tapping on the window. Worried people all around.

'It slid out from under the seat when we spun,' said Milo. 'It slid out and it was here.'

'Where did—'

'It was here all along,' he insisted. 'Under the seat.'

She glanced at Jesse, his huge whites of eyes, no help there.

Tapping on the car window, *tap*, *tap*, *tap*.

'You'd better give it to me,' she said.

Now oblivious to everything else, Vanessa took the treasure, turned it over in her hands.

It was decorative, antique, and the blade coiled, kind of.

Chris Light, alone in the dimly lit doctors' lounge, watched fresh coffee drip through the filter and tried not to worry. Dr Cortez, whom he considered reliable almost to the point of being boring, had been conclusively proved wrong in his diagnosis of Frank Tsang. Perhaps worse, he had disappeared once Dr Hubbard returned from his emergency dental appointment, and had not left word as to where he was going.

The upper endoscopy on Frank Tsang had shown no traces of a tear to the oesophagus; the patient hadn't bled into his stomach at all. Sparky had pestered the gastroenterologist to check twice, even as far down as the duodenum, and they were going to biopsy for ulcers, but that would mean yet *another* symptom on top of the cut to the thigh. Additionally, Tsang's bizarre drugged condition was now suggesting an intoxication more ominous than alcohol.

Of course, an incorrect initial diagnosis was far from unusual. But *something* here was far from usual, though as Nurse Francesca liked to point out – with her typical trace of reprimand – there was nothing new under the sun.

As if cued, she popped her head around the door.

'Mr Tsang awake yet?' said Sparky, before she had the opportunity to speak.

'No, Dr Light,' she said. 'But we have his blood work. You wanted to be informed?'

'Come in, come in,' he said, trying not to sound too eager. 'Frank Tsang was drugged, right?'

'Are you telling me, Doctor, or am I telling you?'

'Chloral Hydrate?'

'You're way off.'

'I'm way off?'

She nodded. 'Although the blood in his veins is swimming in sedatives.'

'What do you mean, the blood *in his veins*?'

'Oh, you'll want to see. But the blood in the pail, the blood he was puking?'

'Yes . . .?'

'That blood *wasn't his*.'

'What?'

'A different type altogether.'

Sparky was stunned, stared at the coffee dripping through the filter. 'But that means . . . at some point Frank Tsang swallowed approximately two thousand ccs of *someone else's blood*.'

'At some point,' said Nurse Francesca, hands on hips.

'Can we please find Dr Cortez?' said Sparky. 'I think we need to find Charlie.'

Charlie Cortez expected gloom and murk, a dark projection of his memory. Instead, he was treated to the low, bright Atlanta sun, framed by a window that had been thrown open, and he shielded his eyes. Threadbare curtains moved on a fine breeze, surprisingly fragrant.

'She isn't here,' he said to Tiffany, but when he turned, she had already gone.

The low motel bed was properly made, corners neatly tucked, and he experienced a curious pang of loss. The various medications on the night table remained in situ, neatly lined up, and it seemed like an obvious place to start.

To start . . . what?

It was more than professional curiosity. Here was excitement, an opportunity to peek into the private life of a woman who had grabbed a little piece of his soul.

It did not take long, and nothing particularly illuminating was revealed. Still, one bottle stood out from the others. Alongside almost every over-the-counter and prescription insomnia medication Charlie could think of was 100mg of Elmiron, or pentosan polysulphate. It was empty.

This was no sleeping drug.

It immediately suggested to Charlie that Leona was probably suffering from interstitial cystitis, a urinary disease of uncertain cause. But this in itself was problematic, given her line of work. It was hardly impossible, IC is not an uncommon complaint, but outside of uniquely specialist establishments it would not do for a hooker to be voiding her bladder every fifteen minutes or so, let alone suffering serious pain in her vagina.

A multitude of inner voices spoke up in argument against this wavy logic.

Of course she has cystitis. People are desperate. They don't have your middle-class choices.

She needs the money. She can take the pain.

Look – the bottle is almost empty. Perhaps it cleared up.

And IC could explain her sleeplessness. What's the word . . . nocturia?

'I don't think so,' Charlie whispered, wondering if the bottle had contained the correct pills.

It was more than a little bizarre that there should be no pain-control medication amongst this extensive personal pharmacy. Where were even the most likely household drugs, the aspirin, the Tylenol? IC hurts, can be agony.

All right, fair enough. Still, is that all you have?

It was a long shot, and he knew it. IC was the most likely – and probably only – reason for the presence of this drug. Charlie hadn't even looked in the bathroom cabinet yet; lord knew what would be in there. Maybe there was something *else* about pentosan polysulphate; perhaps some research paper from Europe that he'd seen a few years ago, back when he was reading every document that crossed his desk . . .

The rest of the apartment received a cursory inspection. The only unusual ornamentation that Charlie could find was a small collection of antique music boxes on the window sill, objects that he hadn't noticed on his first visit. Many looked very old, and possibly expensive.

Beyond this, there was scarcely enough to suggest that a breathing soul had ever existed in the place, although he caught subliminal glimpses: the scent of her perfume when he pulled open a dresser drawer, the impatient hand-swipe prints on the mirror above the sink that appeared in the steam when he ran hot water to wash his hands.

There was nothing in the bathroom cabinet except for a crusty tube of toothpaste and a sad eraser of cracked, forgotten soap. Charlie resisted the urge to smell the fresh bottle of imported shampoo on the shower soap tray.

'What the hell is *this*?' said a strong voice from the other room, startling him.

Charlie strode back into the bedroom, found Tiffany inspecting the small fridge beneath the desk. She'd been hovering in the corridor all along, and he wondered how many of his thoughts he had spoken out loud, and at what volume.

'What is it?' said Charlie.

'We don't lock the mini-bars,' said Tiffany. 'Hell, we don't even stock them any more.'

Charlie bent down to look. She was right, the fridge was padlocked, and it didn't take a craftsman to identify a botched, amateurish job, an inappropriate drill-and-screw effort that had ruined the thin wood in the cheap surround.

'Your cleaner didn't notice this?' said Charlie, glancing up.

'Cleaner?' said Tiffany, using a lacquered nail to trace a shallow pattern in the dust on the desktop.

'Why would Leo lock the fridge, you think?'

'I don't know,' said Tiffany.

Charlie turned back to the fridge.

Pentosan polysulphate. I know I read about some other use for it What was it . . . ?

'I'll get a bolt cutter,' said Tiffany.

'No need,' said Charlie.

There was just enough space to work his fingers between the icebox and the desktop and slide the key out, after an anxious moment where he thought he'd pushed it out of reach.

Still he hesitated. Something told Charlie that he shouldn't look in there, that this had gone far enough, maybe too far already.

'What are you waiting for?' said Tiffany.

Aching from his awkward crouch, Charlie Cortez inserted the key into the padlock and turned it slowly, feeling the springs release in the locking mechanism. He removed it from the shackle as carefully as he might a catheter from a patient.

'Okay,' said Charlie, and he took a deep breath.

The fridge opened with the light pull of air typical of such appliances, but nothing about the contents were typical. It was warm inside, for one thing, bordering on humid, the long screws used to apply the padlock mechanism having damaged the cooling lines.

The stench came next.

There was only one shelf, and the rest of the interior was splattered with dried blood. Resting on this shelf was a recognisably mammalian brain, surrounded by various cuts of truly unidentifiable meat – mostly offal, perhaps a heart – and the whole horrific smorgasbord boiled with maggots. They writhed so furiously that the contents could have been mistaken for a single, blind, satanic abortion. A few drunken flies hopped around the base of the unit, testing their sticky wings.

As if on cue, a heaving morsel detached from the whole, dropping through the bars of the shelf and plopping into a small pool of long-congealed blood, gorged white passengers clinging on.

'*Fuck me*,' said Tiffany.

Charlie, recoiling on his haunches, became aware of his cell phone ringing. He reached for it and, in an automatic motion, checked who was calling.

Vanessa.

Midnight.

Frank Tsang awoke, felt an unusual presence in the space with him.

Sure enough, one of the shadows in the darkened hospital room isolated itself from the others and began to move.

'I'm not ready to die,' said Frank Tsang, when the shadow representing the fellow human was close enough for him to hear it breathe.

'And yet, you had your whole life to prepare,' Leona said in her husky, cracked tone.

'I don't want to die. Do I look like I want to die?'

'No, Frank. But trust me. After yesterday, you really, *really* don't want to live.'

'What happened?'

'I tried to take you where you wanted to go.'

'Where was that?'

'The island, Frank.'

'What island?'

'But now you're back.'

'Back?'

'Not for long.'

'Oh God,' said Tsang, realising. 'Oh God, you're you – you're the whore. Please don't tell anyone about what happened. This was the first time, you know, I ever *paid*.'

Leo traced a long, white finger over his fat chins. 'Oh Frank, you're not seeing the big picture. It isn't important to me that anyone knows.'

'Great. I mean, *great*.' His breath came heavy. 'Man, I talk some crap when I'm drunk. Some real crap. You want more money? My wallet is, I don't know. They can get it.'

'I don't need money, Frank.'

'How did you get in here?'

Leo flipped on the overhead light, studied the huge grey face with something approaching affection.

For Frank Tsang, the brightness was immediate and horrible, and he was introduced for the first time to the mask of madness, wan and beautiful.

Even drugged and weak and woozy, Frank Tsang had hefty, useful bones beneath his excess. Yet when he tried to raise his arm beneath the sheet, he found that he could not. He had been strapped to the gurney with electrical tape.

Jerking around at the limits of his strength produced a series of pathetic rattles, the exertion of which caused his head to throb and his ears to ring.

'Look, Frank,' said Leona. '*Look*.'

And he did, despite himself.

She was flashing a knife stolen from a decent steak restaurant – she had gifted her beautiful weapon from the island to her last client – and she inserted it without hesitation into the vein in her own left wrist, slicing vertically to best work open the fleshy tube.

Leona's eyes only left Frank's to drop the weapon with a bloody clatter and pick up a glass beaker that she had taken from an unlocked hospital lab.

'Little more for you, Frank?'

The beaker was filling.

'Christ, you're going to kill yourself. Nurse! NURSE!'

Leo's eyes rolled.

'NURSE!'

Frank Tsang's screams were not totally in vain. Two nurses and an orderly appeared in the glass wall separating the room from the corridor. They looked for a moment in disbelief, although they were not yet privy to all the bright red splatter.

Leona had dug too deep, and the blood began to pulse out of her in twin arcs.

'NURSE!'

Leona had jammed the door with a lounge chair, although it shifted a little when the big orderly put his shoulder to it.

'Frank, Frank,' she said, scolding. 'You're with *me* now.'

'You're out of your *fucking mind*.'

Thump! The chair rocked up. The legs were going to give.

'All right, Frank,' said Leona, who always knew when time was short. 'Have it your way.'

She allowed the beaker to slither through her fingers, and it hit the floor, a red tide reaching across the linoleum.

She scrambled again for the steak knife. It was slippery in her hands, and when she stood, the jets from her gaping wrist threw blood across Tsang's fat face and his white linen sheets.

He was screaming now, blinded by her wet copper heat, a taste in his mouth that he'd known only too recently.

Leona was dizzy, perhaps dying herself, but with madness comes strength, and the raised knife hacked deep into his throat with remarkable ease.

Frank Tsang's final sounds were involuntary, bubbling gurgles.

'Pray you don't make land,' whispered Leo, as she lost consciousness. 'Pray . . .'

She collapsed to the floor as the nurses stormed into the room.

Two

Vienna, Austria.

'I believe that cannibalism can be a remarkably positive thing.'

Dr Reeta Kapoor paused for emphasis, glancing around her quarter-capacity audience in the *Redoutensaal*, a fine theatre within the Hofburg Imperial Palace.

'Unfortunately,' she said, 'there has, historically, been a sensational thirst for barbaric and graphic accounts that threaten to corrupt impartial study. Yet this subject strikes at the very question of civilisation, and what it means to be civilised. It is no coincidence that Hans Staden's *Warhaftige Historia*, a gloriously overblown 1557 account of a German soldier's experience with the Tupinambá in Brazil, became one of the world's first bestsellers – complete with explicit, orgiastic woodcuts. But this was merely a precursor; it is hardly necessary for me to cite the ubiquitous examples in modern media that grace our cinema screens and fly from the shelves of our bookshops.'

The large room was warm, almost uncomfortably so, and Reeta cleared her throat. She had been hoping for a greater turnout from her Anthropology students, but the dimly lit faces in the audience belonged to a handful of impassive academics, curious tourists and elderly Viennese who had come to the free lecture in order to escape a snowstorm that was gathering force outside.

All three demographics were threatening to snooze.

'Of course, I am not interested in cannibalism as lunatic pre-occupation, murder or sex crime. Nor as the necessary consumption of human flesh for basic survival, such as that which occurred during, say, the siege of Leningrad. What I would term *positive cannibalism* stems from religious, mystical or magical causes. The most obvious example is the Christian Eucharist, whereby to the patristical Catholic, the rejection of transubstantiation is anathema. This provides me with at least one case to suggest that the notion of cannibalism as unacceptable is not innate to humans, as long as it is ritualised in a certain way. Outside of such rituals, why should something be morally repugnant to us, simply because it is nauseating? I believe it is our so-called civilised conditioning, rather than our instinct, that leads us to make the choice not to practise.'

From the floor, some rattles of dry coughing.

'Of course, as many scurrilous academic publications have delighted in insinuating, I, Reeta Kapoor, do not condone the eating of human flesh, or indeed any flesh – I am a vegetarian.'

There was a mild scuffling to the left of the room, a scraping of chairs, and movement out of the corner of her eye. Reeta did not turn to look.

'Can we not call today's human/donor transplant system a form of cannibalism? My point is that we need to remove from our own customs any air of inherent rightness, and our ingrained prejudice about cannibalism is as good a place as any in which to start. Why? Precisely because it provokes such strong opinion.'

A voice called out. It was young, confident and English-accented. 'What about *The Future of the Savages*?'

The audience greeted this interruption with a surprised silence, then began to murmur like an enchanted forest.

'I would be extremely pleased to welcome questions at the end,' Reeta said, arranging her notes.

'Ten years ago, you published a paper with that title,' said the man, rising to his feet.

'What of it?' Reeta regarded her heckler. He was in his late-twenties, Asian, handsome, and clad in fashionably scruffy clothes. Standing next to him was a striking blonde girl of comparable age. She was several inches taller than the man, but seemed to wilt a little under the scrutiny of the room.

'At that time,' he continued, 'you were employed by the Indian Union Territories, reporting to the Lieutenant Governor of the Okojuwoi, Andaman and Nicobar Islands. You were cultural liaison to the native peoples there.'

Reeta turned and motioned through the bare branches of metal music stands that had been left on the stage. She needed to stop the Austrian translator from placing her lecture notes in German upon the overhead projector.

'Do you have a point to make, sir?'

'In your paper, you expressed serious concerns about the methods employed to assimilate the many indigenous tribes of these islands. You drew particular attention to an island more remote than the rest, one known to be occupied by an unusually aggressive tribe. In your estimation, they had yet to be contacted in any responsible way. In fact, the protection of these people appears to have been of particular concern to you.'

'They know it locally as *Savage Island*,' Reeta said to her audience. 'The tribe and island were officially known as the *Lombe*, after Claude Lombe, the first man able to photograph them through a long lens. But that name never stuck.'

'Let me quote a specific instance from the distant past,' said the man. 'Following the accidental marooning of three local fisher-men and the Myanmar who chartered their boat, you rejected any idea of rescue. Presumably, everyone was murdered by the savages.'

'I remember that tragedy,' said Reeta. 'And if you'd read my reports at the time, you would know I don't believe that boat landed accidentally.'

'The Governor may have supported your decision on that occasion. But because of the publication of *The Future of the Savages* – a paper containing strong criticism of the local government's handling of many native groups – you were fired, is that not true?'

The audience turned from speaker to speaker, anticipating blood.

'My role within the administration was dissolved,' Reeta said. 'There was no successor.'

'And now you lecture.'

'I would if you'd sit back down.'

'But *we* don't think you were fired because of your paper.' He turned to his companion, who was now studying her feet, face obscured by the blonde hair.

'The position had become untenable,' said Reeta.

'But I don't think it was because of the *paper*,' said the man. 'It became untenable because the Indian government negotiated a sixty-year lease of Savage Island to a private corporation for reasons unknown. It was a baffling contract with many strange caveats, and unavailable to the general public until recently. Given the lack of detail about the future of these islanders about whom you cared so much, this is something that you will strongly have opposed, yet there were several hundred million dollars in it for the government.'

'I voiced my apprehensions at the time.'

'But you were ignored.'

'Yes.'

'Because you had already been forced out of the Okojuwois, and had taken up a number of teaching positions in Europe.'

'Young man, whatever protest you feel you may be lodging here needs to become both concise and a lot more respectful, or I will have you escorted from the building.'

'Dr Kapoor, we represent *SARPI* – Survival and Repatriation

International. We run worldwide campaigns, fighting for the basic rights of tribal peoples.'

'Yes, I know about SARPI.'

The man's voice was rising. 'A decade has passed since this despicable deal was struck for Savage Island. We now need to draw your attention to the ambitious plans of one Professor Edward Quinn, which are finally approaching fruition. As the closest person to an expert on this island and her peoples, you must be *extremely* concerned.'

Reeta smiled.

'Is something amusing, Dr Kapoor?'

'Very good, Valmik,' said Reeta. 'Once more, you have earned my undivided attention, and, naturally, when I least expected it. Ladies and Gentlemen, please welcome Valmik Kapoor, my younger brother. You'll have to forgive him, he has an unfortunate flair for the dramatic.'

Feet freezing in his shoes, Father Alain Gélamur glanced at his watch and took a last bite of bratwurst, salty fat bursting across his tongue. His fellow diners at the sausage stand had their collars turned up against increasing snow flurries, heads sunk deep into thick coats, nursing pilsner from tall cans. Across Stephansplatz, home-bound commuters scurried towards the crowded *U-Bahn* through in an evening fog that threatened to obscure the floodlit Gothic mass of the white-capped cathedral.

It would be almost impossible for Alain to mark the arrival of Kallmus in such conditions. But Werner Kallmus, ever enigmatic, presumably wanted it this way.

Gélamur wiped his fingers of sweet mustard and joined the throng, licking his cracked lips as he made his way to the Riesentor, pausing, as he had on his last visit some four years ago, to study the curious figures depicted in the tympanum surrounding Christ Pantocrator.

Once inside, he crossed himself. The huge, gloomy nave of the Stephansdom was hardly warmer, but, as per his instructions, the old Frenchman attached himself to a gaggle of tourists loitering around a stairway in the north transept, all waiting for the day's last tour of the catacombs.

The catacombs.

It was characteristic of Kallmus to arrange a meeting in this dramatic location, as if Gélamur could forget the morbid turn that their relationship had taken since the loss of Werner's only son. No, it would be necessary for them to converse while surrounded by the human remains of some 11,000 mortals, because that was the prerogative of Werner Kallmus, and the Viennese supplicant had vast resources of both money and grief on his side.

The guide gave her tour of the various crypts in German, and Alain, lingering alone at the back of the group, did not bother to request a translation. After an interminable time stumbling around dimly lit tunnels on the heels of a snotty-nosed child and her stage-whispering mother, he felt in dire need of some fresh air.

It was at this moment that Kallmus placed a hand on his shoulder, and Alain jumped.

'Father Gélamur,' he said. 'I thank God you found the time for me.'

Alain forced a smile, and they gripped leather-gloved hands. 'Werner,' he said. 'Of course. You were hiding down here? I mean, it is permitted?'

Kallmus chuckled. 'The *Probst* is a friend of mine.' The catacombs exited directly to the street, and he looked to where the tourists were re-emerging onto Stephansplatz. 'I think we can be trusted to remain alone.'

'Excellent,' said Gélamur, staring at Kallmus with what he hoped would be interpreted as loving appraisal.

Werner had aged, that was certain. Perhaps ten years in three, if not more, but no parent should have to outlive their child.

Everything about the Viennese was grey, from his suit and tie to his thinning hair to the steel-rimmed spectacles pushed high on a face devoid of animation. Only his fit, narrow body looked poised for action; Kallmus always bent slightly forward whilst talking, imposing himself into the personal space of his conversant in a habit that might have been developed during years as a cut-throat financier.

Or maybe he just liked to make people feel uncomfortable. It didn't make him godless.

'Well,' said Father Alain, stamping his feet.

'How is Avignon?' said Kallmus, once satisfied they were alone. Gélamur had no German, and Kallmus spoke appalling French, so English became the lingua franca.

Father Alain smiled. 'Pawned to the tourists.'

'Of course. And the Church?'

'We endure. In great part thanks to your continued financial contribution.'

'The new reredos?'

'Beautiful, Werner. Our thanks. *My* thanks.'

'I could give more.'

Gélamur shrugged. 'We could all give more.'

Kallmus ducked through a stone archway, and Alain followed. The next chamber was even darker, and the Frenchman took moments to consider. If this was to be a negotiation, it was probably not about money. Werner Kallmus had made a considerable investment in Father Alain Gélamur and the Sedevacantists that filled his small medieval church, but always from a distance; Kallmus did not require recognition, and shunned gratitude.

What did he want?

The deeper catacombs were warmer, and there was a smell, although it took a while to manifest. It was not exactly decay; more like old tea, or forgotten antiques.

The smell of the comfortably dead.

Alain looked at Werner. The Austrian had turned his back, was studying bones revealed by a strategically broken wall. They were artfully lit, and picked clean of flesh.

Would that Sebastian Kallmus could rest so comfortably.

'Remarkably calming here,' said Werner Kallmus. 'Nowadays, there are so few places in which I can find peace.'

'I don't doubt,' said Gélamur.

'The rich and the poor,' said Kallmus. 'Lifeless together for eternity. I consider it appropriate. Appropriate, and humbling.'

'The Habsburgs were progressive.'

'They were visionary, in that they only allowed their viscera to moulder in public. The royal organs are divided between churches. Maria Theresa was obsessed with autopsy.'

'This city seems to hold a fascination for the ritual of death,' said Gélamur.

'After an outbreak of black death in the eighteenth century, cemeteries in *Wien* were closed. Charnel houses were emptied, remains thrown into pits beneath this cathedral. Imagine, Father. The smell of rotting corpses was so strong that religious services had to be abandoned.'

'God rest their souls.'

'The solution was to send down prisoners,' said Kallmus. 'They spent their wretched, penal lifetimes by candlelight, scrubbing rotten flesh from plague-ridden bodies, stacking the bones like you see here today. Can you imagine such a fate?'

Gélamur nodded, sniffed. 'I have taken a personal tour through the Paris crypts.'

'Nowadays, I see greater respect for the future of our eternal souls in the black eyes of this skull wall than in the attitude of any number of the living.'

'Perhaps.'

'Perhaps? Sometimes we need reminding that those destined for Heaven and those destined for Hell can end up remarkably close together.'

They were into another crypt now, one with multiple exits. Alain was becoming lost, and the stone-clad tunnels seemed to slope ever downward.

'I do not know what you mean,' said Gélamur.

'Do your letters on behalf of my son still go unanswered? Your calls?'

'It has been years.'

'Four years to the week,' said Kallmus. 'As if I could forget. But still you write?'

'Yes,' said Gélamur. 'And I endorse your continued campaign. I am sorry, Werner.'

'I do not need your apology, Father. I need your faith.'

'My faith is strong.'

'And mine?'

'Werner, you are a model for both the young and those in doubt,' said Gélamur. 'You would be a worthy model for any man. You still hear His words? You draw strength from the scriptures?'

'Yes, yes,' said Kallmus. 'But surely, more than ever, our faith exists for the living?' He had a tear in the corner of his eye, or perhaps it was an illusion of the candlelight.

'I would not necessarily agree,' said Gélamur. He motioned towards sarcophagi, encased at head-height. 'But yes, the deceased are in capable hands.'

'You have never lost a son.'

'For all my sins, no.'

'My boy was a fool?'

'Sebastian was many things, but he was not a fool.'

'He was unprepared. I let him go, and he was not ready. Father, I *encouraged* him.'

Gélamur was well aware of this. 'He was overwhelmed by a strength of faith that few of us are lucky enough to know,' he said.

'Recently, I have been haunted by the notion that his faith was not strong enough.'

'Preposterous,' said Alain.

'Why else would the mission fail?'

Alain thought: *What made you think it would succeed?*

Madness, enticing your son to abandon his studies. Madness, to send him to the heart of darkness, all because he liked sex too much to enter the priesthood. Madness to encourage him into contact with a colony of savages who were rumoured to eat missionaries for breakfast and then dig the errant flesh from their teeth with wax Bible bindings.

'You cannot be certain that his mission failed,' Alain said carefully.

This did not receive the expected reaction.

'*Precisely*,' said Kallmus, clasping his fist. 'Because Sebastian is *not dead*.'

'No,' said Alain. 'He lives on in our hearts.'

'Do not patronise me, Father. Sebastian wanted for nothing, at least in equipment.'

'Pardon?'

'Amongst many other useful items, he carried with him a high-grade silicon solar panel. It resulted in a phenomenal output.'

'Werner, I don't know what that—'

'A satellite phone. It never lost power, and for as long as the sun shines in that part of the world, it never will.'

'Yes, I remember now.'

'I call him every day. The one remaining contact with my son.'

'But he cannot answer, Werner. Not now. But we will continue to pray.'

'You are incorrect, Father. There *is* an answer. But for some reason there is no reply. He has been lost for four years in that godless place.'

'*Je suis désolé* . . . an unimaginable loss.'

Kallmus appeared to sneer. 'And yet you are still here for me, yes?'

'Of course.' Gélamur could not see the meeting ending well,

and prepared to push for a painless conclusion. 'Let me take you back to the hotel,' he said. 'Drink some schnapps, listen to the piano player, like the old days.'

Kallmus sighed. 'Father Gélamur, you need to hear me.'

'Yes.'

'After four years, *he is answering my calls.*'

'What?'

'Calls to the island. To my lost boy.'

'Surely impossible,' said Gélamur.

'I admit,' said Kallmus, 'I cannot be certain it is Sebastian. But I *can* confirm that someone has access to my son's phone. Are you not excited, Father?'

Excited was not the word. Gélamur was baffled, and concerned.

If this news was more than grief-ridden delusion, then fresh interest in the case would be inevitable, again drawing fire from religious authorities greater than his. There would be more personal publicity, and more debate. Werner Kallmus would certainly welcome the invigorated interest in his missing son, but while Alain's concern for Sebastian was very real, he did not want a repeat of events surrounding the original disappearance, when his humble assembly of conservative Christians had been thoroughly derided for their apparent encouragement of suicide missions.

True faith might be individual, yes, but it was not to exist in isolation.

The situation in that part of India might be the same, but France, for Alain Gélamur, had changed. He had less influence in Avignon now, and his congregation was dwindling. Yet Kallmus, for all his pain-fuelled, self-serving needs, had more money than ever to donate.

'Can you be certain that you are communicating with the island when you call?' Gélamur asked.

Kallmus nodded.

'What kind of messages are you hearing in response?'

'I do not know exactly.'

'From Sebastian?'

'Not in voice, not yet.'

'Then . . . ?'

'He plays *music*, Father.'

On Herrengasse, a few streets away, Reeta and Valmik Kapoor were brushing snow from their coats and getting comfortable in the cozy opulence of the Café Central, a traditional Viennese *Kaffeehaus* that had once played host to the likes of Lenin and Trotsky.

'A new girlfriend, a new cause,' Reeta said, smiling at her younger brother.

Isabel, the beautiful Austrian blonde who had helped Valmik interrupt her lecture, had gone to freshen up.

'Both worthy of your attention,' said Valmik. 'She's a very clever girl; a philosophy student.'

'I'm sure she is.'

Candlelight flickered off the vaulted ceiling.

'I know what you think,' said Valmik. 'I'm some fly-by-night, travelling around the world on Dad's money, picking up white girls with good cheekbones. I'm the first to admit, I never had your academic discipline. What you *don't* see are my worthwhile achievements.'

'I hardly ever see you at all,' said Reeta. 'Or at least, I don't see you enough. And when was the last time you went to see Dad? Anyway, I thought you were with Greenpeace at the moment.'

'We had our differences. But I'll continue to support those projects that I believe strongly in.'

Isabel returned from the bathroom, enveloping them both in freshly spritzed perfume. She gave Valmik a broad smile, showing perfect teeth.

'And *this* is a project that you're in a unique position to help us with,' Valmik said to Reeta, squeezing Isabel through her cashmere.

'I've heard so much about you, Dr Kapoor,' said the girl. She was much more confident away from the scrutiny of the *Redoutensaal* audience.

A waiter appeared, and they ordered coffee.

'So, how did Savage Island cross the radar of SARPI?' said Reeta.

'SARPI has known about the delicate tribal situation in the Okojuwoi for years,' Isabel said, in her lightly accented English. 'And the Andamans, and the Nicobarese. What we didn't know until recently was that Edward Quinn had negotiated a deal.'

'What did he achieve? What does he have in mind?'

'We don't know yet, exactly. We know he's managed to build some kind of structure on the island, or a series of structures. He's been employing local people, even bringing skilled labour from mainland India, guaranteeing huge sums to the families of the workforce in case of death or injury.'

'Have there been deaths?'

'The whole thing is awash with secrecy,' said Valmik.

'I met Professor Quinn, briefly,' said Reeta. 'He was skulking around the Andamans for a week or two at Port Blair, ten years past. I met him in my office. He wanted a permit to travel to the Okojuwoi: I don't remember if it was granted. He had a fine reputation, so I suspect that it was. But I do believe that he then attempted illegal travel to Savage Island, after it was reported that a family of fishermen and their boat had disappeared. Savage Island has *always* been strictly off-limits. Witnesses reported a white man travelling up the spine of Great Island with a con-artist who was well known to the bereaved family. There were hidden moorings there that they could have used.'

'You thought that he had died on Savage Island,' said Valmik.

'That was the assumption,' said Reeta. 'A great loss for the academic community. At one point Edward Quinn was considered to be a great anthropologist, a billionaire who could self-fund different kinds of projects around the world. He built schools, pioneered field technology and safety, and never seemed to be motivated by religion or personal glory. Years ago I remember reading that Quinn had been disgraced – some relationship that went sour. The girl wasn't a minor, but she was very young, and it was enough to hurt his philanthropic reputation. Anyway, I suspect he was a greater administrator than a scientist, but I never really knew him.'

'There was no rescue attempt?'

'A navy vessel will have sailed around Savage Island, as they do occasionally. But there was no evidence of a wreck, and making land would only lead to further loss of life.'

'But we know that Quinn survived,' said Isabel. 'He became a recluse, but he survived. For all these years, and for whatever reason, Edward Quinn needed to distance himself from the world.'

'Until now,' said Valmik.

'Savage Island is remote from the Okojuwoi Islands, an archipelago a hundred and seventy miles west of the Ten Degree Channel,' said Reeta. 'The Okojuwoi are, in themselves, remote from the Andamans and Nicobarese Islands. All together, they form roughly two hundred and fifty islands; India's most hard-to-reach state.'

'A four-day eastward sail from Chennai,' said Valmik.

'There are some scheduled flights now,' said Reeta, sipping her coffee. 'All but the Andamans are off limits to tourists. Even then, you need a permit.'

'SARPI has a database of photographs,' said Isabel. 'It looks beautiful.'

'The geography of the islands is astonishing, no doubt about that. The reefs are impeccable, the beaches a tourist operator's dream; there are misty, jungle-clad mountains and sparkling blue seas. Even during my tenure there were moves to open the resources up to holiday-makers.'

'Why didn't they?' said Valmik.

'They will.' Reeta shrugged. 'The islands still lack decent runways, infrastructure, hotels, investment, I could go on. Swamps, tree cover and heavy rains combine to form the perfect breeding ground for mosquitoes, so malaria is rife. There are sandfly, too, and the risk of tropical ulcers. Many visitors fall sick. Then, of course, the Asian tsunami in 2004 set things back indefinitely.'

'What happened to the tribes?'

'Short answer: they were fine. To the best of our knowledge, not a single indigenous person living in a traditional way was known to have died in the floods.'

'How come?'

'We don't know. Perhaps wildlife became agitated before the impact, so the natives sought higher ground. Testament to the power of living so close to nature.'

More coffee arrived on small silver trays, accompanied, as is the Viennese way, by glasses of cold water.

'And the Okojuwoi archipelago?' said Isabel. 'And Savage Island?'

'The Okojuwois are currently off limits while the local government attempt to keep the *Jaman* tribe within their designated reserve. The settlers have been trying to complete a tarmac road from Port Barren to the northern tip for the last twelve years, connecting the only two immigrant settlements – both on the main island, incidentally – but, as was my advice at the time of the initial consultation, this road will split up the main *Jaman* hunting grounds. As a result, there have been deaths.'

'Typical of how indigenous people have been handled over the centuries,' said Isabel.

'The British had documented no less than twelve tribes in the Okojuwois by the end of the nineteenth century,' said Reeta. 'But with the exception of the largest tribe – the *Jaman* – who withdrew into the deepest jungles and protected their land with poisoned arrows, these twelve tribes now exist only as a series of names. Of course, I'm excluding the natives of Savage Island.'

'Where did they all go?' said Valmik, stirring his drink.

'Assimilated, decimated, consigned to the pages of history.'

'But today?'

'I would presume that little has changed. In Port Barren, mixed-blood beggars will plead for money outside tea shops and alcoholic half-castes will lounge in abandoned wartime bunkers.'

Valmik looked at Isabel, and she gave him a little smile of encouragement. 'It doesn't sound all that dangerous,' he said.

'Valmik, this is not the South Pacific, only recently discovered in relative terms. Savage Island has been known to Western civilisation for far, far longer, yet it remains untouched. What makes you think that you can walk amongst this tribe when others have been unable for centuries?'

'There must have been *some* contact.'

'What little documentation exists is patchy. Marco Polo was the first recorder, describing savage cannibals with animalistic teeth, although it is unlikely he set foot on land—'

'*Are* they cannibals?' Isabel said, her eyes wide.

'We don't know. We know that the main islanders, the *Jaman*, for instance, are not. But the Savage Islanders are unique in many ways.'

'What ways?'

'For one, sometimes they wear bleached human jawbones around their necks.'

'Good lord.'

'Look, comparisons with the natives on other islands are almost all we have, but comparisons are inconclusive. There is even a theory that they might be a different race from the main islanders altogether.'

'What do you mean?'

'Most of the Savage Islanders are over six feet tall, even the women. Compared to this, the *Jaman*, presumably from Negrito stock, are pygmies.'

'And the similarities?'

'Here we get into the realm of theory alone. To my mind, they will all be hunter-gatherers. They will live on wild pigs, fish and shellfish, turtles, and the eggs of seabirds. Their island supports tubers and fruit and there will be honey to collect. They get flotsam off the beaches from which to make tools, and, of course, weapons. The *Jaman* never learned to create fire; they would preserve embers from the occasional lightning strike and then tend to them within hollow trees. I believe that the Savage Islanders will be the same. This puts them very low on the scale of civilisation indeed. And all are naked, save for belts and the occasional ornamental trinket.'

'Then we don't really know if they eat people?'

'We know that Malaysian pirates put about imaginative legends to ward away other looters from Far Eastern trade routes. It worked, until the British established penal colonies at Port Blair and Port Barren in which to lose Indian and Burmese freedom fighters. If anything, the reality was *worse* than the Malaysian legends; the Okojuwoi are still the world leaders in dermal leishmaniasis – the squaddies who reclaimed the islands from the Japanese in nineteen forty-five nicknamed it *face-rot*.'

Isabel let out a low whistle.

'There must still have been interest in Savage Island,' said Valmik. 'Was there ever an attempt at legitimate study? A first contact?'

'Once, in the seventies,' said Reeta. '*National Geographic* sponsored an effort to win over the natives with gifts. Dinghies full of scientists, anthropologists and armed police were met with a hail of arrows, although one of their boats was able to land once the sun had set.'

'Where did the savages go at night?'

'We don't know. Anyway, they left their gifts on the beach, then retreated to a safe distance to watch.'

'What kind of gifts?'

'Well, a child's doll, a live pig tethered to a pole, aluminium cookware, some red and green buckets. Fresh coconuts. Then they waited for daylight, for the islanders to return.'

'What happened?'

'They buried the doll, took the cookware and ate the coconuts.'

'And the pig?'

'Slaughtered.'

'What about the buckets?'

'They took the green ones and threw the red into the water. Maybe the other way around.'

'And then?'

'When the dinghies attempted to get close again, they were met with another hail of arrows. This time, a cameraman was hit in the shoulder, and a female ethnographer took one through the thigh. Both survived, the arrows weren't poisoned, but it was reason enough to retreat. Shortly afterwards, the Indian government issued their decree that the sanctity of Savage Island was never to be breached. People paid attention. Besides, excepting the shallowest crafts, the surrounding reef is only realistically passable for two months a year.'

'What about the shipwrecks?'

'Over time, there have been countless fishing vessels lost, blown over by the sudden storms that are typical. Sometimes you hear of crackpot missionaries or a lost diving vessel – ignorant tourists pitching up for a lunchtime picnic. Of those believed to have landed, there have never been any known survivors.'

'What about the YM *Fortune II*?' said Isabel.

'I was getting to that. The two highest profile wrecks were centuries apart. In 1670, a solitary Portuguese ship sank five miles to the west of the island, all hands lost. Her name was the *São Francisco Xavier*. She was headed back from Macau, I don't know the purpose of the mission. But this disaster doesn't seem to be related to the island or reef, and there exists no knowledge as to why she was scuppered, probably pirates.'

'And the YM *Fortune II*?'

'That made international news six years ago. You probably know as much about it as I do.'

'A cargo ship,' said Isabel to Valmik. 'On her return voyage from Calcutta to Taiwan. It ran aground on a reef during a night-time tropical storm. The reef was adjacent to Savage Island. The sea was too rough for lifeboats, but the vessel wasn't sinking, so they decided to stay on board and wait for help. They sent out an SOS, but it took a week for the Indian navy to send a helicopter and tugboat.'

'And the crew?' said Valmik.

'Escaped on lifeboats, apparently. Then airlifted to safety.'

'It would have been interesting to hear the content of those calls for help,' said Reeta. 'But they were never released. The crew were never interviewed publicly.'

'Foul play?' said Valmik.

Reeta raised an eyebrow. 'I don't know where Edward Quinn was, or if he had any role in the rescue – I suppose the island was, technically, leased to him at this point.'

'Whatever he has planned now, SARPI thinks that Edward Quinn needs to be stopped,' said Isabel. 'At the very least, the world needs a long-overdue explanation of his motives.'

'Right,' said Valmik to Reeta. 'Will you help us?'

'Other than giving you information, I don't see what possible use I could be. My contract at the *Universität Wien* runs out at the end of this semester. After that I thought I'd go back to Britain, maybe teach in Edinburgh again.'

'But your field experience would be vital,' said Isabel. 'Not to mention your local knowledge.'

'Who better to lead a safe expedition?' said Valmik. 'You're one of the world's greatest explorers.'

'A long time ago,' said Reeta. 'Wait a moment. You're not actually planning on *going* there?'

'We need to make a protest,' said Valmik. 'We need to focus attention. I mean, I've been to the islands before, back when you were working with the tribes.'

'You've been to the *Andamans*, Valmik. You snorkelled and you sat in a hammock. The Andamans are not the Okojuwoi, and the Okojuwoi is certainly not Savage Island.'

'We probably wouldn't try to land on Savage Island *itself*,' Isabel said, somewhat sheepish in the face of Reeta's conviction.

'Bloody right you won't,' said Reeta, motioning to the waiter that she was ready to pay. 'Interrupting my lecture is one thing, throwing away your lives is another.'

'Look, I can make a difference,' Valmik said. 'I *want* to make a difference.'

'I know,' said Reeta, 'but don't risk your life. Look, we'll sniff out what Quinn is up to, and I'll help SARPI all I can. Just because I'm not endorsing a suicide mission doesn't mean that I'm not interested.'

The men had driven several kilometres without seeing another vehicle, the silver-clad trees of the *Wienerwald* looming on either side like a parted sea of bones and the steel sky fading rapidly to black. Before leaving the city limits, local radio had repeatedly warned of *Eisige Straßen*, and although the salt trucks had done their job, the weather out in the woods was coming in stronger than ever.

Werner Kallmus swung his four-door Maserati off the main thoroughfare and Alain Gélamur awoke with a start in the passenger seat. They were cruising through a tunnel of skeletal branches, the headlights beaming onto fresh snow that crunched under the tyres.

Ten minutes of unpaved, single-lane track, and the car emerged into a large clearing in front of *Die Ruhehauss*, Werner's restored eighteenth-century hunting lodge. Light blazed from long, baroque windows. They looped a frozen fountain, where icicles hung from the noses of stone cherubs, and pulled up outside the portico.

'*Guten Abend,*' said the craggy butler who had appeared from the house to open Alain's door. Kallmus would garage the car, motioned for Alain to get out of the weather.

The grand hallway of the lodge was cold enough for Alain to see his breath, despite the many candles that burned in vast iron candelabras. The electric lights shone also, giving the place an unusual, stage-lit quality. This was a family home without a family, Alain knew; Werner's wife had died in a skiing accident some fifteen years ago, and he had never remarried.

'If you please, sir.' The butler spoke in a heavy accent.

Gélamur permitted his wet overcoat to be peeled from his body, and followed the man through ornate, antler-infested living rooms to Werner's low-ceilinged private chapel. It was a recent addition, and still smelled of wet plaster. Alone at last, he arranged himself and his small Bible on one of the four cold pews while the wind howled outside, trying to focus on the eternal flame that Werner had hung above the altar.

'When I lost Sebastian, I allowed that light to die.' Kallmus had appeared, taking a seat across the aisle.

'The light still burned,' said Gélamur, tapping his chest. 'In here.'

'I was angry,' said Kallmus.

'Understandable.'

Kallmus handed over one of two hot mugs of mulled wine. He had mixed hot red Bordeaux with Amaretto, and the rising vapour from the alcohol was warm on their faces.

'Will I call the island now?' said Kallmus.

Alain nodded.

'I am so nervous, Father.'

It was true; Kallmus was shaking with anticipation. Alain had never seen him this way, the Austrian was usually so cool, so self-contained.

'You have nothing to prove here,' said Gélamur.

Werner Kallmus could dial without looking at the wireless

handset. His eyes were focused on his purpose-built altar, or perhaps someplace further away.

Gélamur could hear the ringing, a lost receiver on the other side of the earth.

Ten rings, fifteen.

Twenty.

'Werner,' said Alain.

'Sometimes this happens,' said Kallmus. 'Sometimes he takes time to answer.'

Thirty rings.

Alain cleared his throat.

'Please,' said Kallmus. 'Wait longer.'

Father Alain Gélamur surprised himself by placing a hand on Werner's knee. This was a person whom, instinctively, he would have preferred not to touch.

Kallmus lowered the receiver.

'It took me a lifetime to find a worthy spiritual leader,' he said. 'A lifetime to find *you*, Father. I see weakness all around me.'

'You see weakness in the modern Church,' said Gélamur. 'In this regard we are the same.'

'Where were you four years ago?' said Kallmus.

'Do you require a priest, or do you require a man to validate your personal faith?'

Fifty rings.

'Father, I only brought you to *Wien* once before,' said Kallmus. 'When I first lost Sebastian. Up until then, I was a loyal supplicant to the church in Avignon, if from afar.'

'I responded to your grief, and your insistence,' said Alain. 'I threw the reputation of my ministry into a public relations battle that we could only lose. This damned Indian island was not a Petri dish for your boy and his egoist, pseudo-Franciscan faith.'

'On that island there exist unsaved souls by the hundred, if not thousand.'

'Staunchly inaccessible, violently primitive and protected by legislation too complex to comprehend.'

'Your opinion was a little different when Sebastian was still with us.'

'To my detriment.'

'"What greater challenge?" Were these not your words?'

'I am not a man to be bought and sold.'

'You were four years ago.'

'By God, I was,' said Alain, shaking his head.

'And now? Here in Sebastian's chapel?'

'This is *madness*, Werner. For all we need your contributions, this is madness. Sebastian is gone, but through God, I can help you with his *loss*.'

'You fear humiliation.'

'Not now,' said Alain. 'Before, yes. Now I am too old. I will support you, but I cannot legitimise an ill-advised rescue attempt.'

'You pre-empt me,' said Kallmus. 'A rescue attempt?'

'I could scarcely endorse the original mission.'

'Then you believe that Sebastian is alive?'

One hundred rings. Alain prised the phone from Werner's hand.

'I have no idea,' he said. 'But there will be no more deaths here, not in God's name.'

On the other end of the phone, someone picked up.

The two men looked at one other.

Father Alain Gélamur was anticipating static or distortion. Instead, he heard music, clearly broadcast; an imperfect, chiming melody in a time so strictly enforced as to be awkward in its honesty.

A music box?

Kallmus grabbed the receiver from his priest, babbled in German, even placed his hand in such a way that Gélamur might not see his mouth form whispers of love.

The call concluded.

Werner sobbed, crossed himself.

'Only this?' said Alain. 'Never a voice?'

'Not yet.'

'Take care now,' Alain said slowly. 'Let us recognise what we do hear, and what we do not.'

'This is not your son,' Kallmus said through tears.

'I will return to Avignon tomorrow,' said Alain. 'You will be in our prayers.'

'You should stay here,' said Kallmus. 'I will have Gustav prepare a room for you.'

'I would be glad to return to Vienna,' said Alain.

Kallmus was breathless. 'Of course.'

'Beware an uncertain desire, Werner. You are correct not to let this rest, but remember that I know you, and God knows you. Again, we will push through official channels, petition the Indian government. Until we can be certain that this is indeed Sebastian, it is the only way.'

'What?' said Kallmus bitterly. 'You think this is some devil sent to tempt me?'

'I understand that you are not a man to be beaten, but I hope – for your sake and the memory of your son – that nothing exists in your heart but honest grief.'

'Grief and hope,' said Kallmus.

'This alone?'

'Of course,' said Kallmus.

Three weeks later.

After an indulgent Friday night of Schubert and Bruckner at the *Musikverein*, Reeta Kapoor was ready for bed. She was looking forward to a long weekend of lounging around her apartment, digesting the twenty or so newspapers from around the world that she typically had delivered.

Any belief that a peaceful sleep was forthcoming dissolved as soon as she reached for the handle to her front door and discovered that it had been jimmied by clumsy hands.

Surrounding wood had splintered, it was off the latch.

The corridor was dark. The apartment was dark. There was no sound from within.

Reeta swung open the door on silent hinges and regarded the dark living room.

Nothing moved.

Reeta's instinct had taught her to remember which floorboards squeaked and which did not. In the past, she had lived for months in makeshift huts where armed locals would rifle backpacks for little more than glucose tablets, and she had personally shaken angry scorpions from children's shoes. By comparison, there was nothing to fear in Vienna.

Or was there?

The kitchenette was clear, as was the bathroom off the small hallway. Reeta was about to reach for the phone and hit 133 for the *polizie* when she heard a noise from the bedroom; a strange keening, like the surrender of a trapped animal.

The bedroom door was ajar, but because it lacked a street-facing window, it was the darkest place in the apartment.

Blood rushing in her ears, Reeta charged.

A tall shadow presented itself immediately, so she dived for it, throwing a willowy body against the open wardrobe with as much force as she could. There was a feminine shriek, and then Reeta was one half of an untidy, writhing heap, rolling over and over by the side of the bed.

'*Anschlag!*' screamed a familiar voice. '*Stoppen Sie bitte . . . please!*'

Reeta was now on top of the woman, concentrating her weight on the middle of the narrow ribcage below. There was no further struggle, only a wheezy release of breath.

'*Reeta . . .*' came the voice.

Dr Kapoor scrambled for the cord to the bedside lamp, and the room pooled with light. She found herself face to face with Isabel, Valmik's girlfriend, clad in a tight black jumpsuit: a sexy cat burglar. There was an extinguished flashlight in her hand, and, an arm's length away, a crowbar.

Reeta did not let up the pressure.

'What the hell are you doing here?'

'Dr Kapoor, I'm so sorry—'

'What are you doing here?'

'Valmik's *gone*.'

'What?'

'He's gone to the island.'

'The island?'

'Savage Island. He took off alone, no warning.'

'When?'

'Yesterday.'

'I don't believe it.'

'He left a note in my purse.'

Reeta eased her pressure on the woman's chest, looked over to the bag on the chest of drawers.

'Stay there,' Reeta said, getting up and taking away the crowbar.

She upended the contents of the bag onto the bed. The typed note that she found was on Valmik's personalised vanity notepaper, and had been composed in his typical, somewhat theatrical style:

My darling: we should never argue. By the time you get this, I will be in the air; destination, the Okojuwoi Islands. Forgive my cowardice for further confrontation, but I could not stand to have you plead with me again to stay. Please understand this work was my destiny from the day we met, but it is a path that I now realise I should walk alone.

The danger is real, but I am fully prepared. It is the fight I have waited for my entire life.

Take comfort in the knowledge that you are the first person to have made me believe I can truly make a difference in the world. Powered by your confidence, I will be back before you know it.

This is a short farewell, never adieu.

With the strongest love for you,

V.

Reeta lowered the page.

'This is the first time he said he loved me,' said Isabel, raising herself on her elbows.

'When did you find this?'

'Lunchtime.' She started to cry. 'Last night, Valmik went over to my college, left it at the department for me to find. Then he came out to stay with me in *Leopoldstadt*. Of course, he said nothing about his plans.'

'Impossible,' said Reeta, her mind racing. 'Valmik promised me he wouldn't go.'

Impossible, Reeta? Or exactly like him?

'He said the same thing to me,' said Isabel. 'He told me he would not go. But later, he was so angry.'

'I was explicit about the risks,' said Reeta. 'There were more useful things he could have done.'

'But his research turned up a new name in connection with the island,' said Isabel.

'What name?'

'There's a picture.' Isabel nodded at the detritus spread over the bed.

Reeta sifted through make-up, gum and tissues and found a photocopied print-out of a scratched Polaroid. Staring out at her was an astonishingly ugly man.

He had a vast, pale, soccer-ball-shaped head, which was bald and scarred. Hairy eyebrows arched high above small, rage-filled eyes. Beneath a pug nose, bloated lips formed a contemptible smile, and the jacket that Reeta could see beneath the thick jaw was a dirty off-white.

She shuddered, and turned the mugshot over. Scribbled in Biro on the back, in Valmik's handwriting, were two words: *Otto Lix*.

'Otto Lix?' Reeta looked over at Isabel.

'This man is employed by Professor Edward Quinn,' she said. 'But we don't know what he does for him. He's some kind of mercenary – he has a criminal record on three continents. In South Africa for example, where he was born, he's linked to extortion and even murder.'

'Murder?'

'I don't know for sure. But in 2002 he was employed by DrillCorp, an Alaskan oil speculator who neglected to upkeep a section of piping. Two hundred and sixty thousand gallons spilled over multiple acres near Camden Bay, destroying unspoiled wilderness. They got away with a nominal fine. Valmik led the protest to blockade a DrillCorp tanker in Prince William Sound.'

'I never heard about this before,' said Reeta, gazing at the photograph.

'Otto Lix attached two limpet mines to the hull of the *Pacifica*, then threatened remote detonation if the ship didn't move. It may have been a bluff, but it worked. Greenpeace couldn't risk loss of life or further damage to the environment, but the mines were *not* duds.'

'You can be certain it was this man?'

Isabel shrugged. 'I wasn't there. But he's very dangerous. His paper trail is like a bad smell. I think Valmik wants revenge.'

'Why did you break into my apartment?'

Isabel swallowed, and the words stumbled out. 'I didn't know what else to do. I have to follow Valmik, but I don't have any of the information he gathered about the islands, or about Professor Quinn's scheme. He took it all with him when he checked out of his hotel.'

'Typical. He's such a silly boy.'

'You're the world's expert on the subject; I thought I might find something useful, but I always remembered how strongly you felt about the idea of going. I don't know – I wanted notes, information, anything—'

'Inside my wardrobe?'

'I found a machete, and a hunting knife.'

'Antiques.'

Isabel blinked. 'You keep them very sharp.'

'I can't believe Valmik would do this,' said Reeta, biting her lip. 'Bloody idiot.'

'Do you think I can get there in time to stop him?'

'What was he planning to do?'

'I don't know,' said Isabel. 'Find a way onto to Savage Island?'

'Bloody *idiot*,' said Reeta, again. 'Do you have a valid passport?'

'What?'

'I'm coming with you, of course.'

At midnight, Werner Kallmus switched off the muted nonsense that projected from the portable television in the kitchen of his mansion and sat for long moments in the semi-darkness. He waited with bedlamite concentration, watching huge blocks of filtered moonlight inch slowly over a central workbench and state-of-the-art cooking equipment.

Eventually, the clock in the hallway struck one, the sound shivering up through the house.

Over on blankets in the corner, one of two Great Danes kicked out in her sleep.

Gustav Wrabetz, the butler, would also be asleep by now, and his room was at the front of the building on the top floor. Werner considered how much Gustav might know, and, if nothing, whether or not the man had his suspicions. Herr Gustav, a confirmed bachelor, had been the family retainer since long before the death of

Arianne, and he had watched Werner's gradual mental unravelling with stoic support; never directly offering comfort, nor daring to intervene.

The kitchen porch contained boots, cross-country skis and a plastic drawer of old ham bones for the dogs, sealed well from mice. Werner, clad in multiple layers of clothing and carrying a wicker hamper, unlocked the back door and stepped into the night. Fifty paces away, in a purpose-built shed, his two-stroke Alpina snow-mobile was waiting.

Directly, it was a scant half-mile to the redundant ice-house that had once been shared by the scattered hunting lodges whose various acreages converged at a deep, carp-filled lake. Werner selected a far longer route, one he had found and memorised, that led down ancient forest paths, and his passage across the virgin snow beneath the full moon and stars was illuminated as brightly as day.

Werner, you're enjoying this.

He relished the throttle in his cold, gloved hand, and the crystal powder under the outriggers. But more than anything, he delighted in his new, lunatic confidence that somehow, somewhere . . .

Sebastian was still alive.

I shouldn't be enjoying this.

The ice-house, built to store winter ice throughout the year, prior to the invention of the refrigerator, was uncommonly large. It had a domed roof, and was half-sunk into a shaded rise, double doors facing north towards the frozen, tree-lined lake. Werner had person-ally converted and refurbished the structure, ensuring it was water-proof and insulated. He had even constructed a small generator to provide electricity. From the outside, the ice-house looked much as it ever had, but that was the point; inside, Werner had a great secret to protect.

Werner Kallmus parked outside, and when he killed the engine, the silence was complete. He trudged towards the sloped wooden doors and unfastened the heavy padlock. For the purposes of muting any sound within, the doors led to a small anti-chamber, where there was a further metal door, set in a thick wall and studded with rivets.

At this point Werner could hear chatter from the little television he had purchased.

He raised his fist, and pounded hard, twice.

After a moment, the television fell silent.

Werner placed his hamper on the ground and opened it. He had packed a loaf of black bread, a wheel of smoked cheese, hard sausage with white rind, and half a litre of *Marillenschnaps* in a violin-shaped bottle. On top of this hastily assembled picnic was a loaded handgun wrapped in a dark ski-mask, a competition-oriented Glock 35.

Kallmus pulled the ski-mask over his face, obscuring his features. Then he tapped twice on the metal wall with his gun. This was the second signal, a communication to the prisoner that the door was to be unlocked, and that he should be certain to be sitting cross-legged at the rear of the room, hands held high.

The interior was humid and somewhat airless, and Werner made a mental note to double-check the ventilation. There was also a strong smell of sewage from the toilet and drain that he had plumbed into the corner. Other than this, the place still seemed comfortable enough; people across the world lived in far worse conditions.

Werner had provided piles of carpeting, a makeshift bed, and light shone from a single bulb, dangling on a short wire. The low ceiling meant that the room was scarcely high enough to stand up in, but there was nothing Werner could do about that now; attempting to lower the floor had been one concession too many.

'Good evening, Valmik,' he said, placing the hamper of food inside the door.

From his position in the far corner, Valmik Kapoor said nothing. His face was grey and his eyes wide. Werner considered: was he losing weight?

No, it's too soon for that.

Kallmus felt a pang of concern. He didn't want to traumatise the young Indian any more than necessary, and he had no intention of killing him.

'Next time I will bring bleach,' said Kallmus, nodding towards the smelly latrine.

'What do you want with me?' said Valmik.

'Do not concern yourself,' said Kallmus. 'Be patient, and soon enough you will be free.'

'Why are you keeping me here?'

Werner took a final look around the cell. Satisfied, he turned to leave.

'*Where am I?*' said Valmik, real panic in his voice.

Kallmus turned to look at him, then sneered beneath his mask. 'Amongst the savages,' he said, and slammed the heavy door.

Three

The Sharjah Desert, 70 miles west of Dubai, United Arab Emirates.

'Where is he, Mommy? I don't see him.'

'Hush, peanut. He's right there.'

'You see him?'

'Hush!'

'Mom?'

'Well, I can't see him *now*,' whispered Constance. 'He's still by the riverbank, I guess. I think he's eating.'

'Gross!' Eleven-year-old Liza was entranced.

'You saw him swipe the water? You saw him make the catch?'

'Yeah. This is *so* cool.'

And it *was* cool. *Very* cool. Flooded by artificially enhanced moonlight, and across an invisible but man-made barrier, a motionless leopard had been staring with lethal intent into shallow, fast-flowing rapids. Mother and daughter had watched with comparable bloodlust as the sleek animal eventually pounced on a trout and wrestled it onto the grass. The carnage that ensued was worthy of multiple shots from Liza's new camera phone, and, following a messy kill and much smacking of feline lips, the fish carcass had been dragged beneath a mass of skeletal scrub.

Now, the stage was quiet again, perhaps awaiting the next performers.

Constance Roper was a retired tennis pro with two singles victories at Flushing Meadows. She was also one of that weekend's celebrity VIP guests, and she really had to hand it to the Arabs: it had only taken two short years to construct a night safari in the grounds of the Yadub Hotel and Miracle Resort. The 1,400-room Yadub was only eight months old in itself, and marooned in beautiful red desert, miles away from the emirate of Dubai's overdeveloped coast, with its hot, greasy sea and curiously priced real estate.

In a country that thrived on excess, The Yadub Miracle was a relatively classy coup. Dubai needed something new, it always did. A cable car perhaps, or an underwater hotel, or a refrigerated beach to keep the sand cool. But the night safari was the latest effort at attracting international attention, and it was already being triumphed as a great success. They had even constructed their own desalination plant – complete with a mind-boggling amount of underground piping – to provide the 25 square hectares of imported dry broadleaf forest with the annual 800mm of rain necessary to maintain the diverse biome. The whole project had cost a recession-defying $600 million, and thanks to dozens of retractable 40-foot sprinklers disguised within giant dhok trees and a fully integrated control room, technicians could even simulate the monsoon season that was required for absolute realism.

Constance was just one of the many big names invited to that afternoon's inauguration lunch, and the blueprint for the future, as PowerPointed during the dessert course by Dr Rashid Al Shindagha, was even more incredible. Should certain visitor targets be met, it would only be another five years before an entire savannah could be constructed to the south, based on a miniature Serengeti of, say, 100 square kilometres. At this point, free-roaming elephants, giraffes, zebras and lions would be added to the bewildering menagerie. Guests could go on jeep safaris during the day, as well as watch the big cats hunt at night; that was, if they could find time between the numerous beauty therapies, hot stone massages and yoga lessons also on offer.

Constance herself, while no expert on the subject, was unsure about the precise implications of any of it. A one-time anti-fur campaigner, she had her doubts about the morality of captive breeding and the wild animal trade, as well as concerns about the welfare of any creature kept behind barriers, however well disguised those barriers were. Additionally, the environmental credentials of the project were proving to be a bit of a joke, the operation of the small Yadub multi-stage flash distillatory unit only serving to dump more brine into the Persian Gulf.

Lastly, there was just a sort of *feeling* that Constance had, something about the way the scientists behind the night safari were able to stage-manage the climate. They could click their fingers and create rain in the desert. They could use theatrical lighting to increase the quality of the moonlight, simply to illuminate nocturnal animals. It felt like the ultimate manipulation of nature, and all for the benefit of wealthy tourists who were ballooning their own carbon footprints.

'Mom, Jesus, what is *that?*'

Liza was reaching for her camera phone again.

Constance Roper turned to look, and, as had happened many times during that weekend, her concerns were quashed by sheer amazement. Surprise existed around every corner in this place, although due to sheer proximity, this one was perhaps the most astonishing.

The park was connected to the hotel by several kilometres of gently winding footpaths, illuminated only by the restrained glow of lights sunk into either side of the tile. Elaborate and beautiful mosaics on the ground informed the visitor what they could expect to see at each viewing platform, and the verges were neatly manicured.

In keeping with the concept of an open zoo, there were no visible barriers. Instead, concealed cattle grids and cunningly disguised hotwire augmented man-made moats constructed to resemble rivers and streams.

'Mom?' said Liza. 'What is it?'

'I don't know, honey. Can you find it in your guidebook?'

It was getting late. Constance and Liza had lost the crowd a while ago, and were now making their way back to their residence. A perk for the VIP guests was that they got to choose from one of forty luxurious tents, each hidden within the park itself, though *tent* was a somewhat misleading description. Entirely stationary, and complete with four-poster bed, freestanding roll-top bath and regally embroidered interior canopy, the units also enjoyed a private swimming pool, sun deck and air conditioning. Obeisant staff whizzed around on khaki-painted Segways, delivering fluffy white towels and chocolate-dipped strawberries.

Yet because of the size and design of the park, guests were also provided with an all-too-real experience of jungle solitude, albeit one with wireless internet access.

Constance, while impressed, was now feeling a little more of that solitude than she might have liked. Mother and daughter were not lost – the park signing was far too helpful for that – but they were alone, and both a little shocked to see an animal, and a large one, so close to the path. It was pale in colour, and looked like a cross between an antelope and a large goat. It also had unusual but threatening-looking horns that corkscrewed up from a thickly bearded head.

'It's a *markhor*,' said Liza, pleased. She was squinting into the glossy guide that had been handed to every visitor. 'Strange . . . on the map, it looks like their enclosure is somewhere else.'

'What's a markhor, Peanut?'

'National animal of Pakistan,' Liza read out.

Constance watched as the creature lost interest in them and

began to snuffle at the ground. It could only have been three metres away, yet there was no barrier in sight.

How is the illusion achieved?

It was incredible, and not a little spooky.

'Is it . . . ah, *dangerous*, Peanut?'

'I don't think so. Can we watch what it does?'

'We can come back tomorrow,' said Constance. 'Don't you want to take a swim in the pool?'

'Yeah!' said Liza, and hands interlocked, they carried on their way.

Once mother and daughter had gone, the markhor moved forward, nose still to the ground. Confused at first by the terracotta it found underfoot, the big animal stepped up onto the path where the humans had been standing, moments before.

The blond American major with the flat-top haircut was in the peak of physical condition. Squaring up in front of the F-16 fighter jet that served as a backdrop to this one-on-one combat, he moved in on his opponent with what was supposed to be the decisive blow.

It was a fight that had been long, arduous, and almost impossible to call.

At the last second, his adversary – a semi-naked Indian with a phenomenal torso and emaciated waist – somehow emerged from his dizzied trance and dropped to the ground. He slid forward with unlikely speed, using bare feet to knock his aggressor backwards through a wooden crate.

The major remained on the tarmac. Fight over.

Kelly Maelzel was furious.

'*Fuck IT*, and fuck *YOU!*' she said, in her raspy Australian accent. 'You said you were taking a *weaker* character this time.'

Kelly mashed the buttons on the SNES, plastic rattling under her strong thumbs. Duncan Cho had already dropped his own controller. He raised his palms towards her, a gesture of surrender.

'I thought you had the edge there,' he said. 'Honestly, I did.'

'Well,' said Kelly, 'we didn't all spend our youth masturbating over computer games.'

'Unfair advantage,' said Cho. 'Sorry.'

Kelly Maelzel and Duncan Cho had been colleagues for months and friends for weeks, trapped together in the cloying luxury of the Yadub Miracle Resort. It only took a moment before a twinkle crept into Duncan's eye, and the corner of his mouth twitched into a smile.

'I said, *fuck YOU!*' said Kelly, lunging out of her plastic chair and upending a can of lager. Cho fell backwards as she applied a vicious noogie to his bald spot, the sound of his laughter muffled by her headlock. There had been no battle in Kelly's life, however trivial, that she did not take with absolute seriousness, and every defeat was personal.

Lurking in the shadows of a side-door to the enormous, cathedral-like ballroom, a British-born night-manager called Samuel Trigger was not witnessing the Kelly Maelzel explosion for the first time. Even so, such aggression was still irritating to him. It was also, in his mind, very unprofessional, particularly considering the woman was essentially responsible for the safety of the entire park.

He chose his moment to pick his way across the deserted space, careful not to tread on exposed cabling left by the workforce. The architectonic lighting designer had not seen eye-to-eye with his employers, and construction was on hold until a replacement could be found.

It was typical that Kelly would squirrel herself away here he thought; the last room in the Yadub that anyone would think to look for her, yet probably the only one grand enough for her ego.

'You shouldn't be in here,' Trigger said. 'This is still a hard-hat area.'

Kelly wasn't releasing her hold on the computer technician. She dug her nails into Duncan's earlobe, forcing a scream. She liked Duncan a lot, considered him particularly loyal to her methods.

'Get yourself a brew,' Kelly said to Trigger, gesturing at a half-empty box of Castlemaine XXXX. 'You ever play this old console? Duncan just bought it on eBay; only turns out he's a bloody natural.'

'There's a problem,' said Trigger.

'Then deal with it,' said Kelly. 'The hotel is all but deserted. That's why they call it a soft opening. Even you can't have a bung up your arse right now.'

'A problem with the animals,' said Trigger.

'Impossible.'

'Some of the staff have been reporting in from the park. The VIP tents.'

'So what?' said Kelly, tossing Cho another beer.

'A couple of the guests are worried. I need you to take a look at something.'

Kelly and Duncan stared at him.

'This better not be your usual jobsworth horseshit,' said Kelly, popping open her can. 'This park is the most secure animal preserve on the planet. I know, because I built it.'

Constance Roper was sitting up in bed, removing her make-up and watching CNN.

She jumped in surprise as there was a crash of foliage above. Something heavy had landed on the roof of her tent.

This wasn't too unusual, Constance reminded herself. Certain animals in the park, like the peacocks and some small, tame monkeys, were permitted to roam freely. She had heard frantic scrabbling from above on more than one occasion, as well as the kind of strange howling and hooting never experienced in her six-bedroom home on Palm Jumeirah.

Animal disturbances, however, usually occurred at dawn. This intrusion was large enough to get her out of bed and reaching for the complimentary Ugg slippers.

Liza was still outside in the pool. A born athlete, she could swim for hours, but she might want to stop and get a photograph of whatever this was.

Constance hesitated, listening to more loud thrashing from above. She emerged from her four-poster bed in time to see the shape of what looked like a giant bat struggling for purchase on one side of the diagonal canvas roof.

Her jaw dropped.

Silhouetted by a strong desert moon, the shadow of two monstrous, ungainly wings gradually emerged from either side of a thick torso and began to beat at the thick covering. It was no use; despite all the noise and activity, the bulky creature was beginning to slide.

Constance reached for the telephone.

Whatever this was, it needed recapturing, not photographing. It was obviously in distress.

The Hide was what Kelly Maelzel had called the faux-colonial country house that served as the nerve centre for the zoological and security staff. Getting there from the main hotel required a ten-minute ride on a golf-cart, which was ten minutes too long for Samuel Trigger. The radio at his belt had been crackling constantly whilst Kelly had been driving along the service road, the switchboard having received at least half-a-dozen calls from guests concerned about aggressive or unusual animal sightings.

'If the visitors take food into the park, they are going to attract attention,' said Kelly.

'You don't know that's what happened here.'

'I told management: no food in the park. Not even loose food in the tents, to be safe. But no, people need bloody Toblerone in their mini-bar.'

'You know,' said Duncan Cho, who was holding onto the cart with both hands to stop himself skidding off the rear seat, 'this concept of landscape immersion is probably new to a lot of people. I mean, there are no barriers anywhere to be seen.'

'Right,' said Kelly. 'Getting spooked by nearby animals is part of the fun.'

Trigger did not think that being spooked was much fun. Multi-starred hotels were his business. Smooth facilitation of conferences and weddings was his business. This artificial park was eerie – hundreds of aggressive eyes staring out of the imported foliage at their open-sided cart.

They aren't supposed to be here, these animals. This isn't even their continent. They don't want to be here.

The country club façade of *The Hide* presented a far more civilised front to the guests than the rear of the structure, which contained darkened veterinary suites, craftsmen's workshops and any amount of junk-filled storage space. Kelly drove up to a wide, electronically locked side gate and tapped a six-digit number onto the keypad.

After a series of security checkpoints, the three senior staff found themselves upstairs in the control room of the main building. Two terrified-looking Sri Lankan men were staring at a bank of video screens as though Armageddon might be enfolding.

Kelly joined them, her eyes everywhere.

'There's nothing happening,' she said, bewildered. 'There's nothing happening.'

Five shrilling, unanswered telephones on the left-hand side of the room suggested that she might be mistaken.

'Integrity of the fences is solid,' said Cho, punching at the keyboard of a mobile terminal. 'One tapir fence is flashing yellow, but that's a misfire from two days ago. Park is secure.'

'Secure?' said Trigger, reaching for his radio.

Nobody spoke.

'Park is secure?' said Trigger to Kelly.

Kelly Maelzel had become distracted, was watching something in the monitor bank. One screen was showing movement.

Through a thermographic camera, she could see a bright blob.

The Sri Lankans could see it too. Then Cho. Then Trigger. Then the blob disappeared.

'Sweet Jesus,' said Kelly.

The individual private swimming pools adjacent to every tent were small and square, but enjoyed some innovative design features. At the push of a button, strong jets could pump water from one end to the other, simulating a current to exercise against.

Liza Roper, proud of her backstroke, relished the unusual sensation of the water pushing her long hair down the sides of her head and stared up at the stars, uncommonly bright in the clear sky.

When the cycle ended and all was quiet again, Liza allowed her legs to drop and tread water. The base of the pool was still one growth spurt out of reach.

There was a noise from the surrounding undergrowth, and Liza turned to see the largest Royal Bengal tiger in existence emerge from the carefully landscaped border.

Unfazed by the strange clearing he had found himself in, the monster predator shrugged stray leaves from his coat and dived into the water.

Motionless but afloat, Liza could only watch in terror. The tiger did not paddle, he remained fully submerged, swimming underwater. She had never realised that tigers could do that. And he was swimming fast, with great power.

Swimming towards her.

Instinctively, her arms and her legs gave a strong spasm and she floated backwards. The tiger did not divert from his course, and Liza felt a strong flux of water as he passed, the majestic body inches from her bare legs.

Even in this diffused, underwater light, there was no mistaking the strong muscles beneath the orange and black fur, nor the size of the teeth, bared by the resistance of the water.

In seconds, he had passed. The tiger leapt up the steps to the shallows, shaking his body in an arc of spray that spotted the pool and made Liza blink.

Then the tiger padded through the open door and into the tent.

Justice descended quickly, and did not ask too many questions.

On top of the expensive private prosecution being planned by the board of the Yadub, Kelly Maelzel had to spend a month in the Sharjah Punitive and Rehabilitation Centre while the Court of First Instance decided what charges to bring about for her apparent negligence. One of the six prostitutes sharing Kelly's baking concrete cage had an advanced case of scabies, and she scratched her body until it bled onto her six-month-old baby.

The child howled incessantly.

Meanwhile, Kelly stewed, mentally preparing herself for the future. She knew her situation was grim. She had no family or local sponsors to campaign for her, and the Australian embassy in Abu Dhabi remained curiously quiet.

After an interminable daily routine of mindless, self-regulated exercise and a diet of fermented camel meat, Kelly Maelzel was thoroughly ready for a fight. She was filthy, she stank and her eyes blazed. This was a high-profile case with international interest, so special dispensation was to be permitted, at least in the speed of the proceedings.

The accommodation at the courthouse was more hygienic. Still handcuffed, Kelly was shown to a white cell enclosed by black bars made of a synthetic plastic. After the extreme heat of the prison, the air conditioning was barely tolerable. She noted the clean sheets on the bench, and an unmarked toilet seat. Kelly was alone for the first time in weeks.

In the evening, a meal of lentil curry was served by a female guard who would not make eye contact. Ten minutes after her tray had been removed, Kelly heard different footsteps approaching, heavy on the highly polished floor.

A shadow appeared, long before the person.

The man it belonged to was remarkably ugly. Perhaps he knew it, because he paused, as if to give her time to accept his appearance.

The first thing Kelly noticed were the eyebrows, which were untrimmed, ginger and arched way up towards the crest of a huge bald head, badly scarred by repeated sunburn. The man must have been fully six feet seven inches tall, and the irregularly shaped body – brawny across the shoulders and arms, paunchy in the middle – was clad in a tight white safari suit, stained under the armpits. More red hair escaped from the collar and cuffs.

The overall effect could have been comical, but Kelly found herself staring at the angry veins in his muscular neck, and recognised a dangerous temper in the grey eyes that now studied her like a specimen in a tank.

The man stepped forward. In one hand he held a thick cardboard tube, sealed at either end; in the other, a small brick wrapped in wax paper and a battered brown briefcase.

He placed the briefcase on the ground, and held the brick up to the bars.

'What's this?' said Kelly.

'Soap,' the man said, nodding towards the sink in her cell.

His voice was cultured, but she couldn't quite place the accent. Kelly noted his hands: huge, machine-like. They made her want to shudder.

'Thanks,' said Kelly.

The man then held up the cardboard tube as if to pass that to her also, but appeared to think better of it, and lodged a joyless smile in his face.

Kelly regained her composure. This did not look like an ally – this looked like trouble. She stepped forward herself, the man's enormous body filling her vision; the bars and his suited body, black/white, black/white.

'My name is Otto Lix,' he said.

'Otterlix?'

The smile grew a little wider, and, as if it were possible, a little uglier. Kelly bristled.

'Why should I care, mate?'

He ran the cardboard tube along the bars of her cage. Kelly watched his sausage-like fingers, the knuckles forested with wiry ginger hair.

'It seems to me,' he said, 'that a woman in your position would need friends right now.'

'I've never needed friends.'

'That belief is your first mistake.'

'And my second?'

'Where should I start?' said Lix. 'Let's see, a year after graduation, you were part of the original team in New Zealand who planned the extension to the *Springs of the Gods*. I've never been there myself.'

Kelly looked again at his cardboard tube. It was thick as a drainpipe, but the big man could twirl it in one massive hand.

'I've seen photographs,' said Lix, studying a fingernail. 'Greatest thermal wonderland in the world. Terrestrial hot springs all the colours of the rainbow. Of course, you remember what happened to the tourist numbers after Mrs Julie Rousseau?'

'Julie Rousseau was nothing to do with me.'

'Forty-year-old mother of three, waist deep in volcanically superheated mud.' Otto Lix clicked his tongue against the roof of his mouth. 'You know how hot those pools get? You left those kids with *half a parent*.'

'I was exonerated.'

'You designed the pathways, decided where was safe to walk. You ignored the geologists.'

'No, the geologists ignored me.'

'Yet, as you say, no charges were brought. You have a remarkable CV, but this has got to be the most astonishing thing about it. You continue to be valuable.'

'I work hard to create experiences for people.'

'Exactly.' Lix seemed pleased, gave the tube an extra spin. 'You're like the ringleader of a circus, and beneath your tent, you put the natural world on show. You're also an escape artist, but I think your time has come. Tell me, why can you never again set foot in Kenya?'

'I was framed.'

'Because, Kelly Maelzel, you are on the KWS list of most-wanted poachers.'

'The animals were always my priority,' said Kelly.

'You never fired a gun. But you brokered a deal between Ugandan ivory dealers and the Japanese.'

'I was in the wrong room at the wrong time.'

'No, the room was in the wrong place,' said Lix. 'You can't have that kind of conversation in Nairobi.'

'I was set up by the local news. A white scapegoat made for good public relations.'

'Don't worry, I'm not on the side of the conservationists.' His voice was sympathetic, condescending. 'You don't have to justify yourself to me.'

'I'm not.'

'Lots of elephants in Kenya,' said Lix. 'Elephants and farming are not mutually sustainable in sub-Saharan Africa. Did the statistics validate your ethical dilemma?'

'Tell me one thing,' said Kelly.

'Of course,' said Lix.

'What's in the fucking tube?'

'And it isn't even the craziest thing,' said Otto Lix, as though she hadn't spoken. 'By all accounts, you personally turned Kenya's dilapidated Noah Conservancy into the most visited national park in the country. That was against entrenched competition. You oversaw the construction of twelve new eco-lodges, half as many new jeep trails and the resurgence of the antelope and black rhinoceros populations. All on-time and under-budget. Despite the many, many controversies, your stock continued to rise.'

Kelly said nothing.

'Then there's your penultimate contract, the short-lived consultancy at Sydney Zoo. At first, the figures demonstrate that you did astonishing work. You introduced technology that slashed payroll and operating costs. But then, we also know that this isn't your first big cat escape, is it, Kelly?'

'Everyone was fine in Sydney.'

'But that's not the case here. You have the world's most famous tiger attacking a much-loved American tennis professional, and in her two-thousand-dollar-a-night tent. Constance Roper lived, she was resourceful. Imagine, she put a glass shower door between herself and a man-eater, and that tiger was *strong*. Her daughter had the good sense to run for help, but who knows what could have got *her* in the meantime. Twenty per-cent of your systems had failed.'

'Impossible.' Kelly ran hands through her grimy blonde hair.

'The night safari was your baby,' said Lix. 'Your budget was practically unlimited, but you had financial bonuses specifically tied to completing it on time. I think you cut corners.'

'Show me the evidence.'

'If only the Arabs had as much knowledge of your CV as I do.'

'And that's where you come in.'

'Yes.'

'You're going to give them my history, the one you've so painstakingly researched. What are you, some kind of freelance vigilante *shithead*?'

For the first time, Otto Lix looked surprised, the thick ginger eyebrows inching further up his forehead. The cardboard tube received an extra twirl, and then he pressed it horizontally against the bars, leaning forward as if to steady himself.

Kelly was on her feet again, squaring up to him.

'Are you sure you don't need friends right now?' Lix said quietly.

Kelly cleared her throat, spat on the floor.

'I don't want to help put you away,' said Lix. 'They don't need me for that.'

'Then *what*?'

'Kelly Maelzel, I've come here to offer you a job.'

'A *job*?'

'Right.'

'Who are you again?' said Kelly.

'I'm Otto Lix.'

'Of course you are. And what do you do, exactly?'

'Today, I'm a head-hunter.' The phrase seemed to amuse him.

'Well, in case you hadn't noticed,' said Kelly, 'I'm not available right now.'

'Wrong again,' said Lix. 'You accept the offer I have for you, and my company will pay off the Yadub, as well as posting the extortionate bail that they're going to set tomorrow.'

'What company is that?'

'We have a fully fuelled turboprop on standby at a private runway in Ajman. It'll take us to India. You'll be out of the Emirates before you're missed.'

'Why India?'

Holding her gaze, Otto Lix popped the top off his cardboard tube.

He unfurled four large scrolls, each covered in bright colours. Two of the scrolls were maps of the same island, one schematic, one topographic. A third scroll was an aerial photograph. He passed them through the bars.

Kelly spread the scrolls out on the bench.

'You're building a zoo,' she said, her back to him.

'Of sorts,' said Lix. 'We have a sixty-year lease on this island from the Indian government, with an option to extend. But there are special circumstances.'

Kelly was busy with the maps. The island was the shape of an inverted ankh, a mountain range dividing east from west. The loop of the ankh consisted of three small volcanoes filled with crater lakes of striking green water, foliage dropping straight into the sea. There were also several inviting white beaches, and a modern human settlement on the smaller western arm. Multiple reefs were visible, the sea surrounding the island changing from light to dark in splashes of varying blues.

'What's this line?' said Kelly, tracing with her finger.

'A monorail, under construction. The whole island is the *zoo*, as you put it.'

She turned and held up the schematic. 'And this?'

'Approximate location of a shipwreck; Portuguese, seventeenth century. You're a PADI instructor – you could help recce the dive site, perhaps with an eye to developing an additional visitor attraction.'

'What are these?'

'We're proposing a series of campsites for visitors. If the design goes according to plan, they'll double as hides. There's an awful lot to take in, of course. I have reams of documents for you on the plane. As you can see, we've already constructed a visitor centre, a lodge and a small port.'

Kelly flipped the map over, the back was blank. She searched through the other papers.

'I don't see, ah, any barriers on your maps. You're using naturalistic barriers?'

'Of sorts,' said Lix. 'It isn't in our interest to impose barriers.'

'Visitors want to see the big predators,' she said. 'You won't have a going concern without them.'

'This,' said Lix, 'we already know.'

'There are ways to disguise barriers. You saw what I did at the Yadub?'

'No barriers. Of any kind.'

'Look,' said Kelly, 'big cats are territorial. Even if you bloat the island with prey, I don't think you could sustain more than maybe, what, four or five adult tigers here. That doesn't give your customers great opportunity for sightings.'

'There'll be no tigers,' said Lix.

'No?'

'The only exhibits planned are those that already inhabit the island.'

Kelly blinked.

'Don't be simple, mate. People aren't going to travel thousands of miles to view butterflies and bush pigs. These are your only indigenous animals here.'

'Our exhibits aren't what you would call typical animals.'

'How's that?'

'Well, for one thing, they're *human*.'

The sun was relentless, the stone terrace baking.

'I appreciate you seeing me this morning, Dr Rashid,' said Constance Roper.

Dr Rashid Al Shindagha lowered the mouthpiece of his shisha, the hose coiling towards a beautifully ornate water jar.

'Of course, Ms Roper.' He expelled fruit-scented smoke through his broad smile. 'Tell me, how is your daughter these days?'

'Her nightmares have stopped. Of course, she's still obsessed with tigers.'

'Regrettable,' said Dr Rashid.

'On the contrary. She keeps asking when we can come back here.'

'Ah.'

'Business seems good,' said Constance, gesturing around the tables of Petit Four, the Yadub's bakery and coffee shop. It was almost full, the clientele predominantly happy, rich, white families. The heat would have been unbearable but for the fine mists of cool water spraying from nozzles disguised in the parasols.

'The Yadub has luck,' said Dr Rashid. 'Advance reservations are exceeding even the most optimistic predictions of our accountants. The website receives millions of hits.'

'This was hardly the case one month ago. Remarkable recovery, given the global economy.'

Dr Rashid stroked his beard, then picked imaginary dust from his spotless dishdasha.

'I won't sugar-coat it,' said Constance. 'My near-tragedy generated all this publicity for you.'

'Bad publicity,' said Dr Rashid, shaking his head.

'Evidently not.'

Somewhere out in the safari park, there was a scream from some unseen, exotic creature. A few people looked up from their Viennoiserie to stare at the surrounding foliage. Constance herself twitched at the sound, working hard to maintain eye contact. Her own nightmares were ongoing, and not yet receptive to therapy.

'I've taken legal advice,' she said, leaning forward. 'As discussed, there will be no lawsuit. But you will *not* euthanise the tiger.'

'I will do everything in my power.'

'Your obligation to Liza, at the very least, is to save the tiger. She's in love.'

'He has survived so far, and the veterinarians do not think it necessary.'

'Did you find out what caused your systems to fail?'

'The investigation is ongoing.'

'Yet the park is operational.'

'There is no further threat, Ms Roper. Of this were are certain.'

Constance considered. 'In October I will play the charity doubles match on the Burj helipad. I talked to Agassi, he didn't take much persuading.'

'Ha!' Dr Rashid slapped the table. 'My brother will be delighted. After all, I am taking business from him now.' He smirked. 'You are a good friend to this family.'

'At this moment, I would say invaluable,' said Constance. 'But you have another brother, in the office of the public prosecutor.'

Rashid Al Shindagha began to look distinctly uncomfortable.

'Don't worry,' said Constance. 'I think this is a dispensation well within your power. It will *guarantee* the life of the tiger, and maybe provide the insight you need into the security lapse that almost took my life.'

'I see,' said Dr Rashid. 'It is very important to me that we come to an agreement.'

'I know,' said Constance Roper.

Three weeks later.

The plucky plumber in the green overalls rounded the final bend, easy on the acceleration so as not to drop off the rainbow-coloured track.

The finish line was in sight.

Impossibly, and with only seconds until victory, the small cart was thrown into a violent tail-spin, whirling off the racecourse and into the ether. A red shell, a missile with homing power, had caught him in the nick of time, and a small toadstool overtook, sailing past for the win.

'I *hate* you,' said Duncan Cho, throttling his controller.

'I know,' said Kelly, her face shiny in the subterranean light of the recently completed aquarium complex. 'You should, mate.'

Cho sighed.

'Another game?' said Kelly, watching her score tally on the screen.

'Of course,' said Cho. 'But later. I need to go to *The Hide*.'

'Back-up restarts automatically, it can wait until tomorrow,' Kelly said, yawning. 'Besides, Trigger will call if there's a problem.'

'Still,' said Cho.

Kelly considered. Prior to her arrest and subsequent reinstatement, she would have chided her deputy for this unnecessary concern, his lack of faith in her networks; may even have accused him of running away from their pixelated battle of wills.

But things had changed. She knew she was lucky to be reinstated. She knew that the case against her had been thrown out in order to recast the story of the tiger escape, and all she had been required to do in return was testify to a bored-looking committee of locals.

Kelly had been fed her lines by one of Rashid's stooges. She claimed that the problem in the park was due to faulty hardware imported from a South Korean company, a company that had already gone out of business. Yet Kelly still had no real idea why the park systems had failed.

But this way, perhaps, there would be no victims; the tiger was permitted to live, promoted to a larger and more impressive compound, now a global celebrity. The Yadub publicists were happy to admit that they had overreacted, because naturally, security was their number-one concern. And the publicity surrounding the miraculous survival of Constance Roper and her daughter, although initially negative, had impacted very positively on visitor numbers.

Publically, Kelly had received a short, swift apology for her incarceration. Privately, she was on her final warning. She had met with Constance Roper, and was under no illusion who her saviour had been. But should anything else go wrong on her watch at the Yadub, then Kelly would certainly be locked back up in that hellhole, and this time they would throw away the key.

Then there was the mysterious man-monster Otto Lix, who had taken her murky employment history apart and then *still* offered her a job. Thankfully, she no longer needed to accept his insane offer, but it would have been interesting to have discovered some more information about him.

Lix, however, seemed to have disappeared.

Once again, Kelly Maelzel had been lucky. What was it that Lix had said?

You're an escape artist, but I think your time has come.

'Kelly?' said Duncan Cho, watching her carefully. 'Are you okay?'

'You're right,' said Kelly. 'Check the cycle: do it now. Give my computers some love.'

Cho dragged himself to his feet. Behind aquarium glass, a school of pompano chased down silt-like plankton, casting mottled shadows across the dark space.

A hungry nurse shark watched on, motionless at the bottom of the tank.

Duncan Cho knocked on the door in what he hoped was a confident, forthright manner.

He was nervous about confrontation, knew he could never thrive on it the way Kelly did. He also imagined that the man in suite 706 would be pretty capable in that regard, although Cho had only ever dealt with a voice on the phone once, and from then on by proxy through a lawyer in the Cayman Islands.

Otto Lix answered the door in a hotel robe that was far too small for him. Legs like hairy tree-trunks dropped into naked feet stuffed with obscene blue veins.

'Good evening,' said Lix. 'Please, close the door behind you.'

Cho swallowed. The man was enormous and phenomenally ugly.

The hotel room looked tidy and unlived in. The lights were low, so behind Lix, through a large window, Cho could see pools of artificial illumination out in the park, highlighting the various exhibits for visitors on the ground. The setting was almost romantic.

'Your money has been in the Caribbean for six weeks,' said Otto Lix.

'I know that,' said Cho. 'But there's a problem, Mr Lix.'

'Oh?' Lix seemed disinterested.

Cho swallowed again. 'It isn't enough, Mr Lix. Not any more. You're asking for further work, and the risk is greater now.'

Lix studied the lights in the park. 'Kelly Maelzel is out of jail,' he said. 'I had it on good authority that she would never accept my job unless she was compelled. Leverage is everything.'

'How was I to know the tennis player would get involved?'

'Our deal was explicit. You were to generate the appearance of guilt on her part. Reasons for the park failure proved ambiguous at best.'

'The risk was too great.'

'Do *not* talk to me about risk calculation. It was the level of risk that dictated your considerable compensation.'

'I couldn't have pointed the finger any more than I did. Kelly Maelzel is too smart.'

'At this point, the problem is exclusively yours. Release another tiger, inject a gorilla with PCP – I really don't care.'

'Security is tighter now.'

'Because of *your* failure, Mr Cho. People are paranoid about sabotage, as well they should be.'

'Deal's off, Mr Lix. Sorry.'

Otto Lix said nothing. Cho could feel the walls closing in.

'Well then,' said Duncan Cho, in what he considered a tone of finality. 'You can have the money back. I never touched a penny.'

After an eternity, Lix held out his hand to shake. 'I think I understand your situation,' he said.

Cho's relief was palpable, but when he took the gigantic hand, Lix switched his grip, folding Cho's thumb inwards and exerting massive pressure, rotating the knuckles with a sickening series of crunches, and using his own thumbnail to dig deep into Cho's pulse.

Cho screamed at the sudden, extraordinary pain, and Lix moved rapidly, taking the opportunity to force the four fingers of his other hand into Cho's gaping mouth.

His left thumb wedged into the soft skin beneath the jawbone and worked upwards and inwards, always moving, searching for pressure points.

Cho tried to bring his teeth together, but to no avail; there was insufficient momentum, and the hand seemed to fill his entire head. Instead, he lashed out with his legs, caught the huge man on the shin. It was like kicking a goalpost.

'No, no, no,' whispered Lix, rooting further and further back into Cho's head, cutting off air, wiggling his vile, monstrous fingers. Cho was induced to vomit partially digested cheeseburger, his nasal passages blocking up with bile.

'There we go,' said Lix, manoeuvring Cho down onto his knees.

Otto Lix drew his face close to the other man. His breath smelled like hot garbage.

'You *will* frame Kelly Maelzel as we agreed, or I will *find* you,' he said. 'You can't nod or speak right now, but you can make noise. I've done this enough to know a negative from a positive.'

Cho's eyes and nose were streaming.

'So,' said Lix. 'Do we have a deal?'

Cho grunted.

'Take your time,' said Lix. 'I'd hate to think you'd been rushed.'

Cho grunted.

'What was that?'

Cho grunted again.

'If I rotate my hand, I could entirely destroy your soft palate with my fingers.'

Cho tried to scream.

'You see,' said Lix. 'It works out if we all just do our jobs.'

He withdrew his hands, pulling thick spittle from Cho's mouth. Cho dropped forward onto his face, grabbing at his injured throat.

Otto Lix walked to the bathroom for a clean towel. When he returned, Cho was still on his knees, trying to say something.

'What's that?' said Lix.

'Why . . . Kelly Maelzel?' said Cho, a little blood running down his chin. 'What's so fucking *important* about her?'

Otto Lix shrugged. 'How should I know?' he said, wiping his

fingers and forearm. 'Something to do with Edward Quinn. Some kind of unfinished business there.'

'Who?' Cho went into a coughing fit.

'Forget it,' said Lix, throwing the towel at him. 'Now, I'm going to call room service, get this puke cleared up, and maybe order a shrimp cocktail. You want anything?'

Four

'The patient is stable,' Chris Light told Charlie Cortez. 'At least, she's stable from her self-inflicted knife wounds. We don't know what's going on with her brain.'

'Her brain?' said Charlie.

'Do you think Leona Bride meant to kill herself?'

'How would I know?'

'I thought you were taking a personal interest.'

Gossip travels fast.

'A what?' said Charlie.

Does Sparky know that I know Leona already? That I was her client last week?

'I mean, you're in here so late.' Sparky shrugged, offered up a sympathetic smile. 'Your wife has been calling the switchboard.'

'My cell, too,' said Charlie. 'She knows I'm working. She'd leave a message if it was important.' He looked again through the glass wall into the room where Leona lay in the semi-dark, faceless beneath a clean sheet. He could just make out her one uninjured wrist, which was cuffed to the bed, white and bare.

'I don't know it if was attempted suicide,' he said. 'I can't speculate. I suppose she did a pretty good job on Frank Tsang.'

'She *murdered* Tsang,' said Sparky. 'And in this hospital.'

There was a cop and a senior member of hospital security posted outside. They looked nowhere, but saw everything.

'She might have been a suicide,' said Charlie, almost to himself. 'But does Leona Bride seem like a murderer to you?'

'We don't know what's going on with her brain,' said Sparky.

'I heard you the first time,' said Charlie.

Chris sighed. 'Well, for one thing, she should be unconscious.'

'Tell me why.'

'Loss of blood. Shock. Exhaustion. She's underweight and her system is swimming in sedatives. Tox-screen shows a lot of the same stuff she presumably used to tranquillise Tsang.'

Bottles and bottles of pills on the night table.

I never sleep.

'She's awake?' said Charlie. 'Now?'

'Her eyes are open. There's significant brain activity. She might be in an ASC; we need to do more tests.'

'Did you medicate?'

'Neilson, initially – two mg Lorazepam. Ms Bride was manic even after she collapsed and dropped the steak knife. She was still trying to fight.'

'Has she said anything?'

'Nothing sensible. She recognises visitors, but they agitate her. It doesn't make any sense.'

'Agitate her?'

'To put it mildly. She tries to attack, and hurts herself on the restraints without care for self-injury. I gave her another two mg about an hour ago, but it didn't seem to do anything. With all that stuff already in her system already, I daren't administer another antipsychotic. Even without external stimulus, she suffers from hallucinations and panic attacks.'

'I'm not surprised.'

'That she's awake?'

'No, that she's hallucinating,' said Charlie. 'Given that she's full of sedatives and still conscious. The question is, *how* is she awake?'

'She's *more* than awake,' said Sparky. 'She claws, she bites . . . sometimes she behaves like, I don't know, something from *Dawn of the Dead*.'

'Highly scientific,' Charlie said.

'Scientific? Earlier today, before tracking him here and killing him, that woman carved a slice out of Frank Tsang's thigh.'

'I know what happened.'

'She also had time to eat it. We know, because she vomited it all up. She didn't chew slowly.'

Charlie said nothing.

'And it was hardly a leap of faith to cross type the blood vomited by Tsang with the blood in Leona's veins,' said Sparky. 'An exact match.'

'I saw the notes,' said Charlie.

'Do you want to go in and see her?'

How did it come to this? It was never supposed to be like this.

'I won't see her now,' said Charlie. 'She needs to rest.'

'Unless something has changed in the last ten minutes, she isn't resting.'

Charlie made up his mind, put a little authority into his voice. 'Okay. Get the psychologist Dan Demus and meet me in the usual conference room. I believe we can diagnose, but we might not have much time.'

Charlie seemed to be struggling with something personal, and Sparky knew it wasn't his place to intrude. Fresh action was very welcome; he showed enthusiasm, bounced in his sneakers.

'So what are we fixing, exactly?'

Maintenance was rewiring in Conference Room 1.11, but they had finished for the day; some small bulbs dangled like dislocated eyeballs from the dark rectangles of missing ceiling tiles.

Dan Demus brushed workman's dust from the table with his hand, and gnawed a white slug of nicotine gum. Dr Light and Dr Neilson had already left with their instructions; Charlie had ordered a barrage of tests for Leona. Now he and Dan regarded one another.

The clock on the wall showed midnight, and Dan's watch beeped in sync, more or less.

'Why have you got them looking for cystitis?' Dan asked.

'Because the answer, one way or the other, will be very telling.'

'Yes?'

'Of all the pharmaceuticals I saw on Leona's night table, there was one joker in the pack. Elmiron is not a sedative, she wasn't using it to try to sleep. That drug is used to treat cystitis.'

'But you think she *doesn't* have cystitis.'

'The KCI test will soon tell us.'

'And if she doesn't?'

'The British have pioneered another use for pentosan polysulphate, though they have little definitive evidence yet as to the effectiveness. I'm thinking that maybe Leona self-diagnosed, she's a smart girl. Perhaps she was using the Elmiron to try to treat herself for something different.'

'What?'

'Transmissible spongiform encephalopathies.'

Dan's eyes opened wide. 'CJD?'

'That would be the most likely prion disease. And many of the symptoms fit.'

'The insomnia? The . . . what, the *cannibalism?*'

'Okay, not all of them.'

'Have you considered the possibility that she could just be insane?'

'No,' said Charlie. 'I haven't.'

'If she thought she was treating herself for Creutzfeldt-Jakob, why was she still eating raw meat? The stuff in the fridge?'

'We don't know for sure she *was* eating it. It looked pretty ripe.'

'Then why keep it?'

'I think all this behaviour was caused by her encroaching dementia,' said Charlie. 'The MRI should tell us something.'

'Okay, say you're right.' The psychologist leaned forward. 'Mad Cow disease? In the United States? Do you know what you're talking about here?'

'Given the rates of diagnosis, a one-in-a-million possibility,' said Charlie. 'Unless there's some tainted cattle somewhere, in which case we might start seeing some new cases.'

'This could be huge,' said Dan. 'Are you going to contact the Center for Disease Control?'

'I'm not inclined to bring in the CDC until we have some results,' said Charlie. 'Meantime, I'm going back to the motel to collect samples of the mystery meat in Leona's refrigerator. If she has variant CJD, then the incubation time would be too fast for that stuff to have infected her. But if she's been eating bits of animal from the same source for a while, then . . .'

'We need to find that source.'

'Right.'

'You do know that if your diagnosis is correct, then your new girlfriend is certain to die.' Dan put a trace of sympathy into his voice. 'There's no cure.'

No cure but music, lights and laughter.

'She's not my girlfriend,' said Charlie.

'Okay,' said Dan. He tried to smile for the benefit of his friend, but his mouth only shivered. 'All the same, let's hope she just has the cystitis.'

No cure for what we have, Charlie Cortez.

No cure but death.

Reggie Owens was twenty minutes late for his 11 a.m. appointment at the diner on Cheshire Bridge Road, but his client was nowhere to be seen. He hoped he hadn't missed her. Mrs Vanessa Cortez did not seem like the kind of woman who was used to waiting around, especially in a grease-spot designed to steal early-hour custom from a nearby Waffle House.

He was halfway down his second root beer when an exotic sports car swung into the grubby lot. A few heads turned to goggle through the window.

Reggie smiled and shook his head. If this was Mrs Cortez's idea of discretion then she wouldn't be finding a job with him at Safe Harbor Investigations anytime soon; not that he wouldn't have appreciated such a beautiful colleague. The statuesque figure that strode towards the restaurant looked like the world's most glamorous widow, clad from top to toe in form-fitting black, hands dripping with gold jewellery, huge sunglasses covering half of her face.

When she saw the private investigator in his scruffy overcoat, she wrinkled her nose in displeasure, although it could have been the overpowering smell of fried sausage. Vanessa dismissed the waitress without words and squeezed her tightly clad rear into the booth.

'Hi,' said Reggie, as impressed as he had been the last time they met.

'What do you have, Mr Owens?'

'Photographs.' He reached into his attaché case and extracted a manila envelope. 'It was as you thought, I'm afraid.'

'Let me see,' said Vanessa.

Reggie Owens slid the envelope over, watched the woman digesting evidence of her husband's infidelity. Impressive rack she had.

Why did men always cheat on the hot ones?

'Where is this?' said Vanessa.

'Motel above a dive bar on Ponce de Leon. I have a document with the complete timeline.' Reggie tapped one of the pictures. 'Dr Cortez went after work, was drinking with this man.'

'Dan Demus,' said Vanessa, as though cursing.

'Dr Cortez met the girl in the bar downstairs. Afterwards, they were quite a while in the room. You want to know about the girl? I don't have much.'

'It doesn't matter,' said Vanessa.

'To be fair to the guy, he only saw her once,' said Reggie. 'No other evidence.'

'Once is enough.'

'As you say.'

'That man, *my husband*, hasn't been right in the head for weeks.'

Reggie used his bottom lip to remove a little soda foam from his moustache.

'What about the knife?' said Vanessa. 'You know, the dagger I found in our car?'

'Right,' said Reggie. 'See, he got it the same night I took these pictures.'

'Why the delay in telling me?'

'You said you'd only talk in person. Besides, I wanted to give you the full story.'

'Which is?'

'The guys at my disposal don't exactly work for the Smithsonian, but the thing is valuable. Not an item a working girl would have, let alone give away to a one-time client.'

'Maybe Charlie had it with him already?'

'No, ma'am. See this picture? He doesn't have the knife walking in, and here he is carrying it out. He looks really damn messed up: wonder what she did to him?'

Vanessa sneered. 'He's a drunken goddam mess.'

'There are a dozen different fingerprints on there. Think he stole it?'

'At this point, anything's possible.'

'Anyway, see here,' said Reggie, taking a folded-up newspaper page from his pocket and flattening it out. 'Item like that, expensive dagger, someone is probably going to want it back. I put a notice in the paper with a description, claimed it had been found, and if there are any enquiries to get in touch.'

'Why?'

'Solve the mystery.'

'What mystery?'

'Who does it belong to? Where did it come from? There might be a reward.'

'I didn't ask you to do that,' said Vanessa.

Reggie sat back, smiled. 'No charge to you. A friend on the classifieds owes me a favour.'

'Well, quit it.' She tapped one long, squared-off fingernail on the table. 'This meeting is over.'

'Your retainer is still good,' said Reggie. 'Want me to keep watching him?'

'No, I've seen enough.'

Vanessa Cortez stood to leave, and Reggie caught a whiff of fragrant cleavage. He began to stammer a little, unusual for him, but he couldn't let the opportunity pass.

'Ma'am, you *are* the same Mrs Cortez, right?'

'Excuse me?'

'Vanessa Cortez who, you know, writes books for children. *Wilkins the Worm*.'

'Right, right. Yes, that's me.'

Reggie brought his hand down on the table. 'I knew it was you, you look so much better than your picture. My daughters, they love old Wilkins.'

Vanessa considered removing her sunglasses, but decided against it. 'That's very kind,' she said. 'Thank you.'

'No, thank *you*. They gonna make a cartoon for TV anytime soon? Give ol' *Spongebob* a run for his money?'

'I don't know,' said Vanessa.

'I'm sorry, I have a . . . do you mind?' Reggie rifled through his case, brought out a copy from the second series, not a first edition or anything.

Vanessa took his pen, signed her initials.

'I never read anything to my kids before Wilkins,' said Reggie, smiling. 'But they eat that stuff up. Do you do all the drawings as well, or . . . ?'

Vanessa looked at her watch. 'The artist does that.'

'Because our family love the pictures. We really love the pictures.'

Vanessa was leaving. 'Well, pictures don't always tell the full story, Mr Owens.'

'So often the truth,' he said.

Charlie couldn't get into the parking lot of the Clearmont Lounge and Motor Hotel. It was crowded with police cars, both marked and unmarked, and a barrier of red and black caution tape had been rolled around the entire property, the perimeter guarded by men in dark suits.

Cops directed curious pedestrians towards the other side of the road, and, further towards the building, two large, ominous white vans displayed the biohazard trefoil.

The scene was ablaze with the flashing lights of emergency vehicles and the air vibrated with the chatter of radios. Excited children chased each other on bikes in the road outside, oblivious to traffic whose occupants slowed down to stare.

It looked like a major operation.

Charlie announced himself to a suit who carried an air of seniority, and messages were fired into a walkie-talkie. Charlie was not kept waiting for long. Two more men appeared from the building and regarded him from some distance. One was tall, in sunglasses and an ear-mic, the other short and slender in a white lab coat, squinting in the sunshine.

Lab-coat gave instructions to sunglasses, and sunglasses strode away. Lab-coat approached alone, and Charlie saw then that he had nostrils cavernous enough to lodge bats.

'Speak of the devil,' said the man, having ducked under the caution tape.

'I don't understand.'

'We were about to contact you, Dr Cortez. Yet here you are.'

'Who are you?'

'My name is Dr Ira Mardy. I'm from Health and Human Services. I work out of Emory, although I sometimes consult at Fort Detrick.'

'What is your concern here, Dr Mardy? Why the three-ring circus?'

'I'm a little surprised to hear you ask, Dr Cortez. As you are already aware, we have a reported food safety threat at the Clearmont.'

'I haven't confirmed that yet.'

'The confirmation has been made. We had a call from Alexandra Lindemulder. She calls herself Tiffany.'

'I know Tiffany,' said Charlie.

'Mrs Lindemulder and her husband own this place; the motel and the bar below.'

'I know,' said Charlie.

'I know you know,' said Mardy, his voice smug. 'She told me all about you, a doctor from Grundy sneaking around here and asking questions, and, a few weeks ago, getting up to god-knows-what in the early hours. Mrs Lindemulder is a very concerned citizen, and so she should be. Leona Bride, one of this motel's long-term residents, has disappeared.'

'And for this reason Tiffany called the CDC?'

'Mrs Lindemulder believes that Leona Bride is very sick, due both to the bearing of Ms Bride in the days before her disappearance, and to the contaminated meat she seemed to be eating. Meat that Ms Lindemulder said you discovered in Ms Bride's room.'

'I haven't confirmed that the meat is contaminated,' said Charlie. 'Or that Leona was eating it. That's why I'm here now.'

'It seems you haven't confirmed very much, Dr Cortez. Is Ms Bride a patient of yours?'

'You know she is, or you wouldn't have been about to contact me.'

'Yes. Your administrator at Grundy, Dr Krohn, was very forthcoming when I contacted him. But I like to give a man the opportunity to answer for himself. Tell me, are you also in a sexual relationship with Ms Bride?'

'What business is that of the CDC?'

'Just something that Ms Lindemulder said.' Mardy waved his hand as though Charlie could be swatted away. 'Anyway, I'm going to arrange to have Leona Bride transferred to Clifton Road. This is my investigation now.'

'She's my patient,' said Charlie. 'You don't have the authority.'

Mardy sighed. 'What about Barry Petrovitch? I suppose you know him as well.'

'Who?'

Mardy stroked his chin. 'It'll be curious to learn whether Mr Petrovitch is a regular customer of the Clearmont, some of his family live nearby. Or, I should say, whether he *was* a customer.'

'I don't know the name.'

'Petrovitch has something in common with a woman called Mary-Anne Sellers, although I doubt Mrs Sellers would ever have set foot in a dive like this, devout Christian that she is.'

'What are you talking about?' said Charlie. He was tired, he hadn't been home in two days.

'Precisely,' said Mardy. 'You have no idea. There are a handful of others as well, one a child from South Carolina. You're way out of your league, Dr Cortez, so I suggest you stop asking questions and start answering them.'

They were interrupted by two men in hazmat suits who squeezed past, the barrier temporarily parted by another suited agent in an FBI baseball cap. High above, helicopters buzzed.

'Is all this necessary?' said Charlie.

'You and your patient are only one part of a much bigger puzzle,' said Dr Mardy. 'Mr Petrovitch died yesterday of acute kidney failure. Mary-Anne Sellers is on a drip at the CDC. Fortunately, both had already given stool samples. My lab found enterohaemorrhagic E. coli bacteria.'

'E. coli?' said Charlie. 'That doesn't fit my diagnosis of Leona Bride.'

'No?'

'I think Leona Bride could be suffering from variant CJD.'

Dr Mardy laughed through his extraordinary nose. It was a very unpleasant sound. 'Unlikely,' he said.

'Unlikely, but possible. Or perhaps she has some other kind of prion disease.'

'Prion disease?'

'Yes.'

'And what would you say your specialty was, Dr Cortez?'

'Emergency medicine.'

Mardy laughed again; it rapidly became a sneer. 'What we're dealing with here is a terrible case of food poisoning.'

'That much I might agree with,' said Charlie.

'We'll have Ms Bride transferred into my care,' said Mardy. 'Will you expedite?'

'Ms Bride is undergoing an MRI and lumbar puncture,' said Charlie. 'We're checking out her cerebrospinal fluid. In the mean-time, her situation is being carefully monitored.'

Dr Ira Mardy's patience, brittle at the best of times, shattered completely. His temples turned the colour of beef. 'You don't know what you're looking for, Cortez.'

'14-3-3 protein?'

'Listen to me,' he said. 'You're stumbling about in the fucking *dark*. The Clearmont has been slinging bad burgers. So has the counter at The Eat & Go, as has anyone who serves anything that was ever stored in a contaminated unit at Polski's Wholesale on Kingsboro.'

'You can trace?'

'Of course. There's been a recall out for months, but it seems management at the Clearmont utilise particularly deep freezers and have an aversion to watching the news. I suppose I should be grateful. If it wasn't for you and Leona Bride, we might never have found this place.'

'Polski's Wholesale?'

'All on the label; ground whole muscle cuts, some of which are downstairs, defrosting now. They were meant for tonight's potential victims. It couldn't be clearer, the date of production matches other proven source material. Now, I don't know why Ms Bride was hoarding unusual bits of edible veal in her mini-bar, but you can be sure that we're having it tested.' Mardy smirked. 'Perhaps you might suggest a reason, since you seem to have such a close relationship with her.'

Charlie was undeterred. 'Any signs of dementia in your patients?' he said. 'Speech impairment, things like that?'

'Of course not,' said Mardy.

'Hallucinations? Personality changes? Violent psychosis?'

'No, no.'

'Sleeplessness?'

Dr Mardy pushed forward into Charlie's personal space; he had to stretch his neck to do so. 'Are you actually *looking* to create a new health scare? We already have media on the scene. The FSIS is embattled on this, and my job is medicine, not finessing the Department of Agriculture.'

'Diplomacy not your strong suit, I can see.'

'Back off, Cortez. The American consumer doesn't trust science but wants to eat hamburgers. Any scandal will be on your head, given the evidence of your personal involvement here. Besides, if you're correct about Creutzfeldt-Jakob – which would, frankly, be pretty damn incredible – then Leona Bride is dead anyway.'

'It seems I have nothing to lose,' said Charlie Cortez, walking away.

Charlie crossed the street, rested for a moment against the hood of his car.

'Excuse me? Sir?'

He turned to greet the gentle voice, found himself looking at a little white lady holding a closed, frilly umbrella. She was younger than sixty, but her deportment and countrified accent made her seem older.

'Can you tell me what's happening here?'

'Public health scare,' said Charlie.

'My,' said the woman, looking over at the Clearmont. 'They don't tell you anything, do they?'

'No,' said Charlie. 'They don't.'

'I think my daughter is in there. I haven't heard from her for weeks. I don't know what I hate more, coming to the city or using the buses while I'm here.'

'Figures,' said Charlie. His cell phone was buzzing in his pocket. He was finding it easier and easier to ignore; if there was news from Grundy, he would be paged.

'I don't drive,' said the woman. She was more insistent than her initial frailty suggested. 'Why she chose to live here, I will never for the life of me know. She was never the same after travelling. I don't truck with going abroad, not at that age. Still so *young*.'

'Need to watch those foreign people,' said Charlie.

'Don't condescend to me,' said the woman, tapping his ankle with her brolly. 'Sorry to have bothered you. You looked like someone who might have had answers, was all.'

'Wait,' said Charlie, realising. 'Who's your daughter?'

'She isn't really my daughter,' said the woman. 'I run an orphanage up in Cobb County. Fifteen kids right now.'

'Leona Bride?'

'How did you know?'

'What's your name, ma'am?'

'Martha Calloway.'

'Can you answer some questions?' said Charlie. 'It could be very important.'

'Who are you?' said the woman.

'I'm Leona's doctor,' said Charlie.

As there was no way to stop Leona's uncontrollable movement and no way to put her to sleep, the only way to keep her still enough to perform the MRI was to introduce a paralytic agent, which also meant that she had to enter the scanner wearing a compatible respirator to keep the air moving in her lungs. Many patients reported that putting their heads inside of the large cylinder was a traumatic experience in itself, so Dr Chris Light could not imagine what was passing through Leona's conscious mind as she was subjected to the test while denied control of her own body. It must have felt like being buried alive.

She's insane, he reminded himself.

But since the aminosteroid injection that had left her body motionless, it seemed to Chris that Leona had been looking up at him with new comprehension in her eyes.

Is it fear?

'Sparky, look at the thalamus.'

Chris Light and Dr Sara Neilson were studying scans that appeared on the monitors, a soft glow diffused across their faces.

'Full of small holes,' said Sparky. 'Like a sponge.'

'Of course she can't sleep,' said Sara. 'The thalamus regulates wakefulness.'

'Cortez was right,' said Sparky. 'This is neurodegenerative; her brain is attacking itself. She's losing far more than sleep. No wonder she's going mad.'

'Well, it certainly isn't cystitis or E. coli,' said Sara. Charlie had called to inform them of his conversation at the motel.

'Unlucky for us.'

'Variant CJD?'

'That's the thing,' said Sparky. 'She has a prion disease, but with an unfamiliar etiology. Her SPF more likely suggests *sporadic CJD*, which would mean . . .'

'A genetic disorder. Leona didn't catch it from something she ate.'

'So it might be something that runs in her family,' said Sparky. 'Some protein mutation. You see the amyloid plaques?'

'Still incredibly rare, though,' said Sara.

'But it probably isn't that either.'

'There were no triphasic spikes on the EEG.'

'And there are too many phenotypic expressions,' said Sparky. 'We need experts on this, and we need them *now*.'

Dr Sara Neilson stood and stretched. 'What do you think the chances are that we've discovered something entirely new?' she said.

'At this point,' said Sparky, staring at the scan results, 'I'm prepared to believe anything.'

It only took interstate traffic to turn curiosity into a tiring excursion. Charlie held the car well below the speed limit of the I-75, yet Martha Calloway still leaned forward as though distrusting horses. She grimaced at every overtaken semi, and only began to settle once they had passed The Big Chicken, East Cobb County's favourite fast-food landmark and navigational star.

Finally, the traffic thinned out, and after a few miles of empty country roads, Charlie was directed to a large detached house on the outskirts of Kennesaw. He parked the car in a hard-mud yard, parting a ten-strong crowd of happy, multicoloured children. They were skipping rope and playing tag, and unlike in the Cortez household, no hand-held electronic device seemed necessary to divert boredom.

It might have been Leona's childhood home, but Charlie felt instinctively that this was a place where the trail of madness had gone very cold.

'You want coffee, Doctor?' Martha said to him, struggling to unclip her seatbelt. 'I can get Jonas to heat you a slice of pie, yesterday was baking day.'

'Thank you,' said Charlie.

Returned to her familiar universe, Martha became far more comfortable, striding towards the wraparound porch with Charlie and a bunch of the kids in tow. She had a remark for each of them; sometimes praise, sometimes a matronly scolding, but all delivered with good-humoured affection.

Dr Cortez was shown into the chintzy living room, probably the only place in the house untouched by the happy mess that surrounded the orphans. The quiet was a little disorientating, and Charlie realised then that he had been glad of Martha's company.

Why could I never create a place like this for my own family?

Maybe I still can.

He squeezed the arms of his overstuffed chair. This orphanage, untouched by modernity and nestled amongst the abandoned tree-houses of generations past, looked like a damn good substitute for home. At that point, given the way Charlie felt about the complications in his life, it was tempting to find a sleeping bag and maybe bunk up in the basement.

A black girl, one of the eldest at eighteen or so, brought Charlie a mug of oversweet coffee, then disappeared with a polite smile. She was humble and beautiful enough to turn him a little awkward. Charlie fiddled with his cell phone until Martha Calloway returned to show him up the two flights of stairs to Leona's old room, which was in one of the eaves of the attic.

'You think this will help, Dr Cortez?'

'I'm certain,' said Charlie, who had no idea. He had already convinced Martha to delay her visit to Grundy, ostensibly because of Leona's ongoing medical tests, but predominantly because of his own curiosity to peek into his patient's old private life as soon as possible.

The room was nothing like Leona's accommodation in the motel. That space had felt transient and hollow, somewhere spirits went to die. Here, a full, messy life spilled from the cluttered walls: books, photographs, posters, keepsakes.

Of course, it would have been unnatural for Leona not to have changed since she had lived in the orphanage. Charlie knew he was looking at a snapshot of her late teenage years, and she was now a young adult. Yet none of her insanity-tinged self-consciousness was present in here.

Or was it?

Leona's face beamed out from framed pictures on the walls; crowded headshots with tanned friends; a sun-faded Polaroid in school uniform, and a playful, leggy portrait on one of the tyre swings outside the house. Many more pictures were pinned to corkboards, along with ribbons and postcards, notes and numbers.

Why did she change?

Charlie's instinct was to search for psychological trauma, both because he couldn't quite believe his own unlikely theory about a prion disease and because a disorder without viral or bacterial specificity would be far easier to treat. Yet within six years of these cheery photographs, something had conspired to turn Leona into a cannibalistic psychopath with a terminal illness.

'I don't think I'd ever have picked these colours,' said Martha, gesturing at the chaotically patterned wallpaper. 'Leona was never a *girly girl*, if that makes any sense to you, just a strong young woman who wanted a little pink in her life.'

Charlie ran his hand down a wall of books. 'A reader?'

'Lord, yes. A reader, a collector, a critic. Victoriana was her specialty. She loved travel writing and essayists.'

'Did you know her real parents? Her genetic family?'

'No,' said Martha. 'And she never had any desire to track them down.'

'She have any plans for the future?'

'She wanted to be a nurse. Leona liked to help people.'

'A nurse?'

'Even applied to The School of Medicine in Druid Hills,' said Martha. 'She had her acceptance letter, a scholarship, was all ready to go.'

'What happened?'

'She dropped out. Never set foot on campus. She took up a place in that God-forsaken motel, started working for the lowlifes of Atlanta. The more time passed, the less she called.'

'I'm sorry,' said Charlie.

'We're pushed for space here, but I kept her room just the same. Lord knows, I shouldn't have favourites, but Leona was one of my first, and she used to be so good with the little ones.'

'I can imagine,' said Charlie.

'As you can see, she left everything behind – everything but her musical boxes. But she only started collecting them after she got back from India.'

'India?'

'Right. She went travelling in the year after high-school graduation, had saved her money from the late shift at Dairy Queen for an age. It was supposed to be nine months, visit different countries, but it turned out so much longer than that. She was never the same again.'

'What happened in India?'

'I don't know,' said Martha. 'She wouldn't talk about it. But like I say, she returned a completely different person, and the change continued. She just sort of . . . disappeared into herself.'

'Do you know where in India she went?'

Martha shook her head. 'I could never keep up. She used to

telephone every week, but in the last year of her trip we heard nothing, until one day she returned home, pale and ill and silent. You can imagine how we worried. Soon she was gone again, this time to Atlanta. But she wrote diaries while she was in India, pages and pages of diaries.'

Charlie's heart leapt. 'Can I see them?'

Martha shook her head again, and tears rolled down her cheeks. 'I'm sorry, Dr Cortez.'

'Please?' said Charlie. 'It could be useful.'

'She burned them,' said Martha. 'First thing she did when she returned was burn her diaries, in a garbage can outside. We couldn't stop her. But that girl sure loved to write. She was a good girl, not like the person you see today. She was such a good person, I hope you can believe me.'

'I do,' said Charlie.

Milo, the eldest of Charlie's twins, was mildly asthmatic, and found his inhaler running on empty following a particularly tense quest on WoW. His mom kept several spares, one in her handbag, but before he pushed into the kitchen to ask, he heard her weeping down the telephone to a friend. Milo did not want to interrupt, but neither did he bother to hang around and listen to the conversation; Mom's tears had become commonplace in recent weeks.

Beginning to breathe heavily, he entered his parents' bedroom. There was another emergency inhaler in Mom's nightstand, although this place was usually off limits. He found it in a drawer, hidden beneath the strange dagger that had caused so much ruckus the day before. He puffed thoughtfully on his inhaler, curling his lips around the mouthpiece as his airways became clear.

'What are you doing, faggot?'

'Clear off, Jesse,' Milo said, not turning around. 'You shouldn't be in here.'

'You suck on that thing like such a fag.'

Milo ignored him. Too much sugar turned Jesse aggressive, and he'd already been given a hard time at school that day. Jesse seemed to get chewed out even when trying hard in double math, while Milo wouldn't attempt to hold a basketball during gym class.

'*I* shouldn't be in here?' said Jesse. 'Are your MSN boyfriends making you feel all grown up?'

'What do you think it means?' said Milo, meaning the dagger. He picked it up with two hands, held it up to the light.

'Let me see,' said Jesse. 'I'll show you what it means.'

Milo's reaction was immediate.

'You shouldn't be touching that! You shouldn't be in here!'

Jesse pushed Milo back onto the bed. It was barely a nudge, but Milo sprawled.

'*Aaarrr!*' shouted Jesse. 'I be *Captain Jack Sparrow!*'

Jesse clambered up, pinning Milo's knees with his own. He brandished the knife, then brought it down, believing that he could predict exactly where Milo would move to escape him.

He was correct.

'Get off me, you fucking maniac!'

Jesse laughed, the game was almost over. Beneath him, Milo bucked and writhed. Jesse loved his brother, but Milo was such a predictable snob, and sometimes he needed to be taught a lesson.

Jesse decided to risk one more stab, knew this time Milo would move in the other direction.

Milo was so predictable.

'Hello,' said Charlie.

'Hello,' said Leona, eyes opening. She tried to move her head, winced at some pain or other. 'Where am I?'

'You're in hospital,' said Charlie. 'My name is Dr Charlie Cortez.'

'I know who you are,' said Leona. 'What am I doing here?'

'You were sleeping,' Charlie said gently.

'That's impossible,' said Leona. 'I never sleep. I can't.'

'Don't try to move,' said Charlie. 'You're very weak now.'

'Okay,' said Leona.

'Do you want to see Martha? She's waiting downstairs. She came all the way from East Cobb, and she's been so worried about you.'

'Beautiful Martha,' said Leona. 'No, I don't want her to see me like this.'

'Maybe later?' said Charlie.

'Maybe.'

'Look,' he said, trying a different tack, 'I brought you something. I know you collect these, you had so many of them in your room at the motel.'

Charlie reached into the paper bag he had carried in with him, produced a music box.

When he opened it, a tiny ballerina pirouetted before the mirror in the lid, and delicate chimes played a melody from *Swan Lake*.

'Thank you,' said Leona, attempting a smile. 'But it doesn't play the correct tune. None of them ever do. That's why I have so many, I have to keep looking.'

'What's the correct tune?' said Charlie.

'I don't remember,' said Leona. 'I'm a stupid girl. I make mistakes.'

'I don't think you're stupid,' said Charlie. 'I think you're very clever.'

'Smart keeps you alive,' said Leona. 'Not clever.'

'You can be both,' said Charlie, sliding the box onto a nearby table. 'For one thing, you were correct about the pentosan polysulphate. It eases your symptoms, but not in pill form, the way you were administering it to yourself. We had to infuse it into your lateral ventricle. It was an experiment that allowed you to sleep, and, right now, is the reason that you and I can have this conversation without you descending into mania.'

'Was I right? Do I have Creutzfeldt-Jakob?'

'I don't know. But you're certainly suffering from a degenerative neurological condition.'

'Am I cured now?'

'I don't know that either. In fact, I don't even know if, or for how long, your consciousness will remain stable. We need to do another MRI.'

Leona closed her eyes. Charlie thought she might be sleeping again, but when she opened them, she looked at him with something like tenderness.

'When these symptoms first started,' said Charlie, 'the insomnia, the mania – why didn't you go to a doctor?'

'I did,' said Leona. 'But the free clinic prescribed anti-depressants and sleeping tablets. That was when I started my own research, found the PPS. It used to help, but I got worse and worse.'

'Do you know your real parents?'

'You think this might be something hereditary?'

'Yes,' said Charlie. 'There's another rare prion disease called Fatal Familial Insomnia. Normal proteins in your brain tissue can mutate. Several of your symptoms are compatible.'

'But not all.'

'No.'

'My real parents don't want to be found,' said Leona. 'I tried. But it doesn't matter.'

'Why?'

'Because what I have isn't genetic.'

'How do you know?'

'I got it from the island.'

'The island?'

'I can't prove it, but I'm certain all the same.'

'What island?'

Leona rolled her eyes as if Charlie was supposed to know everything already. She rattled her uninjured wrist in the plastic handcuff that attached her to the bed.

'Can you undo this, please?'

'I can't do that,' said Charlie, and he saw then that their scene together was a reversal of the last time he remembered speaking to her, when Leona had tied him with silk in the motel.

'Don't worry,' she said. 'Your secret is safe with me, Charlie.'

'I'll try to keep the police out of this for as long as possible, but you're going to have to talk.'

'Frank Tsang?'

'Yes.'

'You know, when you get the taste for raw meat, it doesn't ever leave you. Of course, I resisted for as long as possible. I even bandaged him, don't suppose that made any difference, some of my medication must have been kicking in again.'

'What are you talking about?'

'It all comes back to the island.'

'You mean India? I know you were in India.'

'It isn't India. Not really. It might say so on a map, but that means nothing. They call it *Savage Island*. I kept my return ticket from a place called Port Barren, but I should never have been anywhere near. Ask Martha to show it to you.'

'What happened there?'

'You strip a person to the truth, and you might find they have nothing left,' said Leona. 'You should have let me kill myself.'

She grinned with the practised ease of a conjuror, and Charlie shuddered. It hardly mattered that she was tied down; Leona suddenly seemed very dangerous again.

'I don't understand,' he said.

'Neither did Frank Tsang.'

'And now he's dead.'

'You don't know how lucky he is,' said Leona. 'But you soon will.'

'What do you mean?'

Leona wasn't listening. 'I gifted you my dagger,' she said. 'I thought you were special. I even gave you my real name – I wasn't just Amber or Violet or Candy.'

'What dagger? What are you talking about?'

'For a moment I believed you were different, a lost little boy. But you were just another stoned fool. You gulped down my sleeping tablets like an addict. You were so desperate to escape, but I keep the gates of hell.'

'Let me help you,' said Charlie. 'Please?'

'I'm not the one who needs help,' said Leona. 'Not any more.'

Charlie looked down at her face; it was changing, the eyes lacquered and fierce. Perhaps the PPS was wearing off. His hand was within reach, and when she grabbed it, he yelped in pain.

'I tried to warn you, but you wanted to see what I could see. You were so desperate, so *greedy*.' Her nails dug deeper. 'If I were you, Doctor, I'd get back to work and *find a cure*.'

'You mean . . .?'

'Yes. Frank Tsang was the *second* client to drink my blood, Charlie.'

The moment the elevator spat Charlie Cortez into the corridor outside his apartment, he could see that something was seriously wrong. His front door was wide open, and the table in the hallway had been cleared of ornaments.

A few fallen packing peanuts led inside like a sinister trail of breadcrumbs.

It was cold within – the air conditioner had been running all day – and there was a lingering smell of sweat and grime from the men who had removed most of the furniture, leaving it bachelor bare. Nobody had bothered to vacuum up, yet all the lights blazed, and it was with dumb sadness that Charlie realised how easy it was to return their home to the soulless shell they had bought all those years ago.

Vanessa was waiting for him in the kitchen. She had a bottle of bourbon and a shot glass on the counter, although the bottle was full and the glass dry; she rarely, if ever, drank.

'I see there's another cockroach here,' said Vanessa.

'Where?' said Charlie.

Vanessa thumbed towards the place where a vase of fresh flowers usually stood, and Charlie walked over to look. He saw a set of grainy photographs – Charlie outside the Clearmont Lounge, Charlie holding onto Leona like a sailor on shore leave.

He felt the blood drain from his face.

'Where are the kids?' he said, already knowing the answer.

'With my parents. That's where I'm going.'

Vanessa was past raising her voice; she was into territories of rage that he had never seen before. She stood up.

'Can I see them?'

'You can go to hell. You don't answer your phone now?'

'Work,' said Charlie, uselessly. 'An important case.'

'I'm sure. I know how you spend your time.'

'Vanessa—'

'And I don't care. But I came into our bedroom to find Jesse and Milo trying to kill each other. They were using the knife that you got from that *whore*. That's what happens when there isn't a decent God-fearing man around. You get *bedlam*; this family is in chaos.'

'What knife?'

Vanessa wound up to slap him. She took her time, the signals were obvious, but Charlie let her do it anyway. Even so, the blow hit him less across the face and more across the right ear. It would sing for days; all those weeks with her personal trainer had paid off.

'You must think I am *so fucking stupid*,' she said. 'Yet you are the weakest individual I ever met. And to think I agreed to share my life with you, to give you my support. I must be a *saint*.'

Charlie looked again at the photographs. Him, Leona, the Clearmont.

Leona's voice: *I gifted you my dagger.*

'I have more for your scrapbook, if you're interested,' said Vanessa. 'Thank the Lord God I can get Milo and Jesse away now, before you corrupt them. My mother was correct, it isn't just that we were wrong for each other, it was that I never *needed* you. You call yourself a man, Charlie Cortez, but you're *nothing*.'

Vanessa poured herself a solitary drink, then killed it.

'Say something to me, you *fucking loser*.'

'I'm sorry,' said Charlie. 'It wasn't meant to be like this.'

'No?'

'Not tonight. I mean . . . not ever.'

'Not tonight?' Vanessa grabbed her bag and the photographs, then breezed past him.

'I'm so sorry,' he said, although he could see he had lost her; knew that he had probably lost her weeks ago, well before Leona. 'I'm so *sorry*, and there are things you need to know . . .'

'My lawyer will bleed you to death,' she shouted, and the front door slammed.

The desert island was exactly circular, and small enough to see the flat, dark ocean on all sides; a complete circuit paddling in the shallows would have taken less than a minute. There were three plastic palm trees in the exact centre, cast-offs from some cheap movie, and a few rocks strewn about for good measure. Charlie was clad in one of his nicest suits, but his feet were bare, which was fine, as there was no wind and the humidity was almost unbearable.

He glanced over his shoulder to see Frank Tsang, the obese patient that Leona had murdered. Naked and drained of colour, he lay on his back, tongue lolling and feet trailing in the water.

Leona was there too, similarly naked but very much alive. She was on all fours, tearing sinewy flesh from a gaping wound in Frank's stomach with razor-sharp teeth. Judging from all the blood that slicked her body, she had been enjoying her meal for some time.

'Hello,' she said, slurping purple intestines like spaghetti.

'Hello,' said Charlie, penis stirring to life in his pants.

'You can't blame yourself,' she said, mouth full. 'Vanessa was gone anyway, you just had to give her a reason. Ask Frank here. In life, it is always easier to be the victim.'

Frank Tsang raised his head.

'She's right,' he said. 'She's always right.'

Charlie couldn't remember how Frank had sounded in reality, so Charlie attributed to him the clichéd Southern tones of Wilkins the Worm. At least it was the last time he would have to hear that particular voice.

'Are you a victim, Charlie?' said Leona. 'I suppose that's your test now.'

'No,' he said, 'I'm not.'

'Then what are you waiting for?'

Charlie kicked off his clothes and clambered over Tsang; somehow the fat man's body was bloating to whale-like proportions. Once Charlie was shoulder to shoulder with Leona, he took her lead and buried his face in Tsang's raw wound, felt his head surrounded on all sides by cold wet flesh and the stink of the cadaver.

It was like entering a poisoned womb.

Bad meat filled his mouth and nose and ears, and he screamed and laughed and Tsang screamed and laughed, and then Charlie couldn't breathe any more.

The phone was ringing.

Charlie Cortez believed he was awake, but he was only dreaming about lying in bed.

He found himself on the floor of the master bedroom, mouth dry as an ashtray and his cheek hot from carpet friction. The moonlight through the window was like the beam of a torch, and it was bright enough for him to idiotically consider the empty bottle of whisky that lay within arm's reach.

He managed to stand, reeling as though beaten, and the city below him twinkled.

Charlie collared the phone on the tenth ring.

'Vanessa?' he said, voice thick. '*Vanessa?*'

'Chris Light,' said the caller. 'Sorry, Dr Cortez. Did I wake you?'

'Sparky,' said Charlie. 'No problem.'

He glanced at the alarm clock: 3:30 a.m.

'You wanted to know if there were any developments,' said Chris.

'Developments?'

'Thirty minutes ago, Leona Bride passed away,' said Sparky. 'She's dead, Charlie.'

'I'm pretty sure,' said Dan Demus, 'that once a patient gets a bed down here, there's not a lot more we can do for them.'

'Yes,' said Charlie. 'But there are still some things that the patient can do for *us*.'

The two doctors were marching down the long concrete corridor towards the hospital's huge morgue. Overhead, there were miles of exposed pipes and wires and cabling.

'Are you all right?' said Dan. 'No offense, but you look terrible.'

'Leona died from a prion disease,' said Charlie. 'This much we proved.'

'Right,' said Dan. 'CJD, Fatal Familial Insomnia, something like that.'

'Correct, but it was none of those. There's another unusual disease called *Kuru*. It was first diagnosed in the Eastern Highlands of Papua New Guinea, amongst an endocannibalistic tribe. This was in the fifties. They used to eat their dead relatives as a mark of respect. The word is *transumption*. Just as cows shouldn't eat other dead cows, humans shouldn't eat other dead humans. In the long term, bad things can start to happen.'

'You think Leona ate parts of another infected human.'

'Exactly.'

'But if this disease is fatal and linked to ritualistic practice, why didn't it destroy the tribe?'

'I've been studying. It almost did, until Christian missionaries eliminated cannibalism in the region. Kuru can have a latency of forty years.'

'Even so, there'd be little chance that Leona could catch it.'

'And besides,' said Charlie, 'she never travelled to Papua New Guinea.'

'Then how did she contract it?'

'I didn't say she did.'

Charlie and Dan reached the desk of the solitary night-shift attendant, who sat before spring-loaded double doors as though guarding somewhere people wanted to go. Out in the world, the sun had not yet risen, yet the man was considering a half-eaten salami sub the size of his forearm, and the meaty reek did not help Charlie's nausea.

'Good morning,' said Charlie.

The attendant nodded, staring at their identification and chewing like a disinterested bullock.

'Where's Joe Loder?' Charlie asked. Loder was usually in charge of the graveyard shift.

'Loder got called upstairs,' said the attendant, eyeing Charlie's unkempt appearance. 'Important paperwork.'

'Strange time of day,' said Dan.

'Strange sort of place,' said the attendant.

'We want to see Leona Bride,' said Charlie. 'She arrived here about two hours ago.'

'Little early for visitors, ain't it?'

'Will we wake anyone?'

The attendant was hunting through the print-outs on his desk. The information he wanted was right in front of him, but he seemed to need to work from the bottom.

'Room three,' he said, thumbing towards the doors. 'Then, alphabetical, A, B, C. You want B.'

Charlie and Dan pushed through the double doors.

Grundy's basement did not contain the pristine, stainless-steel vaults of flashy, neon-drenched crime shows; visitors were greeted by an interconnected succession of icy dungeons packed with white body bags atop metal gurneys, each room bright enough to cause the uninitiated to squint.

The smell of death versus disinfectant often travelled up the elevator shafts.

Dan's breath was steaming in the cold. 'Are you going to tell me what we're doing here?'

'Leona's symptoms were a little different from Kuru,' said Charlie. 'She suffered from sleeplessness and a kind of violent psychosis, whereas sufferers of Kuru experience excessive shaking and pathologic laughter. Secondly, her incubation period was far, far faster. But I think something *similar* to Kuru – another prion disease transmitted in the same way – might be endemic amongst a different tribe, one that she encountered in a remote part of India.'

They were walking past rows and rows of bodies, Charlie counting off names.

'Same question,' said Dan. 'Why wouldn't your new, hypothetical disease have destroyed this other tribe before Leona had time to contract it?'

'I don't know,' said Charlie. 'Different disease, different behaviour. Different tribe, different physiognomy, different ritual practices ... maybe they developed an immunity that, as an outsider, Leona didn't have.'

'Why haven't there been other reported cases?'

'There are a lot of pieces to this puzzle, but we can find a big one today.'

'How's that?' said Dan.

'Mice,' said Charlie.

'Mice?'

'We don't know who Leona's real parents were,' said Charlie. 'Kuru, my new model, can be transmitted into other primates by inoculation with autopsy-derived brain tissue. I'm going to prove that whatever this is, it isn't a genetic disease. I need to know if it has the potential to be an epidemic.'

'By taking her brain.'

'Part of it.'

'And injecting the tissue into mice.'

'This disease progresses faster than any other known TSE. Faster than Kuru, faster than variant CJD.'

Charlie stopped walking, turned to his friend. 'Of course,' he said, 'there is another reason.'

'There always is,' said Dan.

'If I can prove that Leona's sickness was genetic, then it means that *I* can't have contracted it from her. But if it isn't genetic, if it *is* transmissible, then . . .'

'You're going to die,' said Dan. 'Maybe.'

Charlie nodded.

'Here she is.' Dan gestured at the row of bodies they had reached.

Charlie had brought along his old-fashioned leather bag, a gift from his father-in-law upon graduating from medical school. It contained all the required equipment, but Charlie didn't get time to unclasp it.

'She should be on this one,' said Dan, standing before an empty metal gurney and rereading the ID tags on either side. Charlie knelt down, where another tag had fallen to the bare floor.

It read: *Leona Bride: 96–1456.*

'She's gone,' he said. 'Someone's taken the body.'

It was a minor miracle, but Charlie managed to catch up with Dr Ira Mardy on the Health Department parking deck, in the section reserved for VIP visitors. Dawn was breaking, the first pink fingers of sunlight reaching over an industrial horizon.

Mardy was just leaving, dressed for the golf course, and loading his briefcase into the trunk of his Lexus.

'What did you do with my patient?' Charlie said, breathing heavily.

'Dr Cortez,' said Mardy, in a businesslike fashion. 'You truly stink. Did you sleep under a bridge?'

'I know you just took her out of here; I talked to Joe Loder.'

Mardy sighed. 'Leona Bride isn't your patient any more. Leona Bride is dead. I had her transferred to the CDC so we can get a better opportunity to learn what killed her.'

'You don't have the authority.'

'I have written permission from Martha Calloway, Leona's next of kin.'

'You got to Martha?'

'Nice woman. Very distressed, naturally.' Mardy smirked, flexing his incredible nostrils. 'While you were lost in the bottom of a bottle, time was wasting.'

'Time had already run out,' said Charlie. 'When we first met, you wouldn't consider my diagnosis. You were chasing an E. coli outbreak.'

'Then you admit you couldn't help her. You admit that you needed us.'

'That was the point,' said Charlie. 'Of course I needed you. But later, I think you suspected – you *learned* – that Leona had a disease without a cure. Instead of transferring her while she was alive, like you said you were going to, you let her die on my watch. All for the sake of convenience and your own goddam stats.'

'Now you can read minds, Dr Cortez? You're sloppy drunk. Get out of my way before I call Security.'

'No,' said Charlie. 'You're a thief and a liar.'

'Anything else?' said Mardy, as though he'd heard it all before. 'I'm due at the Highlands Course before nine.'

'Yes there is,' said Charlie. 'I have proof. After I discovered you'd raided our morgue, I learned that you'd been requesting all my test results from Dr Krohn. You always knew exactly what was going on. You were monitoring Leona Bride from afar.'

'Guilty as charged.' Mardy shrugged. 'What are you going to do about it?'

Charlie could feel the fury simmering inside him. He welcomed it, allowing it to free him. He had never felt quite this way before.

Is this the first symptom of the madness?

'Still, I'm sorry you couldn't find a cure,' Mardy said. He screwed insincere sympathy into his angular face. 'Better luck next time.'

'Was the E. coli outbreak even real? Or was that another part of your lie?'

'Don't be absurd.'

'Do you have any other patients with this disease, Dr Mardy? Any other casualties? Do you know what's really going on? Because God help you if another one turns up.'

'Get out of my way, Cortez.'

'I want access to Leona.'

'Forget it.' He glanced at his watch.

'Why?'

'Because you're in no position to make demands. And besides, I don't like you.'

'I think the government was more interested in her dead than alive,' said Charlie. 'You hovered like vultures, waiting for her to die. Why would you do that?'

'It doesn't matter what you think,' said Mardy. 'At least, not any more. I mean, are you also concerned that we might now use her brain for some good? For some worthwhile, life-saving research? Or are you bothered that we might be acting in the public interest?'

'For these reasons, you come here in the middle of the night?' said Charlie. 'Who removes a body in the middle of the night?'

'We're early risers.'

'Enough bullshit. What are you trying to cover up?'

'Get out of my way, I won't ask again.'

'What are you trying to cover up?'

'Okay,' said Mardy. 'Calm yourself down, pal. Let me give you one piece of advice; something they should have taught you at med school, but evidently didn't. Because believe me, despite appearances, we're all on the same team.'

Charlie waited.

'Sticking your cock in the terminal patients is strictly off limits,' said Mardy. 'Especially once they're dead. Go and sedate one of the cleaners, I'll even write you the fucking prescription.'

Charlie drew back his fist and punched Dr Mardy in the mouth, hard enough to skin his knuckles against the man's expensive dentures.

Ira Mardy slid down the side of his car like an empty sack, but his face didn't particularly register surprise; maybe he was used to being hated.

After a moment's reflection on the ground, Mardy checked his jaw for fractures.

'Were you quite finished, Cortez?' he said, spitting blood across Charlie's sneakers. 'Because you are now, you dumb *fuck*.'

Some days later. It was a cool, clear afternoon.

Two men walked outside and stood for a while in the rundown hospital garden, listening to the roar of freeway traffic far above them. The garden was a forgotten donation from someone-or-other, and plagued by shadow from the overpass. It was a profoundly depressing place with concrete sculpture and failed plants, visited by few.

'I don't want to shitcan you, Charlie,' said Dr Brett Krohn, once he imagined a sufficient silence had passed between them. 'But you give me little choice.'

'Yes,' said Charlie Cortez.

'You're a good doctor, and an even better teacher. I know, I've been your supervisor for three years. We're short of staff and we can't afford to lose you, but you've made a hell of a mess here.'

Charlie had stopped listening.

'Until he started asking about Leona Bride, I'd never heard of

Ira Mardy,' said Krohn. 'But you can be sure he has friends in high places.'

'I'll bet,' said Charlie, absently.

'There's one piece of good news,' said Krohn. 'Mardy isn't going to prosecute. He wants your medical licence, but I don't think he'll push for it. He says he doesn't want the publicity.'

'Of course he doesn't,' said Charlie. 'This is a cover-up.'

'What kind of cover-up?'

'I don't know yet.'

'Jesus, Charlie. If the CDC or some other government agency wants this mess, I say let them have it. They have resources that we can only *dream* of.'

Charlie said nothing.

'Why can't you accept that it'll be better for your career – and better for this hospital – that the body of Leona Bride has attracted the interest of a greater authority? Grundy is not about diagnostics. We don't have a surplus of neuropathologists. We stumble from one financial crisis to the next, and we allocate our limited funds to help the community, not grab headlines.'

'Ira Mardy stole a corpse from our morgue.'

'Even if you're right about a cover-up, it will certainly be for the best.'

'Not for me, Brett.'

'You knew the girl. You saw her condition. Think of the other patients you could have helped while trying to find treatments for an incurable disease.'

'Incurable?'

'This wasn't going to be a story with a happy ending.'

'They rarely are,' said Charlie.

'Just be careful who you decide to attack next. I gave Mardy your test results because he asked for them, and I saw no reason not to. You weren't here most of the time, and you weren't answering your cell. You paid for all this treatment yourself, I assume?'

'Yes.'

'Look,' said Krohn, 'I know your wife just left you. I know you might lose your kids. I know that you got too close to the patient. I can't imagine what you're going through, and I don't really want to. But you can't go talking with your fists, damn it. There's no excuse.'

Charlie said nothing.

Krohn sighed. 'I can't believe we're having this conversation,' he said. 'You're on six months' administrative leave. Go today, go quietly, and don't practise medicine in the state of Georgia.'

If Dr Krohn was expecting a reaction, he didn't get one.

'I seriously advise you not to challenge, Charlie. I negotiated hard for this, and you're getting off very, very lightly.'

'Don't worry,' said Charlie. 'I won't challenge.'

Dr Brett Krohn sighed again, reached for his cigarettes. He pulled smoke into his lungs as though drawing strength.

'Any idea what you'll do now?' he said eventually.

Charlie looked at him.

I kept my return ticket from a place called Port Barren.

They call it Savage Island.

'I thought I might travel,' said Charlie.

The pale young man with the damp, haunted face stepped down from the MARTA bus at Decatur, unsteady on spindly legs.

He turned and pulled a sickly, insane grin at his fellow passengers.

The driver felt relieved to have avoided an incident. The young man, who couldn't have seen more than twenty-five years, had the bruised, sunken eyes of a geriatric wino, and carried with him the primitive stench of something far more than unwashed clothes.

This person was dying.

In fact, he already looked like a walking corpse.

The driver shook his head.

Always with the young people and drugs these days. He pulled the lever to close the doors and glanced across at the huge hospital. *At least he's come to the right place.*

Scarcely upright, the young man weaved across the bright plaza to the main entrance. It was busy with people on lunch-break who made a studied effort to get out of his way.

'Hello,' he said to one of Grundy's receptionists.

The man fell forward and the receptionist caught the full force of his breath, which reeked of disease and raw meat.

She immediately went for a triage nurse.

'Hello,' he whispered to the triage nurse.

'Sir? Are you all right?'

'I'm here to visit a patient . . . her employer at the Clearmont Lounge said she was here.'

The man collapsed on the floor in a heap of clothes and bones.

The triage nurse was called John.

'My God,' said John, kneeling. 'What happened to you?'

'I don't know,' said the man, and when he stared, John saw damnation behind his eyes. 'I never sleep any more. I can't. I haven't slept for, like, *weeks*.'

'What's your name?'

'Todd.'

'Todd, we need to get you to a doctor.'

'First, I have to see Leona Bride. I think she's a patient here.'

The young man gripped John's arm with strong, spectral fingers. His nails were like talons, and his strength was both surprising and painful.

'Todd?' said John. *'Todd?'*

'She's my *wife*,' said the man.

Then he started to scream.

Five

New Delhi, India.

By the reckoning of Dr Reeta Kapoor, Valmik had at least a two-day head start, possibly three. If the note he had left for his girlfriend was accurate, then Isabel had come to Reeta's apartment on the night following his departure. At that point they had wasted twenty-four hours in Vienna arranging flights and securing an Indian visa for the Austrian. Then there had then been a further day in the air, punctuated by a frustrating six-hour layover in Istanbul.

Valmik, who had presumably made less spontaneous travel arrangements, could well have made it to the Andaman Islands by now.

Delhi was where Reeta hoped they might make up time. Her brother was capable of organisation, but more often than not he was impulsive, and there had been little warning that a solitary incursion of Savage Island was his intention. Reeta knew the administrative system in the Andamans would be many hours slower than in Delhi, even with the baksheesh that Valmik had to throw around. There was no hurrying a permit to the Okojuwoi, and no private vessel in the Andamans prepared to voyage so far. Furthermore, even with the right documents, catching the irregular passenger seaplane from Port Blair to Port Barren could be a nightmare in itself. More than half the time the company that operated the service had the plane docked, awaiting repairs.

But what about a cargo vessel? Boats carrying emergency medical supplies?

Potential shortcuts did exist for Valmik, yet all were impossible to predict. A veteran of such inconsistencies, Reeta felt well placed to put her faith in the notion that her brother had been held up somewhere.

Instead of worrying, Reeta threw her energy into gambling with the complex bureaucracy that is one of Delhi's multiple heartbeats. A few well-placed calls could limit their time spent in the Andamans, and even cut Valmik off before he boarded another plane.

Reeta took a chance, and booked two nights at the Imperial Hotel instead of one.

It was soon proved that telephone calls would not be enough. Reeta scarcely got further than the secretaries, and even name-dropping her once-influential father failed to guarantee an all-island visa from Mr Benjamin Gupta, the man in charge of such matters. A meeting was scheduled, and then cancelled. As was a second.

Meanwhile, the airlines would not confirm the presence of Mr Valmik Kapoor on any manifest. A call to immigration at Port Blair was equally useless; no one from Reeta's tenure in the islands was still operative, and the new Chief Officer had no intention of releasing information about the comings and goings at his small airport. But he did express concern when Reeta informed him of Valmik's likely intentions, which gave her another idea.

Reeta's next call was to the Governor's office in the Okojuwoi. Here, Reeta's identity actually seemed to work against her: her opposition to policy had never been forgotten. But it made sense to talk about Valmik, and to overemphasise what his intentions might be. If nothing else, the navy patrol might get an extra announcement at their morning briefing.

Finally, Reeta checked in on Valmik's personal website. Here, he detailed his life, and particularly his activism, in a blog. But the website had not been updated.

It seemed strange to Reeta that Valmik was not informing his fellow campaigners about this latest adventure. How else was he supposed to spread awareness about Savage Island?

There was something about this whole caper that refused to make sense.

Reeta sweated through her jetlag at the hotel's well-appointed gym, knocking back plastic cups of ice-cold water. She wondered if the old malaria tablets she had brought would keep both her and Isabel safe, and how effective they were without one week of dosing in advance.

In the early evening, the Imperial reception received word that Mr Benjamin Gupta wanted to take tea with Dr Kapoor in the atrium. Not tomorrow, but that day.

The switchboard also relayed to Reeta that Benjamin Gupta wanted to apologise for the lateness of the appointment, but it was very important to him that they meet. Many years ago, his father had played wicket-keeper to Dr Kapoor Snr's, left-arm unorthodox spin, and they had once shared time together in an amateur Maharashtrian league. It would be wonderful to hear news.

Up in her suite, Reeta kept his office waiting for forty minutes, then called back, agreeing.

Forms were stamped within the hour.

Reeta and Isabel were cleared to fly to Chennai, then Port Blair, then Port Barren. Mr Gupta even rang ahead to guarantee that the seaplane was operating.

Towards midnight, believing herself without appetite, Reeta surprised herself by consuming a full plate of *Tahiri Biryani* and two glasses of salted *lassi*. Clad in a towelling robe, she pushed the room-service trolley into the half-light of the corridor while her laptop booted.

One message in the spam file had the subject line: *Savage Island*.

Reeta's heart skipped a beat.

The sender was one *rgodsfer102*. The return address was *JuN6ErKxqjC@hucksley.ibm.com*.

Reeta clicked.

It was blank, save for an executable file. The file was called *The Diary of Leona Bride: 1 of 2*.

Reeta began the download.

Scanned pages in PDF. Diary pages. Plenty of them.

The handwriting was poor, often hasty, but always legible.

Reeta dialled down to room service for a pot of coffee and began to read.

Wednesday 05/31
It seems unbelievable, but the adventures are over.

We have reached the end of our path!

Calcutta, Kolkata, city of revolution and pride of Bengal. Only the sea remains.

But disaster! The MV Akbar has sailed, a day earlier than we thought!

Of course, we should never have booked in advance, this is not a country for schedules and preparation, but for drifting and exploring. Except for the railways, which run to their own beautiful logic.

Here I go again! The gods only know what Edward said would make of my "subtle prejudice" and "romanticized images". All I can offer in defence is my love-affair with this country, corrupt plutocrat that I am, bewildered outsider looking in.

I blame myself, though Todd is far more circumspect. I know a steady diet of chillums and bhang drinks have altered him for ever, or perhaps it is mother India herself: a journey across this country has changed our lives. Strange to think, our first night was only three months ago – a bonfire in the street before our rotting hotel in Majnu Ka Tilla, Todd's battle with the pre-paid taxi man, sweat dripping from my boyfriend's red face!

He couldn't be more different now, although I worry about the drugs. Some part of me cannot forget my "real life" ambitions in medicine, but then my boyfriends have always said: "Leona, you are old before your time." I look now in the fractured mirror above the sink in our room and only hope they mean my mind, and not my dusty traveller's skin!

Anyway, there will be no other passenger boat for five days, but truthfully, I cannot imagine a greater conclusion to our trip than the teeming streets of this city. No more travelogue from me today, I cringe when I read over my purple prose about the "toy train" to Darjeeling, even though that was only weeks ago! Have I improved as a writer? Only time will tell . . .

This week, the dreary prospect of arranging flights back to America, but then Georgia, my sweet state, how I miss you! Am I so wrong to crave pecan pie and tailgate parties? I wonder what Mary Kingsley or Rebecca West would think of such down-home cravings . . .

I found Todd on the roof, sitting in a circle with a group of Bangladeshi businessmen. Of course there was smoke — tobacco and ganja. He was watching these men like an honor student, taking hits as they did, forming a tight chamber with his hands, lips never touching the pipe.

I looked across cracked rooftops at a polluted sky, and decided it was time for bed. My stomach is a little better, it will be nice to eat something other than bananas.

Friday 06/02
As ever with this man I love, so many mixed emotions.

60 rupees for tar and melted cola bottles; you would think Todd had learned his lesson by now. He must be

desperate, always these misadventures down strong-smelling alleyways. Either there are no touts or they are everywhere (where do they all go sometimes?) yet all want to sell bullshit hash while dogs try to lick the salt from your shins. At least they are friendly, these dogs, from a lifetime belonging only to the street.

Life here is harsh, but not without kindnesses that can sometimes overwhelm. Lost and exhausted, we were taken home by two men on mopeds who wanted nothing more in return than to share a cup of chai, which they themselves paid for. Students, like us, but who could talk for hours in an interesting manner without chemical stimulation.

I will never understand this country!

Todd does not want to go home. Neither do I, but I can recognise a timely conclusion.

Todd is an artist, it is for him to break down walls, experience the future that most of us would be satisfied to leave in twilight daydreams of fantasy or nightmare. Todd must always LIVE, shedding blood if necessary, because without pain, he believes critical moments have no resonance.

Great artists are also selfish. Todd is selfish, but his artistry is protean, he would be the first to admit. For every compromise he makes, a weight is added that he must carry.

Will I love him for ever?

Yes, in this way that a single moment of powerful feeling lasts for ever, now and always. Forever is not linear, it does not mean growing wrinkles together and fighting to reach the early bird special. It exists in those moments that we grasp the strongest, those limited memories that remain before death pulls us into oblivion.

The most important moments are for ever.

Fuck.

I need to smoke less, or maybe (do not laugh, beautiful,

married Leona-of-the-future) it is the beer. One damn pint on an empty belly after a week of sobriety feels like a tranq in the eye.

We talk, Todd and I. For once, his head seems clearer than mine.

There are flights further east, but this is not the point. He and I agreed not to board another plane until it was time to return home. What rules existed prior to this adventure soon melted before the colorful anarchy of India, but the belief that we should feel the world turning beneath our feet has remained.

Todd wants to travel onwards.

Impossible, I say. We will not fly, and our boat has already sailed.

There is a month before anyone expects us home, he reminds me.

You want to go south? (I am reluctant.)

Better, he tells me.

Dear Diary, at sunrise this morning, while I slept off the last of my Dramamine, wonderful, blameless Todd was taken down to the port at Kidderpore by one of his new friends. This friend had an idea, a solution to our problem, and Todd swears he was not complicit to the original scheme.

You can imagine what happened next . . . a container ship, the YM Fortune II (great name!), sails for Taiwan the day after tomorrow.

There is a cabin, with just enough space for two American lovers.

Taiwan!!???!

I say again: FUCK. This is not part of the plan.

You always wanted to take a slow boat to China, Todd tells me. I am fairly certain I did NOT say this, although I would be capable of such cliché.

Here, Todd and I shared a long conversation whose sole

purpose seemed to be trumpeting the genius of this man, this manipulative boyfriend, this son-of-a-bitch TODD, because of his ability to haggle. I refuse to quote now the price he agreed with the captain, it is enough to say that a deal was struck, and the money has already changed hands.

We are sailing to Taiwan.

Three phrases always seem to sum up Todd for me: I hate this man, I love this man, I hate myself. Tomorrow I will go to the docks and see this dread crate for myself, a ship that will be my home for a week or more.

Later

Hello, I almost forgot the music box!!!

Now is not the time for a detailed description. I prefer to wait for artistic inspiration to do justice to a narrative sketch of the item, whatever that means. Regardless, it must be documented, as it is here, between my bare feet, as I sit on this tired mattress and scribble my notes!

Todd is elsewhere, as usual, but it is just as well, as I am too angry with him to display my delight with his gift at this point . . .

A music box.

Small and ornate and surely ancient. It contains a miniature ballerina, who turns with a jolting splendour, and plays music from another age when wound up.

I am certain this beautiful trinket is from Russia – I have never visited the country, but only a land of dark fairytales could produce such evocative whimsy and then have it sent so far around the world!

I wonder – did the creator ever suspect that one vile "Yank" boy would discover it in an Indian bric-a-brac shop and then try to appease his furious girlfriend?

It succeeded, Mr Creator!

Sunday 06/04

Our cabin is the most comfortable accommodation we have shared for some time. The room is spotlessly clean — I always notice such things — and surprisingly large, if with all the charm of a dentist's waiting room . . .

Most pleasing of all is our huge, front-facing porthole, where I watched the massive containers being loaded by dockside crane. Each metal box is roughly the same size, but they are in many different colors, and spread out before us like a giant's mosaic.

Details, details . . . this is a 60,000-ton container ship, but has only three passengers on board, including Todd and myself. I have not met all the crew, but it appears there are very few hands for such a huge vessel, perhaps fifteen or sixteen souls (I am told this is typical). Still, I cannot help but be reminded of the Nostromo, which, of course, makes me shiver.

The captain's name is Sheng, and he has the cabin next to us. He is a short man with an open face, forever smiling. I believe that Captain Sheng is glad to have us on board — he will leave his door open for us to borrow from his collection of old videos (80s comedy movies a specialty). He also has a tendency to grip Todd's arm like a family friend when talking to us.

I hope my boyfriend has not gone from user to dealer.

A little further down the highly polished corridor is the purser and steward. Will I be the only woman on board? I suspect so.

There is an ear-splitting announcement over the speaker . . . So we are to set sail, to weigh anchor, to do whatever it is we sailors do! I hope my photographs do all this justice!

Note: the journey to Kaohsiung should take no more than a week.

Later

A voyage down the Hooghly River at sunset is as spectacular as it sounds.

I was unaware, or had forgotten, that the Hooghly stretches many kilometres south of Calcutta, perhaps more than 100, before it reaches the open sea. It is a busy waterway, and heavily silted by soils washed down from as far as the Himalayas. The going is often slow, and we will be asleep in this bunk of ours before the Fortune II passes the extended marshland of the Sunderbans and we can be alone with the horizon.

Todd and I were invited up to the bridge, and checked out the ageing radar, which looks like a prop from a forgettable sci-fi. Looking left and right (port and starboard!) it was interesting to note that we were accompanied at all times by other boats, sometimes huge ones, sometimes the most unseaworthy vessels you could imagine – small, shallow crafts like elongated wooden shells.

All were silhouetted by the glorious flaming sky . . .

All seemed far too close for comfort!!!

At this point I must make a strange remark. It is not for me to make critical comments on those people I have barely had the opportunity to know on the fullness of this journey, and, as with any trip where the traveller only stops briefly in places that probably deserve greater understanding, there have been many short and sweet exchanges it would perhaps be better to forget.

Of course, there have been just as many tiny (but important) moments of shared humanity that I am delighted to have documented for posterity, but I am afraid this will have to be the former and not the latter . . .

The third passenger has revealed himself.

He is vile and nasty.

He was on the bridge when we arrived, staring through binoculars at the river traffic, but recognizably not one of the crew. I would say the distinction could be made because of his lack of uniform – he was clad from top to toe in a dirty white safari suit, the kind of thing that went out of fashion decades ago – but this was the least remarkable difference about him.

To put it bluntly, the man has the appearance and attitude of a monster, well over six feet tall and built like a retired wrestler . . . the kind of fighter who always plays the villain. He is bald and white and hairy (from the eyebrows down), and, I hate to say it, astonishingly ugly.

I could go on.

Otterlix? Ottolicks?

He had a strange name, and a strange accent (from the few words I heard him say in English) but I suspect we will not be talking with him, so there is no point in learning the correct pronunciation.

Here is what happened:

When this man saw us, his face darkened with a terrible rage. He ignored our greeting and then, literally, grabbed poor little Captain Sheng and dragged him out onto the gangway. The crew were as shocked as we were.

Outside, there was much shouting, mostly from the ape in the white suit. All of it was clearly audible (and visible, we could see through the glass) but they spoke in a Chinese dialect (I think), so we could not understand.

After two minutes or so, this Otterlicks character stormed off.

Captain Sheng returned to the bridge, shaking like a leaf. Perhaps because he felt he had been humiliated, the good captain would not say anything about the exchange. But I tell you, Dear Diary, this is all very bizarre and unpleasant, and it makes me feel sad.

Todd is afraid that our presence has somehow created trouble for Sheng and the crew, though I cannot imagine how this could be the case.

Why is our instinct always to blame ourselves? Because we are outsiders? This is India, after all, almost everyone is an outsider. And why would we be of such concern to a man who is, by all accounts, only a passenger? (The purser later told me, Otterlicks is a specialist technician of some kind, in great demand around the world . . . but he is afraid of flying, as if a man like this could be afraid of anything. He has sailed with them on the route before.)

I just know I will have an uncontrollable urge to stick my tongue out every time he turns his back.

Anyway, enough bad news, and enough rambling from me. Let us only hope this gigantic vessel is big enough for the three of us!

Later, Todd and I ate supper alone in the dining room, a delicious beef noodle soup . . . the crew were still busy. Captain Sheng promises further introductions tomorrow – for now I am tired, so this is no bad thing. It will be good to awaken to the refreshing novelty (for me) of sea and sky and emptiness, India is far too full! The forecast is excellent – bright and clear and still, so perhaps there will even be opportunity to tan this flesh of mine . . .

Monday 06/06

Disaster.

It is late in the day, a day that has lasted a long, long time.

I do not know where to start. Probably with the facts, here goes:

Neither Todd nor I are early risers (once again, I shock with my personal revelations). We were aware that some adjustment to our personal schedule might need to be made at sea, but a rude awakening before 6 a.m. was nothing we were prepared for.

All I can tell you is that I was brought to consciousness by noises I could not identify. Shortly afterwards, still in a half-sleep, there was a violent banging on our door.

"Come in," I shouted, lost in my usual stupor.

No one did.

Useless as we are, we slept on. I found out later that the garbled sound was the PA announcing, apparently, "General quarters."

An hour later, with some subliminal awareness that not all was as it should be, I dressed. Todd still snored, great adventurer that he is.

I struggled alone down to the bar/diner area.

I could be the only person on the boat at this goddam point, so it should have been a relief to see our friendly purser, but he was dressed in a boiler suit, and told me there had been a fire.

A fire?

A FIRE???

Did I forget to mention that the boat was listing?

Walk down an enclosed staircase with your body leaning entirely to one side, fully aware that there is nothing but the cold ocean beneath you and tell me it does not inspire panic.

Mr Purser, I said, a fire??? I wanted to shake information out of the man. I would have throttled him, if it would have made him speak faster.

He recognised all this, chose to dissipate my fears with cereal, of all things. It worked, kind of. We poured milk and ate.

He told me there was nothing to worry about. There was no fire. A chippie has gone missing.

What the hell is a chippie?

Chippie is a term for a junior seaman.

A junior seaman has gone missing?

Yes. A Filipino. (Most of the crew are Filipino).

Where could he have gone?

Dear Diary, this explained the listing of the boat. Try turning 60,000 tons around in open seas as hard as physics will permit. No wonder we were leaning as we walked.

The crew believed they had a man overboard, and had turned the Fortune II around to look for him.

There was never a fire (why the purser lied and then retracted it, I will never know).

Listen: I am not hysterical. I am NOT squeamish. I hope, if you have stayed with me through this journal, that you will be able to recognise that I have a rational, intelligent mind, albeit imperfect.

Sometimes I feel I am the only sane person in an insane world.

Why?

Because the ongoing physical search of this gigantic boat – with all her hidden nooks and rat-infested crannies – yes, I've seen them scurrying around – has a far greater chance of turning up a missing man than any retracing of our progress through warm, open sea. We are now hundreds of miles from land, and the likelihood of happening upon this poor crewmember afloat somewhere is not a bet anyone would take.

Still, I took a set of binoculars and joined the watch.

The search of the sea felt perfunctory and it was mere hours before we were heading south again, full steam ahead.

This happens, I am told, sometimes.

We are at sea.

This happens.

*Still my mind struggles to accept. We are on a steady ship.
I am in a well-lit cabin. I can scarcely hear the engines. I
can barely hear the container refrigeration noises.*

We are on a steady ship.

No one falls off this vessel by accident, everyone knows.

They JUMP, or they are PUSHED.

*The crew is well aware, I see it in their eyes. But what can
they do?*

*The formal but friendly dinner, when introductions were
planned, has been postponed. Everyone is busy checking
and rechecking the ship. Again, I will try to help, but
all I can think about is falling 200 feet into bottomless
water.*

Our cabin door has interior locks, two of them.

Both work well.

Tuesday 06/07

*I must confess to being a little spaced out now, I have taken
something for my nerves.*

Perspective is a strange thing.

Yet, in these moments, perspective is my favourite word.
PERSPECTIVE.

*Let me talk more about Varanasi, take a trip back in time,
review my own notes.*

*A place, hundreds of miles inland, where dung is spread
over the threshold to keep mosquitoes away.*

Here, on the Fortune II, *we lost a crewman. A chippie.*

*A man died by murder or suicide, but most of the crew
continue in their duties as if nothing has happened. There is
even laughter again, sometimes, although one man, a third
engineer (a relation of the missing man, I think), continues
to search, with panic in his eyes.*

Other men fill his duties, without comment or complaint.

More than ever, I realise, we are on a vast, lonely, metal comet.

In my American world, death means something else. So I reach back to Varanasi . . . the bodies burning by the river.

The taste was . . . not bad.

Where is Todd in this memory? Where was my great love? I don't remember. He might have been there, he might not, in this vision I cannot see him.

Against better advice, I walked alone one night in Varanasi. I climbed over a railing and sat upon a cement ledge to face the Ganges together with the oldest man I have ever seen. He ignited a stick from the burning corpse and waved it at me as if in warning.

These were the ghats.

I breathed the smoke from burning human flesh.

Death is different here.

On this boat, everyone looks to the skies, to the Transit of Venus, where a new age of love, wisdom and understanding will be ushered in.

A chippie is lost.

I am again reminded of fragility and respect, and the ongoing cycle of humanity.

Despite my fear, today I sought solitude. When the sun was highest, I made it to the bow.

It is a scarce 200 yards to the front of the ship, but with six flights of stairs and lots of greasy handrails. I had a towel and sun cream, the sky was blue. The sea air was warm and wonderful, it blew back my hair. But the bow is also an abandoned place – ropes and oil and waterproof paint. My plan was to sunbathe, but something told me to return immediately.

I imagined eyes were watching me.

The bridge is one floor above our cabin. Attempting to

prove to myself that I am not deranged, I went up there, came away with nothing but a weather report.

We are sailing rapidly towards a storm front.

Thursday 06/09

Probably for the first time since I began this journal, there is nothing to report.

Perhaps this in itself is noteworthy, so here I am, telling you nothing.

Two days have passed, and the monotony that is typical of being a passenger on a long voyage has reasserted itself. The storm that was forecast has not happened, and the sky remains clear, although the temperature is getting hotter and hotter. The sea is like a millpond.

These are the doldrums.

Yesterday, Todd and I slept past breakfast, which is scheduled each day for 7 a.m. Then we were awoken by the emergency klaxon at 10.30, which almost caused my heart to fail.

It was, of course, only a drill.

We stumbled upstairs in our personal flotation devices, and were shown the lifeboats, which are capable of taking five times more crewmembers than we have.

There was a roll call. It is the first time I have seen the white monster Ottolicks since that day on the bridge, and he makes a big show of attempting to be nice to us.

I hate to say it, but I preferred it when he was horrible.

There is something very, very strange about this man. Perhaps he sensed my reluctance, because he did not prolong the small talk, thank God.

Tonight, Todd and I will eat dinner with the crew on the third deck, an improvement on the dining room, as we can watch the sunset.

Morale on the boat seems low.

Todd is dealing Diazepam to the engineers. I wondered how he would cope with the boredom – now I know. I shouldn't indulge, but what can you do?

Friday 06/10
The storm surprised us all.

I have never known one like it, and I am from the South, where the Christian God occasionally goes insane in the skies following our humid, bacchanalian summer evenings.

I wish I was at home now.

The night is black – there is nothing to be seen but for horizontal downpour in the floodlights outside the window of the cabin. No stars, no moon, nothing. Even the lightning has ceased, there is just the endless pounding of rain against glass.

I will pull the sheets over my head, child/woman that I sometimes am.

Friday/Saturday?
An hour ago, we were thrown from our bunk.

There has been a collision of some kind, of that I am certain.

I want to talk about the DiCaprio Titanic movie, the iceberg. If I thought someone else was reading this, I would never make such a pop-culture comparison, but it is the closest reference to current events that I can think of.

Anyway, we are still alive.

This boat is going nowhere. It does not seem to be sinking, but it is certainly not moving. The electricity fails, and after minutes it returns.

At the moment, the lights are off. I am writing these words by a fragrant candle that we bartered for in Fatehpur Sikri.

I wish I could kill the scent, it seems so ridiculous – scented relaxation in these moments of extreme tension.

I repeat. We were thrown from our bunk.

I still struggle to find a description for the noise. It was a kind of unwilling, cleaving sound, like driving a hacksaw through a can of rusty nails, only on a grand scale. Try to imagine you were living on that can, you get somewhere close.

Following the – what, the collision??! – it was a matter of minutes before we heard hasty footsteps in the corridor, and calls across the speakers to remain in our cabins. (Strange, what happened to the drill we practised?)

So much time has passed without information, giving me time to record my thoughts here.

The floors beneath us barely move (although much uneasy creaking echoes up from the depths of the ship – to me it sounds alive, like an ancient beast in pain). But to glance out of the porthole across our cargo is to see nothing.

Was there ever a night so black?

Todd will not leave the cabin, so perhaps it is up to me to find out what is going on.

Saturday 06/11
Good news and bad news today, all of it exciting!

The bad? The Fortune II has run aground on a shallow coral reef.

The good? I was correct in my guess – we are not sinking. There is no danger.

Additionally, once the sun began to rise, it became obvious that we are only a few hundred yards from land . . . and what land! I can see out past the bow to lush green mountains, and beaches of clean white sand haloed by the bluest water. It looks like a tropical paradise!

*It would be wonderful to get ashore and sunbathe
(anything to put my bare feet on a surface other than metal
or cheap carpet) but I am too shy to make this (frankly
girlish) suggestion.*

*Captain Sheng has checked and rechecked his charts, and
believes that the storm has likely stranded us on a small
westerly island of the Indian-owned Okojuwoi archipelago,
wherever that is.*

*The weather has improved, but the sea is still VERY
rough. For this reason, the decision has been made not to
lower the lifeboats, but to remain on board and await rescue.*

*No one is optimistic about this happening quickly (we are
on one of the most remote places on the planet) but our
metal world is very big and well-stocked, and the electrical
power has returned.*

*I feel bad for the crew, as someone will presumably be
held accountable for this expensive mistake, but there is no
denying my reawakened sense of adventure. Everyone is being
wonderful to me, asking if I am all right, if I need anything.*

*Of course I am fine . . . I feel like a steamship passenger in
the Age of Discovery!*

Sunday 06/12
Noon.

Disturbing developments.

*It was clear at roll-call this morning that over half the
crew have gone missing.*

*There was a perfunctory search. We found that, overnight,
two of the lifeboats had been taken. Even more worryingly,
the rest have been sabotaged.*

Unless they can be repaired, we are imprisoned on board.

*Why have they done this? Why would crewmembers want
to escape alone? Why the bizarre exodus?*

If the charts are correct, the nameless island upon whose reef we are wrecked is uninhabited, and many miles from any other. Yet no significant supplies of food and water have been taken.

Ottolicks is one of those who have disappeared.

Captain Sheng remains aboard, but he will not speak to me, let alone share his theories on the situation. He sends wireless messages to the company operator in Taipei with increasing desperation.

Once Todd heard about the deserted men, he went straight back to the cabin. He sleeps now, doped up to the eyeballs on his goddam stash of Diazepam.

Perhaps he believes, as I do, that this ship is cursed.

Later

There are men on the island.

It carries a native community.

Presumably there are women as well, though I only saw men. Beautiful, naked, black men of great height and powerful stature, who appeared on the beach while I was up on watch.

They wear belts around their waists, but nothing else. They have small, hand-crafted boats, probably shallow enough to break the reef – though such crafts will surely be too fragile for the open sea, which is still whipped up by the recent monsoon. I suspect their boats are built for fishing?

Towards sunset, they tried to sail towards us, but were turned back by the waves. I saw men draw arrows, pointing towards our hull, but they did not fire.

Others carried spears.

They are VERY aggressive, faces twisted in hatred.

Later Again

I took it upon myself to take another watch (no one left on this boat seems to care, are they satisfied with their fate?).

Towards the setting of the sun, I saw the natives gather on the beach. They were building bigger rafts from their many existing vessels, binding them together.

As it grew dark, they lit a fire, and I imagined I could hear chanting of some kind, their shouts drifting across the hot, still air. Perhaps it is was a war-like ritual.

They mean to reach us.

Monday 06/13

Captain Sheng is dead. He took an arrow to his neck.

Apart from the gaping flesh wound, he appeared to suffer an immediate and violent toxicological reaction, writhing on the deck and puking white spume.

The tips must be poisoned, maybe an extract from snake or frog.

The accuracy was incredible. A young savage with a white birthmark on his forehead, not more than seventeen-years-old, shot from a range of probably 200 feet in moderate winds while still bobbing on the ocean.

It was his first arrow.

It preceded an onslaught.

Everyone onboard has dropped back.

Later

The savages have home-made rope and grapples. They are expert climbers.

Later

Manny, a third engineer, has taken over the radio. I left him on the bridge, screaming for an immediate drop of weapons.

We watched from our cabin as the savages swarmed aboard. They are careful, they seemed uncertain (at first) with their unfamiliar territory. But I do not believe these men feel fear.

Those crew that remained on deck to fight were massacred without hesitation.

Those crew that fell to their knees to plead for mercy were torn apart.

I can still hear the screams.

This reality will not go away.

Night
Banging on the door. Rhythmic, brutal, continuous.

They know we are in here.

There is a red smear on the locked porthole where a lump of flesh was thrown at us.

As far as I know, this room is the last on the ship to fall.

They know we are in here.

I have looked through the window for the final time. Men were atop the containers, enormous and bloodied and naked. One held Sheng's head like a trophy.

They run screaming through the corridors.

They are everywhere.

All is dark now. The power has failed again, yet there is a constant whine through the PA, as though the ship itself is dying a slow death. Todd sits on the floor, knees to his chest, rocking.

Let this journal be found, let it be a record of the events on this ship.

Time now for thoughts and prayers, and to give thanks for my life.

The door will give way soon.

*

A tall Sikh porter swept open the door to the waiting taxi, sunlight glinting off the golden buttons of his uniform. Bleary-eyed from a night of poor sleep, Dr Reeta Kapoor pushed a wad of change into his white-gloved hand and took her place next to Isabel as their luggage was loaded swiftly into the trunk of the car.

'Good morning,' Isabel said, concerned at the appearance of her companion.

Reeta said nothing, rubbed her temples with thumb and forefinger.

'Are you okay?'

'Of course.'

Long lashes fluttered as Reeta looked her over. Isabel no longer seemed fazed by their predicament; she was perky, even. Her face was perfectly, if simply, made-up, and she had swathed her body in light, colourful fabrics that must have been bought locally.

It was a little curious that, if anything, Isabel had become more buoyant since the disappearance of Valmik.

'I'm fine,' said Reeta. 'Forgive me, I have a lot on my mind.'

'Me too,' Isabel said, lowering her sunglasses.

The taxi set off, and Reeta stared out at the decorative king palms that flanked the hotel driveway, dark green leaves fluttering beneath an azure sky.

Her thoughts were still running over the astonishing document that she had received. She had replied to the anonymous account as coolly as she'd been able; requested further information, a name, a telephone number.

Why me? She wanted to know. *Why send this now?*

The *Fortune II* disaster was six years ago, no one was supposed to have died, and there were never any reports of Americans on the ship.

If this diary is in any way authentic, how did it get out?

Some instinct told her that she wouldn't be getting verification from the sender anytime soon, but the idea didn't bother her as much as it could have. Even if the story on the pages was un-related to Valmik's current situation, there would be a lot of new and interesting questions to ask once they reached the Okojuwoi Islands.

The finely-dressed young operator of their white Hindustan Ambassador was named Kumar Chand. He spoke fluent English, and had many worthwhile opinions to share on a diversity of topics. Kumar took extreme pride in his professionalism, which meant that he felt it personally upon discovering that his chosen route to Indira Ghandi Airport had been closed due to roadwork. They would have to take a far more tortuous passage.

Once Kumar had been temporarily silenced by an impenetrable wall of immobile but truly anarchic traffic, Reeta took the oppor-tunity to turn her head and address the Austrian.

'I talked to SARPI yesterday, their office in England.'

'Oh?'

'I thought it was worth getting their thoughts about Edward Quinn and Savage Island. You were right, Isabel. As more information gets out, this is growing into a high priority for them.'

'Finally, they listen.'

'Savage Island is a primitive civilisation under great threat.'

'Yes.'

'I even got to talk to Sir James Renwick,' said Reeta. 'We'd never spoken before. He must be approaching ninety now.'

'Yet he seems so young.'

'I'm afraid there was no great revelation.' Reeta shook her head. 'Renwick is a pragmatist. He knows that so much of the decisions regards funding allocation have to be made in the court of public opinion.'

'Hence Valmik's vigilantism. Reeta, I am so sorry for all this.'

Reeta smiled. 'You know my brother well.'

'As well as a person can, after such a short time.'

'Given your conviction, I was surprised that James Renwick had never heard of you. *Isabel Kallmus* is correct, yes? Of course, I had to use your passport to secure the Okojuwoi permits.'

Isabel laughed. It was a pretty, lyrical sound.

'I'm not surprised he's forgotten,' she said. 'I only met Renwick once, at a party in London, and he was very preoccupied; there were politicians in the room and men of big business. I don't begrudge his hazy memory, I'm only interested in our shared passion.'

'Quite,' said Reeta, and they both fell silent.

Reeta considered. It was not particularly curious to her that Sir James Renwick could not recall his meeting with Isabel Kallmus. Octogenarian British philanthropists are not renowned for their photographic memories. It concerned her more that Sir James Renwick did not exist in any capacity whatsoever, and had a name and personality that Reeta herself had invented, about two minutes ago.

The traffic finally began to move, many horns blaring.

Kumar inched forwards, threatening auto-rickshaws. After ten minutes or so, the source of the congestion became apparent, lying by the side of the road and surrounded by worried-looking men.

'Very good luck to see an elephant in the morning,' said Kumar, pleased.

Six

The Chief was dying.

Two cycles of the moon had passed since Sool stepped on razor-sharp coral that sliced deep into his foot. The wound should not have been fatal, but it had become infected, then gangrenous.

The traditional medicines of the tribe were ineffectual. Prayers to El, the god who lived inside the great mountain that cast shade over much of the island, went unanswered.

Now the Chief's leg was rotting, his toeless foot like cracked tree bark, and volcanic with pus.

Tam, one of Sool's two eldest sons, had seen twenty seasons, one less than his brother Udumi. They were the only contenders for future leadership. Udumi may have been a little older, but the next leader would be chosen not on age but on merit, or on a sign from El, or for some other reason yet to be divined.

Tam was alone on a deserted beach, watching the sun setting across the lagoon.

There was no love lost between the two brothers. Udumi was a great warrior, perhaps the greatest the island had ever seen. Every tribesman, Tam included, was proficient with bow and spear, but Udumi was capable of truly incredible feats, and this, combined with his decisive and aggressive personality, inspired awe and devotion from many in the community.

Tam's power came from a different source. His intellect was undisputed. All understood that he had a sensitivity and awareness that the others did not. He was a master craftsman, a spiritualist, a fine teller-of-tales, and even, through Mo and Sew, had managed to learn some of the language of the Owbs.

There were none more feared than the Owbs.

Some of those who loved Udumi actually hated and feared Tam, although they would never say this to his face. Many, particularly amongst the elders, considered Tam to have turned his back on the true god El, and embraced both Apis and a new type of god. Tam had tried to explain time and time again – he did not consider Apis to be dangerous, merely a way to connect with the Owbs, a messenger perhaps, a harmless being from whom they could learn.

Through his studies with Apis (and Mo and Sew), Tam now understood more about the Owbs than anyone in the history of the island. Even if some suspected Tam of being in league with them – and he certainly was not – it gave Tam a credibility and mystique that the living could not fail to respect. It had also earned him several loyal followers.

Tam, however, was frustrated. He could not believe that all Owbs were evil. By extension, he was also curious about the tribal legends that were accepted simply because their existence pre-empted historical memory. The danger of the Owbs, the all-powerfulness of El and the wisdom of The Qesem were all things that Udumi and his like believed without question. But encouraging the others to debate their inherited mythology was proving impossible.

It had been a little easier when Apis first arrived, but few now wanted to know.

Tam grabbed his long, barbed spear and waded into the clear

water. It was blood-warm. He did not stop until he was almost waist-deep, his bare feet on soft, patterned sand.

The lagoon was teeming with blacktip reef shark of varying sizes, some very large indeed.

Indifferent to their intruder, they swam around Tam in wide, lazy loops, awaiting prey. He felt no fear amongst the predators, only anger at the ignorance of his fellow men.

Hunting in this way was not a skill in which Tam had proved himself adept. Having selected a medium-sized beast as his target, he did not correctly account for optical refraction of the waterline.

He lunged.

It was a hit, but a poor shot.

The sea boiled and turned red.

Tam could see little beneath his beltline, so was taken by surprise when he was slammed from behind, falling face-first into the lagoon and tasting salt water.

Had he been bitten? The currents generated by big, manic fish beat at him from all sides.

Tam struggled to stand, discovering he was still holding onto his spear, the shark having tugged free of the barb. He dug into the seafloor, using the pole to regain balance.

Fully righted, he successfully fought down the adrenalin, managed to clear his mind.

Apart from inhabiting very shallow waters, the blacktip is one of the few sharks that can leap fully from the ocean. Tam was about to stab again into the maelstrom when a different fish reared up, powering towards him through the air, mouth agape.

Tam raised his spear, and the creature impaled itself.

This time Tam's footing was more solid, and the tribesman heaved backwards, dragging the dying shark towards the shore.

Later, the sun was huge, orange, sinking, Tam sat on the beach, hugging his knees to his chest. He knew he was lucky not to have been injured, or destroyed.

A few feet away, the shark's mouth yawned, still angry in death, staining the sand with blood. It was smaller than he had remembered at the killing moment.

My beautiful warrior.

Tam's head turned at the voice.

This is a fine catch. Will I build a fire?

Lea, his wife, had sought him out. She stood at the threshold of the jungle. Her face was serious, but Tam knew, should he smile, that she would smile back.

Tam smiled.

He decided to tell her the truth.

My Lea, this fish had no courage for attack. It was confused. At first, I did not aim true. It jumped into danger because it did not have vision. It flew above the water because it needed to see.

Lea considered.

Will the flesh not taste the same?

Tam stood and walked over to the woman he loved, held her close.

The rain fell hard that night. It turned the village tracks to mud and many higher trails into small but powerful rivers.

Chief Sool, aided by two of his wives and a thick, roughly hewn crutch, fell three times while climbing through the jungle. He was attempting to reach the hut of The Qesem – also known as Medea – the wise woman of the tribe, who lived apart from the rest. Only on the third fall did he scream, more out of frustration than pain.

Finally, they reached a clearing, shielded from the worst of the storm by canopy jungle. Outside a solitary wooden structure were the soggy remains of a fire, and from the door hung a chaplet of bleached skulls.

Inside, it was dark, the only light shining through cracks where the walls met the floor. Sool was helped to sit, and he and his wives waited for The Qesem to return from whatever business she was attending to.

Sool felt himself passing in and out of consciousness, but, ever disciplined, he tried not to embrace the peaceful tunnel that would lead towards death.

He had one final, crucial act of chiefdom to enact, although he had no idea how to go about it.

Hello, Sool.

The Chief did not answer, was reserving his strength.

Your mind is prepared for the passing, said The Qesem. *Your body is prepared to return to El.*

You know why I am here, said Sool.

The Chief waited while Medea took her place on the floor opposite him, sitting with crossed legs. She was the only member of the tribe to wear more than one item of clothing: decorative bands of leaf criss-crossed her lean old body, and her necklace and piercings were of human bone.

She pressed her fingers into the viscous goo of Sool's leg, then brought them to her nose and sniffed.

There is nothing more I can do, she said after a moment.

Udumi and Tam, said Sool.

The Qesem closed her eyes.

There cannot be war within the tribe, said Sool, sweat shining on his bare head. *Not now.*

No, said Medea.

These are troubled times, said Sool. *There are more Owbs than ever before, some with magical weapons. Udumi travels deep into the jungle, dares to approach El. He brings back stories of metal trees, and metal nets that divide forests.*

He has told me, said Medea. *He is a strong boy.*

Meanwhile, Tam talks about Apis, and using her to forge alliance with the Owbs. He speaks with confidence, and there are many others who listen, and would follow him.

I have also talked to Tam, said Medea. *He has wisdom.*

The tribe cannot have two leaders, said Sool. *We cannot be divided.*

This is not a question for a dying man.

I am the Chief.

Then let this be your final act, said Medea.

What?

There must be a contest.

Sool raised his fists in irritation. He had thought of this.

Tam would lose, he said. *Or worse, Tam will refuse to fight. There will still be division.*

You do not listen, Sool. It must be a contest that enables each brother to use that ability which comes most naturally to him. Udumi has bravery and skill as a warrior. Tam has a quickness of thought, and a powerful mind.

But what contest?

Medea scratched her breasts.

Tomorrow, gather the tribe, she said. *Let there be a great feast on the high plateau. Sool, you are to take your sacred arrow and fire it as far as you can into the Biota. Can you do this? Will your strength hold?*

Of course.

The following day, when the sun breaks the waterline, the contest will begin. Without weapons, Tam and Udumi must set out alone from opposing beaches, and search for the arrow in the jungle. Whoever finds it must then track the other, and, without bow, use the arrow to kill him.

It could take days, said Sool.

Yes, said Medea. *And it cannot end without a death.*

Sool had known this from the start; it was the price of the tribe's future.

A worthy contest, he said.

Medea said nothing.

Sool was considering. *I still cannot see how Tam would have an opportunity to prevail,* he said. *A battle in the jungle? It sounds like a test for a warrior.*

This is because you, my Chief, are also a warrior. Tam believes he has some control of the future. He will agree to the contest because his battle will not be with Udumi.

No?

It will be with himself.

Sool did not understand, but the Chief could not show ignorance. Instead, he nodded.

Then it is decided, he said. *A worthy contest.*

A worthy contest.

Outside, thunder crashed down through the mountains, and the power of the rain redoubled.

El was giving His approval.

Udumi stood alone in the rain, staring at the lightning as it danced around the mighty peak of El. Water bounced off his enormous pectorals and his wet face shone in the bursts of flashes.

What would you have me do?

Fear was not a familiar emotion for Udumi. Yet El seemed to be telling him that there was reason to be afraid.

Udumi believed that the tribe had become complacent, slow to respond to the threat of the Owbs. Previously, any Owbs that had arrived on the island had been slaughtered without question, and then The Qesem had been able to divine the future from their spilled intestines.

This had all changed with the arrival of Apis. Then, sometime later, Mo and Sew had been permitted to escape.

Afterwards came the Christian god, of whose existence Udumi had personally disproved.

Now there were strange constructions appearing on those parts of the island where few men but Udumi dared to walk. Every area of the island held spirits, some benign, some malevolent, and the tribe's very respect for those spirits was compromising their land to the Owbs.

His fellow tribesmen gazed in ignorance and disbelief as Udumi, returning from a solitary trip into the forest, described great man-made trees without branches, and barriers hewn from ornate metal. What next? Soon the Owbs – the reanimated bodies of tribesmen cursed to return, and voided of language, personality and colour – would walk amongst them.

Udumi screamed into the next thunderous roar. This could not be allowed to happen.

Why did The Qesem not simply take Apis and slice her up the middle? Why not peel off her skin? If she was such an important Owb, might not great power and wisdom exist within? It had been many seasons since the last *Coning*, and this, in the opinion of Udumi, was one of the reasons for the confusion that had unsettled the tribe.

Udumi blamed Tam. Tam and the weakness of Sool, who would soon perish due to his own foolishness.

This was the one positive event. There was shortly to be a new Chief. Udumi swore then to El that it would be him.

It had to be.

The following evening was clear, the view from the high plateau phenomenal.

At the moment the sun kissed the lagoon, pooling burnt-orange fire into the water, Sool struggled to his feet and raised his flatbow.

He stood unaided in front of his tribe, jaw clenched, sweat pouring from his forehead. The gathered, including Tam and Udumi (but not Medea, who was curiously absent) watched and waited.

Had he still strength?

The sacred arrow was tipped with bronze, and centuries old. Sool drew back and paused for a long moment, eyes closed.

The Biota was a stretch of virgin forest, revered as a hunting ground for the native wild pigs, which, for conservation purposes, were only slaughtered on special occasions. As a result, this flat finger of jungle, enclosed on three sides by the lagoon, was rarely entered by the tribe, and only then by the best warriors. It stretched almost 2,000 paces to the sea, from where the high plateau dropped sharply away. Sool was aiming as close to the centre as possible.

The arrow hissed through the air, sailing high and far.

It was a worthy shot.

The tribe yelled and leapt with delight, and Sool sank back, his bow clattering to the rock.

This was the signal for a great feast to begin. A huge fire sprang to life, and the musicians began their rhythmic pounding of hollow logs. Naked children darted between the legs of the women, flames dancing in dark, mischievous eyes. Great bounty from across the island was laid out: meat and fish, and tubers wrapped in wet leaves that would bake amongst the embers. Soon there was the savoury smoke from roasted boar, and the mouth-watering crackle of hot flesh.

Tam walked away from the group to the edge of the plateau, watched the dusk gathering in the heart of the jungle. That was where the sacred arrow now rested; perhaps stuck high in a tree, perhaps hidden beneath foliage on the ground. He was lost in thought, trying to calculate the approximate area where it might have landed.

Has this been my last sunset?

A few feet away, Udumi watched Tam.

Tam could not sleep. He marked time by the passage of the moon, those few slivers of light that could pierce the tightly bound wooden roof of his dwelling.

A senior member of the tribe, his family did not inhabit a communal hut, and his children slept in their own, partitioned quarters. Nearby, on the raised floor, Lea snored gently.

Tam heard footsteps outside. Some instinct told him to remain quiet.

The Qesem entered the hut, shuffled her feet until she could be sure Tam was awake. Nobody crept up on another member of the tribe by accident.

What are you doing here?

Tam's spear was within reach. Both he and Medea could see well enough in the dark. Tam looked over to where Lea was still sleeping.

Do not worry. She will not wake until morning. I have placed a spell on her.

A spell? Why?

Because I have a great secret to tell you, and no one else must hear.

What secret?

Tomorrow, you have a choice. You can live, or you can die. You cannot compete with Udumi in the jungle. He is too great a warrior.

What choice do I have?

Tam, I have the sacred arrow.

What?

I have been into the Biota. The spirit of El guided me. I have the sacred arrow.

Where is it?

I do not have it with me. I did not dare bring it into the village.

Tam waited for more.

Listen to me, she said. *When the trial begins, walk down the beach until you reach a bowed palm where three leaves touch the water. Ten paces inland, you will find a pig run. Follow it to the second clearing. Wait for me there.*

And then?

Then, you will claim the arrow. The rest is up to you. Udumi is strong, but you have cunning.

I do not understand.

What do you need to understand? I am The Qesem. I have made my choice. Tam, you are to lead the tribe. Is this not what you want?

Of course.

Udumi is not guided by wisdom. He is guided by rage.

What about El?

Tam, you would speak to me of El?

Medea, you have no love for Apis, and believe the Owbs would destroy us. Before today you have accused me of blasphemy. Why would you offer this support now? I am not your ally. I believe you use fear to maintain your power.

Medea shook her head. Tam could see the whites of her eyes.

You have much to learn, Tam. I can give you this advantage only because El is the one true god. As such, He does not need to prove Himself in the face of Apis, or you, or me, or any being that walks amongst us. The battle to become Chief is also a battle of faith, and true faith will always prevail. You do not see it yet, but this is your choice. You can live tomorrow or you can die.

One of Tam's babies cried out, but the howl was short, and did not wake the others. His wife muttered in her sleep, turned over as though trying to pull away from something.

I believe a victory for Udumi will be disastrous for the tribe, said Tam.

It is good that you think of the tribe, and not of yourself, said Medea.

I want to live, said Tam.

I know, said Medea. *I know.*

Udumi moved with caution through the Biota, his bare feet silent over fallen leaves.

It was a bright day, but beneath the broadleaf canopy it was dim and cool. His eyes were everywhere, searching for the arrow, and searching for his brother; Tam did not have a warrior's strength, but Udumi knew he had a gifted mind, and the patience of a good tracker.

The trial was far from a foregone conclusion. Unless—

Udumi!

He spun around to meet the whisper, dropping into a crouch, ready to pounce.

Medea was standing behind him, a little distance away. She raised her palms, walked forward.

My brave warrior, she said.

What are you doing here?

I have something for you.

She reached behind her back, pulled a metal-tipped arrow from her belt.

Udumi blinked. The sacred arrow? Had she found it? No. This arrowhead was not bronze. It was no different from any other used by the tribe, hewn from flotsam that frequently washed up on the beaches.

Udumi was mystified.

For me?

A weapon. You will use it to kill Tam.

Medea, this is not the sacred arrow.

The Qesem smiled.

You do not think, my warrior. Use this to kill Tam, and then we will find the sacred arrow together. It will be faster if the search is made by two.

Udumi took the plain weapon, turned it over in his hands. His face became alert once more; there had been the distant crashing of branches, quickly receding; probably one of the wild pigs.

Medea, you must go now. You should not be seen here. I still must find Tam.

The Qesem smiled. *I know exactly where he will be.*

You do?

Of course, Udumi. He will be waiting to meet me.

Yes?

I spoke with him last night. I made him trust me.

You lied to him?

I did what was best for the tribe.

Of course. You are The Qesem.

Medea reached up with one hand, ran her fingers over Udumi's face, his strong features, the white birthmark above his left eyebrow.

You must kill him, my brave chief. You must kill him now, and then we will rule our people together, in the name of El.

Udumi considered. This was a very fine idea indeed.

The sacred arrow was stuck fast in a tree.

Tam, his thighs wrapped around the trunk, had a little trouble dislodging the bronze bodkin, skinning his palms as he did so. He dropped back to earth, wincing at the noise he made.

Udumi was nowhere to be seen. But Tam suspected where his brother might be found.

Other weapons were not permitted at the start of the trial, but when Tam had presented himself before sunrise with a length of catgut hanging from his belt, it had not been questioned by the elders. The fibre had been sourced from hog intestine and prepared some days ago.

He needed to find one branch from a suitable palm. He hoped this would take him less time than it had to find the arrow. Tam knew he had been lucky in that regard, although he had been able to make approximate calculations following Sool's shot the day before.

Within one hour Tam had fashioned himself a very crude self-bow. A couple of practice shots proved that the accuracy was entirely inadequate, but he did not intend to kill Udumi at range.

He only needed power.

You can live tomorrow or you can die.

Tam did not know the precise nature of Medea's plans for the future, but he believed the purpose of her night-time visit was clear: Medea wanted to serve him to Udumi in an ambush, because she could not risk Tam's victory, no matter how unlikely.

The battle to become Chief is also a battle of faith, and true faith will always prevail.

Now, Tam would put Medea, Udumi and even El to the test.

*

Udumi waited by the edge of the clearing, well hidden. He was very uneasy.

Firstly, Tam was not where Medea had said he would be, and The Qesem was never wrong.

Secondly, there had been a strange noise in the forest, an unfamiliar noise, like the drone of a huge flying bug, only far, far louder.

It had come closer, then further away. Yet Udumi had seen nothing.

Do not move.

Udumi clenched his teeth.

Do not move, Udumi.

Tam had crept up on him.

The buzzing sound returned, distant, but closing. Udumi ignored it.

You would kill me, my brother?

Walk into the clearing, said Tam. *Then turn and see.*

Udumi did so. Tam had the sacred arrow drawn in a makeshift bow. It was trembling slightly under the tension, inches away from Udumi's neck.

Udumi saw death, understood then that he was beaten, that he had lost the trial.

The droning sound became impossible to ignore. It was like nothing ever previously heard on the island. Tam blinked and glanced towards the source, the pig run.

The distraction gave Udumi the seconds he needed. He threw himself to the floor, and the rest was confusion.

Tam was lost, taken by the Owbs.

Lying on the ground beneath a bed of fallen yellow palm, Udumi counted and counted his breaths until he felt at one with the forest.

Then, he found and claimed the arrow, which Tam had misfired. His brother had been dropped by some other magical weapon, and then thrown, either unconscious or dead, onto one of the noisy, two-wheeled devices that had broken cover.

The Owbs had vanished on these vehicles with supernatural speed.

Udumi had escaped into the jungle. The Owbs had not followed him.

Tam awoke to an unfamiliar world.

He was staring up at a studded metal roof. The sky was gone. The floor beneath his body was padded. He was unnaturally cold, and there were no sounds of the jungle, no breath of wind.

Tam shook his head to clear the dull, persistent ache he found there. This did not work, so he chose to ignore the pain. In an instant, it was forgotten.

His last conscious memory returning, he tore a hand to his shoulder, discovered nothing more than a bruised lump comparable to the bite of a large insect.

Had he been beaten? Had he lost the trial?

Why had Udumi allowed him to live?

Death was acceptable. Humiliation was not. Tam bristled.

Then perhaps Udumi really DID deserve to die.

Yet his brother was not capable of this, of transportation between worlds.

Tam sprang to his feet.

It was certainly another world.

The bars that surrounded him on all sides were wrapped in rubber. He was in a square cage, isolated in the middle of a far larger chamber, and there was no furniture of any kind. Narrow, reinforced, rectangular windows let in a little light. They were set in a concrete wall that sloped up towards the roof. Tam could see foliage from a perspective that suggested that the room was sunk into the ground.

Three people shared the bunker with him. Two tall men and a muscular woman. All pale-skinned. They stared at him through the bars.

Owbs . . . ?

Tam snarled. He charged, hit the side of the cage with as much force as possible, which was considerable, given the tiny space. He fell back, heavily bruised, then jumped up, charged again.

This time, one of the men fired an X26 Taser into the cage. The cartridge hit the flesh above Tam's heart.

Before muscular incapacitation, the tribesman had time to recognise that this Owb was huge, perhaps larger than the biggest warrior in the tribe, and all white, from his skin to his clothes to the long teeth in his grin.

'*Fuck yourself!*' Kelly Maelzel shouted at Otto Lix, diving across to stop the torture.

Lix continued to shock the naked black body until Kelly managed to knock the weapon from his hands. It clattered to the floor, wires still stretching into the cage.

Ever calm, the third person in the bunker ignored the squabbling of his senior employees. He approached the bars, head to one side as though examining a particularly interesting specimen.

'Hello,' he said gently.

Remarkably, Tam was able to tear the cartridge from his chest.

'Yes,' said the man, in his smooth, mature tones. 'I'm sorry about that.'

Tam fought for breath, unable to stand.

'We're very glad you could join us.'

Tam said nothing, but he found the man's eyes.

'Welcome,' said Professor Edward Quinn. He smiled, and tucked his spectacles neatly into his breast pocket. 'Welcome to Savage Island.'

Part Two

And yet they will follow you when their life is done; others have perished before, just like you, and will perish hereafter.

Lucretius
The Nature of Things, III, 969

Seven

'They say that on Savage Island, the men have the heads of dogs.'

'Uh-huh,' said Charlie Cortez, swigging his beer.

'*Arooo-oo!*' shouted Ben, banging the table hard enough to make Charlie jump, and the three young drinkers opposite cracked up with laughter.

It was clear Charlie had come to the wrong place. He had been four days in the Okojuwoi Islands, and was as sick of the superstitious nonsense as he was of the inescapable humidity. This bar was the latest in a series of 'fine tourist restaurants' recommended to him by his obliging hotelier, who, without prompting, had also been the first man in Port Barren to tell him that the men of Savage Island had the heads of dogs.

It was not that people refused to talk about the island, it was that everyone was far too keen, yet never seemed to have anything helpful to say. Was he asking the wrong questions?

'Any of you ever get close?' said Charlie. 'I hear the reefs are pretty incredible.'

Thad was American, model-handsome, and thinking of relocating to St Croix. 'The reefs, the surfing, the beaches, bird watching, if that's your shit . . . yeah, and the diving is supposed to be *soo* sweet.

But, y'know, all the islands are good around here. Don't need to risk your life.'

'You never thought to charter a boat?'

'You can't get a boat to go over. A few years ago, maybe, with enough *bak*. But there's this new development on the island, everyone's so secretive. The locals pretty much toe the line, and the investor supplements the navy patrol, or whatever they call themselves now. He got himself in league with the governor, must have money to burn.'

'Development?' said Charlie.

Tom was Australian, sunburnt above a blond beard. 'Look around you,' he said, and Charlie did so. 'These islands are going to take off. You believe how busy it is in here?'

The place was barely a quarter-full, although most who had stopped by for a post-lunch beverage were European tourists in clean clothes, some of whom Charlie recognised from his hotel.

'You should have seen it six years ago when that cargo ship ran aground,' said Tom. 'Even four years ago, when the missionary disappeared. Dead as you like.'

'The missionary?'

'The bar, the town, the missionary – all dead. I was in and out of these islands when it was still difficult to find booze. What was he, Swiss, German?'

'German,' said Thad.

'Bloody idiot,' said Tom.

'Did you know him?'

The three drinkers shook their heads.

'What do you know about him?'

'Fuck all,' said Tom, and his eyes narrowed. 'You're not one of them, are you?'

'One of what? A missionary?'

'I haven't seen such a well-ironed shirt in a while.'

'Of course I'm not,' said Charlie.

'I was gonna open a dive shop,' said Thad, lighting a cigarette. 'Make a fortune.'

'We'd been talking about it for years,' said Willow, his girlfriend.

'We couldn't get the permits,' said Thad.

'Who is the Savage Island investor?' said Charlie.

'Why do you care so bloody much?'

Charlie feigned a yawn, as though he didn't. 'Another round?' he said.

This met with general approval, so Charlie stood and made his way to the bar. He placed the order, listening to the white noise of steady rain on the tin roof.

Viper's was perched on a low hill above Port Barren's narrow, torturous streets, and the breeze occasionally blew streams of water in from the guttering; the room was only walled in on three sides.

Charlie sighed. It would have been a relief to open up to someone, but he didn't feel ready to share information with these kids just yet. They were a self-consciously bohemian group: perpetually slumming-it adventure sports types who would soon have to go home and drift into a real job or find themselves marooned in the life for ever.

Besides, their reaction to Charlie's story might well have brought him back to reality, a place he currently had no intention of returning to.

A voice cut into his thoughts: 'Anyone with an opinion about what happens on that island has probably never been.'

'What's that?' said Charlie.

'My name is Vijay,' said the solitary barman. He had dark pools for eyes, and a voice so soft that Charlie had to strain to hear.

'And you,' said Charlie, leaning forward, 'you have opinions?'

'Of course,' said Vijay. 'I have never been to Savage Island, and I never will.'

'And your opinions?'

'Like all opinions, not worth sharing. You don't look like a typical tourist.'

Charlie dabbed sweat from his brow. 'What do I look like?'

'A man on a mission, and asking about the one place you shouldn't. I've seen it before.'

'Charlie Cortez,' said Charlie, and they shook hands. 'Don't worry, I'm not a madman.'

'Then perhaps you travelled to the wrong place.'

'I lost someone close to me,' said Charlie. 'I need to know what happened to her.'

'What is that knowledge worth?'

'I don't understand.'

'Is it worth dying for?'

'Dying?'

'That will be your sacrifice if you go to the island.'

'In your *opinion*,' said Charlie.

The barman smiled.

'Can you help me?'

'No.' Vijay sighed. 'I have more knowledge than I need on that subject, and a family to think about. You may travel to the island, and then you will have your answers, but at what price?'

Charlie was a veteran of one week on the subcontinent, and it was too soon to have his expectations defied. The barman cut him off before he could reach for his wallet.

'As far as I am aware,' said Vijay, 'there is only one local man who has travelled to Savage Island and returned. It is a feat he managed to accomplish on two occasions.'

'How did he do this?'

Vijay shook his head. 'I do not know, I do not want to know.' He appeared to make up his mind. 'If you were to meet this man, perhaps you would feel the same way as I do.'

'What do you mean?'

'Because of his experiences, he is not . . . *well*.'

'I'm a doctor,' said Charlie. 'Perhaps I can help him.'

'Perhaps.'

'Where can he be found?'

'I will try to make the introduction. Meet me here at midnight.'

'Thank you,' said Charlie. 'Thank you, Vijay.'

'There is one other thing,' said Vijay, as another customer sidled up to the bar. 'Something very important you have to know.'

'What?'

'Do you believe in God, Charlie Cortez?'

'God? Why?'

'With this man, you will need to.'

The world was blue, magnified and dream-like.

Such was the weight of her expectation, Kelly Maelzel imagined she could sense the gigantic shipwreck on the edge of her consciousness even before it materialised through the underwater fog. Although partially bitten down to a frail skeletal ribcage and half-buried in the soft sea floor, the *São Francisco Xavier* had an astonishing, other-worldly presence.

Visibility was exceptional, twenty-five feet or more, and this helped Kelly to comprehend the size. Closer, almost close enough to touch, a school of cute, rainbow-coloured fish switched direction in a coquettish flash of fins, beckoning her towards the find.

She trod water and puffed harder on her respirator, bubbles escaping towards a lost, turbulent surface. Kelly knew she was a little charged on both adrenalin and a rich heliox mix, and would have to be careful. As with all wrecks, there was danger here.

The *Xavier* was a high-castled Portuguese carrack, built in Lisbon in the late sixteenth century. A detailed history had been hard to find, but Kelly could estimate that she had maybe 160 feet in length and 40 feet of beam; a gigantic ship for her age. The superstructure was gilded, which had aided the remarkable preservation of the exterior, but floating over the deck revealed that she had split wide, like bad fruit. The insides were filled with rotting flotsam, a tempting abyss full of imaginary monsters.

It was amazing for Kelly to think she was the first of only twenty or so divers to visit here; anywhere else in the world and the *Xavier* would have been overrun with tourists, picked apart for souvenirs or exhumed and placed in a museum. The irony was not lost on her that this was exactly the purpose today: to scout with an eye to opening the wreck to well-heeled visitors.

At least she could enforce a degree of responsibility. Kelly had already decided that no one must ever penetrate the perilous hull, and there would always need to be experienced divemasters on hand, supervising parties of less than, say, twenty.

The ship was too old, too fragile, a lethal honey pot.

Kelly was not going to make the mistakes she had made in the past. There would be no more risks with public safety, and, more importantly, no more blood on her hands. The *Xavier* would have to remain expensive, exclusive, unique.

In other words, a perfect addition to the park, which would delight the wreck's new tenant: Edward Quinn.

Kelly swam closer, and a long shadow appeared, fluttering over the deck. She looked up to see a large, looping conger eel maintaining a safe distance.

Her eyes widened behind the double-dome diving mask.

It was longer than she was tall and seemed interested in her escaping bubbles. Unusual for it to be so far from cover in the daytime.

This, presumably, was the *current* tenant.

Even as Kelly turned her head for a better look, the conger eel broke pattern and swam slowly around the portside of the wreck, where there was another gap in the hull.

After it had vanished back into hiding, Kelly realised she had been holding her breath, which, while diving, was a particularly stupid thing to do.

It made no sense that she should be so nervous; the likelihood of attack was slim. It was probably her mindset following the recent weeks on Savage Island with a morbid and monosyllabic workforce – she had never experienced such low morale. That and working on a project which seemed to her to have a shaky moral justification, no matter how many times it was explained to her.

Moral justification never stopped you before.

Yet despite Kelly's lack of PR experience, she guessed that ethical salesmanship of the project would be an essential part of the job for anyone who worked on Savage Island. Humanitarian awareness would certainly be key to the tourist experience for the lucky few.

Is it enough?

She had her doubts. Anyway, it was good to be away from Savage Island, even for a few hours, and by a few nautical miles.

Kelly checked the dive computer on her wrist; she was over 100 feet down. Then she stared longingly at the tear in the deck. She could allow herself another twenty minutes of exploration, not including her two planned safety stops and the emergency 500 PSI in reserve.

She swam closer, almost close enough to touch the base of the mast, noting the decay of the wood in minute detail.

The *Xavier* was also a treasure ship, she knew; sister to the famous *Madre de Deus*, which had been taken by the English near the Azores with some 500 tons of valuables. Could anything remain here? There was no documented reason for the sinking of the *Xavier*, and no known survivors. Kelly looked forward to bringing in the maritime archaeologists, figuring out such mysteries.

Shining her torch into the guts of the ship, Kelly felt a tug on her fin, and then a sharp pain in her ankle when she spun around to look. Her teeth tightened around the breathing apparatus.

She was becoming entangled in something unseen, probably a discarded monofilament fishing line, virtually invisible underwater. As she twisted again, attempting to reverse her actions, she saw the head of the huge eel, poking out of the darkness a few feet away.

Kelly reached for her dive knife, accidentally kicking the deck and sending up plumes of silt. In an instant, visibility was slashed to nothing.

Long moments passed while she probed the grey walls for unseen attackers. Kelly was straining to listen, to hear for advance warning, but got nothing but indistinct ocean noises and the blood rushing through her highly pressurised eardrums. The frequency in her skull felt unbearable.

What she imagined were jaws closing on her shoulder was actually a strong hand.

Still, she jerked and twisted in surprise, but in seconds, she was free. She kicked hard through the fog until the world became blue again.

Edward Quinn, sheathing his own dive knife, directed her around to the lee of the wreck, out of the tidal flow, and visibility was fully restored.

Kelly looked back at the decaying underwater city, where a mast had toppled and the slowly pluming silt looked like discharge from an explosion.

Kneeling together on the seabed, Quinn gave her the *Okay* signal. Kelly returned it with a shaking hand, feeling numb. The fishing line had split her skin, and thin red smoke floated up between them.

It was time to get out of the water.

The boy emerged from the jungle, a blurry phantom behind a wall of rain.

Reeta Kapoor blinked at him through the greasy windscreen of her yellow-top taxi, heart beating a little faster. The driver was outside, cursing the weather and changing a tyre that had burst in one of the many craters that pockmarked the Great Okojuwoi trunk road.

Reeta tapped on the window, gesturing to him; he had not yet seen the boy.

The anthropologist's concern was ten years old, and stemmed from her time on the island as Director of Tribal Welfare. The marginalised but two-hundred-strong indigenous population of Great Okojuwoi were called the *Jaman*, and in her experience they rarely travelled through the forest alone; when encountered, there were usually violent repercussions of some kind. This was why there existed so many signs warning drivers not to stop or slow, commissioned by Reeta herself after the massacre of twelve illegal loggers.

Having seen the boy, the *taxiwala* opened his car door, presumably, Reeta thought, to seek safety inside. Instead, he reached across with one wet arm and retrieved a half-empty packet of chewing gum from the glove compartment.

Reeta watched as the young tribesman approached, his torso slick with clay. He accepted the gift with a blank stare, and the driver returned to his work.

Things had clearly changed. The once-feared *Jaman* youth were now happy to beg for hand-outs, and, in turn, the settlers had become willing to toss out treats like dismissive puppy owners.

It was the beginning of the end for the *Jaman*, Reeta knew.

All heads turned towards the sound of a heavy vehicle approaching. Reeta looked back to see the native boy scamper away, bare feet splashing through deep puddles.

A long flatbed truck rounded the corner and stopped next to the taxi with a hiss of hydraulics. After a moment, the passenger door swung out to reveal a handsome Tamil in silk shirt and tie. He popped up an umbrella, and climbed down to pull open Reeta's door like a chauffeur.

'Dr Kapoor,' said Ashok Khanna. This was the man Reeta had arranged to meet; she was already an hour late for the appointment. 'Might I rescue a beautiful damsel in distress?'

'If you can find one,' said Reeta, shouting into the storm.

*

Engines cut, they bobbed in silence.

Kelly had buoyed the wreck, so they could identify it and return anytime they liked. The two figures were alone on the powerboat.

Quinn wanted it that way.

'We might be saving a culture from modernity and potential destruction,' Kelly was saying, 'but we're doing so by enslaving it.'

'How can you complain?' said Quinn, unbuckling his tank, seawater gleaming. 'You, who made a living keeping animals behind bars.'

Kelly pulled off her fins and peeled the wetsuit to her waist, ignoring Quinn's eyes on her breasts. The bleeding around her ankle had already stopped, in part thanks to the pressure from the rubber skin, so she decided to keep the rest of the suit where it was.

'These are not animals,' she said, gesturing over at Savage Island. 'These are humans.'

'There will be some subtle, inevitable adjustments to their lives,' said Quinn. 'But they won't realise they are imprisoned. Certainly not in the sense that we understand the word. Can unwitting prisoners even be prisoners?'

'I've heard it all before.' Kelly sprayed water on her face from the freshwater hose on the back of the boat, spat some into the sea. 'You can't guarantee any of this.'

'Not yet, although we will do our best. Remember, these islanders are already caged, restricted by the very ocean that has guaranteed their survival as primitives for so long.'

'They're *confined*,' said Kelly, 'not caged.'

'I'm simply extending a boundary of protection that, in time, would no longer have been sufficient. Nature can only keep them safe for so long.'

'The ocean doesn't seek to exploit these people.'

'Exploitation?' said Quinn. 'Maybe. But exploitation for the purpose of educating those who would, inadvertently or otherwise, contribute to their eventual destruction. You're a conservationist. Is this not what you do already?'

'I say again, these are people, not animals.'

'So you're a *speciesist*.'

'A speciesist? What kind of crap is that?'

'Tell me, Kelly. Does a four-week-old baby have more sentience than an adult gorilla?'

'I'm not going to debate human supremacy with you, Edward. My problem is that you don't seek to curb unnecessary suffering.'

'You're incorrect. I will, however, confess to a single-mindedness. I am capable of mistakes.'

'I know you. You never admit to mistakes.'

Quinn said nothing.

'Saying that, I would never have been here if you hadn't offered me that lifeline. I was dead in Dubai.'

Again, Quinn said nothing.

'We're holding an innocent man,' Kelly said, popping open a beer from the cooler.

Quinn shook his head. 'Unfortunate, I know. But you're well aware that the islanders are more violent and insular than we expected. This might appeal to the morbid nature of a certain type of tourist, but the safety of visitors has to be our primary concern. I'm appointing our temporary captive as ambassador for his people.'

Kelly snorted. 'Ambassador? And how does putting someone behind bars fit in with your hands-off concept?'

'This is, and always was, a social experiment.' Quinn took a cold can and pressed it to his temple. 'I'm humble enough to accept that there needs to be a pliability to both the project *and* my own attitude. I can compromise. What I want is a useful exchange of information.'

'Compromise?'

'Yes,' said Quinn.

'You don't compromise.'

'He will be free very, very soon. Have faith, I'll do all the negotiating myself.'

Quinn smiled, towelling his body. Sweat shone on his tight, tan pectorals, and his thick grey hair was otter-sleek. He looked like an ageing movie star.

Still a handsome bastard, Kelly thought. *And he bloody knows it.*

She sighed. 'When we went out into the main part of the island, I had no idea it was to kidnap. Even worse, Lix used a tranquilliser gun. The darts were primed with Etorphine.'

'I think I understand,' said Quinn. 'Your problem is with Otto Lix. Everyone hates Lix, but he's indispensable.'

'*Etorphine*, Edward. That drug would destroy the respiratory system of an average man.'

'Not etorphine,' said Quinn. '*Immobilon*. And we stockpiled the antidote.'

'I don't care what you cut it with, etorphine is more than an incapacitating agent. This is an opioid, synthesised to fall elephants. Your so-called *ambassador* could have died right then.'

'Okay, so no more Immobilon,' said Quinn. 'You know, these kinds of details are the reason I hired you. I wish I'd known you were available sooner. You fell off the map after Sydney.'

He licked his lips while Kelly stretched. Although the skies were threatening rain, it was hot, and the bucket seats on the fibreglass powerboat were extremely comfortable.

'You need to involve me in decisions at the highest level, or I walk,' she said.

'Done.'

'You need to fire Otto Lix.'

'Impossible.' Quinn, slid into the seat next to her. 'None of this would have been possible without Lix.'

'I don't doubt,' said Kelly. 'But his job here is finished. You're not at war any more, you've made the impossible possible. But he's a psychopathic mercenary, and he stinks. Now, with the park months away from opening, he's also a liability. The Bengali and Filipino workforce loathe him – imagine what he'll be like with the paying customers.'

'I'll consider it.'

Kelly reached over, ran one hand through Quinn's wet hair. Just as he began to appreciate the sensation, she bunched her fingers into a fist and tugged hard at his scalp.

'You'd do that for me?' she said, twisting her wrist. 'You'd get rid of Lix?'

Edward Quinn smiled his matinée smile, holding her gaze.

'I thought you knew me,' he said.

'What does *that* mean?'

'I'll do anything for what I can't have.'

'It has been far too long,' Ashok said, waving Reeta over to the leather couch in the two-storey portable cabin that was his office. 'Tell me, how is your father?'

'Fading,' said Reeta. 'Comfortable, but fading.' She dried her hands and face on the towel he had provided.

'I am sorry.'

'And you? That moustache has grown fuller in the years since I used to steal kisses.'

Ashok Khanna grinned, looking through the window at the huge salvage yard and the business to which his family had given their name. It stretched for half a mile of cleared jungle towards the grey, churning sea. Over his shoulder, Reeta could see rusting hulls and twisted metal, surrounding palms bent double in the wind and rain.

'I am prosperous,' he said. 'But I will sell my land when the time is right – the big-name hotels are already sniffing around the Okojuwoi. Business here is finally growing.'

He poured *chai* for them both, then sat back in his chair and laughed. 'But at long last, you return to your kingdom. These crazy islands miss you, Reeta, with your level head and keen eye.'

Reeta smiled.

'Yet, I know my old friend,' said Ashok. 'You rarely make social calls. What will we talk about, I wonder?'

'Savage Island.'

'Never set foot there.'

'What can you tell me about Professor Edward Quinn?'

'Very little.' Ashok shrugged. 'I know he leases the island from the government.'

Reeta sipped her drink. 'Did you salvage the cargo ship that ran aground on the surrounding reef?'

'The *YM Fortune II*,' said Ashok. 'A very unusual job. Much work, of course, but welcome. I had to bring in shallow draft barges, tugs and a sheerlegs.'

'A sheerlegs?'

'A kind of floating crane.'

'Why was the job unusual?'

'A few reasons. We were inundated after the tsunami, but work was tailing off again. Then, because we were expected to move so quickly on the *Fortune II*, we could afford to take on fifteen more labourers. Most of those men are still at work.'

'Here?'

'Not here, not any more. Edward Quinn put them to work on the island.' Ashok smoothed his tie. 'Of course, I received a hefty finder's fee.'

'He has a workforce over there?'

'Mostly made up of the unskilled temporaries I had to let go,' said Ashok. 'Quinn is smart. He knew the legends and how difficult it would be to get local men, so he insisted we hired from the mainland. Then we were guaranteed military protection while we carried out the salvage, and from there it was easy for him to extend the contract for the men to work on Savage Island.

They believed they would be safe, because no harm had come from working on the reef.'

'Quinn pays the military?'

'I assume so.' Ashok laughed. 'Imagine that, scruffy Bengalis peeling metal from a waterlogged crate, guarded like royalty by guards in uniform with guns and speedboats.'

'But you never lost a workman?'

'No. And there was the other incentive: Quinn promised a big pay-off for the families in case of death or misadventure. But I can't tell you what happens on the island now, because you never see the workers in Port Barren. These are men prepared to work apart from family for years on end.'

'Did you meet Quinn?'

'No, no. No one meets Quinn, he's a modern-day Willy Wonka. Everything was arranged through a man calling himself the *operational executive*. Very ugly fellow, name of Licks.'

'Otto Lix?'

'Right. He spoke Bengali, even a little Tamil, but it was clear he thought we were stupid.'

'Did you ever see the natives?'

'From the reef?' said Ashok, and Reeta nodded. 'Frequently. They would light fires on the beaches and thrash drums made from logs – made a remarkable noise. My men were afraid at first, but as the weeks passed, such displays became commonplace. The savages never ventured out when there was a military boat there, which was always. It was as if they knew they would be outgunned. But I believe they were waiting for an opportunity, one they were never given.'

'What about the survivors from the *Fortune*?'

'Only what I saw on the official report. The crew escaped on lifeboats, then were airlifted by a navy helicopter. Very lucky, as the seas were heavy.'

'Any evidence of foul play? Signs of violence?'

'Not that I saw. Violence? Why do you ask?'

'Does the name Leona Bride mean anything to you?'

'No.'

'What about *Kallmus*?'

Ashok shook his head.

'What happened to all the scrap metal?'

'Ah, that was mine,' said Ashok. 'Part of the deal.'

'And Quinn paid for the salvage?'

'Either him or his insurers. I just cashed the cheques.'

'His insurers?'

'A poor joke.' Ashok Khanna laughed again, displaying his excellent veneers. 'You don't know? The *YM Fortune II* was owned and operated by Burrstein Shipping, which is a subsidiary of The Safe Materials Company, Kowloon. Edward Quinn is the majority shareholder.'

'Quinn owned the *Fortune II*?'

'Apparently so,' Ashok said, amused by her reaction. 'Must have been some kind of fraud.'

'Why tell me?' said Reeta.

'Why not? I was never a party to it.'

'There was no confidentiality clause?'

'I tried to talk once I found out, but no one would listen. You think anyone cares about what happens in the Okojuwoi? Six years later, and you're the first person to ask.'

Reeta was stunned. 'Do you really expect me to believe that Edward Quinn wrecked his own cargo ship? Why would he do that?'

'Edward Quinn's boat ran aground on the only island in the Indian Ocean leased by Edward Quinn,' said Ashok, pouring more tea. 'Remarkable coincidence, no?'

Following the rainstorm, the sky cleared to reveal a glittering chart of stars and misty, luminescent nebulae.

Charlie Cortez, addled by Vietnamese whisky, waited for Vijay to lock up the bar, then followed him down the street to what he presumed would be transportation on four wheels. It turned out to be a garaged vintage motorcycle, a Royal Enfield Bullet 350, beautifully preserved in black and gold.

Together, they sped through darkened streets, Charlie helmetless, adrenalin-fuelled, and squeezing Vijay's waist as though his life depended on it.

He felt wonderful, more alive than he had for years, until the bike was forced to stop in downtown traffic and Charlie found himself three feet from a woman in a dangerously trailing sari. She was similarly positioned behind her husband, balancing a child in each arm and staring at him with a cool he could only dream of.

From then on, Charlie tried not to cling so tightly.

Several twists and turns brought them to the outskirts of town and an unlit road where Charlie could hear, rather than see, the ocean.

Vijay gunned the throttle a few times before switching off the engine. Charlie asked him why.

'I don't want to surprise him,' said Vijay. 'He's mad, you know.'

'Who?' said Charlie. 'Who are we meeting?'

Vijay did not reply. He rested his bike on the kickstand and led the way down to a solitary, corrugated shed on an oil-stained, debris-laden beach. A single bulb fizzed outside, surrounded by a dense cloud of mosquitoes.

He banged three times on the wall, each blow shaking the entire structure and sending up flakes of rust. After a moment, the double doors creaked open to reveal an emaciated Asian man, naked but for ragged shorts. His hair was filthy and shoulder-length, and his beard full. He was muttering to himself and twitching, counting off plastic rosary beads on a string around his neck.

The man could not make eye contact, but when he saw Charlie, the muttering became louder, and he reached below his left knee to scratch what might have been a third-degree burn. It stretched down to his ankle and there had never been a skin graft, although it had healed, of sorts.

In the half-light, the old wound looked to Charlie like moistened jerky. The man's bare foot was a clean white sock by comparison, a seemingly cauterised circle where the skin started again.

'Thein Suu Ay,' Vijay said proudly. 'The Savage Island survivor.'

Christ, he's been peeled, Charlie thought, holding out his hand to shake.

'I will take you,' Thein said in his excellent English. 'Twelve thousand rupees.'

Noon the following day.

'This will not work,' Isabel Kallmus said in German.

'With faith, it will work.'

'Father, the anthropologist is far from stupid. She cannot find verification of her brother in these islands, and she is persistent in gathering information. We need to mount a rescue, and there has been no talk of it.'

'We discussed this possibility,' said Werner Kallmus. 'Plant more evidence, Isabel. Create incentive. If Reeta Kapoor is the woman I think she is, she will not have travelled so far to stop here.'

'I will do my best.'

'Still Sebastian answers when I call him. Still he plays music.'

Isabel momentarily lowered her phone. The sun was high, but the concrete box of the hotel balcony was in shade. She reached out with one well-manicured finger and crushed some ants, interrupting a regimented procession and sending the survivors scrambling.

'Do you love your brother?' she heard her father say. 'Do you love Sebastian?'

'More than my own life,' said Isabel. It was true.

'Your mother would be proud,' said Werner, and the line went dead.

It was early in the morning in Austria, but her father did not sound as though he had slept.

These days, Isabel reminded herself, he never slept.

There came a knocking from inside, strong and persistent. It did not sound like the turndown service. Isabel tightened the cord of her short silk robe and hurried through to answer. Her luggage was pristine: Reeta's belongings were spread across the bed.

She opened the door to reveal the largest, ugliest man she had ever seen.

'My name is Otto Lix,' said the man, drinking in her bare legs. 'I'm looking for Dr Reeta Kapoor. I was directed to this suite.'

Isabel recognised Lix from the photograph she had found when researching the island, the one she had presented to Reeta to explain Valmik's disappearance. As far as Isabel knew, Otto Lix had never met Valmik Kapoor, but it was too late to worry about the possible fragmentation of Reeta's deception; much more important to get to Savage Island and find Sebastian.

'The hotel is full,' said Isabel. 'We're sharing.'

'Is she available?' said Lix.

'Dr Kapoor has an appointment in town.'

'Regrettable,' said Lix, scratching the stained armpit of his white safari suit.

Isabel would have liked to close the door, not least to stop herself from staring, but Otto Lix did not appear to be going anywhere.

'Can I pass on a message?' she said eventually.

'If you would be so kind,' said Lix, with forced bonhomie. 'Please say that through his close friend the governor, Professor Edward Quinn has learned about Dr Kapoor's arrival in the Okojuwoi. Her reputation as an anthropologist precedes her, particularly within this local community, and Professor Quinn would be extremely pleased to extend an invitation.'

'An invitation?'

'To Savage Island.' Lix grinned. 'She would be our first official guest.'

Isabel tried not to look too eager.

'Can I come?' she said.

Otto Lix did not offer to shake hands, but he did help Reeta and Isabel onboard with their luggage, which was placed carefully in the storage locker of the modified powerboat.

Reeta had never seen a vessel like this before. Painted in red and white, the 2009 MTI was essentially a space-age catamaran, 55 feet long and capable of 120mph, with a small, well-appointed cabin surrounded by blue-tinted, wraparound glass and open to the sky. The boat's sci-fi opulence was a guaranteed hit with the local children who crowded the wooden wharf, but none of them dared touch it.

The huge, menacing presence of Otto Lix would have been deterrent enough, but he had amplified his threat with two .44 Magnum Colt Anacondas. They hung loosely from holsters attached to his belt, and generated as much wide-eyed interest as the boat.

According to Isabel, this was the man Valmik had fought in Alaska, and the discovery of his involvement with Savage Island might have been the deciding factor in her brother's disappearance. Unfortunately for Reeta, her attempts to engage Lix in conversation, both casual and otherwise, were fruitless. Irritated by his monosyllabic surliness, Reeta had little choice but to sit back and wait to see what Edward Quinn had in store for them.

In seconds, Great Okojuwoi Island was lost to the horizon, and the boat was skimming across open ocean towards a fat, setting sun whose fingers of red flame stretched across the water.

This was not the first time Reeta had set eyes on Savage Island – she had sailed around it once before, many, many years ago – but it had not lost any of its mystique. The beaches were deserted, the foliage as thick as ever, and, of course, there were the unseen inhabitants practising unknown rituals beneath misty haloes of cloud.

Lix squinted behind his sunglasses and made for the western shore, where the mountains dropped almost straight into the sea.

The next cove revealed the extent of Quinn's ambition.

Speed cut, the hull of the big cat fell back into the water, engines bubbling.

Reeta and Isabel gasped at the vision before them.

It looked as though Oscar Niemeyer had crashed a flying saucer into the side of the mountain, three storeys of modernist architecture looming out over the water from steep jungle. Floor-to-ceiling windows peered down at anyone approaching from the seaward side.

'The visitor centre,' said Lix, without a great deal of passion.

Impressive as it was, particularly given the logistics of the location, the whole *Jetsons*-era construction presented a threatening visor to the world: at best a marvel of unrestrained ego from an idealistic plastic-wrap age, at worst a sharp, violent disc embedded in an exposed gum of earth. Bobbing closer, the underside made it seem less remarkable, more like a flattened airport control tower. Spindly hyperboloid pillars suggested the structure was plundering the mountain for support, despite compromising a striking natural silhouette.

Triggered by the encroaching nightfall, neon panels in the steep-sided walls began to flash like a scan bar in the Indian tricolour of orange, white and green. The timing was perfect. It was a pure expression of futurism, one that consummated the UFO effect.

Otto Lix, however, was an insolent, disinterested tour-guide. He did not appear to be impressed by either the structure or the impact it had on first-time visitors. When Reeta tried to comment, he gunned the motors again, drowning her words and almost knocking her back in her seat.

The structure vanished from view.

Hidden in a nearby crease of land, a narrow finger of river led upstream to a solid eraser of dock that jutted into a tranquil plunge pool, and there was fine mist from nearby waterfalls. A Filipino shore-man threw rope, but such was the piloting skill of Lix, it remained slack around the tie-up.

Throttling impatiently, he waited just long enough for Reeta and Isabel to clamber ashore with their luggage. Then he disengaged and vanished into the night, which had already fallen amongst the valleys.

Together, Reeta and Isabel walked towards an overwrought archway where gasoline flames burned in raised, ornate trays. Rose petals floated in an artfully lit fountain, throwing interesting patterns over the roof, but the light also exposed a poured-concrete, theme-park finish. There was a sudden, overpowering scent of lavender.

The Filipino who had tried to tie up the boat was now holding out deep goblets of pink champagne, droplets shining on silver. Another servant produced iced towels, which were very welcome; back on land, the heat was descending once more. The luggage had already disappeared.

A tall white woman stepped forward.

'I'm Kelly Maelzel. Welcome.'

Kelly was wearing a pale linen suit, but her feet were bare. Reeta shook hands with the Australian, while Isabel gulped at her wine. Neither woman spoke in reply.

'Don't worry,' said Kelly. 'The place had that effect on me, too, the first time.'

'Where are we?' said Isabel. 'Some kind of spa?'

'Not exactly,' said Kelly. 'Would you care to follow me?'

Beyond the introductory faux-Romanesque canopy – whose pillars were inscribed with replica Aurignacian cave paintings – there was an eight-seat gondola-type chairlift on a rack-and-pinion track. Kelly motioned that they should climb aboard, and secured the small door behind them.

The ride was almost silent. Further torches lit the way, each dive-bombed by insects, and forest leaves brushed at their arms. Within moments, the saucer was back in view, even larger.

Just as it appeared they might be absorbed by the structure, the gondola veered left and then dropped steeply.

'Professor Quinn thought you might like to spend the night by the beach,' Kelly said, as though reading from a script. 'Very peaceful down there.'

A straggly line of lights was approaching, cut off where the shore met the sea. The sound of the ocean became louder; this part of the island was not as well-protected by the reef.

'Can we see him now?' said Reeta. 'You can imagine, I have a lot of questions.'

'I'm sorry,' said Kelly, 'but Professor Quinn will be delighted to meet you for breakfast.'

The gondola arrived in a siding beneath more ornate arches, and they were helped out by another two servants. Indians this time, Reeta decided, remembering what Ashok had told her.

It was a short walk along a jetty to private cabins built out over the shallows, and Reeta recognised the style from exclusive hotels in the Maldives. An unfinished second branch of residences blossomed to the right, lit by workmen's torches.

Inside, the accommodation was functional but beautiful, like the captain's cabin on a galleon; the walls had been covered in old, framed maps.

Reeta could hear waves lapping beneath the wooden floor.

'I need to see Quinn,' she said, once Isabel had been led out to view her room.

'You must be hungry,' said Kelly.

'Can I see Quinn?' said Reeta.

'Tomorrow,' Kelly said and gestured towards a table laid with linen and silver. The platter was covered by a dome, but there was the smell of Pernod and hot shellfish. A nearby salver boasted *rouille*, Gruyère and a warm *ficelle*.

'I need to see him *now*,' said Reeta, as the luggage arrived. 'There might be a missing person on this island.'

'I'm going to have to lock you in,' Kelly said, apologetically.

'*What?*'

'Professor Quinn wants you to know that this is only a temporary measure, and for all of our safety. If you require anything, you have a telephone. Dial twenty-two.'

'He thinks I'm a threat?'

'No, no,' said Kelly. 'You have it all wrong.'

'Then *why?*'

'They don't come to this side of the mountain. Not yet, anyway. We don't know the reason.'

'What are you talking about?'

'You camp near predators, you hide away food. Goodnight, Dr Kapoor.'

The door clicked shut behind her.

Two drunk fools, they might have been the last men on earth.

When the little engine failed, as it occasionally did, those few noises that remained were far worse than silence. The lapping of dark, featureless water against the wooden hull served to remind Charlie Cortez of the bottomless eternity of monsters that swam and flexed and pulsed below, driven only by instinct and need. The light-bloated stars seemed indifferent, given excessive importance by the desperate wishes of humankind.

Fortunately, Thein Suu Aye knew God. At least: he knew Him as well as the corns on his left foot or his weakness for money.

Thein made for an excellent convert, in part because he had grown mad, and in part because the world became a far more acceptable place when the fight against his personal failings was voided by inevitability. He had been taught that he was imperfect and fallen, and this was a wonderfully liberating idea. Yet both Sebastian Kallmus and Jesus Christ (in that order) had demonstrated to him that even death did not have to be a certainty.

'I never put my foot on Savage Island with Sebastian Kallmus,' Thein said to Charlie, after the motor had failed a third time. 'I didn't have the strength, despite what he had told me. This time, with you, it will be different.'

'How so?' said Charlie, swigging from a bottle and handing it over.

'With Sebastian, I sailed this very boat into the shallows, and then watched him walk onto land with his eyes open. I knew he would die. But Sebastian found eternity.'

'In heaven?'

'Yes,' said Thein, seriously, 'I'm all for an eternity in heaven.'

'You allowed him to go?'

'It was difficult. I turned around and returned to Great Okojuwoi. I was a coward. But that was the strength Sebastian took from God – he had no fear of death. He was a farmer, planting seeds, but a farmer who had more faith in the soil than in himself.'

Charlie nodded.

'That was his gift to me,' said Thein. 'And now, my gift to you. The first time I was there, Savage Island destroyed me. I had a business, I had pride, I had work. All gone.'

'What happened?'

'Edward Quinn and the savages he keeps as pets.' Thein threw the empty bottle over the side, returned his attention to the engine. Charlie waited.

'I owe Edward Quinn,' said Thein. 'I would never have had the knowledge without him.'

'What do you mean?'

'Through Edward Quinn, I knew the devil. You see, I took him there the first time. I was his captain. Without Edward Quinn, I could have never taken Sebastian.'

'What happened when you landed? The time with Quinn?'

Thein ignored the question. He ran his fingernails over his extraordinary leg, a place where the blue veins still pulsed like fat worms beneath the scar tissue.

'I was born an adult,' he said, vaguely. 'Yet I became like children.'

'A foundational experience?'

'Foundational?'

'I'm very envious,' said Charlie, the bullshit coming easy. 'I'm still looking for my God.'

Thein said nothing, he had lost his train of thought.

'I mean, I will never know Christianity as you know it,' said Charlie.

'Sebastian Kallmus gave me the opportunity to close up those hell-gates again,' said Thein. 'He couldn't find anyone to take him to Savage Island, and I was the least likely person.'

Thein yanked again at the cord and the engine spluttered to life. He had a compass and the moon but scarcely glanced at either. They could have been sailing towards the edge of the world.

'Quinn got a fool, Kallmus got a coward,' said Thein. 'What are *you* expecting from me?'

'Good question,' said Charlie.

'That fucking American,' Thein said, to himself.

'But the *first* time,' said Charlie. 'The time they did this to your leg. How did you escape?'

'Escape?' Thein produced a hiccupping, high-pitched whine that sounded like the call of an extinct bird. It took Charlie a while to realise his companion was laughing.

'That's how I can go back,' said Thein. 'I just got away; no one ever escapes.'

Savage Island was at peace, although the jungle itself whispered and creaked.

Exhausted, Charlie Cortez and Thein Suu Ay pulled their little boat up the deserted beach on the eastern side of the island, hastily thrust it into the forest, then disguised it with long leaves.

This accomplished, Thein appeared to have nothing more to say. He wandered down the moonlit shore, scratching himself and clearing his throat and nose at a volume Charlie imagined could have woken the dead, let alone battle-hungry savages.

Charlie did not feel he should follow. For security, he would have liked Thein to sleep closer, but could think of no way to make the request without giving voice to a fear for their safety that, so far, had scarcely been acknowledged.

Once Thein had vanished, Charlie tried to dig himself into the dark, moist sand just beyond the tree-line, within touching distance of the boat.

He was listening to the lap of the waves and considering how he would ever sleep, when a great wave of fatigue rolled through his body. It melted his bones and sapped his muscles of energy, but it was a happy narcosis, and he embraced it like a familiar lover.

His second-to-last conscious thought was that he had willed himself to contract Leona's sickness out of guilt for losing her, and how this heavy desire for sleep contrasted with his expected symptoms. Leona could never sleep.

So why are you feeling such madness? Why are you behaving this way?

His last conscious thought tried to make the unstable distinction between madness and a rejection of oppression. Thein was mad. Leona had gone mad. If the natives of Savage Island were as violent as evidence suggested, then he would surely find them mad as well. Comparably, his wife, Vanessa, would categorise *him* as certifiable for undertaking his current actions.

Yet Charlie Cortez felt as free as his life had permitted until that point.

Insanity does not have to be physical, he thought. *The cultural meaning is uncontained.*

Charlie slept. He would have liked Leona to visit him in his dreams, but she remained silent.

The girl who watched him in his sleep was white-skinned, blue-eyed, and dressed in some of the tattered, modified clothes that her mother had left behind. She was small and delicate, even for five years old, but her figure cast a long shadow.

Given how similar she looked to Leona, she might have been a product of Charlie's troubled imagination, but she was not.

She was there.

Edward Quinn could have sworn on anything sacred to him that he had no bad intentions towards the man he was holding behind bars, but then, he never expected the savage to know any words of English, let alone be able to ask for his release.

For some reason, this changed everything.

Tam had also asked for food and water, and all in a language that Quinn understood. He spoke in broken, imperfect sentences with a strange, American-inflected accent, and had a vocabulary of about forty words. But Tam would not answer questions or say his name, even once Quinn had learned what the tribesman probably could and could not understand. Having realised the extent of his predicament, he appeared to have accepted his fate with total indifference.

Even more infuriating was when he shat and then handed Quinn his foul-smelling potty with a dignity that was painful to witness. It was almost as if he was not a savage at all.

The interrogation – because that was what it had become – had lasted for hours, on and off.

It was two in the morning, and Quinn was shirtless in the heat; Tam had previously expressed how cold he felt in the air conditioning, so it had been switched off.

The room had become unbearably close.

'Who got to you?' said Quinn, after ten minutes of shared silence. 'Who taught you to speak?'

Tam said nothing. He did not appear fazed by the spotlight on his cage.

'You were supposed to be unspoiled. You were supposed to be *perfect.*'

Tam lowered himself to a sitting position and began to tear open a thumbnail with his teeth.

'What are you doing?'

Slowly, carefully, Tam dripped a little blood onto the floor. Quinn watched and waited as he smeared out a shape with his index finger.

A crucifix.

Quinn was stunned. 'Where did you learn this?'

Always maintaining eye contact, Tam stood and backed up until his body pressed against the bars. Then he raised his hands and dropped his head in an unmistakable imitation of the *corpus Christi.*

Quinn lost his cool. 'Where did you learn to do this? *Tell me!'*

Tam lowered his arms and returned the stare.

'You have to understand,' said Quinn, approaching the bars. 'There is no such thing as cultural exchange when your culture has *nothing to offer.* Not one anthropologist would agree with me, but history cannot be denied. It boils down to this: people will gawp at your traditions, and then steal your women. Finally, you will be sold your own destruction on a plate, and you will swallow it like fools. This is a world of *cultural takeover,* in which I was the only one to see your true value. Why didn't you wait for me, so I could protect you? You are the last of your kind on Earth. I could have let you be children for ever.'

Long moments passed.

'Only the dead,' Tam said quietly.

'What?'

'Only the dead can be children for ever.'

Eight

Grundy Memorial Hospital, Atlanta.

The three medical staff met in Conference Room 1.11, Charlie's favourite place to brainstorm. Some of his hastily wiped scribbles still remained on the whiteboard, none of them helpful.

It felt strange without him.

'The full name of the new patient is Todd Julius Parker,' Nurse Francesca said to Dr Chris Light. 'I can find no next of kin or address, fixed or otherwise. There's nothing to prove his repeated claims that he was married to Leona Bride, except that, when lucid, he sure seems to know a lot about her. No wedding ring, maybe he pawned it.'

'How often is he lucid?' said Sparky.

'Not often.'

'But more significantly, and far more worryingly, he has her symptoms,' said Dr Sara Neilson.

'A degenerative brain disease,' said Chris.

'An *unknown* degenerative brain disease,' said Sara, glancing at the nurse. 'Ira Mardy at the Center for Disease Control insists it must be CJD, but he's wrong. His people are coming to take Mr Parker over there tomorrow.'

'What else?'

'Todd Parker presented with different drugs in his system. Leona was full of tranquillisers when she showed up here and killed Tsang. Todd's tox-screen shows stimulants.'

'Cocaine?'

'Cut with procaine, and any number of other things. He had an eight-ball in his pocket. Cheap, plenty of adulterants. But he's a dependant, or at least a heavy user.'

'What do you think?' Chris said to Nurse Francesca.

'He looks like he's been sleeping rough.'

'You find Charlie Cortez?'

'No, Dr Light. You?'

'Even Dan Demus doesn't know where he is,' Sparky said.

'You know that Cortez is suspended,' said Sara. 'If we find him, he can't practise in this hospital.'

'Charlie needs to know about this. He practically *predicted* it.' Sparky turned again to the nurse. 'Did the new patient say anything about an island?'

'An island?'

'Or a trip to India?'

'No and no.'

'What did he say about Leona?'

'Nothing we don't already have. He can prove he knows her through description, but he didn't seem overly concerned to discover she was dead.'

'That could be the madness,' said Sara. 'He was getting worse by the hour.'

'Yeah,' said Sparky, and then he hesitated. 'Did he say anything about . . . *cannibalism?*'

'Cannibalism?'

'Well, did he?'

'No.'

Sparky chewed his thumbnail. 'Charlie had a theory.'

'And Charlie's last patient is *dead*,' Sara Neilson said, shrugging with impatience. 'You think we should start Mr Parker on the pentosan polysulphate infusion? It might give the CDC some more time.'

'What he *wanted* to talk about is a woman called Reeta Kapoor,' Nurse Francesca said to Sparky.

'Who the hell is Reeta Kapoor?'

'A teacher. She works at a university in Austria.'

'Austria, Europe?'

'No, Doctor. Austria, Ohio.'

'You don't need to be sarcastic,' said Sparky. 'What does Todd say about her?'

'He thinks Reeta Kapoor can help him, and thought that maybe she could help Leona, too. Mr Parker calls her an *expert*, and says they've been in e-mail contact. He says he's been scanning hand-written diary pages and saving them to a memory stick, and now he needs to send them to her.'

'What kind of diary pages?'

The nurse shrugged. 'He says they're the last pages, the only ones he could save.'

'Does he have the memory stick with him?'

'No.'

'Dammit,' said Sparky. 'We could use a break. You think we can get it from him?'

'Not any more,' said the nurse.

'Why not?'

'Because he already gave it to me.' Nurse Francesca reached into her apron pocket.

The liver, fat and filmy and tinged with yellow, had been threaded onto sticks and placed over a fire, the flames tempered by seaweed. I could taste this seaweed like a kind of seasoning as I pushed chunks of the grainy flesh into my mouth, urged on by the other women. The meat was hot, but not cooked through, and the texture was not unpleasant. God help me, I took more.

There was approval at my first mouthful, a kind of satisfaction from those present, but my second passed unnoticed, and for the first time I began to feel acceptance. If I am, as I suspect, some kind of ghost to these people, then the consumption of food is proving my physical reality to them.

It is strange that the closer I become to the tribe, the more ghostly I feel in myself.

I am becoming nothing, or at least, I am becoming something I am not.

Todd was delighted with his meal. The women and the men ate separately – the men take the choice cuts, presumably because they need strength, while the women are given liver, kidney and brains; I will never forget tearing a hot raw lobe to my mouth and feeling it dissolve there.

I understand that Todd gorged until he vomited, which is encouraged at a ritual like this, and such shameless indulgence made him very popular indeed, for a time. Lying in our hut, it was clear he was delighted; he talked of steak and of chops and of char-grilled fillet, as though he had just dined at a fine restaurant. It is the first real protein in our diet for months.

Dare I tell him what he has been eating? Does he know?

Tam, the man who has taken it upon himself to be my educator, is a remarkable person. He is beautiful and considerate and I feel a shared humanity that (obviously) transcends our different experiences of life.

We communicate phonetically – is this the word? Which is to say, I repeat his words as best I can, and he repeats mine, and we sketch pictures on the beach with sticks.

The Qesem.

The Qesem is the wise woman of the tribe. Her power is spiritual, as opposed to the Chief, whose power is political, although it seems these boundaries are sometimes indistinct. When the Chief's sister died of extreme old age – she was maybe fifty or sixty, it is very hard to tell – it was to the remote hut of The Qesem that the body was removed.

The Qesem prepared the feast alone, unsighted. I mean, she butchered the corpse. Two warriors, her bodyguards, brought the food down to be cooked piece by piece.

The women did most of the work.

Fat dripped onto the fire. I could recognise thighs and breasts (I am not a cook myself, but anyone could see that the dissolving, nippled mounds were something that would not roast well) and the smell was extremely sweet, almost sickeningly so. Additionally, there was a strangely familiar element that maybe I imagined, something from the real world, like the taste of a chunk of chewed toenail or licking a burn inflected by the kettle.

Perhaps it was just the flavor of the forbidden?

We danced around the thick smoke until we fell in exhaustion and were given rainwater mixed with berries to drink. Then we danced more.

Nowadays I am naked as the rest, but the men do not look at me with sexual interest, at least, not explicitly. I would try to ask Tam about this, but it might lead to misunderstanding.

For months we were kept in a dark hut, awaiting death.

I realise now, the reason we were not killed with the sailors was because of Tam.

His brother, whose name sounds like Udumi, would kill us tomorrow if he could, and I already have suspicions about

*how this fate would occur, although I cannot fully
understand the ritual that Tam describes. It sounds like the
most sacred the tribe have, even more so than the consumption of their own dead, and it happens to any Owb who sets
foot on the island.*

*One thing is certain: the tribe do not eat outsiders, but
only their own. Incredibly, being eaten is the most respectful
ending imaginable here, a kind of ancestor worship, a kind
of passing on of the soul. In addition, there is a genuine fear
of resurrection, and so to eat the body is maybe reassuring to
them.*

*Naturally, Tam was fascinated when I tried to describe the
life of Christ to him, but I am afraid he will never
understand, and I am equally afraid that I will never be able
to describe this faith in an adequate fashion. It is my
lacking, not his, because my knowledge is limited and my
passion non-existent. But he is very, very keen to learn.*

*I thought I had a thirst to learn from him, although
initially this was more about driving away the madness of
fear and solitude by keeping my mind occupied. Yet Tam,
who is some kind of prince amongst his people, has a far
greater thirst for knowledge than I do.*

*The irony is not lost on me that he is studying us as an
anthropologist might. Todd and I are the subjects, and all
conversation is about our society, our people, our gods. We
are watched constantly. He has little or no interest in
describing his tribe and their practices to me, so what small
facts I can report in this tattered journal are gleaned almost
by accident.*

*What will happened when my knowledge has been
exhausted and the tribe have gained as much information
from us as possible, when we are no longer useful?*

*

Tam is relentless in his efforts with me. For all I frustrate him, he will not give up.

He and I sit on the beach and I attempt to describe life beyond the island. It is, as you can imagine, near impossible.

Tam sets the agenda. When it is clear he is not able to comprehend, he sets about teaching himself my language. I would touch a tree, and say tree, and then he would touch the tree and say tree. After a few attempts at this with various objects we were both rolling around in laughter.

For a long time I thought we were discussing skin, but we were really discussing color. The tribal belief is that outsiders are ghosts, malicious spirits returning from the afterworld, who must be destroyed in the elaborate method that I have yet to define. This goes some way to explaining the resurrection anxiety.

Tam has no knowledge of anything beyond the horizons, yet he is the only tribesperson with any interest in the subject. This may be noble, but I always imagine a quest for information is also an expression of dissatisfaction of some kind. He asks about the stars and the moon and the sun, and where they go with the passing of the hours.

Where, if there is dissatisfaction, does this stem from?

I am an Owb, Todd is an Owb. The men who hover around the distant shipwreck of the Fortune II are Owbs, but they have magical weapons, and the tribe are under strict instruction not to attack, unless these Owbs try to land on the island itself.

They are a war-like people when roused, but very far from stupid.

I have only been permitted one glimpse of the shipwreck, which is being slowly picked apart for salvageable parts. It looks like a huge operation. Presumably the tribe are afraid I will try to signal for help, but this is impossible – I have no doubt that I would be killed in an instant. Besides, true sanctity of life cannot exist for me, a being whom most here presume is already dead.

Instead, I stand before the shoreline, well guarded, and listen to the men thrash huge drums made from wooden logs. This is, in theory, to keep the salvage-working Owbs away, but they appear to have no intention of landing here anyway.

I think the drumming has more to do with self-reassurance and a release of frustration – the warriors are like foxes who cannot get at the chickens they crave.

What the hell happened to the white monster Otto Lix?

Can I accept this life?

Can I accept any life? Would the typical American existence – work, consume, die – ever have been enough for me? Perhaps I will never know.

Will we be here for ever?

It must have been a year now, although there is little seasonal change.

Consistency breeds familiarity, no matter how insane that consistency seems to be.

Todd and I have our own hut, where the insects at least have accepted us as one of their own. At sun-up, we eat grilled lizard or (usually) cooked tubers left from the meal the night before. Food is plentiful and abundant, and each finds for themselves, which is easy to do once you have been shown where to look. Fire is not made, but rather kept; there is always a small flame burning somewhere. Meat is provided by the hunters, maybe twice a week. Days are spent swimming, or being teased by rangy giggling children – we are tiny compared to the adults, all of whom are over six feet tall, continually reminding me of my Gulliverism.

In the afternoons, I sit on the beach with Tam and try to talk.

Todd, my husband (we have been married in a tribal ceremony, which I will try to describe at a later moment) is happy here, strangely enough. He is fit and brown and quiet, and although he is never left alone, he is permitted to explore. He has expressed a desire to kill a pig, but the leader of the warriors, Udumi, continues in his suspicion and dislike, and will not so much as look in our direction.

I wait for this fearsome man to attack, or turn the tribe against us, but it does not happen. Perhaps it is the continuing myth in my mind – the unrealistic notion – that a savage society must certainly be, well, savage. Of course they brutalized and murdered the crew of the cargo ship, but I can even forgive them for this now. The island is the extent of their entire world, and it was being invaded. To have such a gigantic vessel wash up on their nearby reef must have been the equivalent of a vast spaceship hovering above our planet.

Taking this as the metaphor, I am not so sure that America, as a civilized society, would have behaved so differently had the equivalent situation been presented to our political leaders. Besides, Tam has explained to me that encounters with the Owbs in the past have always been bloody. Men arrive with guns, and spears and knifes, foolhardy adventurers and treasure hunters with no respect for the fragile and exquisitely balanced existence here.

I wonder where the legend came from, that outsiders are the malevolent returning spirits of the departed. I am doing my best to dispel this nonsense, but Tam is the only one listening.

*

How to write in such a place?

With pen and paper, obviously, and my cherished dictionary. The journal survived, as did our belongings, which, as backpackers, were paltry to begin with. Less satisfactory for a diarist is to have but the vaguest sense of time. It seems less and less important as the days go by, and as a result, it feels increasingly unimportant to record my thoughts here.

When I turn over the reams of pages that existed before our kidnap, I realise that the words were written for me, for a Leona of the future. As time becomes irrelevant, so the future becomes irrelevant, and so the words are sapped of vitality.

My point is this: I no longer write for myself.

Gone is all vestige of vanity or the self-aggrandizing romance of the travel writer. I am writing for others, in the hope that these words can be found. But the more time passes, the more unlikely I believe there will be anyone to read. So I do not write as much!

Why did I pick up pen and paper on this occasion? Because there is news.

I am pregnant.

As my belly grows, so my panic – initially unbearable – subsides. The knowledge that there will soon be a baby is further proof to the tribespeople that I am not a ghost, that I am closer to them than they think. Most are amazed.

The child belongs to Todd – I have taken no other lover for over a year. While Tam looks at me in what I am certain is a sexual way sometimes, it is more from curiosity than lust, and he is highly desirous for his wife, whom he appears to love very much.

It is a curious fact that since the life in my stomach became undeniable, I have grown closer to Tam, and further from my original lover. I suppose that as a science project, I continue to surprise.

Interesting note – only the Chief is permitted to have more than one wife. You might imagine this would make becoming Chief an enviable prospect, but to have more than one wife is to live in a state of perpetual bankruptcy, if the currency on this island is good food and lodging. As a result, the Chief is always in debt to his people, who bring him gifts in order to maintain his household, and this debt is repaid with wisdom, or a decision in their favor, or in some other small token.

It is a kind of benign dictatorship that appears, in my mind, to work very well, not least because power is never concentrated in one place.

The tribe work through their differences with games – physical strength is probably the most highly prized attribute here – and as a result, even the harshest arguments are resolved with a kind of play, watched over by the rest of the group. Dissatisfaction is never permitted to simmer unnoticed, but must be dragged in front of all to be mulled over or scorned.

The one rift that never seems to be reconciled is between Tam and Udumi, the two brothers – barely distinguishable from one another in appearance, except for the unusual white scar above Udumi's eyebrow. When these young men fight it is as though a great storm is rocking the island. Because all acknowledge that Tam and Udumi are the smartest and most capable, it becomes very difficult to satisfactorily conclude their arguments. There are usually days of mourning – heads held low and little meat (Udumi is the most successful hunter) while they figure it out between them.

*

I have my child, my beautiful, beautiful child.

There was no question I would choose a name for this girl myself. Medea, The Qesem, has named every member of the tribe since time immemorial, and did not think to exclude me from this ritual – perhaps I should be pleased.

My little girl is called Apis.

Incidentally, Tam tells me that Medea has given both Todd and I names as well – Mo and Sew.

Mo and Sew.

Strange. It is interesting to be renamed this way – if we were enslaved, I would think of this as some kind of poetically just inversion of the middle passage, where scores of black slaves were renamed by their callous masters. That is, if we were enslaved, and I no longer feel this way.

Anyway, I do not know the logic behind the naming process, or what the names mean (if anything). Perhaps, eventually, I will find out.

The Qesem was my midwife, the only time I have entered her hut, bow-legged and screaming. She is also, Tam has explained, a kind of apothecary, using bottles washed up on the shore to store her potions and poisons.

All I will say is that the arrival of little Apis into this world was not the nightmare I imagined it could have been – how quickly the human body forgets pain.

There are to be celebrations, the celebration of new life! Before, I had felt so alone here. It is a terrible thing to be feared, and both Todd and I, while officially accepted, were rarely spoken to or even looked at, except by Tam and a select few close to him.

I now have unequivocal love, and with it, a sense of peace.

Tam is hilarious. You would not believe it, but there is a lot of laughter here.

He presented my music box to me, an item I had forgotten about — most of our belongings had been removed, taken, but not forgotten. This was an item of particular interest to Tam, for whom it must have seemed an alien artifact. He is not simple, merely cautious, and his presentation to me was like a further test — he, the analyst, taking notes.

The ballerina was stationary, the music silent. Of course, Tam did not realise that the mechanism needed to be wound. He fell on his ass when I showed him how it worked, and then we pirouetted together across the sand in mimicry.

I play the music to Apis and she falls asleep. What a great gift this is.

Gods.

We all need gods, it seems.

There is one here I have become familiar with: El, the all powerful one, who lives in the great mountain, a being who casts a welcome, cooling shadow for most of the day. With my skin that still peels and reddens, I thank Him for that, and for the shade He gives my baby girl.

This mountain, by far the largest on an island of mountains, is a volcano, I am sure. The most persistent legend, at least as I understand it from Tam, is one of immolation, of burning. Tam filled a beach with sketches of an explosion, of fire and brimstone, falling rocks, and stick figures crossed through. Impressive, palpable, realistic wrath.

Of course the natives are penitent. Such natural power destroyed the great civilization of Pompeii, and to this day threatens grown-up countries from an atlas I do not have.

To approach El is a test of strength and character and will-power, and to do so unreadily is to tempt fate. Tam is dismissive, but I can tell he is envious of Udumi's fearlessness

– as a cultural Christian, I can still twitch at the sight of an inverted crucifix or a ransacked church.

Tam is an atheist, I am sure, but there is no such definition here. He seeks to broaden knowledge, which will lead to perspective, but there is, even by his own admission, a long way to go. He rescued us from the ship for this purpose, making himself unpopular in the process. Only the foolish welcome change without question or reservation, even if that change is for the best.

There are other gods in the plants and trees, and in the water – even in the air, or in certain clearings. Most have names, and are older than time. To worship the environment sounds like hippy nonsense, but again, there is a kind of logic to it, as it is the elements that feed and nurture the inhabitants. It seems very reasonable to me that they should be grateful.

Horror.

After many months of peace, horror.

Two fishermen have been washed up on the island after another freak storm. They are here by accident, I am certain – these were NOT adventurers or treasure hunters, they are like scared children.

I have laid eyes on them, and they me. Tam, Udumi and The Qesem watched the exchange, as though there was something I was supposed to do or say or reveal.

What could I do?

The fishermen are local Indians, and we have no common language. When they saw me they became even more afraid, or it could have been the potion that the vile "wise woman" was pouring down their throats.

They will hallucinate and scream and then their insides will be spilled into some plastic buckets that The Qesem guards with jealousy. These buckets must have been washed up at some point.

Tam tells me that The Qesem can divine the future from the intestines of Owbs, and other lunatic prophesies using the material corpse.

There is big, big trouble here. Tam was impassive at my pleading for the mercy of these men, but when we were alone later he tried to explain. This is the situation now, as I understand it:

Udumi has been venturing further and further towards El. He claims to be growing in faith, but he is becoming a fanatic – he scarcely hunts, he scarcely eats, and he disappears for nights at a time, like some native equivalent of the hair-shirt ascetic.

If Udumi's claims are true, he has found evidence that there are other settlers here.

According to Tam, Udumi is not talking about campfires and clothes-lines – he has described complex and modern structures for which the islanders do not even appear to have names.

The balance of power in the camp is disturbed.

The spirits are whirling, the sanctity of El has been breached. It does not require any great insight to realise that the blame must be laid at the feet of outsiders – just as we frequently do in the West at the idea of immigrants, or an influx of cultural abnormality.

Tam and Udumi have had their greatest falling-out yet. Tam would release the fishermen, but, for once, he is entirely alone in his clemency. The tribe are keen to reclaim the old ways, even if this means a return to cold-blooded murder; but worse, Udumi feels he has a real point to prove.

Both The Qesem and Sool, the Chief, are in agreement. God help me, Sool is so fond of my little Apis, as he is with

*the infants in general, they spend hours together in play.
Such a strong man, and yet so gentle. But at a time like this
it is impossible to forget that we are all very, very different.*

*Now, beneath a bright moon, I am a long way from the
clearing of The Qesem, where the evil deed will be taking
place. Men are being murdered – slowly, horribly – probably
as I write.*

My head is full of imagined screams.

Further months without an entry.

*I only put pen to paper now because Todd found my
journal, hidden high in the eves of our hut, in one of the few
places where the rain cannot penetrate.*

*He tells me he is disappointed not to feature more! Cheeky
man.*

*Well, here goes. I must say it is nice to feel the pages in
my hands and the scribble of the Biro (I am down to my
last, so do not expect much more).*

*Todd has found the most remarkable clearing to the east of
the island, an area with no great significance to the tribe,
not even a place greatly explored. It is, he tells me, full of
treasure.*

Treasure.

*I went straight to Tam with the knowledge – he simply
shrugged. Of course, the tribe are well aware of it. Then I
made the journey to see this "treasure" for myself.*

*I learned what sounds like another legend, but must be
real – the story of a shipwreck. I will point out now that this
treasure is no beautiful find – dull coins and slimy jewels
within rotting chests, but remarkable for being almost
untouched by the natives. What trinkets considered valuable
here are hewn from nature – feathers, branches, and so on.
Additionally, they require craftsmanship, and there are few*

tools with which to work metal into anything but arrows and spearheads. A block of gold, while attractive to a magpie, is, as Tam rightly points out, just another element, and as it is known to be from the outside, most leave well alone.

The story is unclear, because the legend is unimportant. Time, as I have mentioned previously, exists to serve life here, and not the other way around as it does in our society.

It is difficult to get a precise history, but there are valuables here that must be several hundred years old. The original owners of the treasure? Massacred, like all Owbs.

The only useful items are those which have already been fashioned into weapons, including a bronze-tipped arrow, which is considered sacred and has never been fired. Sool gifted Todd with a bejeweled dagger simply for expressing interest, and Todd is happy as an infant. It is not particularly sharp, so I doubt he can do much damage with it!

Of course, my romantic notion is piqued yet again. I wish I could hear voices from the past.

A sketch: Apis, on the knee of Sool, the Chief. I am glad to put my faith in this man, there is none in the tribe he will not listen to, but more than anything, his interest in the education and entertainment of the children suggests to me that he cares deeply about the future.

The shared humanity is there, the understanding almost involuntary. No individual is alone in the group, as, I believe now, no society is alone in the world.

She is gone.

Was she ever real? Was any of it ever real?

Tam must not have understood that we cannot return at any time. We were put into the fishermen's boat before we knew what was happening. I had no idea we were to leave, and Apis was left behind in the women's hut. Our scant belongings were there already. Todd, a person for whom I can no longer feel anything, finally became a man and restrained me.

A night-time flight from what was to be certain death.

Todd and I are now imprisoned in a circular jail in Port Barren, having been picked up by an Indian navy patrol at first light. Initial relief turned to fear, and then one long nightmare.

It was a week before we could see each other, and three weeks before we were allowed access to anyone else. Now, after six weeks, I have pen and paper again, and my scribbling here follows multiple letters to the embassy, to the lawyers we are promised, to anyone who will listen. My hand hurts with it, and I do not care.

I want my child back.

Tam explained to me in the day before our departure (and mostly in my own language) that the civil war threatening the peace of the island was close to erupting again. This was clear from our final weeks, as Udumi had reported finding more Owb constructions, more settlements. He thinks there must be a base of some kind being constructed on the far side of El, and maybe tunnels beneath the mountain, as he sees no people.

Of course, we, as fellow Owbs, were to bare the brunt of Udumi's rage.

Tam has remained on the island, but it was clear he was thinking about leaving also. I knew he would stay, he will fight for his people, and for what he believes.

If anyone reads this who can help, please do so. No one will believe our story.

I want my child back.

*

There is no more. The chapter is finished, the book is closed.

Apis is gone, and with her my will-power.

America now, and her artifice and empty-eyed acceptance of the life into which we were born. I am going to Atlanta to die amongst the hive-mind. I feel mad, but it is better to be mad than to have knowledge.

I will leave this house of my childhood, placing the last of my misery here in this diary so as not to cause any more pain to those who have been good to me.

Why will no one listen?

If you had known me before the island, perhaps many years before the island, you would know I was never a particularly sunny person, an outgoing child, a character with promise or prospect beyond the wishes of those closest to me. This used to be fine. I never blamed my real parents – I was adopted, need I remind you. I never even thought about them until recently, but the sense of abandonment has never felt more real, a cycle I have now visited upon my only daughter. Who are we, if we are not our family?

My child has gone, and my life.

I try to reconcile my thoughts by imagining her desire to stay, and I cannot blame her. It is the only world that Apis knew, and perhaps for the best that it will remain that way. I wish I were there now, but to draw attention to my experiences is to draw attention to a world in such a way that could only help to explode it. God knows I have tried, so perhaps it is for the best that no one really listens.

Todd, who I have not seen for a long, long time, returned briefly to my life, and he and I have reached an agreement. He will give me the dagger he cherishes in return for my diary pages. He does not know that so many pages have been destroyed already, burned on a fire in the backyard, but as he

*never paid much notice to anything I have written, he will
not realise until the exchange is made. More importantly, he
is also becoming mad, and threatens suicide – it would be
typically dramatic of him to use an item from the island. So
I will take it.*

*And you take these words, my husband, and with them
our horrific legacy.*

*So one phase ends, another begins – my new life, my next
life, one in which my mind is slipping. Bring on this
madness, let the days of insanity overwhelm the conscious
memory.*

*I suffer from insomnia, and other desires – certain hungers
– that it is better I do not describe.*

3:15 a.m.

Todd awoke in a dimly lit private ward, feeling more like himself
than he had in months. For one thing it was unusual to actually
be waking up, having not slept in weeks; perhaps a little time getting
clean in the hospital would be no bad idea.

All those uppers were bound to mess with my head.

Todd had no idea how sick he was.

What he also could not know was that the doctors had imple-
mented Charlie's trial pentosan therapy, so the symptoms of his
illness were temporarily relieved. Additionally, as he was not as
far progressed as Leona had been at the same point, he was
returning to a temporary state of consciousness that approached
normality.

Todd looked around.

Lot of strange machinery for an overdose.

How did I get here?

He was wired up to a number of devices, including some scary-
looking multi-parameter monitors. The corridor through the glass
wall was dark.

'Hey!' he shouted. '*Hey!*'

Within moments, the night nurse had hurried in.

'You're awake,' she said, unable to hide her surprise.

'I'm hungry.'

The nurse was busy, checking his vitals and making notes.

'Do you have, like, a pizza place near here?'

'I need to call the doctor,' said the nurse. 'You need treatment.'

'What's going on?' said Todd.

'Don't worry,' said the nurse, halfway out the door. 'You're in safe hands.'

'Can I at least watch TV?'

She was apologetic. 'It doesn't work.'

'You have a newspaper?'

Within moments, Todd was alone with the lights on, a plastic cup of water, and copies of *Barbershop Digest* and *Creative Loafing*.

Due to his short attention span, he was down to the classifieds in ten minutes.

Eventually, Todd's eyes narrowed. He was looking at the inch or so of column dedicated to the exotic dagger that Vanessa Cortez had found in her husband's sports car. Reggie Owens, the private detective she had hired, was still not giving up hope that someone would want to claim it and offer a reward.

Todd could hardly believe what he was looking at.

It could only be.

There was a contact telephone number.

Todd looked out into the hospital corridor; it was dark once more. He removed his nasal cannula and oximeter. When the monitors responded with a high-pitched beep, he reached over and switched them off.

Then, he stood up to leave.

Nine

The coconut crab, or *Birgus latro*, is the largest crab in the world. A prehistoric monster with an unusually long lifespan for a crustacean, it lives exclusively on land, and has even been observed catching and eating rats.

Perhaps more remarkably, it can climb trees, where it cuts coconuts from the branch. Back on land, the two front claws are then used to open the fruit, with up to sixty pounds of pressure.

Charlie Cortez did not hear the first coconut fall to the soft sand, a few feet away.

A few minutes later, the second coconut landed closer to his head. He opened his senses to tropical blue sky and the smell of surf. He stretched with all the luxury of a man on vacation.

Raising his head and squinting, he saw a third coconut fall a little beyond his outstretched feet and roll towards him. Charlie's face scrunched in puzzlement.

The giant crab dropped onto his chest like a football full of sand, and Charlie's screams produced an eruption of birdlife from the nearby jungle. Inches from his face, enormous black-and-orange claws waved and snapped at his jugular, and a jagged, alien mask ground towards him with wet, mechanical hate.

The girl had a stick, and she swung at the beast like a pro-golfer, but despite a solid hit, one claw had Charlie by his shirt collar. The crab's torso slid and cracked and oozed, but many legs still tried to scramble up his heaving ribcage.

Charlie screamed again. His shirt ripped, but the beast clung on.

The girl had a new technique. She flipped the crab over, and brushed lightly at the underbelly with her fingers.

As soon as it had released, Charlie rolled away, breathing sand and coughing.

Crawling on hands and knees, the girl followed. She was small and juvenile, and had a message for Charlie. She was not about to wait.

'We need to go,' she said, tugging at his arm.

'Who are you?' said Charlie, but the resemblance was clear.

Her eyes were blue and blazing.

I see fire, he thought.

Leona.

'My name is Apis,' she said.

Suddenly, the girl sat back on her haunches as though listening to something. She looked casual there, almost comfortable. All urgency appeared to have gone, although the eyes still darted.

'We go now,' she said, biting her lower lip.

'Go?'

'Go,' said Apis. 'Now.'

'Why?'

'They are coming.'

Professor Quinn's office was contained in the body of the spaceship-building. He enjoyed a vast, richly decorated space, one wall comprising a curved window through which he could look out over the bay. It boasted a treasure trove of anthropological curiosities, including masks, weaponry, tribal art and a grisly collection of *Jivoran* shrunken heads.

Otto Lix came in through an exterior secure entry that led to a narrow path with low parapets along the top of a tall, whitewashed bulwark. Quinn could hear the waves crashing one hundred feet below and the screeches and squawks of the nearby jungle, but when Lix closed the door, there was only the quiet, efficient hiss of air conditioning.

Edward Quinn was sitting behind his enormous mahogany desk. He waited until Lix crossed the office and had adopted the stance of a soldier at ease. It was early in the morning, but Lix was already sweating through the horrible white safari suit that he never seemed to change.

They exchanged no words of greeting.

'Otto, I'm letting you go,' said Quinn.

Lix remained silent.

'We both knew this day was coming,' said Quinn. 'You're not a man who will appreciate words of thanks, so I'll be brief. There is a bank account in Lugano, Switzerland. It contains a million US dollars. All in your name.'

'Two million,' said Lix.

'One million three: and I will overlook what I recently learned about your activities with the islanders. You're a rapist, you have a sadistic personality disorder, and you *will* put the future of this project at risk. Try to remember, I have conclusive proof that you are a murderer.'

'One million five.'

'No.'

'You knew what you were getting when you hired me,' said Lix.

'Then, I needed you,' said Edward Quinn. 'Now, I don't.'

Sensing danger, Udumi's wife had shooed the village children away, allowing him to spend the morning alone in his hut. He was considering the sacred arrow, which he had placed in the centre of the floor and surrounded with decorative leaves.

A shadow appeared in the doorway. Udumi did not turn his head.

There is an Owb, said the young warrior.

Udumi said nothing. The warrior twitched. He was nervous; Udumi's temper could be fearsome.

The dawn watchers heard shouting. He is not careful. They have seen him, running west.

Did you find a boat?

Not yet.

Did you go to my father with this news?

It was the warrior's turn to hold his tongue.

Why not?

The man bowed his head in penance, yet the question was redundant. Everyone knew that true power had now fallen to Udumi.

It was not the case that the tribe had failed to believe Udumi's story about what had happened to Tam during their trial together in the Biota, it was that they could not comprehend. Besides, why would Udumi lie? It would have been unlike him *not* to champion his victory over the body of his dead brother; indeed, it had been expected. Yet no such thing had happened. And Udumi, who believed himself alone in the true appreciation – if not understanding – of the Owb threat, had brooded over the responsibility of leadership, because it had not been granted to him in the expected way.

Additionally, it was almost as shocking to Udumi that Medea's plan had not come to fruition: The Qesem was always right. He would like to have spoken with her, but she had disappeared back to her retreat in the jungle with strict instructions not to be disturbed.

Udumi said to the warrior: *Why was this Owb not killed?*

Because he is with Apis. She is leading him towards El.

Are you surprised? Apis is one of them.

Also because . . . his skin is dark.

Many Owbs have dark skin.

Never so dark as this.

It will be some trick of the afterworld.

Should we kill him?

Udumi considered. *No. Capture them both, and bring them to me.*

Capture Apis? Tam would never—

Tam is GONE.

The warrior bowed his head.

We never approach El, he said. *Strange things are happening there.*

Do not talk to me about El, and the mysteries behind the mountain, said Udumi. *It is time for you to be a man. It is time for this tribe to be strong.*

Yes, Udumi.

Do it now, bring them to me alive. I will kill them myself.

Yes, Udumi.

Who knows what we may learn from opening the bellies of such unusual creatures?

A series of winding stairs and short rope-bridges over steep streams brought them up through the jungle mountainside to a point just above the saucer, where Professor Quinn was waiting.

It was a hot walk, but the view from the top was incredible.

A deep, circular swimming pool had been sunk into the centre of the disc, surrounded by a well-stocked bar and sun loungers crafted in teak. Rainbow-coloured parrots swooped between carefully chosen foliage and tented pagodas, occasionally dropping to cool themselves in the sparkling water and shake off the droplets.

'Es ist *schön . . .*' said Isabel, mouth open.

Reeta reserved judgement.

'There will be music here in the evenings,' said Edward Quinn, walking over to shake hands. 'We're closing a six-month contract with some traditional Berber Kabylian folk singers.'

'Your detractors might say you prefer the sound of your own voice,' said Reeta.

'My detractors?' Quinn said, smiling at Isabel with his very white teeth. 'I expected you to disapprove, Dr Kapoor, but you could at least be civil.'

'Yes, Professor. You've done an astonishing thing here.'

'Still with that tone!' said Quinn, delighted. 'Don't worry, I'll persuade you. As for the sound of my own voice, there will be lectures, of course – but downstairs, in specially designed multi-media suites. I really look forward to giving you the grand tour, I've rehearsed this in my mind for months. On Savage Island, we seek to educate as well as to entertain.'

'How noble.'

'Quite. But for now, since you're here, I thought we might take the opportunity to talk. It gives me tremendous pleasure to receive such a renowned guest as my first official visitor. And, of course, any friend of yours.'

'Isabel Kallmus,' said Isabel, with a half-curtsey, and Reeta felt a sharp sense of the ridiculous.

'Delighted.' Quinn clasped his hands together. '*Delighted*. Will you take breakfast with me? It would make sense to get into the shade, the sun up here can be brutal.'

Quinn's pagoda boasted a lavish spread. He dismissed the armed Filipino in the bright shirt who had brought them up, and insisted on serving coffee himself.

'Juice?' said Quinn. 'I have iced cupuaçu, imported from Amazonas. The finest fruit you will ever taste.'

'Thank you,' said Isabel.

'Dr Kapoor?'

'Orange juice,' said Reeta.

'Sanguinello? Valencia?'

'Tropicana.'

'We're fresh out.'

'So fuel a jet.'

'The subaltern bites.'

'Is that a cereal?'

'You know,' Quinn said to Isabel, 'when I first heard of Reeta Kapoor, she was a whiny little essentialist, puppyish in her derivation and in awe of her sisters; capable of wit but with no real thoughts of her own. Worse, she was a terrible essayist, truly terrible.'

'Perhaps you caught me in translation,' said Reeta. 'I thought I saw Tropicana on the room-service menu.'

'Well, we're not yet *fully open*.'

'Then I'll take the cupuaçu and a complaint form. Or are they not ready either?'

'This is going better than I expected,' said Quinn, pouring. 'You couldn't protect Savage Island when you worked in the Okojuwoi; what makes you think you can do it from Europe, and with ten years of nothing but the memory of failure?'

'I didn't say I was here to protect the island.'

'But, in principle, you don't like what I'm doing.'

'Based on what I've seen, what I know of the corrupt government of the Okojuwoi, and what I know of you?'

'Okay . . .'

'Yes,' said Reeta. 'Who else is going to speak for the indigenous people here?'

'If all goes according to plan, the indigenous people, will, eventually, speak for themselves.'

'In what language? Under whose terms?'

'Minutiae,' said Quinn. 'How can you be ready with a conclusion? You have next to no data.'

'So what *are* you doing?' said Reeta, selecting a muffin. It was beautifully fresh, although the basket was already attracting insects. Quinn seemed not to notice.

'My rationale is very simple,' he said. 'Savage Island is the last in the Okojuwoi archipelago to be developed. Tribes on the other, larger islands have been assimilated, their traditional way of life compromised. You know this, Dr Kapoor. You are, in part, responsible for failing them.'

'Unchecked progress,' said Reeta. 'Unthinking, opportunistic progress. Relatively speaking, I wasn't just working with a new government, I was working with a new democracy; elected officials who were inexperienced in every sense of the word.'

'Almost all progress is unthinking or opportunistic,' said Quinn. 'Yet progress, for some reason, is what we, as a species, strive for.'

'I will concede, I was trying to swim upstream,' said Reeta. 'Good people, poor administration – the story of much of the developing world.'

'Tribes on the main islands were lost to alcoholism,' Quinn said to Isabel. 'They died of diseases to which they had no developed immune system, and so on. As Dr Kapoor can tell you, these disenfranchised tribes, if they even remain at all, have been herded into compounds, or onto randomly demarked territory, invariably that which is not their own.'

'Why did Savage Island remain untouched?' said Isabel.

'Dr Kapoor?'

'Geography,' said Reeta. 'Lack of a natural port, a reef impassible in most vessels, and a minimum of exploitable resources. Even logging would have been problematic, due to steep terrain.'

'But,' said Quinn, 'with the dawn of cheaper air travel, the Indian government has been looking to develop the touristic potential in these islands. Natural beauty alone is becoming an exploitable resource.'

'I thought air travel was becoming *more* expensive,' said Isabel.

'There's an emerging middle class in the Far East,' said Quinn, with a trace of impatience. 'Look, it was only a matter of time before these primitives were thrown into the modern era, like their cousins all across the world. It was inevitable.'

'A lost tribe?' said Isabel.

'There are no lost tribes,' said Reeta.

'Lesson one,' said Quinn. 'If we know about them, they aren't lost. But yes, the islanders here maintain a Stone Age, or possibly Iron Age existence. They have had next to no contact with the outside world. We know nothing of their language, nothing of their rituals, we know very little at all. We don't even know what they call themselves, but this will change.'

'Inevitably,' said Reeta.

'We're planning the greatest ethnographic experiment in history,' said Quinn. 'And, because the public can be thrust into the heart of the fieldwork – with an element of luxury befitting the modern traveller – the whole thing will, eventually, pay for itself.'

'You're thinking about your bottom line?' said Reeta.

'Hardly,' said Quinn. 'Remunerative study is something most academics can only dream of. The point is, there will be no roughing it. The Japanese alone are crazy for anthropology; investors there have provided much of our financial backing.'

'But what is it?' said Isabel. 'A zoo?'

'I prefer to think of it as a kind of safari. Everyone loves a safari. We're not interfering with the tribe.'

'Not much,' said Reeta.

'There'll have to be some adjustments to their lives, of course. Unobtrusive adjustments.'

'Enlighten us,' said Reeta.

'Well, they'll need to get used to faces of different colour crossing above them on raised bridges, passing by on jeep trails . . . of course, there are a few new constructions. Hopefully, in time, once they're familiar with our presence we can lead camping trips into the jungle. Maybe guests can even live amongst them for short periods of time. We're protecting a way of life here for generations – that has to be worth something, and the Indian government agrees. If my plan works, our intrusion will be minimal, and, on their island, the natives will always be in the majority. If they start to become homogenised, it will be entirely on their own terms.'

'I don't believe anyone who has been forcibly colonised can become homogenised on their own terms,' said Reeta.

'Your teenage idealism is both tiresome and unworkable,' said

Quinn, pouring more coffee. 'Here in the real world, beyond such politically correct classroom hypotheticals, the tribe can decide and debate amongst themselves about lighter fluid, steel, penicillin. We have a romantic notion in the West that primitive societies will always prefer their traditional way of life. This is a fallacy. Maybe they want, say, modern medicine. As accidental colonists, we are so often put in unwinnable situations.'

'Accidental colonists?'

'I consider it irresponsible to pretend that these tribes cannot be helped,' said Quinn. 'But if they can, at what cost to their traditional way of life? We cannot *unlearn* of their existence, and we cannot *relose* them, despite how appropriate this may sometimes seem. This way, *my* way, over time, they can choose for themselves.'

'*Accidental colonists?*'

'I mean, what is done cannot be undone.'

'Unthinking, opportunistic progress?'

'You doubt my motives, Reeta. In time, you will see. Savage Island is a good thing, potentially a model community.'

'What does the tribe think about all this?'

'And there are so many other positive lessons my experiment will yield,' Quinn continued. 'So much information for the biologists, the linguists . . . everyone can be enriched.'

'What does the *tribe* think?' said Reeta.

Quinn coughed. 'That's been problematic.'

'In what way?'

'Well, as yet, the savages are almost entirely unapproachable.'

'Unapproachable?'

'That will change. It has to.'

'What do you mean, *unapproachable?*'

'I should say, uncooperative.'

'Uncooperative?'

'Well, in the last few years, people have had encounters with them and survived. This is positive progress.'

'*Survived?*'

'I mean, lived to tell the tale.'

'They didn't kill outsiders, and this is considered *progress?*'

'Come now. They're fiercely private, and, as you know, notorious for their extreme hostility.'

'Cannibals?' said Isabel, wide-eyed.

Quinn sat back. 'We don't know yet, not for certain. But you have to understand something. This is all part of their legend, and blood-thirsty legend is an integral element in our sales pitch.'

'To the tourists,' said Reeta.

'Yes.'

'You must be out of your mind,' she said. 'Blood-thirsty cannibals? Extreme hostility? You have busboys here carrying sidearms. Are they trained to use these weapons?'

'To paraphrase my new ops director, people want to see the big predators. When we release the stories about Savage Island, promote the myths and legends, travellers will be fascinated. This could capture the imagination of the entire world.'

'Well,' said Reeta Kapoor.

'Well,' said Edward Quinn.

'This is far more than I expected,' said Reeta.

'I've amazed you.'

'Of course you have. You're selling tickets to a very unhappy ending.'

Despite her age and short stature, the girl set a strong pace.

Charlie, torn and scratched by the jungle and panting a few steps behind, watched as her bare feet flew over fallen branches and thick, warty tree roots, which, moments later, threatened to twist his ankles and send him crashing to the ground.

He was aware of little but her urgency and the increasing incline, which further served to boil the breath in his lungs. They had lost the ocean many minutes ago, and Charlie's only geographical marker in the dark, hot forest was the odd glimpse of the great mountain; this on the rare occasion they broke into clearings thick with butterflies.

Charlie had no idea why he was being led this way, only that he believed in the girl, and felt he had no choice but to follow. This was not someone he could lose. He had lost enough people.

Soon, in what must have been the foothills, the mist descended. At first it was licking their shins, then it was like wading through cotton. It made the going treacherous. A few moments after that, visibility was slashed to only a few yards.

Charlie stopped and clasped his hand to his ear. It was an instinctive action, as he imagined some vast insect had dive-bombed his head.

He fell to his knees at the same moment, taking shallow, ragged gulps of air. When he released his hand, he felt blood running down his neck. His palm was covered and sticky and red.

'They are here,' whispered Apis, after running back to him.

Shocked, Charlie showed her his bloodied hand.

'They are here,' she said again.

Wild with fear, Charlie scanned the jungle. He could see nothing but the nearest foliage, wet with dew. Between the trees, the mist curled like smoke.

Another arrow hissed past his head. It came from nowhere, and was too fast to see. Yet he had heard it, and it was now embedded in a thick trunk. The air sang with the impact, and sap oozed where there could have been more blood.

'Run,' said Apis.

There were no more arrows fired, but Charlie had the primal knowledge that he was being pursued, even though he could hear no new sounds in the forest. This fear gave him his second wind, and, fuelled by adrenalin, both man and child were able to get up a decent speed.

They broke into another small clearing, and Charlie almost

sprinted headlong into a vertical concrete pillar, sunk deep into the ground and secured there with large rivets. It was thicker than most of the surrounding trees, and, because of the mist, it reached higher than he could see, perhaps higher than the canopy jungle.

He stared in astonishment at this unexpected manifestation of modern construction.

The girl yelped in delight when she saw it, and ran off in a new direction.

There was another pillar within twenty paces. The girl slapped it as she ran past.

The going was easier now, as a makeshift path had been cleared, presumably with professional equipment. Charlie began to feel euphoria along with his fear and confusion, at least until he heard the hiss of another arrow. This time, he did not bother to look for his attacker.

The next obstacle to emerge through the accumulating ground fog was a chain-link fence. It too stretched higher than Charlie could see. The fence was reinforced, and netted with very narrow mesh, perhaps to stop the passage of arrows.

A few hazy yards beyond, there was another concrete pillar.

What IS all this . . . ?

The girl yelped again, and ran along the edge of the fence, always touching it with her fingertips, as though it might disappear.

Eventually, she reached a gate. It was unlocked, but heavy and powerfully sprung.

They pushed together, Charlie now able to hear the shouts of his trackers. He half expected his life to end at any moment; one of those arrows on target would have the velocity to sever his spine.

The gate swung closed behind them with a heavy clang.

Miraculously, there were sliding deadbolts on the inside, three of them. Charlie rammed them home, locking both man and child within.

Within . . . what?

Charlie was about to stop and rest, he certainly needed to, but the girl tugged at his shirt, pulling him away from the fence until it melted from view in the fog.

They passed the first pillar and found a second; this one was entwined in spiral steps. They were of lightweight metal construction, some kind of aluminium alloy, and came complete with a hollow handrail that was almost cool to the touch.

The girl skipped up on light feet, her tatty dress flashing bare, scraped thighs.

Charlie was about to follow, when he heard a series of loud crashing sounds behind them. It sounded as though many men were attacking the gate.

Charlie, fighting a queasy desire to walk over and see the people who would have caused his destruction, chased the girl.

It was a three-storey climb, but easy compared to racing over the uneven forest floor.

Now it was the girl who seemed uncertain, hesitant. This was an unfamiliar world to her, shiny and non-organic, although she must have known about it before.

They were still not high enough to have cleared the fog, although it had thinned out. There was another gate and fence at the top, a thinner one. A wooden sign read: MAINTENANCE ACCESS and HIGH VOLTAGE. For additional clarity, there was a red *no people* symbol.

Beyond, Charlie could see what looked like an elevated subway platform.

Little surprised him any more – his primary concern was to move forward not back. Unfortunately, this gate was locked from the inside.

Apis was already climbing, her toes hooked through the wire.

It looked achievable, so Charlie followed, tearing clothes and skin on the barbed wire.

Once over, he rested for a moment, back to the fence, ass on the steel, dripping with sweat.

Apis was saying something again, pulling on his arm, telling him to keep moving, but Charlie badly needed to close his eyes for a moment, so he did that.

The first time Otto Lix killed someone was in Dublin, Ireland.

She was a whore in her forties, and he was aged sixteen. It was his first night in the big city, a school trip. The whore looked a little like his mother, the same mother who had masturbated him daily from the age of eight *to get the sin out*. This maternal abuse continued until he was big and strong enough to beat her away.

Lix didn't mean to kill anyone that day; he really liked the whore. He would have married her after ten minutes of listening to her kind words and lascivious promises and given her all the money he had in the world. This made it worse, later.

He was in love for the first and last time.

Her fatal mistake was laughter. She didn't even find him funny, she was only afraid. Otto Lix was just so damn ugly.

Lix was not Irish, not really, although for a long time he identified himself that way because he was red-haired and went to school in County Galway and he wanted to fit in. His grandparents were white migrants to Lesotho who had made a fortune in the diamond trade. His parents did not need to work, but they were highly religious, and they knew guilt.

As soon as Otto Lix could think for himself, he learned how to reject guilt. He became very, very good at it.

But Otto Lix was not without intelligence, or control, or discipline; as a result, his remorseless rage could be channelled into useful action. He was highly valuable to the despotic few, but never quite valuable enough to be able to afford the complete satiation of his unique appetites.

Particularly at this moment, with an entire island at his mercy.

Now, he meant to kill Edward Quinn's savage because he could, and because he would never be culpable, and because he was irritated with Quinn, and because he *really* hated the lack of fear and respect in the eyes of the savage, and because the savage was beautiful and strong and interesting, and because, ultimately, Lix would feel better that day for causing another person agony.

He would destroy the savage with his bare hands, take him apart piece by piece; it was by far the best way.

But all was not as it should have been in the basement storeroom.

The cell was empty. The cell door yawned. The savage had gone.

Otto Lix took a moment to consider.

He had constructed the cell himself. He had secured the room. This was no accident. Someone had allowed the savage to . . . *escape*.

Tam was free, running up a steep, zigzagging jungle path.

There was smooth pale brick underfoot, brushed of leaves, and metal handrails for his hips to bounce off at sharp turns; he had never seen a trail like this before.

It was his world, his island, with all the sounds and smells he knew. Yet at the same time, everything looked so strange. Twice, Tam passed banks of poorly camouflaged surveillance technology, cameras swivelling as he ran by.

He stopped to catch his breath. There was a brightly painted sign written in a jaunty font:

Only a little further!
Scenic Observation Point and Drinking Water: 250m ahead.

Tam understand none of it.

Breaking out into the advertised clearing, he gasped in amazement, but not at the beauty of the view. It had become clear from the position of the sun and the patchwork of ocean colours far below that he had somehow been taken to the south-western tip of the island.

Tam was sceptical about the powers of El, the god responsible for the welfare of the tribe, but, like every other living islander, he had never laid eyes on this, the other side of the mountain. Here was His sacred face, where He bade farewell to the sun each day, and where, legend had it, He poured His molten rage.

Superstition aside, there were other good reasons why the tribe never ventured so far west. One was the basic geography of the narrow cone, which rose very steeply from the sea and was considered impassible by land. Another was that their shallow boats were unsuitable for navigating the heavy seas that crashed against the jagged, volcanic outcrops of the bay.

Further legend had it that, in his fury at being trespassed upon, El could turn a man to dirt, rip the womb from his wife and poison his animals for generations.

Legend said many things, but none worse than the knowledge that Tam now had about the Owbs, and what they were capable of. He had to tell the tribe.

Practically, Tam had three choices.

He could dive into the sea and attempt to swim around the treacherous headland; he could try to find how the Owbs had broken through to the main part of the island and use their route himself; or, he could try to climb over the peak of El and look into the face of God.

Tam would not attempt the swim. Anyone in the water would be highly visible from the main building, and he knew the Owbs had advanced weapons. Besides, the sea could smash him to death.

How the Owbs accessed the main part of the island was a mystery, but their route would be cleverly concealed, as they had evidently been crossing over for some time. Similarly, by snooping around the facility, he was far more likely to encounter the enemy. Tam had no qualms about killing an Owb, not any more, but no tribesperson threw themselves in front of a magical weapon without very good reason, and there were plenty around.

So he decided to climb. Tam was already halfway up the mountain, and could see the white disc of the main building jutting out far below. He jumped off the carefully manicured path and disappeared into the jungle with scarcely a rustle. Going was instantly difficult and steep, but there were roots and branches to cling onto, and he became encouraged when he encountered no more Owb constructions or pathways and the foliage thinned out to reveal the distance he had travelled.

Soon, the ground became looser and drier and the greenery that had scratched at his arms was replaced by shifting mists. The air cooled, although the ground underfoot became warmer. There were clumps of plants he had never seen before, and clutches of burnt-out trees.

After three hours, Tam achieved the summit.

Chest heaving, he put his back to a blackened stump and stared down into the largest of three crater-lakes that had formed in the caldera of the volcano.

His eyes widened as he took in this very alien world.

The lake had a circumference of a mile or so, and the water was paint-pot green. Occasionally, a vast bubble broke the surface and formed ripples. The smell was heady and sulphurous, and sections of the crater walls were smoking. Quartz sand and shiny rocks of black obsidian gave the land a synthetic, manufactured quality.

It should have been a revelatory, life-changing experience; to look into the face of El was to guarantee his place in tribal history for decades to come. But Tam knew that unless he moved now, the tribe was certainly finished. There would be no more stories, no more history; even no more El, at least as they knew Him.

Tam steeled himself to make his way around the edge of the

crater and attempt to descend the eastern flank. It was an almost vertical descent, and possibly fatal.

Battling exhaustion, he righted himself with support from a big white structure.

The Owbs had made it up here before him. They had erected a telecommunications dish, twice Tam's height. Tam squinted at it long and hard, trying to decipher the meaning.

It seemed to point towards the sky.

Thein Suu Aye awoke with the howls of some forgotten nightmare ringing in his ears.

The sun had risen hours ago and he was covered in ants – quickly brushed away – but it was cool in the shade. He was tempted to turn over and sleep off his hangover, but there were more pressing concerns.

When he stood up to take a piss, he was reminded of the snub-nosed Taurus Model 85 tucked into the waistband of his shorts and digging into his full bladder. The gun was used and worn but in working condition, bought from a market trader who claimed he had got it from a retired Singaporean police officer. Thein could not have cared less where the weapon came from; it gave him a physical assurance to match his spiritual confidence.

He was considering calling down to the American to see what the idiot had brought along for breakfast, when his keen eye saw past his own stream of dribbling gold to something glittering in the undergrowth that was neither flora nor fauna.

Thein zipped up his shorts and moved inland for a closer look.

Far enough into the jungle to lose sight, if not sound, of the sea, was a clearing. In the clearing, arranged in a circle, were twelve ancient wooden chests.

Thein Suu Aye, standing outside a boundary of sunlight, was looking at the remaining treasure of from the *São Francisco Xavier*, although he could not have possibly known it. Blinking, Thein stepped forward, reaching out to the chest nearest to him and running his fingertips over the inscription that had been cast into the gold bindings.

The quality of the metal was high, and had scarcely oxidised. The indentations had picked up a little dirt, but some lettering was still legible:

Com a grande gloria de Deus a nossa nação

The other eleven chests boasted the same writing.

The wood was rotted with repeated wettings, but was fairly solid, and holding. In Thein's estimation, this bode very well for the quality of the contents.

He had expected to tussle with the locks, but was amazed to discover that they all came loose from their bindings, and the lids either rocked open or fell off with a firm nudge from his boot.

The contents of the first two boxes were somewhat anticlimactic: just clumps of mud and some soggy, curious smelling resin, which Thein assumed might once have been spices of some kind.

The third was heady with the smell of rotten organic material, maybe silk or calico, and the contents looked like wet black leaves.

The fourth contained chunks of amber.

The fifth, pearls, speckled with dirt.

The sixth, dull silver coins.

The seventh, gold.

Some of it had been fashioned into coins, some into jewellery, some into small statuary.

Gold.

The remaining chests did not disappoint either. All held precious stones of different cuts and colours, damp and entwined in slim weeds that had grown right through the wooden bases and curled around the forgotten fortune in their blind quest for sunlight.

Was it real? Could it be?

Thein thought so. He was no metallurgist or mineralogist, but he had spent a lifetime spotting fakery, from Swiss watches to designer handbags, and his crooked instinct was rarely wrong.

The savages must know about it. Why was it left here?

Because they have no USE for it.

But where did it come from?

Thein threw his head back and laughed. None of this was his problem. His problem was going to be getting it all back to the boat.

Reeta, Isabel and Quinn made their way down a low-lit interior corridor, occasionally pausing at velvet-roped alcoves to view pieces from Quinn's art collection. It was not lost on Reeta that Quinn had chosen to display subjects inspired by Shakespeare's *The Tempest*, including contributions from Joseph Noel Paton, Henry Fuseli and the Pre-Raphaelite style *Ferdinand Lured by Ariel* by John Everett Millais.

They stopped for long moments before a William Hogarth, Caliban leering at Miranda.

'Is this an original?' said Isabel.

Quinn nodded, his eyes bright. 'If Hogarth had been alive today, he would have enjoyed at least one more patron.'

'I think you're patronising enough people already,' said Reeta.

'So easy to throw rocks from the sidelines,' said Quinn. 'You and I are in agreement that, without intervention, these natives will be wiped out by the natural course of history. It isn't enough to say there's a problem and then do nothing. Yet this is all you seem capable of.'

'I believe they will be wiped out *with* intervention.'

'You don't strike me as a pessimist, Reeta. Shall we walk a little further?'

'The savages run off or kill anyone who lands on their island,' said Reeta. 'What is it about this side of the mountain?'

'I don't know.'

'They never come over here?'

'Never,' said Quinn. 'The conclusion was drawn after months of observation, physical and satellite. It left us with limited space to build, but enough to introduce phase one; all of our structural ambitions are in keeping with the low-key presence we want to maintain, and mostly on reclaimed land.'

'This is your idea of low key? You have the USS Enterprise poking out of the hillside.'

'Reclaimed materials, carbon offset; what more do you want?'

'How did you do it?'

'I'm a showman,' said Quinn. 'You'd leave me a few rabbits to pull from hats.'

They reached the end of the corridor and a set of automatic doors. An elevator was revealed. Quinn pushed an unmarked button, and they began to descend.

'Tell me about the YM Fortune II,' said Reeta.

Quinn was facing front, watching the LED. Instead of numbers, pictorials slid by: a cinema screen, a knife and fork, a bed. 'Why don't you tell me?' he said.

'Your cargo ship, stranded on a reef on these shores. Your ship, your cargo, your island. Timber, steel, electronics. Tons of it. We're standing in your shipwreck.'

'It was the fastest way to bypass all kinds of regulation,' said Quinn. 'Cheaper, too.'

'You wrecked your own boat?'

'Don't be naive, Reeta. You think the world cares about the Okojuwoi? You think the financial markets are watching? Yes, I crashed the YM Fortune, and I wrote off millions. It was by far the easiest way to get materials onto the island.'

The elevator doors opened onto another interior corridor, perfectly straight. This one was dressed in a kind of industrial chic, with gleaming walls of black glass and a metallic floor. It was considerably warmer down here, and they could feel a breeze from somewhere, gentle but humid.

'People died in your write-off,' said Reeta.

'Who died?' said Quinn, walking. His footsteps sounded hollow on the walkway.

'Those crew who weren't complicit.'

'There were deaths,' said Quinn. 'I'm not going to deny it. This island is lethal. You run a risk by crashing a manned boat into it. Why the authorities never mounted a rescue, I don't know.'

'The authorities are in your pocket.'

'I would have been glad to support any rescue effort. My donations to local organisations are only one small part of my charitable contribution to this region.'

'I read the press releases,' said Reeta. 'Some claim survivors, some not. Your own companies talked about deaths, then issued a retraction.'

'You really haven't thought this through,' said Quinn. 'You think the Western media cares about missing Filipinos? You have any idea how many ferry disasters there are in that country? I was heartbroken at the loss of life, and I personally compensated the families. Saying that, despite my best efforts, even I can't tell you exactly how many employees were lost.'

'Did you get the Indian military on your side as well?'

'I wish. Ask Otto Lix, my right-hand man. He liaised with the local military.'

'What about the blood on your ship? Did you send someone in to clean that up as well?'

'Blood? What are you talking about?'

'The massacre.'

'Where are you getting this information?'

'The diary of Leona Bride. Someone sent it to me.'

'I don't know that name.'

Reeta sighed. 'I have no source I can prove.'

'Deaths by misadventure,' said Quinn. 'No blood on my boats, no blood on my hands. Not to change the subject, ladies, but we're here.'

Still windowless, the corridor had opened out into a large, futuristic space lit by blue neon. One wall remained unfinished, a bare rock face, and the other contained maps and schematics in sunken glass cabinets, boasting of how the construction had been achieved.

In the centre were two highly polished observation carriages over a solitary narrow track, bookended by smaller, unfamiliar engine-type vehicles whose bizarre internal mechanisms were on display. The train was flush with the platform. Tunnels at either end stretched into darkness.

'You've built an underground railway,' said Isabel.

'No,' said Quinn, unable to disguise his delight. 'I've built the world's only working gyroscopic monorail.'

Reeta and Isabel approached the front engine and peered into the translucent casing.

Contained within, like some steampunk fantasy, were two enormous vertical gyroscopes, mounted on the horizontal axis. They were constructed from brass, and gleamed in the light.

'Each weighs more than half a ton,' said Quinn. 'I designed them myself. The back engine is the same. They patented a prototype idea in England in the early nineteenth century, but I managed to make it a reality.'

'Now this,' said Reeta, 'is beautiful.'

'Each spins in the opposite direction to the other at three thousand rpm,' said Quinn. 'These tunnels pass through the mountain for a little under a mile before emerging onto an elevated rail that runs through the park. Thirty feet up in the air, the train looks terrifying, like thumbtacks in motion along the edge of a knife.'

'I can imagine,' said Reeta.

'The wheels are double flanged, but even so, it can't slip off, because of precession damping and the principles of angular momentum. There's some deep mathematics involved, Newton's third law and all that, but she's quite, quite safe.'

'But without the torque? Wouldn't it just topple?'

'It would, but the carriages lock securely into the station plat-forms. Outside of the stations – of which there are two so far – the gyros will always be spinning. It can stay upright even with a full compliment of passengers standing one side of the carriage. There's a gasoline-powered turbine that also runs the throttle, lighting and so forth. She's my pride and joy.'

'What if the engine fails?' said Reeta.

'There's a smaller back-up,' said Quinn.

'What if *that* fails?'

'It won't,' said Quinn.

'But what if it does?'

'It won't,' said Quinn, thinly.

'How fast can it go?' said Isabel, running her hand over the smooth finish.

'Forty mph on the flat. And it can take curves at a thirty-five-degree radius; it banks like an aircraft. Please, take a look inside. The train was designed so that passengers would have the best view of the gyros.'

Quinn strode away to unlock a Perspex-walled console station. He pushed some buttons and the carriage doors sighed open. Reeta and Isabel peered inside. The interior smelled of polish and fresh paint.

There was a crackle from a speaker somewhere. 'Any more ques-tions?' said Quinn. 'I have a microphone and headset here, the passengers can always be in communication.'

'I suppose it runs in a loop?' said Reeta. 'Can the track bisect, or—'

The doors hissed closed.

'Hey!' said Reeta, spinning around. Quinn was over in his booth, pushing buttons.

'Don't worry,' she heard him saying over the speaker. 'Quite, quite safe . . .'

'Look!' said Isabel.

Reeta turned again. The massive gyroscopes had begun to whirl, faster and faster until they became two blurry globes. Reeta and Isabel hammered on the glass doors, but they were locked solid.

Quinn, safe on the platform, gave them a smile.

'Let me show you the rest of my island,' he said, as the train began to move.

It *was* an overhead subway station of some kind.

Charlie Cortez, ragged and bloody and light-headed from his adrenalin come-down, watched the remaining mist as it sank through the platform and drained slowly into the spaces on either side of the track. High above, the sun shone, and he licked the dried sweat from his cracked lips.

The station was new and futuristic in design, but had already taken on a somewhat abandoned air; it seemed unlikely to Charlie that any train had ever passed through here. Under a wide archway marked EXIT, there were no stairs, simply a drop into the foggy ether, and the computerised terminal he found inside a small, unlocked control room was damp and powerless, save for a single blinking red light. There appeared to be no communication system.

Apis was hopping impatiently at the northern end of the platform, where the thin track – it was a little wider than a gymnastic balance beam – stretched into the distance in a dead straight line.

When she saw him watching her, she jumped from the platform onto the track on her bare, nimble feet, even though the drop between the two was potentially fatal. Charlie tried to shout, but fear trapped the breath in his throat, and he made a noise between a cough and a gargle.

He ran over to save her, but she seemed quite comfortable, if not confused by his concern.

'You want me to go *this* way?' Charlie said, gesturing at the track. 'We'll break our necks.'

Apis shrugged, and bounced back onto the platform.

Without warning, she jumped back, and Charlie reached out to stop her. He became unbalanced, and found himself with one foot on the track and one on the platform, the chasm between his legs.

'Mother *fuck*,' said Charlie.

But Apis was probably correct. Whatever was at the end of this track, it was likely to be civilisation of some sort. And there were an unknown number of savages waiting should they try to retrace their steps.

Will it be so difficult?

It was now or never. The timing was perfect because mist had pooled beneath the track, was thick as cotton. There were men down there with arrows who would kill him, but if Charlie could not see them, they could not see him.

It would be like walking a tightrope over shark-infested water.

Apis gestured that he should go first.

Charlie did a practice walk on the beam within the confines of the platform. It was an awful sensation, but made easier by the fact that the ground was not visible. As long as his knees and ankles were pressed together, he could put his feet side by side with only a little overhang.

'*Fuck*,' he said again.

Imagine there isn't a thirty-foot drop. Imagine there aren't men down there who want to murder you. If it was a fallen log over a brook, you'd be skipping over it.

Charlie was thirty feet out when the first arrow sailed past him. It made no sound, and was far enough away to suggest that he was right – they could not see him.

But they can hear me. And they are waiting.

He stopped, but there was no noise from the ground. Even the birds seemed to have frozen in their chorus.

Waiting was bad. It made him think.

Charlie wobbled.

The second arrow was further away, but this time he heard the twang of the bow, and the weight of his expectation caused panic. He dropped to his knee and then his stomach, knocking the wind from his belly and squeezing the track like a desperate lover.

Seconds passed, feeling like minutes.

There were no more arrows. But there was something else.

The track was beginning to hum.

The monorail careened through the dark tunnel, Reeta and Isabel clinging to the overhead leather straps. The interior had been decorated like a San Francisco streetcar, and seemed to vibrate just as much. What was it that Quinn had said about a top speed?

Forty mph on the flat.

Reeta's ears were popping; they were definitely on a downhill slope.

'Let me give you some more statistics about my island,' said Quinn's voice over the speaker. 'Eight of my workforce disappeared in the park during the construction of this monorail, even though, currently, it passes nowhere near land that the tribe use with any regularity. I lost another five men attempting to make peaceable contact with the savages. They don't seem to appreciate that I'm trying to *help* them, and as long as they cut down on the murder, they will be left in peace. Even with all the funds at my disposal, I'm now having trouble finding people prepared to work for me.'

'He's insane,' Reeta said to Isabel.

'You can push the intercom if you want to reply,' said Quinn. 'Just hold down the button.'

'You're admitting you were *wrong*,' Reeta shouted. 'People are *dying*. Stop this contraption.'

'I'm not wrong,' said Quinn. 'And I never give up. See, I'm appointing you, Dr Reeta Kapoor, as my new tribal liaison.'

Reeta jammed down the button as if trying to force her finger through the wall.

'Forget it,' she yelled. 'You're out of your *mind*.'

'See, you don't appear to have a choice,' said Quinn. 'The gyro will stop at Station Two, out in the park. This is about three miles from the main tribal settlement. It'll go no further, and won't return without my command. If you want to live, you're going to have to make peace with some rather difficult people.'

'You wouldn't dare,' said Reeta. 'If I disappear – if you throw us to the Islanders – you'll get your whole operation shut down. And if I live through this, I'll make it my life's work to shut *you* down.'

'*Focus*, Reeta. You have greater concerns at this moment. Remember, you were once the world's foremost expert on these people.'

'Savage Island? I know *next to nothing*.'

'Which is a tiny fraction more than anyone else. Did you think I would waste this opportunity to use an anthropologist of your pedigree? Now get to work.'

'Fuck you, Quinn.'

'If I were you, I'd be considering more practical matters. There's a combination safe in a long overhead compartment in the second carriage. The code is triple-eight triple-seven one. Inside you'll find a pump-action shotgun. There are five loaded rounds.'

'Five?'

'I wanted to give you enough ammo to make a point, but I can't have you damaging too many of the exhibits. Good luck.'

The speaker crackled into silence.

'Quinn!' Reeta shouted. 'Quinn!'

There was nothing more.

At that moment, the train shot out of the tunnel, and Reeta had the brief, stomach-lurching sensation of flight.

She squinted in the brightness of the midday sun, trying to get her bearings. They had emerged about a third of the way up a sheer side of the great mountain, and the elevated monorail track was running high above the jungle on pylon-like stilts.

The train was descending, fast.

The two women could see the ocean, white crests of waves breaking over the reef. The sky was clear, but patches of ground fog masked the greenery like mutant gauze.

Keeping level with the carriages was a beautiful Andaman Serpent-eagle, his blue speckled plumage shining in the sunlight. One bright eye stared into their precarious vehicle with the acute curiosity of a hungry predator.

'What did Quinn say about cornering?' said Isabel.

'What?'

Isabel pointed ahead, over the wildly spinning gyroscopes. There was a curve in the beam-like track that would have been better suited to a roller-coaster.

'Hold on,' said Reeta.

The car leaned with the force of the turn, but righted itself immediately.

They were below the line of trees now and levelling off, though it was hard to gauge their elevation due to the ground fog. Great flocks of multicoloured birds took off and resettled on branches as they passed, and Reeta had the impression that the train was slowing.

They rounded another corner to enter a long straight stretch, and Isabel screamed.

Maybe sixty yards away, there was a man on the track, flat on his belly, clinging on as though his life depended on it.

Behind him, balancing carefully on bare feet, stood a little white girl.

They were all going to die.

Tam, battered, bruised and on the point of complete exhaustion, was amazed to find his village empty. He was prepared for anything, but not for silence. Where were the children?

Everyone must be in hiding.

Did you really expect your world to look the same?

In a time of crisis, it was accepted that the women and children would flee into the jungle, and the men would congregate for battle. But crisis of that severity was very unusual. Tam hadn't known anything like it since the tsunami, or since . . .

Mo and Sew and Apis.

And, a few seasons later, the coming of Sebastian Kallmus and the news about Jesus Christ.

Tam's realisation was more crushing than any bodily pain.

Udumi had been right. Udumi had been right all along. Admittedly, there was no all-powerful El, no vengeful mountain-god, but that was unimportant, a minor detail.

Important is that the Owbs mean to destroy us all, and my brother knew it.

The truth had been masked by superstition and ritual, but it was still the truth.

Tam staggered towards his father's hut, the largest in the village, which also doubled as the meeting place of the tribal leaders.

Tears sprang to his eyes when he saw Udumi. His brother threw back the wooden door and jumped down from the raised floor, concern and fear in his face.

My brother. What happened?

The sound of his voice gave Tam great comfort.

You were correct, Udumi. I have been a fool.

Do not speak now, Tam. Save your strength.

Can you forgive me?

Udumi said nothing, but dug his shoulder into Tam's belly and carried him bodily into the hut.

Tam felt relief, and love.

Perhaps it will not be too late.

The hut was cool and dark. Tam was laid before Sool, his

ailing father, who wore his ceremonial bones. The Qesem was absent, but the room was filled with the other elders, all silent.

Where were the warriors?

Sool said: *What news?*

Tam cleared his throat and raised his head to speak. They had to be told. Even if it meant admitting he was wrong.

At the same moment, Udumi reached to his back, where the sacred arrow had been stored in his belt. He stabbed it into Tam's eye.

Tam screamed.

Udumi's grip was slippery around the shaft, and Tam went into spasms.

The arrowhead came back-up with Tam's eyeball and optic nerve. Udumi secured his brother's head with one powerful hand to ensure that the second blow would be fatal.

Brain pierced, Tam expelled his final breath.

There was silence, save for the sound of blood dripping through the floorboards.

Gory from murder, Udumi looked to his father, then to the elders. All watched in horror.

It was not the reaction that Udumi had expected.

The competition is over, he said.

Even his white teeth were splattered.

Behold, your next Chief.

Charlie leapt to his feet, his balance now instinctive.

Behind him, the girl had almost reached the platform again.

He turned once more to see the approaching vehicle. It looked like some kind of bulky bus, but seemed to be balancing on one wheel.

Impossible.

Impossible, but happening.

He wasted seconds staring, before measuring distance.

You'll never make it.

Charlie turned and ran back towards the station, arms windmilling. The savages were still masked by the fog below, but they could hear the monorail too.

There was a sudden hail of arrows.

Charlie barely noticed.

He covered in seconds what had previously taken him minutes, and at the last moment leapt for safety, the track vibrating under his feet. He crashed and rolled onto unforgiving metal, exhilarated to have landed on something solid.

He spun over to his front to watch the bizarre train enter the station, the ridges on the sides locking into the platform and dragging it to a halting stop.

Doors slid opened to reveal a muscular Indian woman in boots, jeans and T-shirt, and a tall, willowy blonde who might have been dressed for a day at the beach. Both looked as shaken as he did, but it was the Indian woman who stepped down and spoke first.

'Who the hell are you?' said Reeta Kapoor.

'I'm Dr Charlie Cortez,' Charlie said, into the floor.

Otto Lix found Kelly Maelzel alone on the roof of the saucer, swimming underwater in the circular swimming pool. She stopped once his giant shadow crossed the pool, and spat water when she surfaced. It landed just short of his size-18 shoes.

'Are you here to rub oil on my back?'

'You let the savage escape,' said Lix. It wasn't a question.

'I don't know what you're talking about.'

'You let him out the cage. You let him out the room. You let him out of the building. He's gone.'

'Wait one moment,' said Kelly.

She pulled herself from the pool and walked towards a lounger and her towel. She swigged bottled water while Lix leered at her round backside and clingy swimsuit.

'Quinn must have finally decided to do the right thing,' Kelly said. 'Because it wasn't me.'

'Of course it was you,' said Lix.

'I didn't let him out,' said Kelly. 'Cross my heart.'

'Bullshit,' said Lix.

'But tell me,' said Kelly, squeezing her wet hair, 'even if I *had* let the native escape, what *fucking business* would it be of yours?'

Otto Lix hated the sunlight. He hated the way it burned his skin and pierced his eyes. He was a creature of the night, and of the darkness. Although he had lived most of his life in the tropics, heat made him crazy, and it was particularly unbearable up here.

'Don't come any closer to me,' Kelly said to him. 'Don't you bloody *dare*.'

Lix grinned at the challenge, and then lunged.

Kelly dropped the towel she was holding in her right hand and fired the Taser she had picked up and concealed. She was aiming for his heart.

Lix wasn't fast enough to dodge, but he did bring up his left hand.

The cartridge embedded itself in his palm. He shuddered and twitched, but remained upright, and, after a moment, even began to laugh through the excruciating pain.

He opened his fingers to show her.

Kelly backed away in amazement.

'What the bloody hell *are* you . . .?'

Lix tore his hand away, tugging at the wires and sending the gun and cartridge splashing into the pool.

He lunged again, but Kelly managed to duck the huge hands and drop between his legs. She brought up her whole forearm into his testicles, producing a satisfying yelp.

She tried to back away to strike again, but he caught her with one lucky swipe, catching her on the temple and sending her sprawling.

Backing towards to the lounger, Kelly watched again as his vast head blocked out the sun. Lix was panting, and the sweat poured off him.

Somehow, I need to get him off his feet.

Lix felt his blood boil. He threw himself towards her, but his timing was telegraphed, and Kelly rolled out of the way.

The lounger splintered and cracked with the impact of his shoulder, and Kelly was up at once, kicking and stomping at his face. She made little headway; her feet were bare, and the man seemed to be made of iron. When Lix turned over, she jammed her heel into his Adam's apple with as much force as she could, and he closed his eyes.

Khaaahh . . .

But before she could move away, Lix had his fingers wrapped around her ankle, and he lifted her bodily into the air. Kelly flailed and fell, her slippery hands scarcely breaking the fall.

Her face slapped hard into the concrete, knocking her silly.

Lix was up again. He bunched his hands into Kelly's hair, and lifted her that way. He spun her, like a hammer-thrower, and flung her body into the small parrot aviary, wrecking it, and causing the birds to fly shrieking into the air.

Kelly coughed blood and lost consciousness.

The idea suited him, so he strode over and grabbed her by the hair again, this time with one hand, twisting his arm upwards for maximum grip.

He dragged Kelly's body towards the edge of the roof like a wet sack. The drop would be fatal, a quarter-mile fall onto jagged rocks and turbulent sea.

Lix was still holding her that way when he slapped her awake. Kelly couldn't tilt her neck to see, but she pedalled air, knowing exactly where she was.

'I never liked you,' she said to Lix, and spat in his face.

Otto Lix looked curious for a moment, almost sympathetic. His fat pink tongue poked out to taste her bloody saliva.

Then he opened his hand and dropped her over the edge.

Now it was Udumi who had to run.

Bas, his young wife, who had been present at the time of Tam's murder, ran with him. Although newly pregnant, she was lean and strong and almost capable of keeping stride. Udumi feared for reprisals against his family, such was the outcry over his cold-blooded murder of his brother.

This was not how it was supposed to be. Had he not won the competition fairly?

No one in the ceremonial hut had wanted to see further death at that moment, so a general confusion had reigned, allowing Udumi and Bas to make their escape. Perhaps this was deliberate. Even as they left, there had been cries of *kill him* and *vengeance* – predominantly from those loyal to Tam – but it was clear that Sool was uncertain, or perhaps it was only that he had been over-whelmed by grief and surprise.

Udumi and his wife had been pursued, but without real heart, and no arrows had been fired.

This was encouraging. It proved the tribe was without capable direction, and the warriors were scattered due to Apis and the appearance of the strange black-skinned Owb.

Someone would have to claim the chiefdom.

Udumi made for the Biota, an area of the island he knew well, and a place where he could lose even the tribe's best trackers. His intention was to wait out the crisis – and, if necessary, the shortening days of his father – until he could return and claim his rightful leadership.

With Tam dead, the title was his, especially if there was to be a violent war against the Owbs; he would simply need The Qesem to reassure the elders. His battle now was with time.

Emerging from the jungle onto the shore, the Chief-in-waiting was surprised to see a small boat sitting very low in the water. It was a few feet out, anchored, and of basic Owb design.

Udumi approached carefully, leaving his wife among the shadows of the shoreline. Peering into the hull, he could see it had been loaded with loose treasure.

Who . . . ?

Further down the beach, Thein Suu Aye emerged from the jungle on his twentieth trip from the clearing, his torn, folded shirt stuffed with more riches.

The two men saw each other at the same time.

'I think I can get us out of here,' said Reeta.

'They are coming,' said Apis.

The girl did not sound afraid, or even concerned; it was just a statement of fact.

'Can you stop her from saying that?' Reeta said to Charlie.

Charlie shook his head. The girl's pronouncements might have been unnerving, especially with her wide eyes and blank face, but only because she was right.

The metal fence downstairs was not going to keep the warriors out of the station for ever. Whether the fence was eventually broken down or scaled, the band of tribesmen that had pursued Charlie sounded as though their numbers had swollen to over a dozen, at least based on all the hollers and shouts.

Reeta and Charlie had smashed open the see-through casing to the front engine using a loose metal bench on the platform, and Reeta had been studying the device for five minutes.

'I think we can start the gyroscopes,' said Reeta. 'There's a fail-safe mechanism, and even if Quinn is controlling the train from his control room, I think he'll be automatically overridden because the integrity of the train is crucial. His back-up engine still has electrical power.'

'So what are we waiting for?' said Isabel.

Reeta swallowed. 'Well, we'll need to release the train from the platform.'

'What?'

'The track here is on a slight downhill slope, so we will have a little kinetic energy to play with. As soon as the train begins to move, the back-up should kick in. The gyros will come up to speed, and we'll also get more forward momentum. Despite appearances, this train was designed so it would never topple.'

'What if the back-up engine doesn't start?' said Charlie.

'It will,' said Reeta. 'Quinn was quite clear.'

'What if it doesn't?'

'The train will fall off the track,' said Reeta.

'I see,' said Charlie. 'And I suppose we only get one chance to test this theory?'

'Yes,' said Reeta.

'Wait,' said Isabel. 'Why?'

'Because the train will be moving,' said Reeta. 'We'll all need to be inside it.'

'*Scheiße*,' said Isabel. 'What about the shotgun? Can we not stand and fight?'

'Five rounds,' said Reeta.

'There's a hoard of savages down there,' Charlie said sourly. 'If we manage to shoot five of them, do you think the rest will get the message?'

'Then what do we do?' said Isabel.

'Okay,' said Reeta. 'There must be some way to release the train from the platform, but I'm guessing that if we manage it, the doors will probably close.'

'Why?'

'Well, Quinn must have built in *some* safety features.'

'Let's use the bench,' said Charlie.

He and Isabel busied themselves jamming open the door to the front carriage as Reeta inspected the front and the back of the train, at one point swinging down onto the track for a better look.

There was a loud clatter from somewhere on the ground, and an excited yell from the warriors.

'They are coming,' Apis said again.

'There's a brake run,' said Reeta. 'But the breaks are magnetic. There are retractable fins in the platforms. Get on board, I'm going to have another look in the control room.'

'Wait,' said Charlie. 'I know what to do, I've been in there before.'

Reeta opened her mouth to say something, but Charlie had already turned his back. Reeta watched him while Isabel helped Apis on board.

Inside the control room, parts of the terminal were now lit up and blinking.

There was a red button beneath a protective plastic covering. A small white plaque boasted the following information in red letters: EMERGENCY RELEASE/MANUAL: ENG. WITH 344/K SWITCH

'Here goes nothing,' Charlie said, pushing with one greasy thumb.

Through the glass pane of the booth, the monorail remained motionless.

He pushed again, and again.

But when he next looked up, Reeta and Isabel were frantically gesturing.

Charlie ran outside to see the train start to slip from the platform. Were the gyroscopes turning? If not, it would be suicide to jump on board.

Apis . . .

If he had been in any doubt, the decision was soon made for him.

Naked warriors poured onto the far end of the platform. They showed no confusion at their surroundings, and screamed when they saw him. For the second time that day Charlie was forced to take a running dive, leaping over the bench that had wedged open the door, and crashing into the carriage. He had scarcely landed before spinning over to kick the bench out.

The first arrows were hitting the rear engine car. But the gyros were spinning.

The gyros are spinning.

'Okay,' said Reeta as the train picked up speed. 'We're okay.'

'What the hell are you doing?' said Edward Quinn over the speakers, making them all jump.

Reeta was up, jamming down the button to talk.

'You're in for it now, Quinn. We're coming back, and you'd better be ready for a fight.'

'You're not coming back,' said Quinn. He didn't sounded annoyed, he sounded . . . *scared?*

'You'd use this deathtrap to kill us?' she said. 'You don't have the balls.'

'You're killing yourself,' said Quinn. 'There's nothing I can do about it.'

Reeta shrugged. She looked at Charlie, then Isabel, then Apis. All faces were blank.

She pushed the button again. 'What are you talking about, you fucking *lunatic?*'

'The loop isn't closed,' said Quinn. 'The track isn't finished yet.'

'I know you,' Thein shouted over the buzz of the outboard motor. 'I've seen you before.'

He was referring to the white birthmark on the tribesman's forehead.

Udumi said nothing, not understanding the words. What he did understand, perhaps instinctively, or perhaps because he had seen such weapons before, was the gun in Thein's right hand.

It was pointing into his face.

'I'm going to kill you now,' Thein Suu Aye said. He was knee-deep in the shallows, preparing to drop the propeller into the water and make his escape.

There was a scream from the jungle, and Udumi's wife, previously unseen by Thein, stumbled forwards onto the wide belt of sand. There was an arrow sticking out of her left calf.

The warriors are here.

Udumi took advantage of the distraction, first knocking the gun from Thein's hand, and then smashing his fist into his face.

Thein fell backwards and inhaled brine.

Large shadows appeared between the trees. Arrows splashed around them, the air vibrating. The tribe meant to kill Udumi after all.

The tribesman threw his fainting wife into the boat and jumped in after her.

Thein Suu Aye attempted to crawl back onto the gem-littered beach, but immediately took an arrow into his shoulder. His gun was lost to the sea. With remarkable presence of mind, he grabbed the anchor chain just as Udumi dropped the spinning propeller.

It churned water, and they were away.

'I can't stop it,' said Charlie. 'There's no way to stop it!'

The end of the track was in sight, there was one more corner to take.

The monorail was above the jungle again, but barely, pointing back at the mountain. There was no mist in this part of the island, so they had an excellent view of their fate.

'Are there no brakes?' Isabel yelled. 'An emergency stop?'

No one answered this; there had been both a hunt and a panicked brainstorm, all in vain.

They were out of options.

Now on a gentle incline, the back-up engine was propelling them towards doom at a scant 10 mph.

'Hold on to something,' said Reeta. 'And get in the middle of the train, away from the gyroscopes. They spin like helicopter rotors, and if they break apart in the fall . . .'

Charlie looked down at Apis as the train began to tilt.

She had taken his big hand in her little one. She squeezed him, as if to say *don't worry*.

When the front of the train fell, the four passengers fell forwards helplessly, crowding *towards* the lethal gyroscopes, and they shared the brief experience of weightlessness.

Branches rushed towards them, shattering glass and tearing at the walls, sunlight splashing around the wrecked carriage.

There were screams, a series of impacts, and then there was darkness.

'This is the endgame, Otto. I saw it all.'

Otto Lix turned back from the precipice to meet Edward Quinn.

'You're finished,' said Quinn.

Kelly Maelzel had fallen to her death like a ragdoll. Sadly for Lix, the wind had rapidly pushed her into the cliff, so he had been unable to witness the precise moment of her destruction.

This was disappointing, but he could make amends now.

Professor Quinn had emerged from the cliffside path at the other side of the saucer. He was aiming a Pneu-Dart CO_2-powered rifle – a tranquilliser gun. Lix knew how effective it could be; he had fired it often enough at live targets.

Even if Otto Lix was capable of negotiation, there was nothing more to say. He was guilty, and he was in the line of fire.

Otto Lix took the first ballistic syringe in his neck, barely missing the carotid artery. He staggered backwards, eyes rolling up in his head. Inches from the edge, he suddenly fell forward onto both knees.

The second dart hit Lix in the heart, red tailpiece fluttering.

Quinn lowered his weapon. '*Die now*,' he whispered.

Slowly, unbelievably, Lix raised a hand. He pulled out one dart, then the other. A little blood stained his white suit, but otherwise he seemed fine.

'Your girlfriend drained out the sedative,' Lix said slowly.

'She . . .'

'Kelly was a real *humanitarian*.'

Quinn blinked in disbelief as Otto Lix got back to his feet.

'See, you can fire empty needles at me all day, but it'll only make me angrier.'

Edward Quinn dropped the rifle and turned to run.

'Now, *this* is the endgame,' said Lix, walking forward.

A half-mile from Savage Island's western shore, well inside the reef, and it was still shallow enough to stand up.

Far from arrow-range, Udumi raised the outboard motor, and the boat drifted a little.

Thein Suu Aye, discovering that he was somehow alive, let go of the anchor chain. He tried to lift his dripping body out of the water, but Udumi slapped him away.

The tribesman's first concern was for his wife, but he was re-assured to see that the arrow was not poisoned. It had not gone deep and the bleeding from her leg had all but stopped. Her eyes were closed, but her breathing was steady.

'You *will* need me,' Thein said, weakly.

Udumi ignored him.

'Someone will have to help you,' said Thein. 'How will you survive in the world?'

Udumi turned to look at the strange little man in the water.

Thein was waist deep, wearing an expression like a sulky child. Blood was clouding around from the wound in his shoulder. It was very, very hot.

'You *will* need me,' he said again.

Udumi, who knew his island and her seas very well, waited to see what would happen next.

Thein yelped in surprise as the first black-tip reef shark nudged at his left buttock.

He turned, and saw that the sharks were legion. Thein howled in fear, and tried once more to scramble on board.

Udumi palmed Thein's face, pushing him backwards.

'But you'll *need* me,' Thein spluttered, finding his feet once more and slapping at the sea in impotent fury. 'Everyone always *needs* me . . .'

The boat was floating away on the eddies, faster than Thein could run through water, which was slower than most nightmares.

His next scream was cut short as a young shark leapt out of the water, felling him, and the ocean erupted with pink.

Udumi nodded in satisfaction when he saw Thein's bobbing torso break the surface like ballast. It was void of a head. Within moments, the seabirds were diving to try to grab a share of the carcass, and the orgy of feeding drifted south with the current.

Udumi, hand on the tiller, forked the anchor chain on board. He pointed the boat away from the haloed peak of El and towards the sun that was still high and fat and strong, his bare feet on warm, bloodied gold.

Ten

Deep in the *Wienerwald*, the snow was falling in fat, soft flakes.

Werner Kallmus, father to a lost missionary, crunched through fresh powder towards the ice-house prison of his own creation. Already half-mad, his insanity was no longer fuelled by grief, but by the embrace of insanity itself. Every so often he would stop to try to identify individual patterns on the ground, as the frozen crystals caught the first rays of the rising sun.

Werner was searching for coherence and logic, but found none. His huge dogs galloped around him, tongues steaming as they chased forgotten scents.

Valmik Kapoor, Reeta's brother, had been imprisoned for eight days.

Werner no longer cared about the welfare of the kidnapped man. Something told him that it had gone too far already – that his son, Sebastian, had been dead all along, and now, probably, Isabel as well. Although he could not entirely bring himself to give up hope, it had become impossible to care about the sanctity of his own life.

As a result, the future of a dark-skinned non-believer was of less than secondary concern.

Two days previously, Herr Gustav, patient butler to the Kallmus family for twenty years, had handed Werner a letter of resignation, effective immediately. Werner knew it was coming, because the man had spent the previous day cleaning out his quarters and muttering plans down the telephone to a woman he was keeping in Melk.

Secretly, Werner was pleased; Gustav's departure would free him from the last civilising factor in his life.

Werner received the letter in his kitchen. It was handwritten in Gustav's elegant script, and talked of loyalty, goodwill and history. Werner said nothing, even when Gustav broke the habit of a professional lifetime and urged his employer to seek help, clasping a hand to Werner's shoulder.

Werner had shrunk from the touch and dropped his head, pretending to study a knot in the wood of the table. He remained that way long after the front door had closed and the sound of the man's car had receded into the distance.

As the hours ticked down to midnight, Werner embraced those unchained spirits that were now permitted full reign to swirl around his ancestral home: the lost, the mad, and the soon-to-be freshly dead. Screaming in unfettered agony, he drew blood from his bare chest with numb fingernails and pissed in the cold, unraked fireplace. He drank himself unconscious and awoke with the dogs.

Werner Kallmus was pleading with God, but no one was answering.

In his bare right hand, the Glock was a black shadow against the snow. In his left, he carried a burlap sack within another sack. He would use the burlap to bury the body, if that was to be the course of action. The snowmobile was out of fuel, but, if required, he could go back for it after the deed was done. Better to toy with the idea of murder now, while the veil of madness was still lowered.

Werner entered the ice-house, his blood hot.

Once in the anti-chamber, he thumped on the metal door to the prison. There was no sound from within, nor light from under the door. Seconds later, he tapped on the metal wall with the butt of the gun, his second signal.

Nothing, no sound of movement.

Impatient, Werner threw open the door, expecting the prisoner to be in his cot.

Valmik Kapoor, eyes bulging and face grey, was hanging from the lighting cable, the smashed bulb dangling loosely around his neck.

No . . .

The corpse was limp in the half-light of dawn.

Werner cursed. He knew there had been many yards of wiring between the light and the generator, but his construction plans had never taken account of this possibility, that the prisoner would smash the fitting and find himself enough slack to hang himself.

But wait, how did he . . .?

Werner approached and saw a glint in the eye of the dead face.

He is ALIVE . . .

Valmik Kapoor lashed out with his foot and knocked Werner Kallmus to the ground with one wild, lucky blow.

Another conference room, another set of harsh lights, this time in the headquarters of Metro Atlanta's Center for Disease Control.

Dr Ira Mardy, wearing an unnecessary lab coat and sporting a cartoon-patterned tie that utterly contradicted his humourless personality, was the only speaker to have got to his feet.

'What we have is an unknown transmissible spongiform encephalopathy,' he said, as though taking credit for the discovery. 'It is related to, but different from, both Kuru and Fatal Familial Insomnia. Comparable to FFI in that the normal conformation of PrP is altered, and, in aggregate form, collects as plaques in the thalamus, causing deterioration. Comparable to Kuru in that this particular prion disease is not genetic, and appears to be spread via a common pathophysiology. But it is neither.'

'Not *so* common,' said Dr Chris Light, quietly enough for the small panel of listeners to want to strain to hear. '*Cannibalism.*'

'Cannibalism?' said the head of the panel. His name was Colonel Patrick Wade, a virologist from the United States Army Medical Research Institute of Infectious Diseases – USAMRIID.

'Endocannibalism, to be precise,' said Sparky.

'Everyone will have the opportunity to put forth an opinion,' said Dr Mardy. He could have been chairing a meeting for the parents of errant schoolchildren.

'I read the diary of your patient,' Colonel Patrick Wade said, ignoring this. 'You have reason to believe any of it was fabricated?'

Sparky liked the colonel, he reminded him a little of his father.

'No, sir,' said Sparky. 'And I think Leona Bride had a shorter gestation period than Todd Parker because, as traditional for a woman in that tribe, she was exposed to meat that had a richer concentration of prion particles. The evident dysmorphism relates to her consumption of, ah, *offaly bits*, brains and so on – while the men in the tribe, Mr Parker included, were encouraged to consume the more, how should I say, palatable cuts. Just a theory, of course.'

Mardy rolled his eyes.

'Dr Mardy? Do you have anything more?'

'Well,' Mardy said, looking skyward for the trump card that so far seemed to be evading him. 'I wonder if Dr Light could tell us the location of Todd Parker. This, of course, is critical.'

'Good question.' Colonel Wade peered at Sparky over his reading glasses.'As the only proven living host of this new disease, his whereabouts could be useful.'

All eyes went to Chris Light.

'Mr Parker walked out of Grundy Memorial unchecked,' said Sparky. 'We don't know where he is.'

The panel from USAMRIID, three men and one woman, exchanged glances.

'Can you explain this, Dr Light?'

'Not really,' said Sparky.

'Then I will explain for you,' said Ira Mardy, sneering. 'The attending, Charlie Cortez—'

'Perhaps *you* could inform Grundy as to the whereabouts of Leona Bride,' said Sparky. 'If Charlie Cortez had been able to perform the autopsy tests that it has taken the CDC two weeks to consider, we might have secured Todd Parker. As it happened, Dr Cortez was suspended, and Todd Parker was merely assumed to have Creutzfeldt-Jakob.'

'Cortez was out of control,' Mardy said, stroking the memory of his facial bruise.

'And Charlie Cortez is gone,' said Sparky. 'Along with his answers. You sent him away.'

'Leona Bride's body is in Maryland,' said Mardy, 'awaiting further tests; the staff on the panel know that.'

'The CDC deliberately misdiagnosed E. coli, then bunny-hopped to CJD, all to protect *what*?'

'The *truth*, Dr Light. The American public. And Creutzfeldt-Jakob *is* serious, you damn intern.'

Chris got to his feet. 'Serious, yes; but not a diagnosis where you expect the patient to stand up and walk out. Grundy Memorial has been misled and misinformed from the start. Charlie Cortez was getting close all along, but you and your pride refuse to admit it. He drew the same conclusions as the CDC, all out of a lab run on Medicare, donations and common sense. Your agency is funded to the tune of nine billion dollars.'

'We're not interested in your conclusions, Dr Light, and we are not interested in airing some sociological conflict. With your limited experience, you're lucky to be in the room.'

'And with your personality, you're lucky to still have your own teeth.'

There was a flurry of activity from the panel of four, a joyous shuffling of papers. They seemed to have taken pleasure in the way the point had played out.

'I've heard enough,' Colonel Wade said, eventually. 'I have to get back to DC, and I can digest these reports on the plane. My suggestion to you, Dr Light, is to find Todd Parker. Young man, you may be a student, but this was your patient, and your hospital. You need to take responsibility.'

'Yes, sir,' said Sparky.

'And my suggestion to you, Dr Mardy . . .'

'Yes?'

'Is to find Todd Parker *before* Dr Light, given that your full-sail opacity is the reason I'm now going to have to bother some important fucking people.'

'Mr Doe is waiting in Hague's office, Reggie.'

'Who?'

'Mr Doe.' T.J. pulled the headphones from her ears and checked the diary; Reggie was treated to a tinny blast of Ludacris.

'Mr Doe?'

'Yeah,' she said. 'He doesn't have a first name. Made the appointment last night, insisted on seeing you. I put him in Hague's office, being as he left it unlocked. Did you get the text?'

Reggie Owens was tired. 'I got it. What does he want?'

'He says he's here about the dagger.' T.J. snapped gum around her glittery French-cut nails, inconveniencing herself for some reason. '*The dagger*. That mean anything to you?'

'Maybe.'

'I gave him a cup of water, but he dropped it when I put it in his hand. I think his depth perception don't work properly or something.'

Reggie Owens thought about Vanessa Cortez, his most glamorous client of recent months, and about Charlie, her doctor husband, whom Reggie had caught with his pants down at the Clearmont Lounge. It was a nasty business, but business it was. Still, the ornamental dagger presented an usual twist, one that Reggie had almost forgotten about.

'Mr Doe, he say anything else?'

'Nah. But be careful, he's fucked up.'

'What does that mean?'

The gum came loose. 'I'm not his doctor. And he calls himself Mr Doe. Ain't that what they call dead bodies?'

'Some private detective you'd make, T.J.'

'What do you want from me? Okay, he looks like a hobo but he ain't. Sometimes he seems like he's forgetting to breathe. He's whiter than highbeams, and his eyes don't stop. Reggie, *be careful.*'

Reggie Owens, surprised by the sudden attention being lavished on him by the office's hot young secretary, switched his attention up a DEFCON.

'Getting late,' he said. 'You can go home.'

'I was gonna. Been the only one here for, like, two hours.'

T.J. clacked towards the elevator while Reggie straightened his tie. If there was some kind of reward to be claimed, he didn't want anyone suggesting he buy all the drinks for the near future.

The name of the company founder was Wayne Hague, and he was the only investigator in the suite to have his own office. It was fortunate that Wayne was semi-retired, as it meant his colleagues could usually count on using this private space for delicate meetings, which was most of them.

Wayne was a decorated former fireman, but in recent years seemed to take greater pride in the accumulation of bowling trophies. It was the faux-marble base of one of these gilded prizes that knocked Reggie to the ground as he entered the office, the lid rolling and clattering over the hard, institutional flooring.

Another of the trophies was a crystal trophy bowl. Reggie turned in time to see it in the hands of a skinny white drug addict, who threw it to the ground like the spell-casting of a petulant wizard.

Shards flew, and Todd Julius Parker reached down to help himself to a jagged triangle.

Reggie closed his eyes in an attempt to clear his head, but then the youth was on him, knees pinning his shoulders, the crotch of his baggy jeans stinking of old urine.

'Where's my dagger?'

'You don't need to do this, kid. If it was yours, you can have it.'

'Where is it?'

'Just relax,' said Reggie. 'One of my clients has it.'

'Who?'

'Her name is Vanessa Cortez.'

'Vanessa Cortez?'

'She's a good citizen, she could help you. She's rich.'

'Where is she?'

'Look,' said Reggie, struggling. '*Look*. Give me twelve hours . . .'

The kid was squeezing his makeshift weapon too hard, and blood dripped from his hand onto Reggie's face.

'*Where is Vanessa Cortez?*'

Reggie Owens, who had made a living on the seamier side of life, could recognise real trouble. This kid was more than a drug addict, he was drawing strength from desperation that Reggie wanted no part of. But there was still humanity there, a quality that suggested all hope was not lost.

'Now listen,' Reggie said. 'I'm gonna get that knife for you. But you need to know—'

Todd brought down the shard of crystal and sliced open Reggie's throat.

Reggie gurgled, and lost consciousness. He bled out fast.

Ten minutes passed while everything became sticky, including the ceiling of the floor below.

'I'm not a killer,' said Todd, into Reggie's surprised, dead face.

What now?

Todd struggled to his feet, and Reggie's jacket fell open.

The killer reached in and found, among other things, a small address book. Reggie had no truck with technology, which was fortunate for Todd, because neither did he.

The killer tried to flick pages, and they became gluey with redness. Eventually, he found what he was looking for.

Cortez, Vanessa.

In an outer office of The Pentagon, lights were burning brightly.

'The *Okojuwoi*,' said Donald Bovee, Deputy Secretary for Defense. He squinted at the satellite images spread over his desk; islands were spattered across the ocean like dripped blood. 'I don't mind admitting, I'd never heard of them.'

'They're a long, long way from the mainland,' said Colonel Patrick Wade, who, forty minutes ago, was being rushed through Reagan National Airport.

'The Bureau just confirmed the travel arrangements of Charlie Cortez,' said the man from the CIA, pocketing his phone. 'We have him on manifests all the way from Atlanta to Port Blair, and he got his Indian visa through a travel agent in Fort Worth.'

'Cortez was the attending doctor.'

'Yes, sir,' said Colonel Wade. 'And the first man to identify this new disease. But there is a strong possibility he became infected somehow; he attacked another doctor.'

'That's two kids and a healthcare professional,' said Bovee, 'in one of our population centres.'

'It isn't so much the transmission that concerns me,' said Wade. 'Before death, the infection leads to violent psychosis, and we have at least one attributable murder: Frank Tsang, a salesman. We think Tsang's death was a direct symptomatic result.'

'A biological threat?'

'Unlikely to be a synthesised weapon.'

'Why not, Colonel?'

'With respect to Colonel Wade,' said the man from the CIA, 'we aren't in a position to speculate about that yet.'

'Now wait a minute —'

'*This* island,' said the man from the CIA, tapping at the map, 'was uninhabited until eight years ago. It was leased from the Indian government by a man called Edward Quinn.'

'Not uninhabited,' said Wade. 'There's a native tribe.'

'We know very little about this tribe,' said the man from the CIA.

'I read the medical report,' said Bovee, grimacing at Colonel Wade. 'Cannibalism makes for a gruesome bedtime story.'

'The leading expert on the people of these islands is an Indian-born anthropologist called Reeta Kapoor,' said the man from the CIA. 'Can you guess where she is right now?'

'Savage Island,' said Wade.

'We pulled her flight manifests too. Why, at this point, would they all be in that region?'

Bovee was flicking through pages. 'What is this Quinn doing? What are his motives?'

'We don't know. There appears to be no way to communicate with the island, and the project is shrouded in secrecy. But sources in New Delhi tell us he's planning on opening it up to the public.'

'When?'

'Reports are still coming in.'

'Colonel Wade, are we going to see more of this? Of American kids with curdled brains?'

'I don't know,' said Wade. 'You'd think cases would have appeared in India first, but our investigation is only days old. As you know, that's a vast country, and the infrastructure—'

'It seems that none of us knows very much,' said the deputy secretary. It was not a criticism; this was a potential crisis, but one still in infancy. Jobs were being done.

A senior assistant knocked twice and pushed her head around the door.

'Major General Ruskin,' she said. Bovee nodded.

'Anything else?' he said when she had gone.

The man from the CIA reached into a thick file and produced a series of glossy photographs, including blurry security stills.

'There is also *this* person,' he said.

Donald Bovee found himself staring into the eyes of the ugliest man he had ever seen.

'Otto Lix,' said the man from the CIA. 'He's been working for Quinn. Here he is in Cape Town, Bogotá, and again on the *Croisette* in Cannes. He's been quiet for a long time, but he's a known terrorist.'

Bovee sighed, and reached for the telephone.

'You just said the magic word, Sam.'

Jesse opened his eyes.

He looked across to where his brother, Milo, should have been sleeping.

As he did so, Milo opened his eyes also, and the boys stared silently at each other for a time, faces petrified by the moonlight pouring through the open window.

Vanessa Cortez had moved herself and the twins back into the family home while she considered her options. This was the place she had been born and raised, a small mansion near the foothills of the Blue Ridge Mountains, surrounded by stunted oaks and natural beauty. Milo and Jesse usually liked these trips upstate because they had generous, indulgent grandparents and the surrounding woods were great to explore.

At night, however, the house could become a dark, creaky factory of nightmares. Imagined horrors in childhood can sometimes be educative rather than damaging, but the tilt is easy, and both Milo and Jesse were experiencing heightened sensitivity because of the departure of their father. Vanessa had refused to share her pain with anyone but her mother, believing private grief to be the best way forward, but it also meant that Milo and Jesse were left to use their imagination to fill in their gaps of knowledge. As a result, they had wound each other up into a mild hysteria.

Dad has gone.

Gone where?

Maybe Mom sent him away.

Maybe he'll never come back.

Then who's downstairs?

It was undeniable, the twins could hear noises from the ground floor.

They were kitchen-type noises, the rattle of drawers and the sharpening of a knife. The sounds were familiar, and should have been comforting; Milo and Jesse were used to waking up to the smell of bacon and pancakes.

But this was the witching hour.

The adults wouldn't be up, they were full of wine and exhausted by shared consolations. Besides, the boys would have been woken by the squeaky landing or the groan of the toilet plumbing.

Jesse, ever the adventurer, was first out of bed.

'Wait,' Milo hissed. But rather than stop his brother, as might have been typical, he followed in his footsteps.

Diffused light from the kitchen was reaching out into the hallway. When Jesse paused at the top of the stairs, Milo took the lead, and together they crept down to peer around the doorway.

Of course it was not their father.

It was Todd Parker, currently Georgia's most wanted man, and his psychosis had returned with a vengeance.

Todd had held it together enough to get two addresses for Vanessa Cortez from the murdered private investigator, but when there was nobody home at the Atlanta apartment, he realised he was going to have to travel out of the city. Hitchhiking got him as far as Gainesville, where he had stolen a car in which someone had been stupid enough to leave their GPS.

Breaking into the residence had been far simpler than gaining access to the Cortez apartment; the wooden hurricane doors that provided exterior access to the basement had been in need of replacement for some time.

Now Todd was sitting on the kitchen floor in the light of the open refrigerator, scooping raw chicken from a carcass with his grimy fingers and stuffing it into his mouth. The knife he had taken from a drawer was within arm's reach.

He became aware of being watched.

'Bring me my dagger,' he said to the twins when he saw them. 'This isn't it.'

'Who are you?' Jesse said, stepping forward.

'My dagger,' said Todd Parker, throwing the carcass away. 'You stole it.'

'He means the knife from the car,' said Milo. 'The one Mom found.'

The intruder nodded, as if Todd could possibly have known where they had found it.

'If I get it,' Milo said, 'will you go away?'

He nodded again, face stuffed with raw chicken.

'Watch him,' said Milo to Jesse.

It might have been ridiculous, but Todd Parker did not seem to be a threat. The exchange had all the surreal terror of a random night-time encounter, but with none of the potency. Perhaps it was because the lunatic was disinterested in his present weapon and cross-legged on his skinny ass and making an easy request, or perhaps it was because he was now communicating that he had a mental capability of a tired five-year-old. Whichever it was, neither twin felt any great fear.

'Don't get up,' Jesse said to Todd, when Milo had gone and they had been left alone.

Todd complied.

Milo knew where Mom had put the jewelled dagger; it was in the small gun safe behind a family portrait in the living room. He also knew that was where Grandpa kept his old .38 Special.

Milo loaded it in the semi-darkness with trembling hands, and when he reappeared in the kitchen door, he had both the dagger and a weapon that was ready to fire.

'Give me my dagger,' said Todd.

'No,' said Milo. It was becoming greasy in his palm.

'Give me my dagger, or you'll have to shoot me.'

Jesse grabbed the dagger from Milo and slid it across the floor.

Todd took the weapon and stared at it, as if reunited with an old lover. He stood up, and Milo raised the gun and cocked it. The boy was shaking very badly.

'Don't move,' said Milo and Jesse together.

Todd was now unaware of them.

He held the handle of the dagger with two hands and turned the blade inwards, his face flooded with the bliss of purest relief.

The boys watched in horror, as, with the last of his strength, Todd plunged it into his heart.

Morris Wiseman, US Ambassador Extraordinary and Plenipotentiary, was shown into a sumptuously furnished office in the South Block of New Delhi's Secretariat Building. Outside, the day was bright but dusty, and Ambassador Wiseman wiped his mouth with his handkerchief while he waited for the Indian Foreign Secretary.

Three minutes later, Mr N. P. Nilekani entered the room through a side door. The two men shook hands, and Foreign Secretary Nilekani sat down in such a way as to protect the razor-sharp crease in his trousers.

Theoretically, the deals on the table had already been made, which should have made the meeting a formality; they were complex, and had taken hours of diplomacy to reach. Yet both men were acutely experienced in spotting deviations from the script.

'I want you to postpone the proposed talks in Karachi,' said Mr Nilekani, once the suitable conversation about children, grandchildren and mutual friends had been concluded. 'We are not prepared to be lectured about our response to Bomai, or, indeed, the wider situation in Kashmir.'

'Those talks have not moved beyond the planning stage, Mr Foreign Secretary.'

'But a postponement of the *proposal*. An American endorsement is unacceptable.'

'We have not endorsed the proposal, which came from President Chaudhry's Islamist generals. We cannot censor the foreign press, or the Chinese.'

'America has remained silent.'

'We need Pakistan onside,' said the American Ambassador.

Mr Nilekani tented his fingers. 'Perhaps we should talk about the civil nuclear deal.'

'As senior advisor to The Bureau of South and Central Asian Affairs, I should advise you that the situation in Bomai will be discussed again at the G-20, but no earlier. This is now our official line.'

Nilekani was pleased. 'A more appropriate juncture. Extremism cannot schedule debate on the national stage.'

'India's secular character is exemplary in the world.'

The Foreign Secretary got to his feet, and Ambassador Wiseman followed suit. The whole business had taken seconds.

'We are in agreement, sir.'

The two men shook hands.

'As you may be aware,' said the American Ambassador, as though it had just occurred to him, 'we are still awaiting final approval to confirm a possible medical emergency in the Okojuwoi Islands, and, if necessary, to evacuate US citizens.'

'The island you refer to is privately leased, sparsely populated, and we are aware of no medical emergency,' said the Foreign Secretary. 'Of course, military action would be expressly forbidden.'

'It is an operation of scientific discovery.'

'The US navy has my government's continuing consent to perform limited Blue-Water Ops training in that region. But only as laid out in the most recent bulletins.'

'We appreciate your generosity in this matter,' said Ambassador Wiseman.

'New coordinates will be sent to the Far Eastern Naval Command. Please update us should your exercises require, say, the USS *Kearsarge* to stray into the Ten Degree Channel.'

'We can report to you hourly.'

'As you wish, sir.'

'There is a lot of ocean out there,' said Ambassador Wiseman.

'Quite,' said Foreign Secretary Nilekani, and the two men shook hands again.

The full circus had arrived, cops and medics and press, crowding the long, narrow driveway; flashing emergency vehicles bounced lights off the branches of spindly trees.

There were also a couple of unmarked government cars. The APB out on Todd Parker had included an ominous warning about national security.

His corpse had been wheeled into a private ambulance and was now speeding towards the CDC in Atlanta. The twins were in the back of another, stationary ambulance, wrapped in blankets and sipping cocoa with their grandparents. The paramedic was great, an amateur comedian who kept them all laughing while showing off the equipment and demonstrating the various uses.

Vanessa was sitting on a step by the open doors, listening to the chatter of her children. She too was wrapped in a shiny mylar blanket, but did not seem to be holding up quite as well.

When the news had come into Grundy, Dan Demus had broken the speed limit to get up to the house. The psychologist knew he was not particularly popular with Vanessa, but through his friendship with Charlie, he had known her for a long time. He thought she might appreciate a familiar face, and he was right, to a point.

Vanessa kept saying the same words, over and over, questioning the incident. Dan thought this might be a good thing, helping her to rationalise the impossible, but she was getting more and more accusatory with each repetition, as though trying to teach herself a self-defeating logic.

'This man had a communicable psychosis,' sad Dan, for the third time. 'He didn't know what he was doing.'

'That makes it worse,' she said.

'What I mean,' said Dan, 'is that he was going to die anyway.'

'How can psychosis be communicable?' Vanessa said, sniffling.

'His brain was degenerating due to rogue proteins. Something a bit like mad cow disease, but only for humans. You can't have caught it, or your sons, because the disease can only be passed through the consumption of contaminated matter.'

'I wish I'd thrown that goddam knife away,' said Vanessa. 'My sons helped a man to kill himself, and it happened because the madness came into our home. Charlie brought that madness into our lives. My boys don't have a bad bone in them. This is not *human nature.*'

Isn't it? thought Dan.

You should work in the emergency department of a hospital for a night or two. All of our physical constructions are artifice and arrogance, not just our unsinkable boats and our falling towers and our broken levies, but the locks on our doors and windows and the barriers we place in our minds to keep us sane. These mental constructions are worse, because they mislead.

This has always been a world without walls.

'I have something else to tell you,' said Dan. 'Something you need to know.'

Vanessa said nothing.

'There's a strong possibility that Charlie has become infected.'

'Infected?'

'If he gets in touch with you, or you find out where he is, will you contact the hospital? Here's my number, and a number belonging to Chris Light.'

'How could Charlie have become infected?' said Vanessa, and she thought for a moment. '*Consumption of contaminated matter?* How the hell did he consume contaminated matter?'

Now it was Dan's turn to remain silent.

'I'll kill him,' said Vanessa, shaking in fear and rage. 'I'll fucking *kill* him.'

'You won't need to,' said Dan. 'If he's got it, there is no cure.'

Darkness.

'Continue Mode Two, Roger. Needles.'

'577, 4 miles, course correcting.'

The AV-8B Harrier dropped below 1,200 feet and there was a fluctuating two-tone warning from the altimeter.

'577 approaching the mile, slightly above.'

'577.'

'Bird, call the ball. Quarter.'

The deck of the Wasp-class assault ship appeared in an instant; one moment there was a speck of light in the distance, the next, a lethally short runway.

The V/STOL training jet could carry an instructor, but on this occasion it carried a passenger: Colonel Patrick Wade from the US Army Medical Research Institute for Infectious Diseases. The Harrier pitched a little left as it touched down and hit the wires, but it was an otherwise perfect instrument approach and landing. The pilot's breathing slowed.

'70071 sending commands. A beauty, Bird. Set yourself up on stand.'

Despite maintaining Indian Standard Time, the Okojuwoi Islands are far eastern territory. On the clock, darkness falls early.

Colonel Wade stepped onto the USS *Kearsarge* beneath the glow of a tropical moon, and the heat struck him as soon as hydraulics raised the cockpit roof. There was a small welcoming committee, blinking in the ship's night-vision lights, and the deck was wet from a recent storm.

'Welcome aboard, Colonel Wade. You can surrender your helmet.'

'Lucky we found you, Captain Lawrence.'

'We're on our way back to join CTF-151,' shouted Lawrence over the roar of another landing. 'Dhaka is swimming in aid workers, if you'll excuse the pun. They didn't need an assault ship hovering around, threatening their sovereignty.'

Wade couldn't decide if Captain Lawrence was being sarcastic. Together, they strolled the flight deck, a small team of personnel trotting behind.

'You have a dozen men from SEAL Team-Six,' said Lawrence, lowering his voice. 'They're looking forward to getting sand between their toes. Brief in your own time. You're going in on F470 Rubber Raiding Craft, we call them CRRC's. I'll let the commander tell you what he has in mind, they're chowing down right now.'

'Thank you, Captain.'

'I know this is black-ops in everything but name, so you'll be shadowed by a Seahawk helicopter, painted to look like the Andaman coastguard. It won't fool anyone who looks twice.'

'I didn't request a helicopter,' said Colonel Wade.

'We're flanked at distance between two Rajput-class destroyers and the *INS Jalashwa*, but as of fifteen thirty today, the Indian navy have started pretending we don't exist. Can you tell me, what kind of biological emergency doesn't require hazmat suits of some kind?'

'This one,' said Colonel Wade.

Lawrence shrugged. 'Let me show you something.'

Two marines were uncovering what resembled a model remote-controlled glider, housed on a pneumatic catapult launcher that pointed it towards the stars. The wingspan was maybe ten feet, and the whole contraption looked like an expensive undergraduate experiment.

'The Boeing NightEagle,' said Captain Lawrence, proudly. 'We're maybe two hours from range of your island, and then we can launch, get a detailed recon. Set you up good and proper for sun-up. This little baby is incredible: unmanned, twenty hours' endurance, infra-red camera on an inertially stabilised turret system. It also contains the world's smallest synthetic aperture radar.' He laughed. 'Don't ask me how the hell it works. The original idea was to track tuna, believe it or not.'

'Incredible,' said Colonel Wade, who was still a little fazed and sweaty from his landing.

'My understanding of the situation is that you have a bunch of primitives over there,' said Lawrence, turning to him. 'Spears, arrows, and so on.'

'Apparently so,' said Wade.

'Well, God bless 'em,' said Captain Lawrence. 'And good luck tomorrow. Here, Tracey will show you to your cabin.'

Valmik Kapoor was running through the forest, weaving through trees, frequently stumbling, frequently sinking to his knees in holes hidden by the soft snow.

He had no breath left to shout for help, and had no reason to believe there was anyone for miles who would hear him. He was close to blind panic, as there was also no reason to believe that the two Great Danes, mouths torn back in delighted snarls of pursuit, would not catch up very soon and tear him limb from limb.

Valmik had Werner's gun, but he had never fired a semi-automatic weapon before, and did not know how to disable the internal locking system.

Mildly concussed, Kallmus himself was jogging some distance behind, shouting incoherently and occasionally stopping to press snow into his bruised and swelling eye where Valmik's toe had connected.

Faking a hanging is an extremely difficult thing to do. If the participant is to spend any length of time in the position, some kind of harness is required, and Valmik did not have that luxury.

But having unscrewed the loose lighting fixture, he had been surprised to find there was about three yards of flex to play with.

It had taken hours of experimenting, early efforts threatening to dislocate his shoulders.

A recreational sailor on occasion, Valmik knew knots, and he also knew that drama was everything, so he had left room for plenty of coils in his noose, even though it would never tighten once he had built in an angler's loop. Eventually, he had discovered that he could pass the light bulb cord twice under his pelvic bone, either side of his scrotum, and then put the remaining slack around his neck. His torso would take his weight, albeit for seconds rather than minutes.

Then he had put on his shirt and trousers, stood on the chair – and waited.

Hours passed.

When Valmik heard the outer door, he had leaned forward so as to avoid any drop, and then nudged away the chair. He had held his breath for the half-minute he was in the position, crotch burning as his pelvis took the strain. Hastily smeared dirt from the floor was supposed to represent bruising around his neck.

Once his captor had been sent sprawling – more by luck than design – Valmik had wasted minutes struggling out of his makeshift harness in the most undignified way, eventually falling back onto the floor and losing one of his shoes in the process.

Valmik knew he should have incapacitated Kallmus then, but could think of nothing but freedom. At least he had remembered to take the gun.

At that point, the dogs, who had not given chase until after Kallmus had regained consciousness, were still bouncing around outside. Initially, they paid Valmik little heed as he made his escape, blinking in the unfamiliar sunlight.

The pursuit had been short, but it felt like hours.

Now, even Valmik's reserves of adrenalin were failing. There were no suitable trees to climb. His next fall, caused by some hidden tree root, was his last.

Valmik struggled to his feet and turned to meet his fate.

The dogs were truly enormous.

The first animal leapt, all teeth and mouth and muscle.

Valmik dropped the useless Glock and raised his hands to shield his face.

The sound of a single gunshot rang out through the forest, the echo dislodging a little powder from overloaded tree branches.

The dog snapped backwards in a fine mist of blood. It lay in the snow, twitching.

The second dog, sensing the game was over, worked through her forward momentum with an apologetic look and trotted over to sniff at her fallen comrade.

Valmik turned back to see four figures emerging over the rise.

Three wore balaclavas and dark jackets with the small red-and-white shoulder patches of the Austrian Federal Police. One of them carried a bolt-action sniper rifle.

The fourth man wore a long coat and leather gloves. Valmik did not recognise him, but he was Gustav Wrabetz, former butler to the Kallmus family.

Werner Kallmus struggled into range. He stopped when he saw the four men, but seemed uncertain how to react.

The butler said something to the sniper, who raised his weapon.

Valmik sensed hesitancy in the policeman; the idea of shooting a lone human is very different from felling a dog, even for a professional. But further killing was unnecessary.

Werner had fallen to his knees, sobbing for forgiveness.

Eleven

This time, Charlie Cortez was less willing to accept his returning consciousness.

It was the gentle but excruciatingly painful removal of a large shard of glass that brought him back to life. Somehow it had become wedged in his mouth between lower lip and gum, and had pierced his cheek. Charlie was face down, but he sat up quickly, coughing blood.

'Easy,' said Reeta Kapoor, pulling back. 'Keep your head forward.'

Charlie coughed some more, coloured lights swirling before his eyes.

'I didn't know whether or not to remove it,' said Reeta, when he had regained some composure. 'But if you'd tried to swallow while you were out, you could have died.'

'You did the right thing,' he said, mouth numb.

The anthropologist herself had remained conscious, but her left arm had been caught in a small explosion from the monorail's gasoline engine, the fire from which still burned. It was crisping the jungle and sending up a vast plume of smoke.

Charlie looked around the shady copse; he had been thrown some distance from the wreckage, which meant Reeta had not had to try to drag him to safety. This, in turn, had probably saved his life.

'It won't spread,' Reeta said, registering Charlie's concern at the flames. 'Trees are too wet.'

'The trees saved our lives,' said Charlie. 'They cushioned the fall.'

'But fire will bring the natives,' said Reeta.

'Or maybe a rescuer.'

Reeta said nothing.

'How long do you think we have?'

'I don't know,' said Reeta. 'Can you walk?'

'I think so.'

'Then we should move.'

'Where's the girl?' said Charlie, remembering.

Reeta shook her head, wincing as she did so. Clothing had fused into her burn. She wondered how bad it was, and if, in time, she would go into shock.

'You're hurt,' said Charlie, testing his own limbs. Apart from cuts and bruises and the blow to his head, he seemed to be fine.

'There was bottled water in the cars,' said Reeta. 'Bottled water and this first-aid kit. I'm clean, for now. And don't worry, my legs work.'

'That will be handy,' said an unseen speaker.

Charlie and Reeta turned towards the voice.

Apis appeared first, emerging from the shadows. Behind her was Isabel Kallmus, training a shotgun at the back of the girl's head.

'Five rounds,' Isabel said. 'Combination for the monorail safe, triple-eight, triple-seven one. Very thoughtful of Mr Quinn to give us a weapon.'

Isabel and Apis were dirty and bloodied, but neither appeared as damaged as Charlie and Reeta. The girl smiled hopefully at Charlie, although it was clear she had acknowledged the danger; she was keeping her hands well above her head.

'Don't get up,' said Isabel, when Charlie made to do so. 'Not yet.'

'You don't need the gun,' said Reeta; she did not seem particularly surprised at this turn of events. 'If we work together, we can all get off this island.'

'Reserve your strength, Dr Kapoor. You're going to need it.'

'We can make for the shore,' said Reeta. 'The fire might have attracted somebody.'

'No,' said Isabel.

'What do you want?' said Charlie, incredulous. And then to Reeta: 'What does she want?'

'We will *not* leave without my brother,' said Isabel.

'Your brother?'

'You see, we are all here on a *mission*.'

Before easing himself quietly out of Edward Quinn's office and onto the path that led over the sea wall, Otto Lix smashed and depressed the green emergency alarm, sending a silent electronic message to the pager carried by each member of staff.

The green alarm represented the highest alert. It was a signal that meant the security of the complex had been breeched by savages.

Lix knew the skeleton crew on the island were very well practised, and as there were no guests to evacuate, they would all be offshore in one of the two vessels that existed for such a purpose within twenty minutes. They would probably assume it was one of the frequent drills and wait at a rendezvous buoy a mile offshore for further instructions.

Otto Lix could not tell what would happen when no such instructions arrived, but he guessed the fearful and superstitious workers were unlikely to return to the island. That just left the powerboat at the tourist dock, which was reserved exclusively for the evacuation of the three senior staff.

Edward Quinn and Kelly Maelzel were not going to make it.

Otto Lix ignored the four-seat tourist gondola and pumped his massive limbs to power him down the wide steps that ran alongside the track. As usual, the sweat poured into his vile safari suit. His left arm was still shivering from where Kelly had electrocuted him, but otherwise he felt excellent, throbbing with energy and potential. The atrocities he could cause now would probably tide him over for months, if not years. Apart from generals and presidents, who could claim they had wiped out an entire civilisation?

By the estimation of Otto Lix, he now had two or three hours to play with before taking the powerboat as far as Port Blair and abandoning it – something that would make more sense to do after dark anyway. He was well known at the little airport, so no one would stop him from commandeering Quinn's private jet and flying it to western Cambodia, where he had some old allies in Pailin. There was no harm in disappearing for a while amongst landmines, teenage prostitutes and uncut gems.

Lix was nothing if not resourceful. He had learned early on that his unique pathology required ingenuity if he was to continue operating in the world, and he intended to be around for a long, long time yet. There was scarcely an employer who had outlived him.

Hidden down a side track, beyond the boat moorings, was a second route through the mountain. It was a narrow, man-made, open-ended cave that, at the moment, also doubled as a garage for three modified rally bikes. On the rare occasions that Quinn had sanctioned incursions onto the main part of the island, the camouflaged KTM Supermotos had proved perfect vehicles for negotiating the pig runs.

Due to the length of the tunnel, no natural light could penetrate the central section, and the far end was sealed with a heavy, electrified metal gate. Quinn's ultimate intention had been to build a paved road, widen the tunnel and eventually run jeep safaris; for now it sufficed as a secret route out into the park. There was no evidence to suggest that the savages had ever discovered this gate.

Lix helped himself to a fully fuelled 950 LC8 and tucked his two shiny guns into his belt, where the butts protruded over his kidneys.

His preference was always for brute physical force, but sometimes there were just too many people to kill.

He eased the motorbike down the sloping tunnel, the echo of the engine roaring off the walls.

In minutes, Lix had opened the security gate and was riding through thick forest, bouncing over roots and easing down soggy tracks, the wind drying the sweat on his face and sticking salt to his sunburn.

Otto Lix knew the noise from the bike would signal his approach, but he also believed that the sight and sound of it was still unfamiliar enough to the islanders to cause confusion and fear. The only times a native had laid eyes on such a device was when he and Kelly had kidnapped the savage, and there had not been retaliation at that point.

Lix was under no illusion about the skill of the natives with bows and arrows, but he also expected them to be stupid and ruled by superstition: far more likely to scatter into the jungle than stand and fight. They were like untrained dogs, mindless aggressors who would back down if you proved yourself to be sufficiently fearless.

Even so, Lix did not head towards the main settlement, but towards higher ground. Months ago, covert recon had informed the colonists that there were specific places where the women and children often gathered during certain times of day.

Women and children.

Lix did not know this part of the island so well. He was a little surprised to burst into an empty clearing that perhaps had some ritualistic purpose. The trees had been cut back to form a perfect circle, and the solitary hut there seemed capably constructed, at least for a savage.

A chaplet of bleached skulls hung from the door.

Lix spun around the clearing a couple of times, revving the engine, wondering if anyone was inside and, if so, whether they would show themselves.

He did not see his attacker: at first, he did not even feel anything.

The dart that struck his thigh was loaded with neurotoxins that had been extracted from a krait, an indigenous snake with sixteen times more venomous potency than a cobra.

Otto Lix was unaware of what had happened even as he fell off the bike.

He hit the ground hard, the frame digging itself into the mud, wheels spinning.

Lix tried to lift himself up on his elbows, then attempted to reach for his guns. He failed on both counts, and his gradual awareness of becoming paralysed made him very angry indeed.

The solar-powered satellite phone brought to the island by Sebastian Kallmus contained a powerful GPS transponder that Isabel's portable reader could pick up. This reader, a hand-held PDA concealed in her bag, had survived the monorail crash.

The group marched through the forest, Reeta in front using the Palm Pre, followed by Charlie and then Apis, upon whom Isabel trained the shotgun.

The going was difficult, not only because of the jungle and the heat, but because of Isabel's requirement that they stop every ten minutes to ensure Reeta was leading them in the right direction.

'I've known who you were since Delhi,' said Reeta, at one of these frequent stops; she was becoming a little delirious from her injuries. 'I know you lost your brother, a missionary – it doesn't take much to Google somebody in this day and age. And I know that you were never a member of SARPI. But I never imagined that you didn't love Valmik, and wouldn't follow him out here.'

'Be quiet,' said Isabel.

'I overestimated him, and I underestimated you,' said Reeta. 'Where is he?'

'Do as I say, and Valmik will be fine.'

'And I never knew she was insane,' said Reeta to Charlie.

'Always the quiet ones,' said Charlie.

'Shut up,' said Isabel.

'What made Sebastian believe that this island needed his help?' said Reeta. 'What made him think this civilisation was already anything other than the perfect expression of his God's innocence? These people were *prelapsarian*.'

Isabel pointed the shotgun into the face of the girl, and they walked on.

Colonel Patrick Wade wanted the SEAL team to land as close to Edward Quinn's visitor centre as possible, but it was decided the waves crashing around the rock face were too dangerous for the rubber raiding crafts. The plan to access the river and man-made dock was temporarily abandoned.

The place seemed deserted, at least from the water.

Plenty of daylight remained, so Commander Lenzi ordered that they motor around the headland and land on the nearest western beach. There, they would wait for the swells to subside.

Colonel Wade was uneasy. The purpose of the mission was to warn the Americans on the island – and anyone else concerned – about a neurobiological risk, and evacuate them for testing. Scientifically, it would have been useful to get a native as well, but Wade was fearful of endangering the indigenous population, and it was outside the remit of his orders anyway. He believed, however, that landing on a beach would greatly increase the chances of encounter.

He was correct.

The soldiers had been ashore for an hour and were considering bivouacking when the first arrow struck one man squarely in the neck.

The SEAL fell to his knees and foamed at the mouth.

'Get back in the boats,' yelled Wade. 'Get back in the boats!'

It was not going to happen.

Further arrows flew as the men dropped to the ground and opened fire, shredding the jungle.

The savages did not know how to retreat. One by one, naked figures fell forward, torn apart, yet somehow the arrows kept falling.

'Reinforcements!' screamed Lenzi, radioing to the *Kearsarge*, although the soldiers were already realising that the arrows could not pierce body armour.

'Drop back!' screamed Wade, despite knowing the SEALS had nowhere to go. 'Drop back!'

'Smoke 'em out,' said Lenzi, to a nearby soldier. The boy had an M203 grenade-launcher fitted to his rifle, and he pointed it into the trees.

It was going to be a massacre.

In the middle of a large, bright clearing was a raised mound of earth.

Atop the mound of earth was a thick wooden cross, damp with lichen. It was roughly hewn, and had been made from two fallen trees.

The crucifix was big and solid enough to have borne a man, and it towered over them all.

'He's here somewhere,' said Reeta. 'We're on top of the signal.'

'Impossible,' said Isabel, staring up at the cross.

There were old stains there, probably blood.

'She's right,' said Charlie, looking at the reader.

'What does it mean?' said Isabel.

'Probably that they didn't have two thieves to crucify at the same time,' said Reeta, wearily. 'Now I'd be looking for, I don't know, a sepulcher.'

'A what?' said Isabel.

'A rock-hewn cave.'

Apis knew where to look. She had been here many times before. Isabel allowed the girl to lead her to the edge of the clearing, a place shadowed by forest. There, the savages had constructed a low tomb from stones they had collected and transported from the base of the mountain. This job had been taken very seriously; there was nothing to bind the structure, but it was solid and almost waterproof.

Reeta was fascinated, despite her flagging health. No one alive on the island would live in such a building.

The largest stone, which also served as an entrance, had been rolled away.

'If he's not in there, then we're at least three days too late,' said Reeta to Charlie.

Apis reached in and brought out Sebastian's sat-phone, and then the music box left behind by her mother, which the child kept in the tomb for safe-keeping. Typically, this was not a place the tribes-people ever visited.

She brought both over and presented them to Charlie, who was remembering his final deathbed conversation with Leona: *What's the correct tune?*

I don't remember. That's why I have so many. I have to keep looking.

At the urging of the girl, Charlie opened the music box.

It was silent, the ballerina motionless. Apis wound up the mechanism, and the figure began to spin, dancing to a delicate, awkward melody.

Next, Apis pushed a green button on the sat-phone.

It was marked *receive*; trial and error had taught her how to find the voices. But nothing happened. It needed to ring first, and Werner Kallmus was indisposed.

'She must bring it out here regularly,' said Reeta. 'Into the sunlight, to find power. Or it wouldn't have been able to broadcast the signal.'

'He's dead,' said Isabel, over by the cave. 'Sebastian is dead. This is his body, I'm certain. Some of his belongings are here, his necklace, his Bible. But he's been dead for years.'

"'If Christ has not been raised, your faith is futile,'" said Reeta. "'You are still in your sins.'"

'Paul the Apostle,' said Charlie.

'But this wasn't a passion play,' said Reeta, gesturing at the cross. 'This was the real thing. I'm no expert in Christian soteriology, but we can be pretty certain the tribe didn't attain salvation here. Somewhat disappointing when your self-promoting Messiah fails to resurrect.'

'He did *not* deserve to die,' said Isabel, cracking.

'Someone in the tribe wanted to keep him alive, at least for a while.'

'How would you know?'

'Because Sebastian must have passed on some of his ideas. I'm not going to tell you he didn't suffer, but if he hung here, he atoned.'

Isabel raised the shotgun, this time pointed it squarely at Reeta.

'Did your brother take the Bible literally?' said Reeta. 'Did this happen because he taught literal truth from a book that requires, at best, selective interpretation?'

'Sebastian was not a martyr,' said Isabel. 'Martyrdom was never his plan.'

'Maybe not,' said Reeta, 'but he certainly wasn't much of a teacher.'

In the distance there was the sound of an exploding grenade, and a great cloud of smoke.

Heat from one concentrated source, and pain in the sockets of his arms.

Otto Lix opened his eyes and snarled. He was still in the clearing where he had fallen.

Lix had not been unconsciousness for long, but he was now hanging upside down, tied to a tree. Despite the continuing power of the sun, a large fire had been lit a few yards away. Below him was a green plastic bucket, empty and scrupulously clean.

A very old-looking native woman approached. She was holding her blowpipe, and Lix realised then that she must have been responsible for his capture. Loitering behind were a couple of muscular warriors, Medea's personal bodyguards. Although armed with spears, they looked nervous, and Lix mistakenly believed it was him they were afraid of.

He had strayed into the territory of The Qesem.

The woman watched with curiosity as Lix began to buck and spasm. Thus began a short period of involuntary overexcitation caused by the snake venom. Left alone, the poisoning would eventually result in further paralysis and probably death, as his lungs became incapable of movement.

It would have been preferable.

The Qesem waited patiently for the violent shuddering to subside, then turned and spoke to her warriors.

This is surely the most powerful and fearsome Owb who has ever existed. Look at him!

The warriors did so, eyes wide.

Our world is under attack, but now, at last, we have the advantage. Can you imagine what we will learn from this monster? Our future can be divined from his blood, our history from his stomach. We can use his eyes to see and open his mind to tell us what to think. I can squeeze the beats from his heart, and feel as he does by wearing his skin over mine.

Medea was not speaking literally.

Lix understood none of it.

'Come closer,' he managed to say. 'I'll bite off your wizened tits and stuff them up your cunt.'

Medea reached out as though touching his aura.

Hello, beautiful, she said, delicately.

The four survivors followed the sound of the blast, which had been followed in quick succession by another. Smoke was curling up towards the sky, maybe half a mile away.

Closer, they heard the splatter of gunfire and yells of battle.

Sool, the aged Chief who had lost both his sons, was the only warrior to have retreated. He had not done so out of cowardice, but because he was no longer capable of fighting, and he did not want to demoralise his followers by collapsing. He fell into a clearing a few hundred yards from the front line, placing his back to a great tree and taking his last breaths in the dappled light.

When he was surprised by the four Owbs, he raised his flatbow with shaking arms.

Sool had not been injured in the battle, but he was very close to death, losing blood and tormented towards unconsciousness by his infected foot.

The sacred arrow, bronze-tipped and gleaming, pointed first at Charlie, then Reeta, then Isabel.

Isabel raised the shotgun.

Time seemed to move very, very slowly.

'Drop it,' said a voice; deep, authoritative, American-accented.

Colonel Patrick Wade pushed into the space, his eyes haunted by the sight of recent bloodshed, his rifle cocked and loaded. The barrel was maybe two feet from the Chief's head.

'Drop the weapon,' Wade said again.

Sool did not lower his bow, but he did not fire.

'Don't do it,' Charlie said to the soldier.

Apis broke free of Charlie's hand and ran towards the old tribesman, arms open in embrace.

Sool quivered.

Wade took the shot, the crack of the weapon echoing through the forest.

The Chief was instantly dead. His arrow flew wide, released into the forest for the final time.

Reeta took advantage of the distraction and leapt at Isabel, knocking her off her feet and kicking the shotgun away.

Apis snuggled into Sool's body, as though trying to push her life-force into his. She howled and howled.

The sight was too much for Charlie. He charged at Wade, taking him completely by surprise and raining down blows on his head and face. Soldiers poured into the clearing, and it took three men to tear him away.

Commander Umberto Lenzi led his troops up a well-trodden jungle path, twitching his trigger finger when a small figure revealed herself. It was an old tribal woman, unarmed, but splattered from head to toe with blood and gore.

Shocked, Lenzi lowered his weapon.

'My God,' he said. 'What happened to you?'

The Qesem looked stunned, having just been released from a spiritual trance. She permitted the soldier to place his hand on her sticky shoulder, perhaps because she had exhausted herself, or perhaps because she had indeed divined the future and knew there was no point in further resistance. Her bodyguards had evaporated at one whispered command, and would be hunted down later.

'Sir,' said the SEAL who had gone up ahead. 'Sir, you need to take a look at this.'

The voice belonged to one of Lenzi's toughest men, but it was wavering in a childlike fashion.

Commander Lenzi strode into the clearing, which was already thick with flies.

Otto Lix had been spread around in a way that might have been ritualistic, but looked more an explosion of bad meat. The majority of the solid parts had been piled centrally to become an agitating creepy-crawly buffet, but worse, they had been bookended by the two halves of his head, which had been split neatly and divided so the portions were several feet apart. These facial fissures were filled with the dark vibration of greedy insect life, and the carefully distanced pale-grey eyes stared delightedly at Lenzi as though requesting his applause for the most horrific carnival trick ever performed.

The lips were gone, revealing busy gums, and one eye fell inward even as he watched.

Weeks later, a panel in DC reviewing the recordings made by the commander's helmet-cam were dismayed to lose his blurry POV of what was already an incomprehensible collection of organic matter. The panel knew what they were looking at because they had read it in the report, and had become a little inured due to the photographs they had been required to see. Anything can become tolerable provided it is looked at for long enough.

More dismay was generated by the technical surveillance officer's decision to switch his edit to the camera of yet another SEAL who was arriving on the scene.

Nobody on the committee particularly wanted to see one of the world's most capable and most highly trained soldiers puking his guts up.

Edward Quinn, who always credited himself with extraordinary self-awareness, had somehow forgotten one of the most formative events in his life.

He had once been a dorky seven-year-old in short pants, his legs red and welting from one of the recent thrashings that meant he had somehow wrested his father's attention from work, which was, in itself, an achievement. Young Edward never wept after such physical ministrations, because he had been repeatedly told that he was *lucky*, he was *blessed*, that they had *money*. Certainly this was his mother's mantra, as she gulped gin and opiates and turned her face from the daylight.

The son of a penniless immigrant, Quinn's father, Edward Senior, had made his fortune through ruthless, hard-won smarts and iron-willed discipline. Entirely self-made in the pharmaceutical business, he believed he was entitled to enjoy his success, at least as much as his personal Catholicism would permit pleasure of any kind. But Edward Junior still had it all to prove; in fact, he had to prove far more because he had been granted greater opportunities, and would never need to walk down harsh streets. As a result, there was real resentment between father and son, a patriarchal jealousy that was a direct result of Edward Senior's achievement.

He doesn't know he's born, Edward Senior liked to say, and because pain is a condition unique to the living, pain became a critical element in Edward Junior's education.

He was serving his father's penance.

Now, a tiny figure perched on a stone bench that never seemed to grow warm, Edward was dwarfed by the family mansion, a dark-windowed twelve-bedroom birthright that loomed over and above his narrow, shivering shoulders. Edward knew more servants than friends, and, although he already had the makings of a disciplined student, he was still inclined to daydream and fantasy.

On the ground, a single ant caught his eye.

It was a scout, as lonely and confused as he, and when it turned to dash over the stones, Edward followed, face bright. It had been an unseasonably cold spring, even for northern Illinois, and although the last of the snows had melted, nature was still mostly in remission on the Quinn estate.

What Edward found, behind a mossy pillar, was a place where life thrived.

His scout joined an excitable black river of fellow ants, streaming from a crack beneath the raised patio. They were racing back and forth between the body of a stricken mouse, one that had been toyed with and killed by the family cat, who had abandoned the scene of her crime.

Edward felt a knot of revulsion in his stomach, and lowered his foot onto the regiments, crushing the insects beneath his shoe.

As he withdrew, the ants went crazy, abandoning the mouse and whirling over the disaster area as though in panic. Lost to sudden disorder, none appeared to notice the arbitrary giant who had caused the atrocity, and who was quite capable of repeating his destruction.

Overcome by a strange sense of childish guilt, Edward backed away and went into the house.

The following day, the mouse had gone – perhaps removed by a fox or carried away and further mutilated by the cat – but the ants were still grief-stricken, dancing at random over their squished brethren. Edward had brought some peanut candy by way of a peace offering, and the placing of the confection soon redirected interest. By a process of experimentation, he discovered that he could lure some ants as far as thirty yards from the nest.

Thus began studies that young Edward undertook in an extremely meticulous way. Copybooks were filled with notes and sketches, records were made of weather conditions and eating habits, and rudimentary estimates of population were made. Although home-schooled, Edward had access to a local library, and was delighted to find that there were many books on *myrmecology* – the study of ants.

From his one nest, Edward was able to create others in the abandoned stables, experimenting and refining, using plaster to build formicariums and surrounding them with moats of vegetable oil to secure his populations. If he rewarded one set of foragers and not another, he could note how the ants that never found food would revert to nest maintenance. He became impressed by their problem-solving abilities, how they could build bridges and circumvent obstacles.

They formed the perfect societies, and they were *his*.

What Quinn had also forgotten was how this childish but worthy fascination was brought to an abrupt end. It was the fault of his mother, for whom loneliness in her child was quite acceptable, but obsession was not. Besides, insects were *dirty*.

There was no rebellion, no confrontation, just the wholesale destruction of Edward's societies by borax and boiling water. Tears had been shed, but were not tolerated for long. Shortly afterwards, Edward had been sent away to boarding school, where he excelled at both leadership and emotional internalisation, and where a whole new set of challenges awaited.

Quinn was gradually regaining consciousness, the memory fresh in his mind.

Once again thrashed into submission – only this time to within an inch of his life – it now occurred to Edward that this flash-back bore some vague resemblance to the origin stories for the kind of mundane super-villains that populated the comic books he had read in his teenage years. As a result, the memory disgusted him, like the gassy resurfacing of a rich, overpriced meal.

Of course this ethnographic project – Savage Island, his greatest achievement – had not come about because of some simple psycho-logical shorthand, just as he had made much more of his life than his father had ever dared to make of his own. Edward Quinn was a real person with a valuable mileage of experience. He was an inventor and a lover, an adventurer and an academic, and, above all, he was a travelling witness to the ever-contracting world, delighting in the curmudgeonly knowledge of his late middle-age, but never having lost his energy or creative spark.

Yet the story of Savage Island was *his* story, and all stories have to start somewhere.

Was it not possible that he could still be the hero?

Otto Lix had been ruthless in his brutality, as was his way. Quinn had been stalked down to his office, where he kept a private stash of weapons, but he fumbled with his keycard at the last moment, and Lix was too fast. The fight had been short, and Lix unstop-pable, pummelling with fists and feet.

Finally, Lix had exhausted himself, and Quinn was propped up in a corner of his office and left to die. Some of his ribs were smashed, and his breathing was shallow. Blood was slowly leaking inside his skull, threatening to flood his brain.

How long had he been out? From the look of the remaining daylight, it had been several hours.

Yet somehow, Quinn was still alive, and managing to stand. When he caught a glimpse of his face reflected in a polished glass cabinet, he saw an unrecognisable mask of swollen slits and bloating bruises.

Not the face of a hero. Not any more.

Resting a little on his desk, Quinn turned and gibbered at a sound outside the wraparound window. He could hear the powerful chop-chop-chop of helicopter blades.

Quinn stumbled over for a better look.

In striking profile, the Seahawk gradually lowered itself into view like a big hungry spider, then turned to face him, nose dipping beneath the flickering rotors as if readying to charge. Quinn could not see the pilots, just the reflective eye of battle staring into the blank visor of his building.

He could see machine guns and missiles. This was not the coastguard.

The Army?

Whose army? The Indians? The Americans?

Why . . . ?

They were coming to take his island, and destroy his people.

Never.

Quinn staggered backwards until he was leaning against the panelled wall.

Still watching the helicopter, his hands scrambled until they found the secret catch that would open the door to his personal armoury.

'Is that one of them?' said the pilot of the Seahawk, nudging the cyclic control. She was cautious. This weird-looking futuristic hotel appeared to have been abandoned.

Edward Quinn staggered outside onto the sea-wall path, having decked himself out in artefacts from his office. Over his face, he was wearing a tall, beautifully grotesque funeral mask from the Dogonese people of Mali, and over his shoulders hung a Chilkat blanket he had bought from the Kwakwaka'wakw of western Canada. Jumping up and down and gesturing wildly at the helicopter, he was a ludicrous parody of a savage.

'What is that in his hands, over?'

Quinn's love of hardware had led him to develop two custom-built machine guns. Their design was similar in appearance to the Manville Gas Gun from the 1930s, but the rotary cylinder was electrically driven at a speed of 900 rpm. He had only ever used them once, in practice, and then one at a time, although they could, just, be fired one-handed. Because of the way his wrist threaded through the rotary system, it looked like he was holding a spinning halo of fire.

The guns fired twelve-gauge shells. His only regret was that he hadn't ordered a rocket launcher. Biceps twitching, Quinn hefted them up and aimed at the helicopter.

'Move!' shouted the tactical officer. 'Get out of range!'

Pouring blood and sweat, Quinn screamed into his mask and pulled the triggers.

It was impossible to aim with any accuracy, but Quinn could dig the steel into his hips and use the rock face behind him to counter the recoil. Most bullets went wide, but others smashed glass and bounced off the airframe of the helicopter.

'Are you okay?' said the pilot. 'Mendel? Is everyone okay?'

'Affirmative, readying weapons.'

The Seahawk swayed backwards a little, then squirted a beam of laser onto the vast blankness of the sea wall that stretched down beneath Quinn's feet. The missile-guidance system was hardly necessary; it was a very big target and in close range.

Seconds later, there was a hiss and flare from beneath the helicopter, and a Hellfire missile screamed towards him.

Edward Quinn's last moments were spent wondering if the warhead they were firing would be anti-tank or MAC. *Thermobaric*, he decided, as his universe exploded around him.

The entire sea wall fragmented with the impact, huge chunks of cement splashing into the ocean; it was a landslide. Quinn fell forward into the rising dust cloud in a perfect swan dive, his body lost to jagged rocks and tons upon tons of falling rubble.

The sun, fat and falling, still had the power to superheat the sand. The exoskeleton-like silhouettes of military helicopters rose and fell in front of the flaming orb like angry, vengeful bugs.

Charlie was the first of the survivors to stumble out of the jungle; he was happy just to escape the damp claustrophobia and breathe in the scent of approaching dusk over salt water. His hands had been cuffed in plastic loops, and, near the tree-line, he almost fell over an empty conch shell.

Strong hands pulled him up and shoved him forward onto a baking beach that had been stained with the blood of many. The strength belonged to Colonel Wade, grim-faced and silent, the man Charlie had wanted to kill in blind rage.

Heavily armed soldiers, anonymous behind helmets and sunglasses, nodded as the group passed. They were guarding a temporary perimeter. No one knew how many warriors remained in the forest, or if they would try to counter-attack.

From her stretcher – she had finally succumbed to her injuries – Reeta Kapoor sucked air through her teeth when she saw the bloodied battlefield. Isabel Kallmus, the fire of her zealotry extinguished, said nothing. Only Apis, the child in the group, now seemed unaffected by all that had happened and all she could see.

The army had set up long white tents. They resembled a field hospital, but it was really a temporary morgue. Charlie glanced through an open flap as they passed.

He saw piles of black, bleeding, fly-blown bodies.

The motley group of mortals – Charlie, Reeta, Isabel, Apis – waited in silence to board the small military craft that would take them back to civilisation. In the distant shimmer, Charlie could see the rectangular blot of the huge American assault ship as it balanced on the horizon. He thought then of the people he had found and lost, the end of innocence and the darkness of the human heart.

Charlie was glad when Apis took him by the hand once more, but a soldier who saw his tears turned away in either pity or disgust.

Twelve

Edinburgh, Scotland.

"'I bring you the stately matron named Christendom,'" said Valmik Kapoor, quoting Mark Twain to his audience. "'Returning bedraggled, besmirched and dishonoured, from pirate raids in Kiao-Chou, Manchuria, South Africa and the Philippines, with her soul full of meanness, her pocket full of boodle, and her mouth full of pious hypocrisies. Give her soap and towel, but hide the looking-glass.'"

Valmik was speaking in The Traverse 2, a fine studio theatre off Lothian Road, normally used to showcase new writing. It is an intimate space, and that day filled to capacity. The Scottish capital was in the height of her summer season, and only a week away from the festivals; Valmik had taken full advantage of the literate and curious crowds that were already beginning to filter into the city.

'Missionaries justify their promotion of Western systems by identifying justice at the heart of the gospels,' he said. 'Salvation is attained through the destruction of what pre-existed. To be taught to read is one thing, but to be taught to read in order to have to digest the Bible is quite another.'

Through canny and rather self-effacing promotion, the

kidnapping and eventual escape of Valmik Kapoor from the converted ice-house of Werner Kallmus had become a story with legs. Additionally, Valmik had been able to parlay his press coverage into wider opinions about the dangers of Christian fanaticism and what he called the 'fascism' of certain types of missionary work. Of course, he liberally interlaced more academic theories with his own remarkable tales of derring-do.

'The idea of indigenisation is particularly vile,' said Valmik, enjoying the way the syllables tripped off his tongue. 'Syncretism, while supposedly a retort to paternalism, is really a smokescreen for engendering the worst kind of mimicry.'

Valmik's new girlfriend was a red-haired Scot called Janey; she lectured in geosciences at the university. This short speaking tour had been her idea, and she sat starry-eyed in the front row.

'As King Frederick the Great of Prussia said, after allowing Protestant refugees from Austria to settle in his country during the eighteenth century: "In my country, everyone can look to his own salvation." A worthy sentiment. I, Valmik Kapoor, do not dispute that these motivated men and women who preach in the name of God have real desire for change, but what the world needs is that they put their considerable energies into what I would call *ecumenical toil*; that is, a fight for religious unification and mutual tolerance.'

Valmik cleared his throat, and waited for the applause, smiling broadly when it came.

'Thank you all very much,' he said. 'I have a little time for questions.'

Several hands shot up, but one person stood.

'Shit,' said Valmik under his breath.

'What are your thoughts on enlightened absolutism, Professor Kapoor?' said the woman.

'Well,' said Valmik, 'a good thing, obviously. And, uh, I'm not a professor.'

'No, that's right. It says *doctor* on the notice outside.'

'An oversight.'

'So, you're not a doctor?'

'Well, I have an equivalent qualification.'

'A *Ch.D*?'

'What?'

'A certificate in the Identification and Safekeeping of Cheese.'

'Cheese?'

'I saw you stealing brie and oatcakes from the cafeteria.'

Valmik studied his shoes. 'I thought those were free.'

'Look,' said Reeta, enjoying the impact she was having on the room, 'I really don't mind you trying to present one of my old lectures as your own, but you could at least have ironed your shirt.'

The following morning, brother and sister met at the castle, then ambled down the sunny Royal Mile, past leaflet-thrusters, locals, and time-wasting troubadours.

'A single blow to the head,' said Valmik, remembering. 'Isabel took me to that disgusting house her family lived in on the pretence that she wanted me to meet her parents. But her mother was dead and her father insane. I walked right into it.'

'You sounded braver in your lecture,' Reeta said, putting her arm around him. 'You've been through a lot, little brother. How are you holding up?'

'A couple of weeks in a windowless prison, and it sounds like I got off lightly.'

'We all got off more lightly than we could have,' said Reeta, thinking of the scar tissue beneath her jacket.

She waited while Valmik ducked into a shop for fish and chips and a can of Irn-Bru. Then the siblings sat on a bench for a while and discussed the recent past.

Charlie, Reeta and Isabel had been taken to an American base in Germany for debriefing. Reeta and Isabel were eventually released, following repeated testimonies and extensive medical tests, after which Isabel Kallmus had been sent back to Austria in handcuffs to be tried alongside her father.

Charlie Cortez had been found to have *P. Vivax* malarial symptoms, and remained hospitalised for several months. Despite his morbid certainty, he had *not* been diagnosed with any prion disease, and seemed almost disappointed at the news.

Testing by USAMRIID on those natives left alive revealed an immunity to the illness that killed Leona Bride and Todd Parker, so it did not matter that their soft tissue contained a high concentration of the rogue proteins. However, as Todd and Leona were the only known sufferers – and the only outsiders to have consumed the flesh of the tribespeople – the disease, while incurable, was now in total remission.

Apis, the daughter of Todd and Leona, was also uninfected.

'Did they find Edward Quinn?' said Valmik, eventually.

'They never recovered the body,' said Reeta. 'They found the body of Kelly Maelzel and, of course, Otto Lix, but Quinn must have been entombed.'

'Was he so deluded?' said Valmik. 'I mean, was Quinn so wrong?'

Reeta considered. 'You can't control life if you really care for it,' she said. 'I believe that for all his despotism and arrogance he did care about those islanders, and more than just a little.'

Valmik shrugged. 'Heavy price to pay for what was basically a holiday resort.'

'I suppose,' said Reeta. 'I think I'm going to do a lecture series on modern tourism. People are no longer satisfied just to marvel; maybe experience has been cheapened by the ease with which pictures can be found.'

'Maybe,' said Valmik.

'Paul Theroux claimed that tourism is usually the mobile rich making a blind, blundering visitation on the inert poor. So many people talk about their holiday plans and say they want to see the *real* India, the *real* Croatia, the *real* Madrid. I wonder what the hell they mean.'

'Easy for someone who loves travel to loathe travellers,' said Valmik. 'The sketches of a good writer might well have value, but valuable observation does not put a copyright on experience.'

'Are you telling me that everyone has a right to be inane?'

'Of course,' said Valmik, digging a fingernail into his teeth to dislodge a little food. 'That was one of the personal tragedies for me – Isabel really made me care about those islanders. Say, what do you think has being happening there in this past year?'

'I can probably imagine,' said Reeta.

Savage Island.

Two men, one tall and dark, the other small and pale, stood at the edge of Quinn's saucer-building and stared out over the bay. There was no moon, and it had been many minutes since the sun vanished over the horizon, yet somehow the ocean still held the light.

'Remarkable,' said Filipe Enzo, the shorter man, his hair blown about by the hot breeze.

The tall man, Ashok Khanna, was one of the people hired by the Governor of the Okojuwoi to broker a new deal for Savage Island, and, perhaps because of his expansive and engaging personality, had become their best hope of success. He had already sold off the shipwreck of the *Xavier* – the Portuguese treasure ship – and his reclamation company was working with the officials of an American museum to oversee the salvage.

'Remarkable,' Enzo repeated.

Ashok did not know whether the Spaniard was referring to the scenery or the structure on which they now stood. He hoped both. Enzo was a man of few words, despite representing a powerful European conglomerate of investors.

'Edward Quinn was a visionary,' said Ashok.

'Quinn was unrealistic,' said Enzo.

The Spaniard was slight, with a narrow, tidy moustache and tinted glasses. His tropical shirt and shorts revealed extremely pale skin covered in thick black hair, which gave his bodily movement the impression of being on a television that was not quite tuned in.

'A labour of love,' said Ashok Khanna.

'Quinn's plans limited him to thirty-eight rooms,' said Enzo. 'If he had taken advantage of the full potential of this building, he could have boarded six times that many guests.'

'You're going to divide it up,' said Ashok. 'Very wise.'

'Dependent on our permission to build a new tarmac runway for Port Barren and our planning approval for another hotel on Great Okojuwoi. But most of the changes here will be cosmetic. Rebuild the sea wall, enlarge the dock. Bigger restaurants, bars. Quinn didn't contemplate that high-end tourists to India might expect to eat deep-pan pizza.'

'They might?'

'Of course. By all accounts, Quinn was a snob, an elitist. We will also need a new swimming pool, this one is far too small.'

'Yes,' said Ashok. 'Far too small.'

The circular pool on the roof had become grey and brown, a slimy cauldron.

Nature had been quick to mount a counter-attack on Quinn's dream. Enzo scuffed at creepers that were picking at cracks in the concrete, and the whole building, which had once been fragrant with fresh paint, now smelt of hot, wet carpet and rodent urine.

'We will keep the name, though,' said Enzo. '*Savage Island* sounds suitably exotic.'

'Good idea,' said Ashok.

'What were Quinn's plans for the rest of the island?' said Enzo. 'That strange train of his. The land is beautiful over there, certainly, but no more beautiful than on this side of the mountain. Besides, he had all the space he needed to build. And he's done an amazing thing; this building is almost self-sufficient in power. A perfect expression of modern green energy.'

Ashok shrugged. 'Perhaps we should get back to the boat,' he said, to hurry things along.

'What about the natives?' Enzo gestured towards a group of a dozen or so islanders who were lounging on the ground beneath the terrace's only remaining cloth awning. They were clad in charity-donated clothing, much of which hung loose from their bodies, and they were surrounded by clouds of small insects which had been attracted to the night lights that were just blinking on.

'Of course,' said Ashok, rubbing his hands together.

He knew Enzo had been putting this off. Anyone who had expressed interest in investment had proved uncomfortable on the subject of the disenfranchised islanders, yet this summit was to be Ashok's pièce de résistance. Hopefully it would be an introduction that would remove the final barrier to a valuable series of signatures and permit the lawyers to move in.

Because they now existed on privately owned land, the natives of Savage Island were not protected by any of the Indian government's Supreme Court rulings intended to limit encroachment and contact. Even if they had been, it would be unlikely to have made any difference to their welfare; the Great Andaman Trunk Road through *Jarawa* land has remained open, despite an order to close it from the highest authority.

'Now,' said Ashok, in businesslike fashion. 'These are the only communicative tribespeople who do not currently have measles. Even so, I do not advise that you shake hands.'

'Yes,' said Enzo.

'Bonded labour will be impossible, I suspect; these people are not workers.'

'It was never part of our plan,' said Enzo. 'They must never become a PR disaster.'

'They have been taught some English, with minor success. Their own language is utterly unintelligible. We know their god is a mountain.'

Enzo laughed. His own god, with whom he was not on particularly great terms, lived everywhere.

'Also,' said Ashok, anticipating the next question, 'please be disabused of the notion that these people are cannibals, or that they are violent. They have voluntarily given up their rudimentary arms in return for government aid, and they eat pigs, berries and lizards.'

'I understand,' Enzo said, approaching the group.

The islanders did not appear to be remotely impressed with either the view or the astonishing architectural structure upon which they now reclined; there was nothing sacred about El any more. The men were cloudy-eyed and passive-resistant; several were drunk.

The solitary woman there stood up when instructed to by Ashok. She seemed to Enzo to be a wizened old hag, a cigarette-smoking homeless person in a dirty *re-elect BUSH!* T-shirt.

'This is Medea,' Ashok said with a flourish; he had coached her himself. 'She leads the tribe.'

'*This* woman?' said Enzo. 'A leader?'

Some of his concerns were already being met; these natives were disinterested, pliable, defeated. Ideally, Enzo wanted them invisible.

'Welcome to our island,' The Qesem said haltingly, but through a subservient smile.

'Yes,' said Enzo. 'Thank you.'

'We hope you be very happy here,' said Medea, and twinkled at him as best she could.

Rancho Mirage, California.

A clear Saturday night, stars framed by palm trees. Everything in the best brochures was there, present and correct.

At midnight it was dry and hot, yet, with enough alcohol, Charlie Cortez's new pad had the potential to be a fine venue for a summit of great importance. It had a low pitched roof, and floor-to-ceiling glass windows; a fine example of mid-century modern architecture, whose previous owner, a woman who claimed to have slept with Sinatra, was long dead.

'I don't believe I could ever love a prostitute,' Dan Demus said from his lounger out back. 'But the first one got my dick off fast, and hard. More importantly, I wanted to go away long before she told me to. That is an ideal I have searched for ever since, through tears, love and denial, acceptance, love and even divorce.'

Charlie hiccupped. 'You said *love* twice, dickhead.'

'Well, love is important.'

The conversation had run out of steam towards the end of one of those occasionally blessed bottles of tequila which creates both geniality and an agreeable, mild, pre-sleep deafness, as opposed to misunderstanding and pure rage.

Jesse and Milo had splashed themselves out in the pool hours ago and had gone to bed, or were perhaps on their all-absorbing computer. There was only the surrounding low-rise light pollution to keep the two doctors company.

Charlie Cortez, resident in that place for six months, welcomed the local neon in a vast desert that could have been the last colonised place on earth. He had a good new job at a local hospital dealing with well-preserved geriatrics, and was fast gaining the respect that he used to crave.

'You even know who's over that wall?' Demus said, waving an empty shot glass towards creepers and poured concrete.

The neighbours were awake as well, pushing a little Los Lobos for their personal party.

'Given the lights, could be Turner Field,' said Charlie. 'But I never heard anything, until now.'

'Excellent,' said Demus. 'Good for you both.'

Light projected over the swimming pool, a thousand rippling butterflies.

'Twice a week I go to the supermarket,' said Charlie, after a time. 'I found it on a cartoon map they gave me at the airport. Even though I live here now, I still have that map, in my *key tray*.'

'By the door?'

'Yes, by the door.'

'You're not so unusual.'

'Inside the supermarket,' said Charlie, 'is pure light. Gargantuan, empty corridors of light. And lunatic logos, a kind of unchanging, unthinking tribute to an impossible shelf-life. Sometimes, I see handsome, muscular men in quite small shorts. They sniff fruit for quality.'

'Small shorts? Hairy legs?'

'Yes.'

'Good for them,' said Demus.

'Dan, do you understand what I mean by empty? Literally, there's no one there.'

'Off-season,' said Demus, shaking his head. 'Wait until winter.'

'I'm grilling food we can't even finish,' said Charlie, gesturing at the cold barbecue. '*Good* food. I mean, the steaks are astonishing. And the shrimp and the lobster. But all this food tonight was just *here*.'

'Yeah.' said Demus. 'You've changed.'

'What do you do?' said Charlie. 'I'm fucking serious.'

Demus considered. 'What I like to do is listen to dead recording artists who were more screwed up than I am.'

Charlie laughed, and the men sat in silence for a while.

'My new dogs broke the air conditioner,' said Charlie, after a time. 'That's why it never gets really cold inside.'

'I don't like it too cold,' said Demus.

'They sit by the floor intake to get cool, and fur siphons off until that fur creates a blockage and I have to call someone out who comes to my house and sucks the fur out of my machine.'

'You have dogs, that's the price.'

'I like my dogs.'

'They like you too. That foggy, bouncy respect, that can take time.'

'My next pet will be an oily walrus.'

'You should go to bed,' said Demus. 'You're drunk.'

'I *am* going to bed.'

'You should go to bed and calm down, and think about how it isn't so bad. You were a survivor, Charlie Cortez. And now you have more knowledge than anyone, I can see it in you.'

'Knowledge about what? I lost them all. Why the hell did I move out here?'

'Your kids are visiting. And Vanessa's talking without lawyers, finally. Tomorrow is a whole other day.' Dan staggered over to the Jacuzzi and polluted it with his bare feet. 'And, y'know, I'm here,' he said. 'I'm a good friend.'

The water was lit red and green and bubbled satanically.

'Stay for a while,' said Charlie. 'You know, stay *around*.'

He walked away.

Dan Demus said nothing, but when Charlie was gone, he called over one of the dogs who had broken the AC, and dug love and promises into his ears.

Leona was there.

'I'm not here,' said Leona.

She looked beautiful. Healthy, strong, happy.

'I know,' said Charlie, his heart full. 'But you used to play on that tyre swing, and upstairs is the room where you slept, before you got sick.'

'I remember,' she said.

'You were a child in this place. I wish we could have known each other then, before it all got so confusing.'

They were standing outside the house of Martha Calloway, a place of tumbling orphans and sloppy, loving, experimental bakery.

But it was quiet now, and the house was empty. They were the only people; the windows dark, the trees bare.

'I attacked that soldier,' said Charlie. 'I wanted to kill him.'

'Not really,' said Leona.

'No? I went to the island, I abandoned my family. I thought it was the sickness, but it was me all along. *It was me all along.* Can you understand how I might have a problem with that?'

Leona kissed him, and it felt good.

'What will you do now?' said Charlie.

'I guess I'll stay here,' said Leona. 'Thanks for being honest with yourself.'

'Thanks for not appearing in another dream about fucking or death,' said Charlie.

Leona laughed in the voice of Dan Demus. Charlie laughed too, it was infectious.

'Where will I go?' said Charlie. 'I don't know who I am any more. I don't know what to do.'

'Go somewhere else,' said Leona. 'You know, music, lights and laughter.'

She kissed him again.

When Charlie opened his eyes, Leona was gone for real, or as realistically as any lover can ever vanish in a dream.

Morning.

Dr Charlie Cortez walked over the cool stone floor of his open-plan house on bare feet. It was very quiet; the kids were asleep in one room, and Demus was snoring in another. The dogs were drowsing by the air-conditioner intake.

Charlie had nowhere to hide from his hangover in the glare of the low desert sun, and he knew if he pulled open the back door it would already be roasting outside.

He slid the bathrobe from his arm and looked at his watch: 0605 in California. It would be three hours later in Philadelphia. Just about an acceptable time to call. He scooped up the cordless phone and dialled.

'Developmental Psychology, please.'

While he waited, Charlie walked over to the kitchen to brew coffee; his mouth was gulch dry.

'Can you put me through to Ludmila Petrova?' said Charlie, when another voice introduced itself. 'Tell her it's Charlie Cortez, I'm an MD.'

'Dr Cortez,' said a cheerful female voice after a few seconds. 'Why am I not surprised?'

'Where's Apis?' said Charlie. 'Is she well?'

'Good morning to you, too,' said Professor Petrova, in her light, eastern-European accent. 'And Apis is fine. As for location, you know I am not at liberty to give out that information.'

'Did you read my petition?' Charlie said.

'These things take months,' said Professor Petrova. 'Months and months, as you know. Don't you think she deserves a mother as well as a father?'

'We don't know *what* she needs,' Charlie said.

'Agreed.'

'This is not a feral child,' said Charlie, trying to find the correct words. 'This is a girl with social and personal skills, who understands give and take. She was never malnourished, or anaemic.'

He became aware that he was babbling somewhat.

'I might be the closest thing to family that Apis will ever have,' he said.

Ludmila sighed. She was a very patient woman, but had heard this before.

'Look,' said Charlie, 'I'm sorry. I know you're doing your job, but—'

'But you *care*,' said Professor Petrova, kindly. 'Don't worry, I know what that feels like.'

'She's fragile,' said Charlie. 'She must be, after what she went through. Ah . . . is she fragile?'

'Maybe less so than we first thought. She eats, she can hold a doll, she cries.'

'She cries?'

'This is important; a good thing. But her vocabulary is very, very limited. If children do not learn speech by the age of five, there can be difficulties. There is a specific window of opportunity to acquire language.'

'She *has* acquired language,' said Charlie. 'Maybe not much English, maybe only the English that her mother taught the natives. But she has the language of her people.'

'It is far too early yet to know anything, Charlie. You need to understand that. And you need to stop calling me twice a week; I promised to be in touch.'

'Her interests are all I care about,' said Charlie, closing his eyes to the brightness of the sun. 'She shouldn't be taken advantage of.'

'She won't be,' said Ludmila Petrova. 'You have my word.'

'Just make sure that you are teaching her, and not the other way around.'

'I hope both,' said Ludmila.

New York City, New York.

Lyle Gruber managed to flag down a cab on East 34th Street seconds before the rain started to fall. He barked the Hell's Kitchen address and sat back, loosening his tie.

'Guess you came along at the right time,' he said.

Mr Gruber was a Sports Entertainment promoter from De Soto, Missouri. He had just failed in his negotiations to convince a company that sold canned hotdogs to sponsor a new monster truck in the *Killer Jam II* series, and was feeling rather lugubrious.

'Hey,' said Gruber, when the driver did not reply. 'A little civility gets you a long way.'

'Sorry,' said the driver. He did this in such an impassioned way that Mr Gruber felt compelled to study the identification card glued to the Perspex wall that separated them.

'Ellis Udumi,' said Gruber. 'Interesting name.'

'I only here short time,' said Udumi.

Udumi had been in New York for eight months. Prior to that – in the years that had passed – he had been in five banks, four countries, three jails and two schools.

He had a vague idea that he would tell his story someday, because it was a good one, a long one, and some people pay good money for stories. Besides, he had not been careful enough with the fortune that his island had granted to him. How could he have known? A good portion of it he had scooped into the ocean to speed the passage of his little boat. But there had been enough left when he found land.

More importantly, he was capable of recognising greed in others, which was all that seemed to matter in the land of the walking dead.

'Then welcome to NYC,' said Gruber. 'Greatest city in the world, they say.'

'Uh-huh,' said Udumi.

'The very height of civilisation,' said Gruber, as they stopped at lights.

Udumi flipped on his indicator and watched a bearded hobo rooting through a small mountain of burst, steaming trash bags and coming up with a deli take-out box. A few steps behind, a young woman bellowed obscenities into her cell phone and spat chewing gum onto the sidewalk.

'My pappy calls it the *urban jungle*,' said Gruber. He became aware he was talking to a black man. 'Now, he don't mean any offence by that.'

'No,' said Udumi, daydreaming about his wife and their young son.

Udumi had never really noticed insects in his old life, but now their Brooklyn apartment seemed to be full of them.

His wife would never adapt to America, had never shown willing to adapt to anywhere. Sometimes she went for groceries in bare feet. Yet it is a woman's job to adapt.

'I wonder where *that* idea came from?' said Gruber, gazing out of the window. 'A *jungle*. I mean, I never really thought about it before.' He chuckled. 'Not so many trees here.'

'Fear?' said Udumi.

'I can tell you,' said Gruber, reaching for his iPhone. 'Technology is a wonderful thing, all the information in the world at the touch of a button. No, wait, I have to answer this e-mail.'

The men journeyed without further conversation, apart from one occasion when Gruber urged Udumi to lean on the horn in response to a stalled delivery truck that was blocking the lane.

You can get away with it now, he had said. *You're practically local*.

The in-cab entertainment kept them company, a dusty touch-screen that broadcast mindless natter in a repetitive loop. *It gets so bad, I have to switch it off on the airport run*, Gruber liked to tell anyone who would listen.

Eventually, Udumi made the turn into a quiet side street.

'Over on the left,' said Gruber. 'They don't advertise, but this is surely the best steak in the city. Gotta get my teeth into some raw meat every now and then.'

Udumi checked his mirrors and pulled over, as Lyle Gruber drummed his fingertips on the back seat of the cab in anticipation of his meal: *thumpa thumpa thumpa*. He was too fat to reach for his wallet without standing up.

'Drive safely,' said Gruber, handing the fare through the cab window, and noticing that the driver had a small, white birthmark on his forehead, just over the left eyebrow. 'And be careful in the city, young man. People here can be vicious, and you never know who you're talking to.'

'Yes, sir,' said Udumi. 'Have a nice day.'

Epilogue

Some years earlier

Far below the cathedral canopy of the jungle, three figures regarded one another. The first, a huge man, powerful and dynamic, was leader of his people. The other two were boys, no more than eight or nine years old.

The man addressed his sons in a stern voice.

A game.

Tam and Udumi were delighted; it was as they had hoped.

I will be the Owb, said Sool, flexing his giant muscles and pulling a fearsome, theatrical face. *I will run and hide, and you must capture me. I am a coward, so I will run fast. I am a fool, so I will not hide well. But I am afraid of strong warriors, and fear will make me powerful in my desperation, and I will want to destroy you.*

The children hopped about in excitement.

Turn your backs, said the Chief. *Turn and cover your eyes, until I am hidden.*

Sool was still hiding from his sons when he encountered the *real* Owbs.

He was shocked and surprised. Three men had come running down the beach. Men with knives.

Just inside the line of the forest – where, years later, his people would be massacred by an invading army – Sool had been ready to play with his boys, a family man. Instead, he was forced into murder, as the first fishermen brought down his great knife in a terrified, instinctive attack.

Sool was fast, agile, well-trained. In seconds the Owb was disarmed and killed.

When the other two saw what they were up against, they ran away.

Sool had no weapon but the one he took one from his assailant. Turning the knife, he removed the eyes of the man he had pinned to the ground, so the spirits could not see out at him. After this, he hacked off the head, to ensure that life would not return to his enemy.

His blood risen, Sool set out in pursuit of the others.

Udumi arrived shortly afterwards, and saw Sool and his prey disappearing around the headland. He had tracked his father well, and now this was a fine prize, a clear victory over Tam.

Udumi, alone, had a dead Owb at his feet.

As the light began to fail, Udumi realised that his father was not likely to return. He picked up the head of the fisherman and made his way back through the jungle.

Emerging onto the beach, Udumi was not particularly surprised to see another Owb.

This Owb was called Thein Suu Aye, a conman from Myanmar. When he saw Udumi and his grisly load, he fell back into his boat.

Udumi could see a tribal fishing party in the distance; they were coming home. He shouted, although they might have been too far away to hear.

Another one! Another one!

Udumi dropped the head onto the sand and watched in curiosity as this new Owb first vomited and then collapsed again, his boat drifting out in the shallows only to bump back ashore.

Fear will make me powerful in my desperation, and I will want to destroy you.

Udumi considered the words of his father and began to laugh. This Owb did not look capable of standing up straight, let alone destroying anything.

He looked at the footprints on the sand. Three were accounted for – the Indian fishermen – but a fourth had run in the other direction.

So there was another, somewhere on the island.

Nightfall.

You are not supposed to be here, said The Qesem, when Tam entered her hut. *You know the hunt is still on. You should be back in the village.*

A huge fire cast light through the open doorway. Outside, in the clearing, they could hear the screams of the three who had been caught.

I am sorry, said Tam.

You are a very curious little warrior.

I wanted to see.

Medea did not turn to the boy, she was busy with her ceremonial preparations.

And so you have, she said. *What was it that you saw?*

I saw that they are men, said Tam.

Men?

I have looked into their eyes.

Tell me. What did they show you, these men?

They showed me . . . they are not spirits.

Yes?

Why would spirits be so afraid?

Knowledge without experience is only the illusion of knowledge. I think it is you who are not afraid, Tam. Yet you should be.

Why, Medea?

Because they have the power to destroy us all.

*

Tam had been sent away from The Qesem's hut with a scolding, but he could not sleep.

After a time, he emerged from his hut into the cool, still night. All was silent; the warriors were out hunting for the fourth Owb. They presumed he would be hiding in the jungle.

They were wrong.

Edward Quinn and the boy saw each other at the same time.

Quinn had been skulking around the edge of Sool's hut, taking pictures with his infrared camera. He walked into the open when he saw he had been spotted. He kept his gun holstered and raised his hands in surrender. His mouth was moving as though forming words, but no sound came out.

Quinn was repeating a mantra to himself: *Compassion is the defining measure of a civilisation.*

Tam watched, unafraid. All he had to do was open his own mouth, make a noise, a yell or a scream, and men and women would pour from huts and tear this man limb from limb.

Had Tam done this, he might have lived to be an adult, and his people free.

Quinn backed away, hands still raised. He did not turn and run until he was under cover of the jungle, and the boy was out of sight.

Soon after, Tam was once more creeping around the edge of the sacrificial clearing. The fire still burned high and strong, and it reflected in his eyes.

Two of the three strung-up men were already dead, one of them eviscerated, the other skinless and bled dry. The third was awake, and still trying to scream.

Medea and her helpers were nowhere to be seen.

Tam tugged at a knot that had been tied around the tree and the rope whipped loose, dumping the man noisily onto the ground.

Run, said Tam.

Wrists still tied, Thein Suu Aye struggled to his feet. He stared at the boy in confusion and pain, and was bleeding heavily; the skin had been peeled back from his leg.

Run, said Tam, again.

Udumi was also awake; he had snuck out of the village several hours ago.

He was fascinated by the Owb boat, which had been pulled up onto the beach, and tomorrow would be stripped by the tribal craftsmen for useable parts. Udumi was particularly fascinated by the engine, and had even, quite by accident, managed to get it started once or twice.

He became startled by sounds from the jungle; men running.

He expected to see warriors, who were returning here often in case the fourth Owb attempted to make an escape. Yet warriors would not make such a careless noise as they moved through the forest.

Both Edward Quinn and Thein Suu Aye broke cover at the same time, and sprinted for the boat. Udumi stepped back in amazement, and was ignored.

Tam was next to break from the jungle. He had been running not far behind.

In moments the men had pushed out the small craft and jumped aboard.

Later.

The boat was gone, and with it the two survivors.

Long moments passed, while Udumi looked at Tam. Neither needed to speak, it was clear what had happened: Tam had somehow permitted the Owbs to escape.

Sometimes Udumi did not understand Tam, but he respected his wisdom. Each brother could recognise that the other was special, and in unity was strength.

No one must know you have done this, Udumi said eventually. *So I will say nothing.*

Tam was surprised. *Why not?.*

Because you are my brother.

The stars were bright, the moon also. Tiny breakers swept up luminescent algae, and beneath drooping palms, the beach sparkled.